Berkley Prime Crime titles by Betty Hechtman

HOOKED ON MURDER

DEAD MEN DON'T CROCHET

BY HOOK OR BY CROOK

A STITCH IN CRIME

YOU BETTER KNOT DIE

BEHIND THE SEAMS

IF HOOKS COULD KILL

FOR BETTER OR WORSTED

"Get hooked on this great new author!"
—Monica Ferris

continued . . .

"Molly's latest adventure is sure to be a favorite of crafters."
—*The Mystery Reader*

"Delightful . . . With *A Stitch in Crime*, Ms. Hechtman has successfully created a craft-centric cozy series not to be missed!"
—*The Romance Readers Connection*

Dead Men Don't Crochet

"Crocheters couldn't ask for a more rollicking read . . . It has mystery, yarn addiction, a bonus cheesecake cupcake recipe, and a shawl pattern in one fun-to-read package."
—*Crochet Today!*

"Fun . . . Has a great hook and a cast of characters that enliven any scene."
—*The Mystery Reader*

"Classic cozy fare . . . Crocheting pattern and recipe are just the icing on the cake."
—*Cozy Library*

Hooked on Murder

"A gentle and charming novel that will warm the reader like a favorite afghan. Its quirky and likable characters are appealing and real."
—Earlene Fowler, national bestselling author of
The Road to Cardinal Valley

"Betty Hechtman has written a charming mystery. Who can resist a sleuth named Pink, a slew of interesting minor characters, and a fun fringe-of-Hollywood setting?"
—Monica Ferris, *USA Today* bestselling author of *Threadbare*

"Hooks the reader from the onset with likable characters . . . Readers will admire the feisty, caring Molly."
—*Genre Go Round Reviews*

"Readers who enjoy craft-and-hobby-related cozies will find lots to like in *Hooked on Murder* . . . Betty Hechtman does it all so well: writing, plotting, and character development."
—*Cozy Library*

If Hooks
Could Kill

BETTY HECHTMAN

BERKLEY PRIME CRIME, NEW YORK

THE BERKLEY PUBLISHING GROUP
Published by the Penguin Group
Penguin Group (USA) LLC
375 Hudson Street, New York, New York 10014

USA • Canada • UK • Ireland • Australia • New Zealand • India • South Africa • China

penguin.com

A Penguin Random House Company

IF HOOKS COULD KILL

A Berkley Prime Crime Book / published by arrangement with the author

Berkley Prime Crime Books are published by The Berkley Publishing Group.
BERKLEY® PRIME CRIME and the PRIME CRIME logo are trademarks of
Penguin Group (USA) LLC.

For information, address: The Berkley Publishing Group,
a division of Penguin Group (USA) LLC,
375 Hudson Street, New York, New York 10014.

ISBN: 978-0-425-25233-8

PUBLISHING HISTORY
Berkley Prime Crime hardcover edition / November 2012
Berkley Prime Crime mass-market edition / November 2013

PRINTED IN THE UNITED STATES OF AMERICA

10 9 8 7 6 5 4 3 2 1

Cover illustration by Cathy Gendron.
Cover design by Rita Frangie.
Interior text design by Kristin del Rosario.

Acknowledgments

Thank you once again to Sandy Harding for being a wonderful editor. My agent, Jessica Faust, is the best. Thank you to Natalee Rosenstein for making Berkley Prime Crime such a great place to be. The Berkley Art department keeps coming up with fabulous covers.

Thank you to Delma Myers and Crochet Guild president Amy Shelton for being my buddies at the Crochet Guild of America's summer and fall shows. Suzann Thompson gave a great class on the bullion stitch.

Thanks to Lee Lofland for putting on the Writer's Police Academy. Where else could I have asked an ATF officer about how to make a silencer, or been able to try on a Kevlar vest, or felt what it was like to be handcuffed or in a jail cell?

Roberta Martia provided the inspiration for the wedding hankie idea and a sample. Dr. Howard Marx offered medical information and Appellate Defender Judy Libby answered legal questions.

A special thank-you to Linda Hopkins for all of her generous help with the crochet patterns and everything else.

Thank you, Thursday knit and crochet group—Rene Biederman, Alice Chiredijan, Terry Cohen, Clara Feeney, Lily Gillis, Sonia Flaum, Winnie Hineson, Linda Hopkins, Debbie Kratofil, Reva Mallon, Elayne Moschin and Vicki Sostman. Paula Tesler keeps us trying new things.

Burl, Max and Samantha—you guys are forever the best.

CHAPTER 1

I HAVE DONE A LOT OF EMBARRASSING THINGS, BUT this morning I topped even myself. . . .

I watched as the detective walked out of the small blue stucco house down the street from my best friend Dinah Lyons's house. Everything about him gave off the vibe of somebody who'd been up all night chasing down evidence. His face featured a day-old beard, his tie was pulled loose from the collar of his pale blue dress shirt, and he gave out a weary sigh as he sauntered down the three steps to the front walk and moved toward the black Crown Victoria parked at the curb.

He was almost to the street when a man in a hooded sweatshirt with a baseball cap on top of the hood darted out from behind a large red oleander bush. The morning sun glinted off the gun in his hand. As he raised his arm and took aim, something triggered in my mind, really someone, namely Barry Greenberg. I'd given up trying to find the right title for Barry. It was enough to say he was my ex-boyfriend, he was a homicide detective and he'd recently been shot. I wasn't about to let that happen to someone else.

Without a second of hesitation, I rushed up behind the guy with the gun. If all the adrenaline hadn't been pumping I never would have had the force to knock him over. And maybe I would have noticed a few things like the detective's shirt had no wrinkles. And he was definitely wearing makeup. And there were cameras, lights and lots of people standing around.

"Cut," a tall man in black jeans and a loose taupe-colored tee shirt yelled as he rushed onto the grass. He glared at me and waved to the uniformed officer hanging by the curb. "Get her out of here," he muttered, pointing to me as I rolled off the presumed assailant. The man I had tackled got up and dusted himself off, and the throng of onlookers surrounded me as I got back on my feet. But they parted for the officer who came through the crowd, linked his arm with mine, and pulled me to the edge of the sidewalk.

"Pink, what have you done now?" Adele Abrams rushed up behind me as Dinah Lyons started explaining to all who would listen why I had done what I'd done. No, this wasn't some kind of bad dream, though at the moment I was wishing it was and hoping I'd wake up twisted in the sheets of my own bed. I admit to often finding myself in trouble, but usually it's for something real. This was all make-believe.

It was summer in the San Fernando Valley and the area had become a back lot for TV and film productions. Caravans of white trucks were on streets all over the Valley. Street corners had yellow signs with arrows to direct the cast and crew to the location. They always disguised the real name of the production with some cryptic phrase, so no one would have guessed by the sign on Ventura Boulevard that the area around Dinah's house had become the set for *L.A. 911.*

If this were a TV show or movie, it would freeze-frame right now. Then I'd step forward and explain that my name was Molly Pink and that after my husband Charlie died, I'd started a whole new chapter in my life that included getting a job as the event coordinator at the bookstore Shedd & Royal Books and More, which was just up the street from all this activity. I might mention that I was also in charge of the yarn department we had recently added.

You might wonder about a yarn department in a bookstore. The yarn department was added because the local crochet group, the Tarzana Hookers, met at the bookstore and quite frankly the owners, Mrs. Shedd and Mr. Royal, were looking for more revenue streams. I think that's the right term. Actually, with a crafting table and available yarn, the Hookers didn't just meet at the bookstore—they almost lived there. Mrs. Shedd liked to joke that if we had cots, the group would probably sleep there, too.

Adele Abrams, the person who just called me Pink, worked at the bookstore, too. There was a little tension between us. She thought she should have been promoted to event coordinator instead of Mrs. Shedd hiring me. As a consolation prize, she had been given the children's department to oversee. Adele didn't really like kids, though she did like to dress up in costumes for story time.

Then, when the yarn department was added, Adele thought she should be in charge of it. Adele, Dinah and I were all part of the crochet group, and no one would dispute that Adele was far superior with a hook, but she had this small problem. All of the Tarzana Hookers thought crochet was the best of the fiber arts, but Adele took it a step further. If you so much as showed her a knitting needle she would throw a hissy fit. Personally, while I know she had a real reason for being nuts about knitters (she'd had a bad stepmother who was a needle head, as Adele called her), I thought it was time she accepted a world where hooks and needles could get along.

Having a needle hater running a yarn department wasn't a good idea—not if you wanted a knitter's business. So, even though I was somewhat of a novice at crochet, Mrs. Shedd wanted me to handle the yarn department.

But none of that explained what I was doing hanging out at a TV shoot. Actually it wasn't planned. Adele, Dinah and I were on our way to one of the newer Hooker's houses to pick up some crochet stuff. Her house was around the corner from Dinah's and we'd had to pass the caravan of trucks and trailers to get there. Even though seeing a set on the street wasn't new, I still found it exciting. It was fun to see what they'd done to the front of the modest stucco house they were using for a location. They'd carted in trees and bushes and arranged them so that the other houses on the block weren't visible and so you couldn't see the open-air tent set up down the street that was acting as a dining room for the cast and crew. A catering truck was parked in the street and the smell of the barbecue wafted down the block.

This is where the freeze frame would end and the action would pick up again. The uniform who'd grabbed my arm had gotten me to the edge of the crowd. Adele followed close behind. "Pink, you'd better thank my boyfriend Eric for saving your skin." Now that we'd reached the sidelines, Eric let go and apologized if he'd been too rough.

"It was fine," I said to the barrel-chested man who towered over me. Eric Humphries was an LAPD motor officer and was using his vacation time to work security on the production. In case there was any doubt, he was also Adele's boyfriend. "Thanks for saving me from the angry mob," I said looking back at the crew as they tried to set up the shot again. Adele glanced around, saw that no one was watching and touched Eric's arm in a possessive manner. He responded by beaming a big smile her way. It was embarrassing to watch them making googie eyes at each other. But at least this time the romance wasn't all in Adele's imagination.

They made an unusual pair. Adele, with her wild clothes and say whatever attitude, was a sharp contrast to the very proper and polite motor officer. He rode his motorcycle with ramrod straight posture and took his security work at the set very seriously. "Cutchykins," he said, winking at her. "I'm glad you stopped by. You look lovely as always."

My eyes started to roll on their own. Didn't the man have eyes? Adele was wearing a one shoulder sundress made out of multicolored granny squares with a red crocheted flounce at the bottom. She looked like she was wearing an afghan. And Adele had crocheted herself a big brimmed cream-colored hat. It had turned out to be a little too floppy in the brim area, and kept dipping down and cutting off her line of sight.

Dinah rejoined us and Eric went back to his post. "Don't worry, I took care of everything," she said. I had no doubt she had. Dinah was a community college English instructor and her specialty was freshman English. She knew how to take charge of an unruly group, no matter who they were. I figured she'd done the same with the production group. "As soon as I explained about your connection to Barry and how he was a homicide detective, and that he'd been shot, and that you were still so sensitive to the whole thing that you'd lost your mind temporarily, they all understood. That North Adams was particularly nice," she said sending back a glance to the seasoned, tall, dark-haired actor who played the homicide detective I'd tried to save. "He even offered to talk to you and help you with 'this difficult time,' as he put it. And the guy who played the shooter seemed to take it as some kind of compliment to his acting ability."

"You said I lost my mind?" I said, skipping over everything else she'd said. "Great, now they think I'm crazy." Normally I might not care what strangers thought of me, but I was probably going to see these people again. The bookstore was just up the street and even though the production was self-contained, providing meals and snacks, the cast and crew still drifted up to the bookstore to hang out, buy books, get coffee drinks and scoop up our barista's great cookies.

"We better go," I said. "We've still got to pick up Kelly's crochet items."

"We don't all have to go," Adele said, reminding us that she was more or less in charge of the crochet group. It was more in her mind and less in reality. CeeCee Collins was technically the leader, but her acting career was so busy right now it was hard for her to handle the group as well. So Adele had jumped in as de facto leader.

"Well, none of us really has to go," I said. "Kelly doesn't know we're coming and we can just wait until she comes to one of our meetings."

Adele snorted. "Maybe you can wait, Pink, but CeeCee and I have our doubts about Kelly's crochet ability. She keeps saying she's going to come to a meeting and she keeps saying she's going to make things for our booth at the Tarzana fair, but I haven't seen anything to make me believe it's true."

"What about the scarf she showed us that she was making?" I said.

"Okay, so she can make a scarf, and so she came to a

couple of meetings, and so whenever we see her at the bookstore she says she's been making stuff at home for the fair. But I want to see proof."

It was useless to argue with Adele, so Dinah and I traded nods and kept silent. It was just a short walk up the street to Dinah's house, which was on the corner. Kelly lived around the next corner on the street that paralleled the one the production company was using. As soon as we got on the other street, it was much quieter. The houses were set on orderly little plots, close to the street. This part of Tarzana had sidewalks and seemed more like a neighborhood than where I lived.

"I don't know why Kelly has to be so difficult," Adele said with a harrumph in her voice. It was all Dinah and I could do to keep from laughing. Adele practically wrote the book on causing a ruckus. Apparently immune to our stifled laughs, Adele continued. "If she's going to be one of the Hookers, she ought to follow the rules."

"Rules?" Dinah repeated with surprise. "What are they, the ten commandments of crochet?"

"I don't know if there are ten, but there should be something that says if you join the Hookers, you have to go along with the group, and show up to the meetings," Adele said as the breeze caught the brim of her hat and pushed it down, covering her eyes. She flipped it up and tried to make it stay. Go along with the group? Did Adele hear what she was saying? She never went along with anything.

As we continued down the block, I noticed that the street was crowded with cars and commercial vehicles. Generally it was empty at this time of day. But then I realized they were all part of the production and probably just being kept there until they were needed. I noticed a truck with open slats up ahead, parked in Kelly's driveway. The back of the truck was filled with greenery in pots and two men in jeans were standing next to it.

Since Dinah's house was just up the street from Kelly's, which made them neighbors, my friend knew more about Kelly's business than the rest of us. "She's got her hands full," Dinah began. "You know both she and her husband have kids from previous marriages. It's always a changing cast of characters in that house. His kids, her kids, no kids. You can't just pick up and hang out at the yarn table when you have kids out of school for the summer, and you have to cart them around to activities."

Adele spent some more time fighting with her hat as we got closer. She didn't seem impressed with Dinah's explanation. "And there's her husband's business," Dinah continued. "Maybe she helps out at his store."

The store was Hollar for a Dolllar, Tarzana's first dollar store. Dinah had heard that Kelly's husband was hoping to make the one location into a big success, so he could develop it into a chain. "He went up and down the block and gave us all goodie bags of merchandise and ten-percent-off coupons to entice us to go into the store."

I'd seen the goodie bags. The specialty factor of Hollar for a Dollar seemed to be that it had almost name-brand stuff. Dinah's goodie bag had contained Uncle Len's rice, Suckers strawberry jam and Wiggly's spearmint gum.

As we got closer, I noticed a woman standing on the sidewalk, watching the action with the truck. She had her hand on her hip and you didn't have to be a body language expert to know she was annoyed. As soon as she saw us, her expression sharpened and she stepped toward us.

"Coming to complain, aren't you," she said focusing on Dinah. "Well, I'm with you. It's not enough that we have that production company around the corner, but thanks to Kelly Donahue, its going to be on this side of the block, too. That is, unless we do something to stop it."

I knew not everyone found having a production company on their street exciting. To some it was nothing but a nuisance. Apparently this woman was one of those.

Dinah nodded a greeting at her. "Hi, Nanci. I don't think you've met Molly Pink and Adele Abrams." Nanci's angry expression broke for a moment as she acknowledged us, and Dinah told us that Nanci Silvers was Kelly's next-door neighbor and PTA president-elect at Wilbur Elementary.

Nanci definitely acted the part of PTA president. In all the years my sons had gone to school, the names and faces of the PTA presidents had changed, but the personas had stayed the same. The words bossy and controlling came to mind. Nanci's champagne blond hair was cut severely short with asymmetrical long dagger-shaped strands on the side that did nothing to soften her sharp features. There was something businesslike in her attire. The black slacks and short-sleeved jacket seemed like a suit. The jacket was embellished with a cluster of bloodred crocheted flowers. I noticed she'd started tapping her toe as one of the jean-clad men pulled a palm tree in a big black pot out of the truck. He nodded a greeting at our little group before continuing down the driveway toward Kelly's backyard.

"Kelly rented out her yard to the production company." Nanci went on to explain that Kelly's yard was directly behind one of the houses they were using on the other block. "Not only that, but she's signed her house up with a location service." Nanci gritted her teeth. "She's got dollar signs in her eyes. This isn't her first marriage, you know. And I think it won't be her last. That woman will do anything to make a buck. And she didn't even consult her husband. I want to take up a petition to stop her before our street becomes like that one." She gestured toward the street behind us.

"Kelly just doesn't get it about rules," Adele interjected.

Nanci nodded in agreement. "Kelly doesn't understand about being part of a group or neighborhood. It's all about money with her."

I knew what Nanci was talking about. Renting out your house to a production company could bring in a nice profit. Sometime back when Charlie was alive, someone had tried to hire him to do PR for their house. Yes, a house. It had become quite a star because it was Todd Jenkins's house in the family saga *The Jenkins*. It had also been used as the home of the matriarch in *Our Family and Friends*. Though a family lived there when it wasn't being used for a show, it had been built with the idea of renting it out to productions, so the interior was designed with an open plan, which made camera setups easy. Charlie had shown me the house and I had laughed when I saw the kitchen. It was designed for cameras not for cooking. I mean, you practically needed a golf cart to bring the dishes from the dining room to the sink.

After getting an assurance that Dinah wasn't thinking of listing her house with the location service and being non-committal about signing any sort of petition, Nanci let us go, but I noticed she followed us as we walked up to Kelly's house. Kelly's place had been given an overhaul since it was originally built. Someone had taken the basic stucco house and added a second story. To me, it looked like a cream-colored box with a red-tiled roof.

Kelly answered the door with a cordless phone to her ear. I guess she was used to people just showing up at her door because even though we hadn't called ahead she didn't seem surprised to see us. Whenever I saw her, I thought of the phrase *cute as a button*, though the saying didn't really make much sense. How was a button cute? But Kelly definitely was. She smiled at us and the two dimples in her cheeks appeared and then quickly disappeared when she saw Nanci lurking in the background. Kelly put her hand over the phone as Nanci fussed about the truck in the driveway and insisted that it was ruining her view. Kelly listened with a tired sigh; clearly she'd heard this before. "It *is* my driveway," Kelly reminded Nanci in a pointed tone.

Nanci made a huffing sound, turned abruptly and left. The cuteness came back into Kelly's face, and while she apologized for the interruption to whoever she was talking to on the phone, she gestured for us to come in. Her chestnut brown ponytail swung from side to side as she led the way. The beige capri pants and loose ivory linen top were casual, but something in the fit and the texture of the fabric said expensive. Still listening to the phone call, she pointed to some small brightly colored blocks in a box and mouthed *watch out*.

Not only did Adele watch out, she picked up the box and examined the side. She pushed it on me with a knowing nod. The front had the words LUGO Blocks printed in big letters and showed some scary looking pictures of things you could build. Whoever had written the copy clearly wasn't too good with English. Did anyone really say, "One thousand and one funs," or "Let's block"?

As Kelly hung up, she saw me reading the box and made a disparaging sound. "Sorry about the blocks. My kids were here last week and Dan brought the blocks home from the store for them. He doesn't understand that kids care about brands. LUGO?" she said with a snort. The phone rang in her hand and she went to answer it. "Go on into my workroom. I'll be in there in a minute." She put the phone to her ear as the three of us went in the direction she'd pointed. Adele pressed ahead mumbling something about wanting to see if there were any crochet supplies.

Dinah pointed at the "No Kids Allowed" sign on the door and gave me a quizzical look. Dinah was all about teaching kids and young adults how to behave, not excluding them. We passed through the door into a large room at the back of the house. A sliding glass door looked out on the backyard, and there were the men we'd seen before, walking around the yard measuring things.

"Hmm, let's just see what she's got," Adele said as her hat brim flopped in front of her face. She lifted it away from her eyes and quickly began to look around the room.

I was less concerned about finding proof that Kelly really crocheted than with checking out the whole room. We all loved seeing each other's craft rooms, hoping they'd be as messy and yarn filled as our own.

Kelly's was neither a mess like mine, with bags of yarn all over the place threatening to trip anyone who walked in without watching their step, nor super perfect looking like the ones I'd seen that were set up like yarn stores. Kelly seemed to favor plastic bins over shelves or cubbies. There were piles of them along the wall and Adele rushed toward one to check the contents. She seemed disappointed when the first one she opened contained yarn. And not just any yarn. When Adele held up a handful of skeins, I recognized the labels as high-end expensive yarn.

The room had a different feeling than what I'd gotten in the rest of the house, where the furniture seemed modest and utilitarian. The living room couch and chairs were plain and could probably live up to the abuse of the assorted kids who stayed there. But Kelly's crafting room was filled with nice things. There was artwork on the walls and all the furnishings were tasteful and eclectic. Her computer sat on a beautifully refinished library table and the Victorian dining chair pushed into it had a dusty rose cushion to soften the back. A Victorian-style love seat was covered in the same dusty rose material. An old trunk served as a table in front of the love seat and held a silver tray with a silver tea service. I guessed that the Mission-style easy chair was Kelly's seat of choice judging by the facedown magazine on the small table next to it and the full-spectrum floor lamp arranged to illuminate it. I was admiring the doll-size figure of a knight next to a small silver bowl of dried rose petals when Kelly came in the room.

"You found my knight in shining armor," she said with a smile. Adele let go of the lid of the plastic bin she was snooping in and turned quickly, no doubt to hide what she'd been doing. The brim of her hat flapped down over her face blocking her view, and Adele suddenly lost her balance and whirled across the room. The burst of wind from her movement flipped the brim back up and Adele reached out to steady herself and almost knocked over a lamp with a leaded glass shade sitting on the end of the computer table. I grabbed the brass base just in time to steady it and knocked a small book to the floor instead. I replaced the book, noting it was some kind of guide to coins.

"That glass shade wouldn't have taken a tumble well," I said. When I asked about the Tiffany-style lamp, Kelly laughed and said it was just a copy. "Just like everything else in here," she said, making a sweeping gesture with her arm. "Is there a reason for your visit?"

I noticed that one of the men had set a potted feathery palm tree in front of the sliding glass door. The other man looked at it and shook his head. The first man pulled it away.

Before Adele could stick her foot in her mouth, I told Kelly we'd come to pick up anything she'd made for our booth at the Jungle Days Fair. Kelly's phone rang, interrupting us. She answered it and listened for a moment before turning to the group.

"I have to go pick up my kids and take them to their father's house. I still have a little finishing to do with the pieces I made. I'm really coming to the group meeting tomorrow. I'll bring everything in then." She ushered us toward the door. "I promise."

When we got outside, Adele gave Dinah and me a knowing glance. "I'll believe it when I see it."

CHAPTER 2

"THAT WAS A WASTE OF TIME," ADELE SAID AS WE walked into Shedd & Royal. The bookstore seemed abuzz with business and Mrs. Shedd was standing at the front near the cashier station watching the activity with a big smile. Dinah had left us when we passed her house. She was teaching summer school and had to get her things together.

"At least you believe Kelly crochets now," I said.

Adele rolled her eyes with consternation. "Pink, I just saw some skeins of yarn, which doesn't prove a thing. I still say she's a crochet pretender. And she was sure in a rush to get rid of us."

"She had to pick up her kids and we did arrive unannounced," I said.

"Watch, if she does come to the meeting tomorrow, she'll have another excuse."

It was useless to argue with Adele. Crochet pretender? Adele was too much.

"I hope they stay forever," Mrs. Shedd said, gesturing toward the crowd in the café and bookstore. I knew the *they* she was referring to was the *L.A. 911* production.

The production had set up shop a little over a week ago and was using the whole area. I'd heard they were filming a number of episodes and would be there for weeks. It looked like Mrs. Shedd was going to get her wish, for a while anyway.

"If it weren't for my Eric," Adele said. "Molly might have messed all that up for you. She almost got arrested." Adele waited a beat before she added "Again."

There was no use denying it. I did seem to walk into trouble a lot, though it was hardly intentional. Mrs. Shedd gave me a stern look.

"I already heard about the incident," my boss said. "Molly, please don't ruffle their feathers. We don't want to chase their business away." She watched two people as they headed for the cashier each holding several books. "In fact, we want to do the opposite. We want to make them feel at home."

Adele mumbled something about spreading the word to the crew. "Everybody knows me, thanks to Eric," she said before heading to her domain. I watched as she made her way across the bookstore to the kids' department, greeting people from the production with nods and pointed fingers in what she seemed to think was some sort of hip gesture.

Was I the only one who saw that Adele got puzzled stares in return? "Mrs. Shedd, I promise I'll be good," I said before moving on. I know she'd told me I could call her Pamela and Mr. Royal, her partner, Joshua, but it felt too weird to change after all this time of calling them by their last names.

When I glanced toward the entrance of the café, I noticed the actor who'd played the homicide detective I'd tried to save had come in. He was carrying a cup with a fluff of white foam on top. Our eyes met as he got closer and his lips curved into a teasing smile.

"I suppose I should thank you," he said. "I heard you were trying to save me from him." He pointed toward the actor who'd had the gun. I barely recognized him now. He'd taken off the hooded sweatshirt and didn't appear threatening at all as he laughed and talked to one of the extras. It must have been a relief to get out of the jacket. Summers in the Valley always sizzled, but lately it had been hovering around one hundred. It was dry heat, but still one hundred was hot however you looked at it. "I don't think we've met. After what you did, it seems like I ought to know your name. North Adams," he said, holding out his hand. He was still wearing his costume of a suit and dress shirt, but his demeanor had changed. Gone was the weary cop face, and now he seemed affable and relaxed.

"Molly Pink," I said, with an embarrassed flutter of my eyes. Of course, I'd recognized him without the introduction. North Adams was a well-known actor who'd been in a number of successful series over the years. I liked the sprinkling of gray in his dark hair and I suspected it was planned by some stylist to make him look serious. When he was younger his features had been almost too even and too handsome. But time had put some character in his face. Still the azure blue eyes were startling in person. His head was slightly too big for the rest of his body, but that seemed common in actors. I guessed that abnormality made them appear better on camera. "I don't usually go around tackling people. I am truly sorry and I hope it didn't cause you a lot of delays." I hadn't realized that Adele had come out of the kids' area and was standing directly behind me.

"It was because of what happened to her boyfriend,"

Adele said. "Correct that to the person who was her boy-friend."

I had taken offense at the "boyfriend" title the whole time Barry and I had been involved. It just sounded too sock hopish for a man in his fifties—the same way saying we were dating sounded silly. But now I just let it go. It was irrelevant. I heard Adele begin to tell the story of what happened. Dinah had just offered the broad strokes when she tried to smooth things over at the shoot, but Adele was going into every detail and I really didn't want to stand there and hear it again.

Without a backward glance I escaped into the yarn department and started straightening the skeins that had been left all over. It was surprising that none of the Hookers were hanging out at the table, but I was just as glad for the peace. I noticed the crowd from the production company begin to thin out, so I was surprised when North Adams walked into the yarn area.

"Now I understand," he said with sincerity in his voice. "I'm so sorry for your loss."

"What exactly did Adele tell you?" I said as he turned to go.

"Everything. Maybe even too many personal details," he said before he left.

CHAPTER 3

I WAS SURPRISED AT WHAT MASON FIELDS SAID when he called suggesting we get dinner. Well, I wasn't surprised about the dinner part. We had been doing that a lot lately. But he said he had some kind of problem. Mason had always been the person who fixed problems. If he'd had any before, he'd never told me about them. But then our relationship was a little odd.

I liked to think of us as friends, though since I'd broken up with Barry, Mason had been trying to knock it up a notch—to what, friends with benefits? It was hard to tell exactly because Mason compartmentalized his life. Other than knowing he was divorced and had two kids, his family had always been off limits to me. In fact that had been the stumbling block to us having more than a friendship before. While we both agreed we weren't looking to get married, I needed a little more than he seemed willing to offer. Mason was in the middle of my life, but I felt like he kept me on the sidelines of his.

When he wasn't spending time with me, Mason was a top-flight attorney to the stars. He was the one naughty celebrities turned to to get out of trouble. Mason was very good at getting people out of trouble. He'd done it for me a number of times.

With the summer days still long, it wasn't completely dark when I walked out of Shedd & Royal. The evening had cooled off only slightly and the air still felt balmy. I drove the greenmobile home. I was beginning to see my son's point about the car. It was a 1993 190E Mercedes in a color I called teal green and while I thought of it as a classic car, it was beginning to show its age. I left it in the driveway and didn't go in my house. To go in was to get sucked into a vortex of animals and things to take care of and never get out and I could see Mason had parked on the street and was leaning against his car, checking his BlackBerry. He put it away as soon as I got close, and his face broke out into a happy grin before he hugged me in greeting.

He was still dressed in his work clothes. The light color of the taupe suit made it seem summery. All of his suits were custom tailored and made out of a fine wool that draped perfectly. His blue dress shirt had the collar opened. As usual a lock of his dark hair had fallen across his forehead. I always thought it made him look earnest and hardworking. And I thought the sprinkling of gray made him look distinguished.

"What's up?" I said as I got in the car. "You said you had a problem." I might have seemed a little too eager, but it was the first time he was letting me into his life.

"It can wait," he said as he steered the car onto the street. "Tell me about your day. I could use a little diversion."

I made a face. Was he backing down? But then I fell for the bait. I mean, who doesn't want to talk about their day?

We ended up at a neighborhood Italian restaurant. Tarzanians had been eating there for decades thanks to the good food and friendly atmosphere. We took a table by the window and picked up our menus. I didn't know why I bothered looking at mine. Mason always did the ordering. He knew what I liked better than I did.

When the waiter came by, Mason ordered a Caesar salad for two. They made their own dressing and it was delicious. When Mason ordered several appetizers for us to share, it was like he'd read my mind. With the hot weather and late hour, I didn't feel like anything too heavy.

The waiter had just brought us a basket of hot home-made bread and I was pouring some olive oil on my bread plate, when I noticed someone come in from the back. Kelly walked through the tables, up to the counter, obviously there for food to go. I started to wave, but she didn't see me and I let it go.

"You know her?" Mason said.

"Not exactly," I answered. I started to explain about going to her house, but then realized it was better to start at the beginning of the whole thing. Mason's eyes widened when he heard about me trying to tackle the actor. Then he laughed.

"I wish I'd been there for that. Anybody I know in the scene?" The Caesar salad had come, and he divided it up on our plates, and asked for fresh pepper.

"I don't know the name of the actor I tackled, but North Adams was the guy I was trying to save."

Mason nodded. "He's a client of the law firm. I know him from charity events and such, but he's never needed my services. At least, not so far."

I mentioned our real destination had been Kelly's. "There's something weird there," I said. Mason's grin widened.

"Great. I love it when you play detective." I rolled my eyes in response. But after being involved in solving a number of murders, I'd developed some skills. I had started to notice things more and infer things from them. I did it at the grocery store all the time and tried to figure out what the people were shopping for by what they were buying. Like the time I figured out someone was having a barbecue and one of the guests was a vegetarian because they had a bag of charcoal brickets, six Spencer steaks, and one frozen vegetarian entree. I'd actually asked the man and he'd told me I was right.

Mason laughed when I told him about the LUGOs. "I saw the store," he said vaguely gesturing toward the street. "How's it doing?"

"I think they're struggling. The neighbor mentioned Kelly would do anything to make some money."

"So tell me Sherlock what did you notice about the Hollar for a Dollar people's house?"

It had gotten to be kind of a game with us. I told him about Kelly's room and how it seemed like a haven. "It was different from the rest of the house and had nicer furniture and doodads." I described the refinished library table she had her computer on. I mentioned that I'd seen a chair like her Mission-styled one in a store for a couple of thousand. "Adele knocked into a leaded glass lamp. Even the modern copies of those aren't cheap. I wouldn't think much of it if the rest of the house, or what I saw of it, went with the things in her room." I stopped for a moment and in my mind's eye, I was seeing it again. "And it wasn't just the furniture. It was the yarn, too."

Mason knew what a mess my craft room was. More than once he'd almost skidded across the floor after getting his fancy shoes caught in a grocery bag full of yarn. "No bags of any kind," I said. Her stuff was all in plastic bins stacked neatly against the wall. I pictured Adele opening one of them and visualized the yarn she'd held up. "I recognized the brands. It was all pricey stuff." Mason still looked a little puzzled.

"The point is, instead of a hodgepodge of stuff like the rest of us have, Kelly's looked like stock. She had a whole container of the same kind of yarn." Mason kind of shrugged and urged me on.

"So what do you think it means?'

"I don't know. We don't even know if she really crochets or is a crochet pretender as Adele called her. Either way, it seems odd she would invest so much money in yarn. It was funny, too, that she didn't have any samples of her work sitting in the room."

"So maybe Adele is right and she's a fake. A fake with fancy taste," Mason said.

"What's the difference if she is or isn't, anyway," I said. We'd started on the thick slices of fresh mozzarella with tomatoes and basil, along with the stuffed mushrooms and grilled asparagus done in garlic and olive oil. "Now you tell me *your* problem."

Mason's face changed. The grin faded and he set down his fork. He took a deep breath and sat back in his chair. "You know my daughter is getting married and you know the wedding invitations have gone out." He watched as I nodded.

As I was agreeing, I was thinking that I didn't even know either of his daughters' names. He just called them my youngest and my oldest. And about those invitations— I hadn't gotten one. I had dropped enough hints, but he'd shrugged them all off. As far as I was concerned not getting invited to the wedding was a definite sign our relationship shouldn't be moving to the next level.

"I just found out the wedding planner declared bankruptcy. It seems her assistant was embezzling money and never paid the deposit on the ballroom at the Belle Vista hotel, which is listed on the wedding invitations. No deposits were paid for flowers, food, the cake, the band . . ." His voice trailed off and I waited for him to say more. He looked at me intently. "Do you know what that means?"

I had a pretty good idea, but I let him say it. "It means we have no location for the wedding. It means two hundred or so guests are going to show up and find somebody else having a birthday party in that ballroom. The food and the rest of it, is fixable. But finding a location at the last minute"—Mason threw up his hands. "And here is the worst part—my ex has known this for weeks. She was going to take care of it and then tell me. Take care of it?" His voice started to rise. "Jaimee took care of it all right," he said sarcastically. "If she'd told me when she first found out, we might have found another place. But now? It's just about impossible."

I'd never seen Mason so upset. Instinctively, I put my hand on his as a sign of sympathy. He squeezed it and sighed. "Sunshine, I knew you would understand." So now I at least knew his ex-wife's name. And I began to wonder about all the stuff he'd told me about them having an amicable divorce.

"I could get buses to take the guests somewhere, if we had a somewhere to take them." He picked up his fork, then dropped it in frustration. "I could just kill my wife."

He said it rather loudly and several diners looked toward us with surprise.

Then Mason pulled himself together and asked if I wanted cheesecake. When I nodded, he ordered us coffees and a piece of cheesecake with extra strawberries to share. "I'm sorry for venting this on you. I suppose you've figured this isn't the first time my ex has made a mess of things and dropped them in my lap to fix."

"So your wife's name is Jaimee," I said with a teasing smile. "My first peek behind the curtain. How about telling me your daughters' names instead of calling them the youngest and oldest." I'd gotten through to Mason and his mouth slipped into a grin as his anger dissipated.

"Thursday is the one getting married and her sister's name is Brooklyn."

"Thursday?" I said.

"It was Jaimee's idea to give her a unique name." He rolled his eyes. "And Thursday is happy with her name. Go figure that."

"See, it isn't so hard to let me into your life."

Mason was back to his usual self and chuckled. "I have been keeping my family separate for so long—it takes time to change. I have to take baby steps," he said. "I suppose you want to know why we got a divorce."

From what he'd just said about Jaimee, it wasn't too hard to figure, but I let him explain anyway. It was another baby step and I was glad he was taking it.

"For a long time I was all work, work, work and we barely spent any time together," he said. "Then, when my daughters went off to college and I finally had younger lawyers working for me to handle of lot of the grunt work, I started spending more time with Jaimee." He shook his head with disbelief. "I'm not sure if she changed or if I just didn't know her in the first place, but I started not wanting to go home." He beamed a big smile my way. "She wasn't any fun like you are."

After he paid the check, we walked down Ventura Boulevard holding hands. All the stores on the main street were closed and we looked in at the illuminated display windows as we headed back to the bookstore parking lot where Mason had left his car. Traffic had thinned out and the air had gotten the typical evening chill that made the summer weather so tolerable. You always needed a blanket at night and could turn off the air-conditioning and throw open the windows.

Mason pulled the car in front of my house and cut the motor. "Shall I come in?"

He'd been asking me that same question every time he brought me home and the answer had always been the same. We both stared at the front of my house and I said something about it not being a good idea.

"When?" he said, which surprised me. He'd never pushed before. I made a helpless shrug.

"When he's gone," I said. "I know what you're thinking. I should have my head examined." I looked toward the front window and just then I saw a familiar form standing in front of it, peering out.

CHAPTER 4

EVEN THOUGH IT WAS A SHORTER DISTANCE UP the walkway to my front door, I took the driveway and went through the backyard to my kitchen door. Inside everything was quiet. Even the dogs and cats didn't rush to greet me.

My plan was to quickly make myself a cup of herbal tea and take it to my room before anyone caught sight of me. I was filling my mug with hot water when Barry Greenberg, my former boyfriend, suddenly walked into the kitchen. It was a relief to see him not in a wheelchair, not in a cast, not on crutches and not leaning on a cane. He was beginning to seem more like his old self, though he was still favoring his left knee.

"You're coming home kind of late." He leaned his tall frame against the counter as I took out the tea things and gave him a dark look. I had to force myself to keep from saying that it was none of his business.

This was awkward with a capital *A*. There always seemed to be an undercurrent of anger when you saw an ex-boyfriend. But if he was living with you—well, not living *with* you, but under the same roof and recovering from something terrible, how could you not feel guilty for the anger.

A videotape began to play in my mind. It was a combination of what I'd been told about Barry's shooting and what I'd seen on TV. It had been just an ordinary day, shortly after Barry and I broke up. Barry was loading his car after a shopping trip to Walmart when he noticed a couple of uniforms taking out a pair of teenage boys in handcuffs and figured they'd been caught shoplifting. One of the cops was helping one of the suspects into the backseat of the cruiser when suddenly the other kid started to struggle with the officer handling him. Without hesitating, Barry rushed in, flashed his badge and tried to help.

This was the part when I had to stop and swallow a few times. How could that kid have been so stupid to go from a shoplifting charge to attempted murder? Somehow he'd managed to get hold of the arresting officer's gun, even with his hands cuffed behind his back, and began shooting wildly. Barry wasn't wearing a Kevlar vest. It was all so unexpected, he couldn't even move. He'd been shot three times. Once in the chest, one in the thigh and once in the knee. Even now, I shuddered just thinking of the pain.

It had been Barry's son Jeffrey who'd called to tell me about his father and to tell me that Barry was asking for me. It was all touch and go then. Barry was delirious, but still worried about his son. I was the only one he wanted his son Jeffrey to stay with. It didn't matter what had gone on between Barry and me, I loved Jeffrey. I'd taken him home with me from the hospital.

Barry's condition kept getting upgraded and eventually

he was ready to go home, but there was a problem. His condo was a two-story place and he couldn't manage stairs. So what did I do? I offered to let him recuperate at my house. What was I thinking? I know what I was thinking— that he would never accept. It was Barry who'd been all or nothing about our relationship, insisting either we got married or were done, and I mean, completely done, not even friends anymore. But he had accepted my offer anyway, saying it was because of Jeffrey. The kid had been through a lot and he seemed happy at my house.

Mason tried to talk Barry into getting a chairlift put in his condo and even offered to get it done, but Barry stuck with staying at my place. As a last ditch effort, Mason suggested both Barry and Jeffrey stay at his place. He lived alone with a toy fox terrier in a huge ranch house. I wasn't surprised when Barry turned that down. Though the two men knew each other, I'd hardly call them friends.

You didn't have to be a brainiac to figure out Mason's motive. He was campaigning for our relationship to be something more than pals, and having Barry staying at my house would definitely be an obstacle.

At first it had worked out okay. My son Samuel had moved back home awhile ago and I gave Barry and Jeffrey rooms down the hall from his. Mine was on the complete other side of the house. I knew there was a constant flow of people coming and going to help Barry out, but I was barely affected by it. We were just ships occasionally passing in the kitchen.

Whoever had designed this house must have known that someday, somebody would need to get away from it all without leaving home. Once I shut the door to the den behind me and entered the short hall, I could forget about everyone and whatever else was going on in the rest of the house. The master suite was really a suite and far away from the other bedrooms. I had a huge bedroom with a fireplace, a generous-size bathroom and a hall area that was like a sitting room. I'd moved some of my crochet stuff and brought in a comfortable chair to work in. I had all the electronic essentials—TV, video player and computer. I'd brought in a stack of romantic comedies and had a pile of books I wanted to read. It had become a habit for me to come home and shut myself in my little haven.

Now that Barry had progressed from a cast with crutches, to just crutches, to a cane and now was down to a small limp, I was even more grateful for my refuge. He was up and around more and I never knew quite what to do when we ran into each other. I was looking forward to his going home. I'd have the run of my house back and we could permanently shut the door on our relationship.

The air filled with the scent of peppermint as I swished the tea bag around in the cup a last time before discarding it. I was all set to grab the cup and my things and head across the house, when Barry started to talk.

"I just want to thank you again for letting me stay here. I know it's been great for Jeffrey." This wasn't the first time Barry had thanked me. I nodded and said I was glad he seemed to be healed. I waited, expecting him to say something about moving home.

"I don't know if you know, but I went back to work," he said. He was watching me from across the room. I was all befuddled about where to look. It was normal to face someone speaking to you and I glanced up from the mug of tea. He must have changed out of his work clothes into the faded jeans and soft blue tee shirt he was now wearing. He'd looked pretty bad when he first got to my house, and I was glad his face had lost the gaunt look. I might have had a little residual anger about the way things had worked out for us, but I still cared about him. I was having a hard time making sense of it but I thought the best way to deal with it, was by keeping a distance.

"You must be glad to get back to it." I picked up the mug but still he didn't move.

"I'm not exactly back to my regular job." He held up a blue binder that had been tucked under his arm. "I'm easing back in by working cold cases." He glanced toward the steaming cup of tea. "That smells good. What kind of tea is it?" I wanted to take the tea and go, but it felt wrong to just rush out, and the way he was looking at my mug, it was obvious he wanted some, too. I certainly wouldn't begrudge him a tea bag. I pointed to the cabinet and told him to help himself.

Without the slightest hesitation, he grabbed a mug and found one of the tea bags. As I made another move to go, he said, "Maybe we could have our tea together. To toast my going back to work."

I was going to beg off, but it was just a cup of tea after all, so I agreed. Barry didn't wait for me to have second thoughts and led the way to the living room.

"Seems like old times," Barry said looking at the couch. When we'd been a couple, we'd spent a lot of time sitting there together. The idea of sitting there now felt strange and uncomfortable. I just wanted to drink my tea fast and escape.

"Let's sit outside," I said, making an abrupt turn. Barry followed me through the kitchen and out the door.

The yard was filled with the night sounds of crickets chirping and birds calling to each other. My gardenia plant was covered with creamy white blossoms and they filled the air with their heady scent. The floodlights along the back of the house illuminated the patio area and I noticed that Barry still seemed a little stiff as he lowered himself into one of the patio chairs. Above us the sky was midnight blue and the full moon peeked through the orange trees.

"It's nice out here," he said setting the mug of aromatic tea on the small glass table between our chairs. He stretched his leg into a more comfortable position. I asked where Jeffrey was and he said he'd gone to bed.

In a certain way, Jeffrey had benefitted from his father being laid up. Barry'd had to let go a little and his fourteen-year-old son had started using his bike for transportation. Jeffrey loved the freedom of getting around the area on his own. I might have kept my distance from Barry, but Jeffrey kept me up-to-date on what was going on in his life.

"The important thing is that you're better. It looks like it's all healed up." I glanced toward his outstretched leg. "I'm sure you're anxious to move back home and get on with your life. So, what do you think it will be? A few days, a week?"

Was it my imagination or did Barry's expression falter. "I don't have an exact date. I'm still getting physical therapy and I'm not feeling ready to tackle all those stairs." As if to make his point, he moved his leg and seemed to feel a twinge of pain. "But if we've overstayed our welcome, I'll try to make some other arrangements."

"No, no. Stay until you can run up and down the stairs," I said. I wanted him to go, but at the same time I didn't want to push him out while he was still healing. What difference did a little more time make, anyway? I drained my cup and prepared to make my exit.

Before I could say anything along the lines of good night, Barry laid the binder he'd been carrying under his arm on the table. "It's the murder book for one of the old cases I'm working on." He'd never even mentioned a murder book before, let alone put one in front of me. We both stared at it for a moment before he invited me to have a look.

I'd become a bit of an amateur sleuth and happened on a number of bodies, but I wasn't prepared for the photos. I guess I'd been lucky, the bodies I'd encountered hadn't been that gory. I gasped at the photo of a man's body sprawled in a pool of blood.

"That's from a murder five years ago. There were no suspects and it seemed like a home-invasion robbery gone bad. The guy worked at a liquor store. He did a lot of deliveries. The girlfriend said he didn't have any enemies, and that all the customers liked him and sometimes invited him to join the events he'd delivered for."

Part of me wanted to close the book and go inside. But I couldn't stop looking at the photograph. I noticed a band of skin on his wrist that was lighter than the rest of it. "It looks like they got his watch," I said.

Barry smiled. "Very good, babe, I mean, Molly. The girlfriend said he'd recently gotten a fancy watch. She wasn't very good about listing what was missing. She thought some household goods had also been taken. The only thing she did say was that something had happened to change things for the guy. He had never given her details, just that he'd recently had some kind of uptick in his life. And that he'd also recently purchased a gun." I gazed at the picture again and noticed something odd on the carpet. It looked like a plastic juice bottle, but there was black tape around the mouth and the bottom seemed to be missing. There was a plastic number next to it, I knew they used to mark evidence. I asked Barry about it.

"The original notes described it as a homemade silencer,"

he said. I knew very little about guns and even less about a silencer. Barry was only too happy to answer when I asked about them.

"The obvious point is to muffle the sound of the gunshot. The homemade ones I've seen were made of two-liter plastic bottles filled with Styrofoam peanuts that were taped onto the end of the guns. It looks like this one was improvised at the last minute from the victim's own bottle of juice." He pointed to the mouth of the bottle and said the notes said they'd swabbed it for DNA and it had matched the victim's. "The original investigators thought, judging by the bullets, that he'd been shot with his own gun, though they never found it."

I'd gotten so involved with the murder book and hearing what a silencer was, I'd forgotten I was trying to leave. Finally I set the binder back on the table and picked up my mug. "I better go in," I said, getting up.

"Oh," he said. "I was going to tell you about the other case I'm working on." I stopped in my tracks. I wanted to go, but I was curious about the other case. Barry had never shared like this before. And I liked being complimented on my sleuthing skills for noticing the missing watch. I sat back down. What harm could there be from spending a few more minutes with him?

"Are there pictures?" I asked sliding back into my chair as I gazed at the binder.

"I didn't bring that binder home with me," he said. "I'll just have to tell you about it with no visual aids." He started to tell me the details. The big difference with this case was the detectives who worked the case were sure who did it. The victim was a wealthy man who lived in a gated community in Chatsworth. He was single, entertained often and liked to surround himself with low-level celebrities. He'd been hit on the head with a large geode. This particular one had amethyst crystals inside, not that it mattered. When it had first been investigated, the detectives had found out that the victim had recently accused the housekeeper of taking pieces of jewelry and collectibles, one item at a time. Though she'd denied it, he had fired her. "It appears she came back, killed him and then took a bunch of collect-ibles and some valuable decorative items. The problem was, the detectives couldn't get enough evidence to make a case against her, and no matter how they tried, she wouldn't con-fess. And none of the stolen items ever surfaced."

Barry seemed more animated than I'd seen him in a long time. "I'm going to have another go at the housekeeper. After all this time, she won't be expecting it." I nodded to show I was listening, though I wanted to make my getaway. I made a move to get up, but Barry continued talking. "I found out some things the earlier guys missed. It seems the liquor store guy delivered to the other victim's house and there's something similar about the items taken."

I heard the clank of the gate by the driveway and a mo-ment later my son Samuel came through the yard. He was carrying a guitar case and looked happy. When he saw Barry and me sitting together with the binder open to a grisly picture, his smiled faded. To cover the awkward pause I asked him about his evening.

"I had a gig up at the country club. All sixties music for a wedding anniversary," he said taking off his sports jacket. Samuel's move back home was only supposed to be tempo-rary, too, but recently he'd gotten his hours cut on his barista job and his night gigs as a musician were undepend-able, so I didn't think he was going to be moving out any-time soon. He tucked the jacket under his arm and focused in on me.

"Tell me you didn't tackle some TV actor with a fake gun," Samuel said. When I looked embarrassed and made a little nod toward Barry, trying to tell my son that Barry didn't know and I wanted to keep it that way, Samuel rolled his eyes and he shook his head with disbelief.

CHAPTER 5

"ONLY YOU WOULD HAVE BEEN ENTICED BY AN offer to see a murder book," Dinah said with a laugh. We'd met for breakfast at the Le Grande Fromage, the French café down the street from the bookstore, and I'd told her, no strike that, more like confessed, about the cup of tea with Barry.

"I just want him to go home so I can get my stuff back from the storage unit and have my crochet room again," I said. "It's too confusing with him there. I'm angry at him for being so stubborn. If I wouldn't marry him, we couldn't even be friends? What kind of logic is that? I should never have offered to let him stay at my house."

"It sounds like he wants to be friends now," Dinah said.

"No, I think he appreciates that I let them live at my place and I think he was bored last night and had no one to talk to. Remember, he's used to keeping crazy hours. He told me he's working nine to five now."

"Did you tell him about the incident on the *L.A. 911* shoot?" Dinah asked as one of the counter people brought over our food. I had a red eye and one of their freshly made cheese croissants. Dinah had ordered café au lait and a plain croissant. As usual, the airy place, with its round tables and black-and-white-checkered floor, was busy, and there was a line of people at the counter waiting to place their orders.

"No. I just left a big silence after Samuel's comment," I said picking up the red eye and checking to see if it was too hot to drink. "Then I rushed inside and left Barry sitting under the stars." The coffee drink needed a few minutes to cool, so I broke off a piece of the cheese croissant. "I suppose having the tea was okay. We just talked about the cases he's working on. It wasn't like it was anything personal. I'm just as ready to shut the door on our relationship as he is. Once he moves home, that's it, we're done."

"You had a busy night. Dinner with Mason first. How's that going?" Dinah simultaneously poured steamed milk and hot coffee into her mug. I told her about Mason's problems with his daughter's wedding. "But did he say anything about inviting you?"

I made a face. "No." I tried the coffee again and took a small sip. I started to defend Mason saying he had a lot on his plate, but Dinah interrupted me.

"You know you could just tell him you want to be invited."

"I want him to do it on his own." I explained what he'd said about taking baby steps. "At least, he's trying."

"I'm just curious," Dinah began. "You said Barry had a lot of people visiting him while he's been staying at your place. Was Detective Heather one of them?" Heather Gilmore was a homicide detective and if she was aiming for perfect, she was succeeding. She was smart, beautiful and I heard she was great with a gun. She'd always had an eye on Barry.

"I don't know. There were all kinds of people coming and going—home health care workers, his cop friends, pizza delivery guys. I think he even got flowers. It's not my business anyway." I pulled off another piece of my roll.

A dark-haired man with a quick gait came into the café and went directly to the counter. He grabbed a coffee, and as he headed back toward the door I caught sight of his face and recognized the sharp features of Kelly's husband, Dan. I didn't really know him, other than he shopped at the bookstore and liked spy novels, but when he looked in my direction, I said hello.

"The bookstore lady," he said, setting his cup on our table as he checked to make sure the top was secure on his coffee. "And Kelly does some kind of activity with you, right?" He seemed a little overly cheery. The kind of cheery that grated on your nerves in the morning. I mentioned the crochet group and introduced Dinah. He picked up his coffee and seemed about to go, but then set it down again. "I want to run a few names past you. I'd like to get input from the locals. I'm not so sure Hollar for a Dollar is the best name for my store. I could feel Dinah twitching in her seat. It bugged her no end that he had misspelled *hollar* so it rhymed with *dollar*. Any day now she was sure some hapless freshmen in her English class would spell holler with an *a* and use the store as the reason why.

"What do you think of *The Dollar Den* or *Dollars to Donuts*?" Before we could answer he went into an explanation. This store was his chance to tweak the concept before he turned them into a chain or franchised them. He was bright-eyed and enthusiastic and said something like every journey starts with a single step or in his case it was a chain or franchise starting with a single store. "Think about the names and come into the store when you've made up your mind. I'm putting a box in the front where you can vote for one of them. Before I even count the votes, I'm going to do a drawing. The winner gets a whole year of shopping at my store, whichever name wins."

"How about calling it More Bang for Your Buck?" Dinah said. "And all spelled the traditional way." Dan's face brightened even more if that was possible.

"That's it. I don't even need to have a contest. Your idea says it all." He hugged Dinah and then took one of our napkins and scribbled the name on it. "When you come in, you're getting the prize. A whole year of shopping. We've got Paul Noman's products, Gray Pooponit mustard, and Conniption dairy products. Just before he left, he pulled out a couple of coupons and gave them to me as a consolation prize.

He left a whirlwind in his wake as he rushed out the door.

When we finished our meal, we headed up the street to Shedd & Royal. My start time wasn't until later in the day, but the Tarzana Hookers were having an official gathering in the morning. Dinah and I walked through the store to the yarn area. Almost everybody was already there and the table was covered with a colorful mélange of yarn and projects.

Dinah and I took seats next to Eduardo and started to pull out our projects. Even though I'd been crocheting with Eduardo Linnares for a long time, I was still amazed to see how this former cover model with huge hands could work a small steel hook with such precision.

He nodded a greeting to us, while I admired his work. Eduardo could crochet with any kind of yarn, but he preferred working with thread. He'd learned Irish crochet from his Irish grandmother and it was natural for him. He laid the white lacy bookmark in progress on the table and stretched.

Rhoda Klein eyed him from across the table. She was a real no-nonsense sort of person. Her hair was brown and short and she didn't wear makeup or trendy clothes. Loose pants and loose tops in neutral shades gave her a rather cylindrical shape. It was hard to judge her age, and I was too polite to ask, but I'd guess she was somewhere in her forties, though she was the type who looked older when she was young and ageless when she got older.

"I don't think the bookmarks are worth all that effort. Not enough perceived value. People want to buy something they can wear," she said. She held up a summer weight shawl she was working on. She was using a thin cotton yarn and a big hook, which gave the shawl a lacy look and let lots of air through.

"Where's Sheila?" Rhoda asked. CeeCee said Sheila hadn't been able to get away from the store down the street where she worked.

Elise was sitting next to Rhoda. The two of them couldn't have seemed more different. Elise was slight with a frizzle of brown curls. I always felt there was something a little scattered about her. Her tiny features and bright eyes went perfectly with her wispy, birdlike voice.

"But a shawl takes much longer to make. Eduardo turns out those bookmarks in no time," Elise chirped. She glanced at Eduardo's work. "I bet you could make some of those vampire style." Elise was still hung up on Anthony, the vampire who crocheted and was featured in a series of books and now a movie, and everything she made was what she called "vampire style." It meant that she used black and white yarn, with a touch of red. And what she called the vampire stitch, which was really a half double crochet, but looked a little like a fang. Thanks to her obsession, Elise had taken to dressing vampire style, too, which meant all she wore was black, white and red. Eduardo just smiled and went back to his bookmark.

CeeCee Collins sat at the head of the table. She was the official leader of the group, no matter what Adele said. CeeCee was our resident celebrity and was far more done up than the rest of us. Her mink brown hair was perfectly colored and styled. She'd gone from being referred to as a veteran actress, which was a nice way of saying over with, to being referred to as the comeback kid. It had started when she got the hosting job of *Making Amends*, a reality show about righting old wrongs, but the real change came when she was cast in the crocheting vampire movie *Caught by a Kiss*. The fact that there was Oscar buzz about her performance had put her back into the spotlight.

"What do you think of this look," she said, standing up so we could see the mint green linen pants and long white tunic. "This new stylist has a pallet of colors for me she calls pastels, but I call them candy colors. When I looked in my closet it was like looking at a box of those French pastel mint patties."

Nobody said anything, which I think was based on the idea if you can't say something nice . . . Adele was a latecomer to the group and came in as we were all looking at CeeCee's clothes.

"What happened to you?" Adele said as her eyes moved up and down CeeCee's outfit. "You look like somebody tried to erase the color of your pants." Adele twirled for all of us. "Now this is green." She wore a long dress with slits up past her knees. I would have called the color grass stain. She'd added a fuchsia-colored crocheted belt that hung low around her hips with a matching headband. Adele stopped the modeling move and looked up and down the table. She pursed her lips when her gaze settled on the empty chair.

"Promised she'd come, did she," Adele said, putting her hand on her hip. "I don't think so. No matter what Kelly said, I don't believe she has any pieces to give us for the Jungle Days Fair. I'm telling you, she's a crochet pretender."

"Dear, sit down," CeeCee said. "I think you're being a little harsh about Kelly. Though I am getting a little concerned she might be a flake, I would like to see what she's got. We just have a few weeks before the fair. And since it's a Tarzana fair and we're the Tarzana Hookers, we want our booth to make us look good."

Dinah told the group what she knew about Kelly and all the things she had going on.

"I'm going over there after the meeting," Adele said. "And I'm not leaving with empty promises. Either she hands over something she's crocheted, or I say we banish her from the group."

CeeCee gave me a worried look. "Molly, we don't want Adele going there alone, do we? Dinah just lives down the street. The two of you could accompany Adele." CeeCee's voice sounded cordial, but her meaning was clear. No way was Adele going to be allowed to go alone.

"How about the three musketeers going there together," I said. Adele had come up with that title for us a while ago.

"Pink, you're so right. It would be much more powerful if I have backup when I pin her against the wall."

"It's only some crocheted items for a street fair," Dinah said, trying to get some reality going in Adele's mind. Good luck on that one. The three of us walked outside. The sun had moved up in the sky and was doing away with the last of the cool morning as we went around the corner.

Whoever had planned this area, didn't like grid-pattern streets. Each of the streets had a curve. I suppose the planner thought it made the area more interesting. The street that went down from Ventura, past Dinah's house and on to the production area had an S curve and we could only see the beginning of the production equipment. Kelly's street cut in just before Dinah's house and curved around before running parallel.

Adele was trying to walk ahead of us, but when she saw Eric sitting astride his motorcycle in the middle of the street, making sure no traffic tried to pass, she made a detour. Despite the heat, his uniform appeared meticulous. Every strand of his short, wavy brown hair was in place. Up ahead, two actors stood in the street as a car drove slowly toward them. The lights and reflectors were positioned around them, and the camera and a bunch of people were in the middle of the street. The caravan of trucks had been moved back and were blocked from view by the curve of the street further up.

This time I didn't even flinch when I saw the tip of a rifle pointing out of the open car window. It was all just make-believe. Dinah and I had slowed to a stop. There was something mesmerizing about watching the other side of the magic.

Suddenly a voice called "Cut." Then there were a bunch of angry voices and I heard someone yelling for "Security." Eric had already popped off his motorcycle and was running to the knot of people. Run might have been the wrong word. It was more like loping. His posture was ramrod straight and there was something proper about him even as he rushed into trouble.

"What did you do this time, Pink?" Adele had rejoined Dinah and me on the street corner.

"Are you kidding?" I said with annoyance in my voice. She countered by saying something to the effect that since I always seemed to be getting into trouble, it was an easy assumption.

Dinah elbowed me and pointed. Eric was coming toward us and he had a kid in tow.

Jeffrey?

"Hi," he said with a weak smile when they got close to us.

Eric appeared tough and all business. "You know them?" Eric said to Jeffrey in his ticket-giving voice. Then his face softened when his eyes met Adele's. "See you later, cutchy-kins," he said in a sweet voice before he caught himself and went back to gruff Eric. "And don't you come back," he said, letting Jeffrey go and returning to his post.

Jeffrey was not the spitting image of his father. Barry had close-cropped no-nonsense hair and was a conservative dresser. It was either suits, slacks and a sports jacket, or well broken-in jeans with a pocket tee shirt, possibly topped with a plaid flannel shirt.

Jeffrey had a "look." But then Jeffrey wanted to be an actor, no strike that, he was an actor. He'd done some plays with the middle school drama club and had gone on some auditions for commercials. There was a debate going on about his name. He wanted to go by Columbia Greenberg and then just Columbia because he thought it made him stand out. Barry thought the whole idea stunk and dealt with it by ignoring it all together.

Jeffrey's hair was longer and spikier than his dad's, thanks to massive amounts of gel. He usually wore a sports jacket and jeans with a graphic tee shirt underneath. But today he'd gone all-American kid. He had on jeans, high-top sneakers and a bloodred tee shirt.

He threw a disappointed look toward the security cop and the production crew. "Geez, I was just trying to get something for my reel." Jeffrey explained that he'd ridden his bike past the action, figuring he'd get in the shot. "Then I could say I'd been on *L.A. 911*." He watched as they reset the scene. "It wasn't like I waved or anything. I was just adding a little background. They ought to realize I was helping, not hurting." He had a pleading look when he locked eyes with me. "You won't tell my dad, will you?"

"It'll be our secret," I said, not mentioning that Barry and I didn't even talk that much. Jeffrey seemed relieved and went back to talking about his reel, which was like a resume for actors with clips of their performances. Then he realized his bike was still where he'd left it when the crew had surrounded him. I was about to offer to retrieve it, when Adele stepped in.

"No problem, I'll just talk to Eric," she said in a grand manner. "Having a boyfriend in law enforcement has its perks."

Once we'd seen Jeffrey take off on his bicycle, we started down the curving street that led to Kelly's. Dinah and I practically had to restrain Adele from rushing on ahead.

The same truck was parked in Kelly's driveway, and the same two men were walking down the driveway to the street. Nanci must have been attending to PTA business because she wasn't standing out front.

"Let me handle it this time, Pink. You're too soft. Kelly keeps saying she's going to come to meetings and she's going to give us things she's made for the Jungle Days Fair. No more broken promises. I think she's used to getting by on her dimples." Adele straightened and appeared formidable.

"They don't do a thing for me. Either we get some actual crochet from her this time or she's out."

In the hopes of toning Adele down, Dinah and I flanked her as we walked up to the small porch and I knocked on the door. Kelly opened the door and invited us in. I heard the two men from the production company call to her.

"Kelly, we're going to be heading over for lunch," one of them said. She called them by name and wished them a good meal. Then she led the way back to her workroom, apologizing for not making the morning meeting.

"Sit, sit," she said indicating the chairs and small couch. "Would you like something to drink?"

"We're not here for any of that Popsi Cola," Adele said, still standing. I tried to give Adele an admonishing look, but she avoided my eye. Just as Adele opened her mouth to speak again, I stepped in.

"We appreciate how busy you are, but CeeCee needs to get an idea of how many crochet pieces we have for the Jungle Days Fair. We really need to pick up whatever you've made."

Kelly smiled at me and her dimples kicked in. "Sure, I have them all in a bin. I'll get them for you." I turned to nod at Adele when Kelly's doorbell rang. She excused herself to answer it. Adele still seemed unconvinced that Kelly would give us something she'd crocheted.

"Watch, she'll come back and make an excuse." The words were barely out of Adele's mouth when Kelly did come back in the room. "Okay, what is it this time?" Adele said with her hand on her hip. I tried to shush her and stepped in front of Adele, not that it stopped her mouth. "You're too busy with whoever came to the door to show us what you crocheted?"

Kelly seemed preoccupied and then after a moment said

it was only a real estate agent handing out brochures. She passed in front of us and went into the closet. After rummaging around, she came out holding a plastic bin that was considerably smaller than the ones stacked in the room. "Here, take this," she said. Adele reached out for it, but Kelly handed it to me. Now that you've gotten what you came for . . ." she said in a dismissive tone. She glanced toward the door to the rest of the house and then hustled the three of us to the sliding glass door. "If you wouldn't mind going out this way," she said, pulling it open.

I had to push aside one of the potted poplar trees that were lined up along the glass to get out. Dinah brought up the rear and put the tree back in place.

"She certainly rushed us out of there," Adele said.

"After what you said, can you blame her," I said. "Well, I guess this means she's still in the group, if she wants to be."

"Maybe, maybe not. Let's see what she gave us."

CHAPTER 6

ADELE WANTED TO OPEN THE BIN AS SOON AS WE got outside, but I held firm and kept walking. As soon as we got to the bookstore, we headed straight back to the yarn department.

"Now I want to see what she gave us," Adele said, pulling the bin out of my arms and laying it on the worktable. With her back to Dinah and me, Adele flipped off the top and hovered over the contents. I was expecting some kind of haughty comment about the quality of Kelly's crochet, but instead Adele squealed and slammed the bin shut.

"We want to see, too," I said, reaching around her and trying to open the container, but Adele leaned on it and held it shut.

"It's nothing," she said. "I'm going to stow the bin over here." Adele pulled the container away and started opening cabinets in the yarn department, looking for a space.

"Hey, we're supposed to bring everything to CeeCee's," I protested, but Adele kept moving things around to make room for the container. What was going on? Adele seemed very upset and was totally ignoring me. Finally, I cornered her and pulled the container from her grasp.

"Don't, Pink," she wailed as I set it on the worktable and prepared to remove the top. Adele lunged at it and made a last attempt to hold the lid closed, but I pulled it off anyway. When I looked inside, I couldn't understand why Adele seemed so upset. Dinah joined me and we ruffled through the contents. There were some odds and ends of yarn, a smaller container, along with a plastic bag with some papers stuck in it, a couple of small crocheted animals and a bunch of crocheted flowers attached to round pieces of felt. I picked one up and turned it over. "I think they're supposed to be pins. If we hadn't pushed her to give them to us, she probably would have finished them and put pin backs on." I could hear Adele's anxious breathing as I pulled out the plastic bag and examined one of the sheets. It had some diagrams and writing.

Adele took the opportunity to grab the container. "Now you know my Achilles' heel," she said with a few dramatic sighs thrown in.

"Achilles' heel?" Dinah repeated. "What are you talking about?"

"This," Adele picked up one of the flowers pins with one hand and put the back of her other hand against her forehead in a sign of distress. "I can't do a bullion stitch."

"A what stitch?" Dinah said, looking at the pin in Adele's hand. I was right there with Dinah. I knew there were single and double crochets, shell stitches, puff stitches, and even picots. But I'd never even heard of a bullion stitch.

Adele pointed to the yellow long coil that made up one

of the flower's petals. "This is a bullion stitch. She leaned in closer to us. "You can't tell CeeCee," she said in a whisper.

I tried to hand the plastic bag with the yellow sheets I was holding to Adele. "Maybe this will help. It looks like it has some directions."

"It's a crocheter's greatest nightmare. I know how to make the stitch; I just can't do it with yarn—yet," Adele said, pushing the bag back on me. "Go home and try to make one of these," she said pointing at one of the coils again, "then we'll talk." When I didn't do anything, Adele took the plastic bag from my arms and shoved it into the tote bag I was using as a carryall. "Subject closed."

Then I got it, Adele was still vying with CeeCee to be the leader of the Hookers and having this stitch disability put her at a disadvantage. Well, anything to keep the peace. I agreed to let her leave the container in the bookstore for the time being. I gathered that the time being was how long it was going to take Adele to master the stitch.

Adele threw her arms around me. "Pink, thank you. You saved my reputation." She was worn out from the emotional outburst and collapsed into a chair next to the worktable. She pulled a hook and some yarn out of her shoulder bag. She made a foundation chain and something to anchor the next row, then she began to wind the yarn around the hook. I watched for a moment as she tried to pull the strand of yarn through the coil but it came unraveled. And as it did Adele came unraveled with it. It was too much to watch so Dinah and I walked away.

As we did, I saw Mrs. Shedd look at me, then at her watch. I'd gotten so caught up in the fuss with Adele, I'd forgotten about the time. My workday had begun. Dinah had her own things to take care of so we walked as far as the customer service desk before parting company.

Though my official title was community relations and event coordinator, when I wasn't planning events, I helped out on the floor of the bookstore. Lately, the "and More" in the name of the bookstore had taken on a new meaning. Mrs. Shedd and Mr. Royal were trying to move with the times and had expanded the stores offerings to include an assortment of e-readers, e-books, some toys, some items of clothing and a whole lot of chocolate.

Mr. Royal wanted the same policy with the e-readers that we had in the yarn department—try before you buy. Really, the idea was try and then you'll buy. So the e-readers sat loose on a table. Mr. Royal had placed the table near the customer service station so we could keep tabs on the expensive items and so far it was working out.

I lost track of time as I helped customers find books, explained how to use the e-readers and gave an opinion on which graphic tee shirt would make the best fortieth birthday gift.

Mrs. Shedd came by the customer service booth. "Those kids are back. Could you keep an eye on them," she said gesturing toward two scrawny looking junior-high-age boys hanging out in the magazine section. With the kids out of school, a lot of them had taken to hanging out in the bookstore and café. These two had been in before and were doing their best to look like tough gangster types with the baggy clothes, bandanas and oddly tilted baseball caps. I thought they were a little too small to really appear as menacing as they hoped. They both sported tattoos, but I bet they were the temporary kind. I knew the kids were local and had the feeling they'd left their houses in normal looking attire and changed after they left.

While keeping my watch on the pair, I noticed a police cruiser go by the window with its light flashing and siren whining. Ventura Boulevard ran in front of the bookstore and as the main street that ran along the southern part of the Valley, it wasn't unusual to hear sirens. But after the third cruiser went by, I began to wonder what was going on. When two more whizzed past, I went to the window to see where they were going. My stomach clenched when I saw them barely slow at the corner and turn toward Dinah's. I made a move for the door and as I passed Mrs. Shedd, I said something about being worried about Dinah.

"Go," she said, with a wave of her hand. "But if it's part of *L.A. 911*, please don't tackle anyone."

I rushed down the street and saw another cruiser pass Dinah's and go down the street that ran in front of Kelly's. I rang Dinah's bell and when I got no answer, followed the trail of the cop car, but didn't get far. One of the cruisers had blocked off the street. Up ahead I saw a cluster of people standing in front of Kelly's house. The truck with the slats was still in the driveway and wasn't going anywhere soon, as yellow police tape had been strung across the driveway and across Kelly's whole front yard.

A black Crown Victoria drove past me and around the cop cars. It pulled in front of the Donahue house and Detective Heather got out. Not a good sign.

CHAPTER 7

"WELL?" MRS. SHEDD SAID WHEN I CAME BACK
into the bookstore. My adrenaline was still pumping from
seeing all the cops, and most of all Detective Heather, and
my mind was out of focus. I gave Mrs. Shedd a puzzled look.
"You were going to see what was going on. Is Dinah okay?"

Her question made me remember why I'd gone down the
street in the first place. "She wasn't even home." I glanced
around, wanting to get back to normal. "Right, I was working customer service," I mumbled to myself.

"If it wasn't Dinah's, then where did the police go?" Mrs.
Shedd asked. I winced at my lack of information. If it had
been any detective other than Detective Heather, I probably
would have tried to find out what happened. But we had a
history and not a good one. I knew there was no chance she'd
give me any information.

And that was fine because I wasn't sure I wanted any

information. Detective Heather was a homicide cop and if she was there, someone was probably dead. Judging by the yellow crime-scene tape, it was a safe bet it was someone from the Donahue house and last time we'd stopped by, the only one home was Kelly. I could just imagine Mrs. Shedd's face if I told her we'd just been to Kelly's and now she might be dead.

I knew what Mrs. Shedd would say, too. "Molly, I don't know what it is about you, but dead bodies seem to show up wherever you go. You visited that poor woman and look what happened to her."

The worst part was I couldn't argue with Mrs. Shedd, because it was true. I certainly didn't plan it, it just seemed to work out that way. I finally answered Mrs. Shedd and simply told her the cops had gone down the street and stopped in front of one of the houses. "I don't really know what happened."

"Some of us can find out," Adele said in a haughty tone that made me want to scream. "Some of us have a boyfriend in law enforcement who is happy to give us important info." I looked at her and thought what have I done? I was the one who'd gotten her fixed up with Eric in the first place. It had been through Barry, though not directly—a friend of a friend of a friend. Adele'd had such a broken heart, I'd foolishly tried to help mend it. I should have realized things with Adele tended to boomerang.

Adele was out the door in a flash. Mrs. Shedd almost wobbled in the wake of her whirlwind exit. "Is it my imagination or is Adele even more full of herself than usual?" my boss said. It seemed to be a rhetorical question because my boss didn't wait for an answer, but checked out the front of the store. Her gaze stopped on the junior high boys in gangster outfits who'd been joined by some look-alikes, all of whom were hanging out in the magazine section. They were jostling each other, jumping around and generally being a nuisance.

"Should we ask them to leave?" I said, but Mrs. Shedd shook her head.

"I had Joshua try that when they came in before. Or I think it was them. With those outfits, they all look the same. One of them said his father was a lawyer and he'd be all over us for discrimination because they were customers. He showed Joshua he was buying a chocolate bar and a graphic novel." Mrs. Shedd told me to keep a watch on them anyway.

I wanted to push whatever was happening down the street out of my mind and headed back to the customer service booth. I was glad there were people waiting.

An author interested in having a launch party at the bookstore had just walked away, when Adele returned. It wasn't a silent entrance, either. "It's just terrible. Oh, the humanity of it all," she said in her loud voice. As she went through the store, the loudness of her voice and her repeating about how horrible it was, attracted the attention of the shoppers and they began to follow her like she was the Pied Piper. Adele snuck a look over her shoulder at the crowd she'd gathered. When they reached an open area, she turned, ready to hold court.

I fought the urge to join the gathering. I did and didn't want to know what happened. As long as I didn't know anything about Kelly for sure, I didn't have to get upset. And there was something else. I'm not proud to admit it, but being in her audience would give Adele the upper hand.

It became a nonissue anyway, because Mrs. Shedd rushed up to the customer service booth and grabbed my arm. Two of the junior gangsters were heading toward the door. Even from here I could see they'd stuck some magazines under their shirts. One of them darted toward the table with the e-readers and grabbed one before rejoining his friend.

"Do something, Molly," Mrs. Shedd said. "I don't care if their father is a lawyer." They were local kids and I knew it was more about the thrill than the actual stuff they'd taken. I ran up behind them and grabbed them both by the back of their shirts.

"Hey, lady, back off," one of them said and tried to squirm away from my grasp. I managed to transfer my hold so I had a grasp on each of their arms, but I was definitely struggling. One of them had started kicking backward toward my shin. I glanced around hoping for some help. The front door opened and Barry came through. I felt a sense of relief, knowing his cop instinct would kick in instantaneously and he'd step in.

But instead, he seemed to freeze before looking away. The boys were about to pull free when North Adams came in behind Barry and tried to help. A moment later, Joshua Royal came into the store and joined in.

When I looked up Barry was gone.

The star of *L.A. 911* became Detective Jake Blake and used his authority voice to try to scare the boys with threats of arrest and prison. Mr. Royal got the kids to hand over the e-readers and magazines and gave them a stern warning before letting them go.

The customers all missed the incident because Adele still had their attention. I couldn't hear what she was saying, just the rise and fall of her voice, with an occasional gasp from the small crowd.

"Molly," a voice called from behind me. I turned and Dinah rushed toward me. I knew she hadn't been home when the chaos had erupted on her street, but still I was relieved to see her in one piece and hugged her tightly. I could feel her heart palpitating and noticed that her breath seemed a little ragged.

"They stopped me when I tried to go into to my own house," she said. I urged her to take a deep breath before she continued. "There are cops everywhere," she said gesturing in the general direction of her street. "Detective Heather is there." I nodded and told Dinah I'd seen the detective when I'd gone down the street. Dinah swallowed hard when our eyes met. "I started asking the cops questions and they started asking me questions about when I left and things like that." Dinah stopped to regroup. "I didn't get many details, but it's Kelly Donahue. Something about her husband came home and found her. It was too late. They think it was a robbery gone bad. I heard some cops talking about looking for the murder weapon. I'm pretty sure she was shot. The cops asked me if I heard anything before I left."

"Did you tell them we were at her house earlier today?"

Dinah shook her head. "It's my policy not to volunteer information that will only cause me trouble. I know I didn't kill her. . . ." Dinah stopped and looked at me.

"Take a deep breath," she ordered. My best friend knew what I was thinking.

"Molly, it isn't personal. No matter what Mrs. Shedd has said about not wanting to go anywhere with you because dead bodies keep showing up. It's not your fault. You're not some kind of jinx."

I was embarrassed to admit that was exactly what I was thinking. "Dinah, I'm terrible. A woman is dead, and here I am thinking about me." Once that was out of the way, I began to ask Dinah for more details, but she didn't have many.

"They blocked off the whole area and shut down the production. I'm guessing they're talking to all the neighbors around Kelly's house," Dinah said.

Adele breezed by after she finally dismissed her crowd. She looked at the two of us. "I didn't see you two in the group when I was explaining what happened. I guess you just wanted to hear it from me personally. It must be kind of embarrassing to not be the one in the know." The last comment was aimed directly at me. All the attention had gotten to her and she looked like her head might float away from all the hot air inside as she straightened the strap on her gauzy sundress. The lime green swirled with purple made me think of a snow cone. She had pulled her brown hair into tiny little pigtails that stuck straight out.

"No problem," I said. "Dinah just filled me in." Trying not to sound too pleased, after all I was talking about somebody who had just died, I told her I already knew that Kelly had been shot and what the cops thought. I watched as Adele deflated like a Mylar balloon with a big leak.

"Oh," she said with a harrumph. Then she brightened. "But I don't suppose you know who they think the killer really is. Eric was the first responder," she said before giving me her spiel how motor cops were often the first ones on the scene in any kind of emergency. "Even though he's technically off duty while he's working as security on the production, in his heart, he's always on duty," Adele said with a flutter in her voice.

"So?" I said, annoyed with myself for falling for her bait.

"So, he saw the crime scene. It was Kelly's workroom," Adele said. "There was stuff tossed around, but he thought it was just a cover-up to make it look like a robbery. He said the first person they'll be looking at is her husband. He's the one who found her. Eric said that's a common ploy to try to cover up being the killer," Adele said, savoring her moment of being in the know. "The cops are questioning everybody, anyway. All the production people and actors."

I thought about seeing Dan and his concern over names for his store. He didn't seem like somebody with murder on his mind. But then Barry had always said you couldn't tell a book by its cover when it came to murderers.

"That's nothing special in the information department," I said, embarrassed that I'd gotten sucked into her game and was trying to one-up her. "In fact, what you just told me is investigation one-oh-one in *The Average Joe's Guide to Criminal Investigation.*" The book had been my personal bible when it came to learning how to sleuth. "You always look at the closest person first. They usually have means and opportunity. All you need to do is find their motive and some incriminating evidence."

Adele tried to dismiss what I'd said. "I was just telling you that in case you get any ideas about investigating. Eric has it under control."

I just smiled and nodded and didn't even bother mentioning that Eric rode a motorcycle and gave out traffic tickets when he was on duty. Yes, he might show up when there was a riot or an earthquake, but he wasn't a detective. He didn't detect or investigate like my boyfr— I stopped the thought in my head, glad I hadn't said anything. I didn't need Adele to remind me again that Barry and I weren't anything any longer.

Adele walked off saying that she had to get back to the children's area. She was in the process of planning a big event. She was going to have Eric as the special guest reader of *Officer Pauly Solves the Case of the Missing Parakeet.*

Dinah hugged me again and said she was going back

home. Before she left she glanced toward the café and saw North sitting at one of the tables. "What's he doing here?" she asked. I just shrugged as an answer.

After the shoplifter's caper, Mrs. Shedd suggested we keep the e-readers behind the information desk and only let people try them right in front of us. Mr. Royal wanted to keep it easy for people to play with them and said he'd figure out a way to keep them on the table.

Eventually, I went into the café for a late afternoon red eye and saw that North Adams was still in there. Nice as the café was, I thought it was odd that he was hanging out there alone.

As I stopped to pick up a lid for my drink and some napkins, the two men who'd been working in Kelly's backyard, putting the trees along the back of her house, came into the café. They made some chitchat with Bob, our barista, and said that they wanted coffees for the road. They seemed surprised to see North and stopped at his table when they'd gotten their coffees. I was curious about their conversation and, shall we say, took my time getting a lid and napkins.

"You do know they shut us down and sent everybody home," the older of the two jean-clad men said to North. When the actor nodded, the man seemed perplexed and asked why North was hanging around. He was going to stay perplexed, too, because North avoided the question by changing the subject.

Instead North asked, "Do you guys know what happened exactly? I was in my trailer."

The older man whose name was Fred said after lunch he and Zeke had been ready to start laying out the props for the next setup, but had gone back to the Donahue yard to add some more bushes. "We never got to do it. Our security guy was out front with the mister from the house. Then a bunch of cop cars came tearing down the street." He explained that as soon as the police heard they'd been working in the Donahue's yard, they wanted to question them. "The cops gave us the bare bones of what happened." Fred paused and let out a sigh before he repeated what the cops had said—that a woman had been found shot in the house.

"Do you know who she was?" Fred said. North answered with a shrug. "You remember Rexford Thomasville?" When North seemed to draw a blank, the prop guy continued. "He's a set designer. Or he was. I heard he has a store in Santa Barbara now. Kelly was his daughter. I didn't recognize her at first, but she remembered me and showed me some things she was selling online in case we needed them for an upcoming production. It turns out back when, she tried working with her dad, and we all worked together on *McCavity*. Of course, when she told me who she was, I remembered her. All you had to do was see her smile. The whole family has matching dimples." North had a glazed look, like he was getting a much longer answer than he'd expected and way too much information. When Fred started talking about Kelly's brother who had the same dimples and had helped out with props before becoming some kind of surfing champion, North cut him off by asking how long they'd be shut down. Neither of the prop guys knew and finally picked up their coffees before leaving.

I finally popped the lid on my drink and prepared to go back to the bookstore. Adele sailed into the café as Eric came in the door from outside.

"Hi cutchykins," he said as a goofy grin spread over his face.

"Oh, Eric, you're such a hero," Adele said, rushing up to

him. She turned to the smattering of people in the café and explained that Eric had been the first responder to the tragedy up the street. "The whole production had to shut down while they process the crime scene," Adele announced to the café patrons. "But Eric, Officer Humphries to the rest of you, is still working. He's never off duty." He didn't seem to mind her effusive comment about how wonderful he was. If anything he just stood a little taller. She linked arms with him and said that after what he'd done, Mrs. Shedd wanted to make sure he got a complimentary drink and cookie snack.

It was all a little too sugary for me and I escaped back into the bookstore, still thinking about the conversation I'd overheard. I'd just sort of glossed over the two prop guys when I'd seen them bringing stuff in the yard. It had never occurred to me that Kelly might have a connection with one of them. Maybe I'd spent too much time thinking about mysteries, but I automatically wondered if Fred had told the whole story. Or just enough to throw someone off the track.

CHAPTER 8

WITH THE PRODUCTION SHUT DOWN, THE BOOK-
store stayed quiet for the rest of the afternoon. Mrs. Shedd
probably wasn't happy, but I was relieved. It was still haunt-
ing me that I'd visited Kelly shortly before she'd been killed
and I figured it was only a matter of time before word got
back to Detective Heather about the timing of my visit.
Instinctively, I glanced toward the door half expecting to see
her walking in ready to question me.

And then tussling with the shoplifters. Why had Mrs.
Shedd left it up to me? Did she think that came under my
title of community relations coordinator? Frankly, I was still
shocked by Barry's reaction, or should I say, lack of reaction.
I called Mason, hoping to talk it over with him, but I got
his voice mail and had to leave a message.

With my thoughts still racing, I took advantage of the
quiet and headed back to the yarn department where I took
out the cowl in progress I'd stowed in the cabinets for times

like this. Adele had given me the pattern, anxious that I turn some out for the upcoming sale. I wasn't so sure about that, but it was a simple and repetitious pattern and was just what I needed. As I sat working the cream-colored cotton yarn, I felt all the tension go out of my shoulders.

Refreshed, I went back to the customer service booth as customers filtered into the bookstore. After helping a woman find a book listing local hiking trails, I was surprised to see North Adams sitting in one of the overstuffed chairs by the window. He had a book open in front of him, but seemed to be staring into space. After a moment he got up and went outside. I thought he'd left, but when I looked back at the chair, he was in it again.

Why was the star of *L.A. 911* sticking around the bookstore?

As I tidied up the customer service booth, I found my eye wandering back to where North was sitting. He had a slight resemblance to Barry—both had close-cropped dark hair and stubborn chins, but North's eyes were the color of those clear blue mints and Barry's were an earthy brown. It was odd seeing North as himself. When I'd seen him on the set, he'd had a very different kind of persona. He'd had an air of authority and seemed like someone who could corner a suspect into a confession. He'd become that person when he'd helped with the shoplifters. But sitting in the bookstore chair, he barely resembled that character. Partly, I suppose it was the clothes. The suit and dress shirt had been replaced with jeans that had no doubt gone through extensive abusive treatments to get the soft worn look. No old cotton tee shirt for him. The fit of his black vee neck had "imported from Italy" written all over it. His detective shoes had been switched out for a pair of tasseled loafers he wore with no socks.

Still, he had charisma. I couldn't put my finger on what it was exactly, but something about him kept drawing my gaze back.

I helped some more customers, and when I looked his way again, he was on his cell phone. I saw him look up at me with interest. Still on the phone, he walked across the bookstore and pushed the phone toward me. "Somebody wants to talk to you," he said.

"Hello," I said tentatively and was surprised to hear my son Peter's voice. Before I could say anything more, he told me just to listen.

"No comments on anything. Just say uh-huh," Peter ordered. There was a pause. "Well?" he said.

"Uh-huh," I answered. Peter was my older son and a talent agent specializing in TV. He didn't share as much of his life with me as Samuel did, so I had no idea, until he explained, that North Adams was one of his clients. I started to express my surprise, but Peter cut me off.

"Mother," he said dragging the word out with disapproval. "I said just to listen. No comments. Don't give away what you're hearing. Just smile."

I forced my lips upward hoping it didn't look too phoney as I said, "Uh-huh."

Peter groaned and said I should do all this while appearing natural. I couldn't help it—despite all his orders I said, "You missed your calling, you should have been a director."

For that I got another drawn out "Mother," with an extra dose of disapproval.

"This isn't some kind of joke," Peter said annoyed that there might have been a touch of sarcasm in my uh-huh. "I need you to take North home with you now. I'll pick him up at the house. Don't ask him any questions. And take the back roads home."

"Uh-huh," I said in a noncommittal tone. It was all very mysterious. Peter entrusting one of his clients to me? Just before he hung up, Peter implored me just to do what he said and not mess anything up. Maybe I had a bit of a reputation of putting my own stamp on things. But not this time. Whatever was going on, I didn't want to cause my son any problems.

I handed the cell phone back to North and told him to hang on for a moment. I was relieved when Mrs. Shedd didn't mind me leaving a little early, though when she saw me walking out with North, she gave me an odd look.

I couldn't blame her. What was going on? Peter was always horrified that I was still driving the greenmobile. And now he actually wanted me to give one of his clients a ride in it—to my house? Peter didn't approve of that, either. He thought I should have downsized to a condo when my husband Charlie died. He hadn't liked Barry when we were a couple and was completely against me letting him stay at my house.

He was also upset about his brother Samuel moving back home and bringing a pair of cats with him. The only thing in my life Peter seemed to approve of was my friendship, or whatever you wanted to call it, with Mason.

North made a comment about my car being a classic as he got in the passenger seat. Already I liked him a little more. I took Wells Drive home as Peter had instructed instead of taking the shorter route via Ventura Boulevard. I tried to make conversation and asked North what he knew about Kelly's murder. I didn't refer to her as Kelly, but instead called her the woman whose backyard they were using, and I never let on I'd overheard his conversation. He didn't seem to want to talk and just muttered something about being in his trailer.

It was just getting dark as I pulled into my driveway be-hind Barry's Tahoe. For weeks the Tahoe had just sat there. He'd only recently been given the okay to drive. North got out of the car and followed me as I went through my back-yard. Peter hadn't said anything, but I wondered if I was supposed to give his client dinner.

As we walked into my kitchen I noticed a bunch of white takeout cartons on the counter and a smell that definitely seemed like Chinese sweet and sour something. A moment later, Jeffrey came in carrying his plate, no doubt for sec-onds. He gave me a hello nod and started to glance back toward the Chinese food, when he did a sudden double take.

"You're that guy," he said to North as awe gushed through his voice. "You're Jake Blake on *L.A. 911*. North Adams, right?"

North smiled at Jeffrey's exuberance as the boy actor put down his plate and stuck out his hand while telling North that he was an actor, too. "You should have seen me as Curly in *Carousel*. Everyone says I really nailed it."

"I bet you did," North said in a friendly voice. Jeffrey seemed to have forgotten why he came in the kitchen and stood watching North with wide adoring eyes.

Barry walked into the kitchen. His brows were furrowed and he clearly had something on his mind. He stopped in front of me before jumping in. "About this afternoon at the bookstore," he began. "I don't know what happened. I'm sorry—" But suddenly he stopped short and his expression went to neutral—he'd noticed there was a visitor present. Ever the cop, he scrutinized the actor's face. I had the feeling Barry thought North looked familiar, but couldn't place him. Was it because he was on a wanted poster somewhere or had they met?

My two dogs came in to check out what was going on. Cosmo, the bolder of the two, sniffed North's shoes before sitting down. Then Samuel's cats, Holstein and Cat Woman, arrived silently and moved through the group before going to check their food bowl.

I stepped in and did introductions, explaining that Barry was an LAPD homicide detective and that North played one.

North seemed interested in meeting Barry and asked Barry if he would pass along some hints. "I like to put in the little touches to make my performance seem real," North explained.

"I don't really watch the show," Barry said, "although I might have caught it once or twice. But for starters, if you want to make it accurate, you could have a few wrinkles in your dress shirt. Try spending all night going over a crime scene, and then knocking on somebody's door at five A.M. to tell them their son's been killed over something stupid like road rage or he owed somebody a few bucks for some weed, followed by getting a lead that takes you to a homeless encampment in the dirt under the freeway, and then see what your shirt looks like." North seemed a little overwhelmed with the information, but said he'd tell the wardrobe people.

When Barry looked away, I caught his expression of distaste. I knew what he thought of TV cops. He said they were all flash with no cash, meaning they had the swagger, but nothing to back it up with. Hoping to avoid an awkward silence, I mentioned that Barry was working cold cases at the moment.

"Oh, yeah?" North sounded interested. "What made you switch?"

There was a flash of irritation on Barry's face. "It's only

temporary. Once I settle the two cases I'm working on, I'm going back to homicide. I just went back to work after an injury." Barry started to talk about the cases as a way to direct the conversation. Not that it worked.

"What kind of injury? Like something in the line of duty?" North asked.

"Something like that." Barry turned toward me as if he was trying to figure out what I was doing with the actor. Meanwhile North tried to ferret out more details.

Remembering that North was an important client of my son's and I was supposed to be keeping him happy, I answered for Barry and said that he'd been shot by a shoplifter. Barry blew out his breath in consternation.

"Molly, you make it sound so lame," Barry said. He glared at North. "If you're looking for something for your show—just remember that any situation can turn deadly."

North's face was suddenly animated. "I remember hearing about that. You're the one who was trying to help the newbie cop arresting the shoplifter at some discount store. The shoplifter got hold of the newbie's gun, right?" Without pausing a beat, North stepped closer and patted Barry on the shoulder as if they were somehow connected. "Our writers loved that story and were writing something like it into an upcoming show. You've got to admit, it's kind of funny being shot by a guy in handcuffs." Barry's response was a glower.

I heard the kitchen door open behind us. "What's going on?" Mason said coming into the room. He joined the group and said hello to Barry and Jeffrey and introduced himself to North.

Both Mason and Barry looked at me with questions in their eyes. I knew they were wondering what I was doing with North. There was nothing to say because I didn't even know what I was doing with him. This was getting more awkward by the minute. Peter had only said he would pick North up, not when or why.

Finally, I heard the front door open and close. At least I'd gotten the answer to when.

CHAPTER 9

"WHAT WAS THAT ABOUT?" MASON SAID WHEN IT was just the three of us. Peter had rushed in, waved to North that they were leaving and barely called a "thank you" to me before they went back out the front door. As the door shut, both Barry and Mason stared at me.

"I have no idea," I said with a shrug. I'd been avoiding having Mason come over while Barry was staying at my house, but Mason had taken matters in his own hands and just walked in.

"Look at you," Mason said turning his attention to Barry. "Your cast is off and you're good as new. I hear you're back to work and driving. So, then you'll be moving out." Mason turned to me. "Then Molly can get her stuff out of storage and life around here can go back to normal." Mason stepped closer to me and put his arm behind me on the counter. It wasn't around me exactly, but it made a point. Barry's eyes rested on the position of Mason's arm.

"When?" Mason asked staring squarely at Barry.

Jeffrey had drifted out of the room as soon as North was gone. I was glad he wasn't there to see this confrontation. Barry hesitated, but something in his posture said he was standing his ground. "I don't know exactly. I haven't gotten the okay from my doctor yet." To punctuate it, Barry moved his leg and grimaced in pain. Was it real or imaginary?

The whole exchange reminded me of something I'd heard about parking spots. When a man saw that someone was waiting for the spot he was in, he took much longer to pull out than if there was no one waiting.

"It's a little crowded here," Mason said, gesturing toward the rest of the house. "Molly, your message said you wanted to talk to me about a murder. I'm here to help."

"C'mon," I said to Mason. He was right, it was too crowded in the kitchen and awkward with a capital A. I led Mason out of the kitchen, across the living room and through the den. As he soon as he went through the doorway into the hall that led to my bedroom, I heard him sigh.

"Finally into the inner sanctum," Mason said. "I'll close the door behind me."

"I know more than he does," Barry said. I hadn't realized Barry was right behind Mason until I heard his voice. Mason pulled the door to the hall shut before Barry could follow.

That was a laugh and a half. When had Barry ever been willing to share what he knew? From him it was stay out of it. The cops have it covered, blah, blah, blah. Mason had always been a better source of information.

"This is more like it," Mason said walking into my bedroom. He looked around and suddenly seemed a little disappointed that with the small couch and wing chair, it looked more like a living room than a den of inequity. "Hmm, no round bed with mirrors on the ceiling," he joked touching the basket of yarn next to the wing chair.

He sat down on the couch and I took the chair, but after a moment I got up. "Let's go get some food or something," I said. "I'm too tense here. I feel like Barry is standing by at the door."

I wasn't too far off. Barry wasn't standing by the door to my wing of the house, but the chair he picked in the den wasn't far from it. He had the TV on, but it was obviously all a ruse. Barry watching a dancing competition? His head swiveled as Mason and I walked through the den toward the living room, but he didn't say anything.

"You need to remind Barry that he gave up all claims on you," Mason said when we got into his car. "Even though I'm glad he did, I still think he's nuts. If a woman said she didn't want to marry me, but wanted to keep things as they were, I'd never tell her it had to be all or nothing." Mason paused a moment. "I think Barry's forgotten that he chose nothing." Mason started the motor and pulled the car away from the curb.

We continued our conversation when we got to a small bar/restaurant that served the best thick-crust pizza. We ordered a large one with cheese and a salad to share.

"When he was laid up, it was no problem. He had people who came over and took care of things and who took him whereever he needed to go. I barely saw him. But now that he's up and around and back to work, it's gotten all strange. I said something to him about being ready to move back to his condo. He gave me the same story about needing his doctor to okay him going up and down stairs. But I'm sure it won't be long." I paused a moment and then told Mason how Barry had frozen when he saw me struggling with the kids stealing the e-readers in the afternoon.

Mason appeared stricken. "I wish I'd been there. I would

have helped you. It sounds like Barry needs to get his edge back." We'd finished off the salad and the pizza arrived in the black round pan. The waitress set it on its own little table after serving us each a piece. For a few minutes we were lost in pizza heaven. The tomato sauce was homemade and the mozzarella made a creamy counterpoint to the zesty sauce. And the crust. It had a little crunch and a delicious buttery flavor.

"Maybe when he takes care of the two cases he's working on and gets back to his old job, it'll come back." I helped Mason and myself to another piece of the delicious pizza.

Mason shook his head. "He can't go back to his old homicide job until he gets his mojo back. If he hesitates at the wrong time, it could get him killed. And anybody working with him. I'm sure he knows that." I felt my shoulders slump. I knew what Mason was saying was true.

"So, tell me, sunshine, who got murdered this time?" Mason said trying to change the subject.

Between bites, I told him about Kelly. The whole story— how Adele, Dinah and I had gone over to her house in the morning and now she was dead.

"Are you three suspects?" Mason asked.

"No. The cops don't even know that we were there." I paused and had visions of Adele talking to Eric. "Yet, anyway." I looked at the two slices still in the pan and debated whether to have one or not. Mason read my thoughts and scooped up one and dropped it on my plate, before taking the last one for himself. "I'm not really worried about being a suspect. I'm more concerned about Dinah. The murder happened a half block from her house. According to Adele, even though it looked like a robbery gone bad, the cops are zeroing in on Kelly's husband. You know who he is. Dan from the Hollar for a Dollar store. Oops, I mean More Bang for Your Buck. I suppose it could have been him. Actually I hope it is him instead of some random robber with a gun."

"So, she was shot?" Mason said. "You'd think someone would have heard something with all those people around."

"It is odd." I said.

With the pizza finished, we ordered espressos and a vanilla gelato to share.

"Sunshine, I hate to say anything, but you do seem to keep getting caught up in murders. Maybe I should be worried," Mason joked as he picked up the small cup of strong coffee. Then his smile faded. "I know I shouldn't joke. It's serious business. Your crochet friend is dead."

I tasted a spoonful of the gelato. The creamy sweet taste was a perfect contrast to the espresso. "If there's anything you can find out, I'd appreciate it. I'm concerned because Dinah lives down the street, but there's something else." I stopped. I knew I should be better than this, and not stoop to Adele's level, but . . . "Adele is making this huge deal out of being the information source. I just need some little edge. I'm not proud of it, but any minute she's going to start referring to herself as Adele Poirot, or Sherlock's sister, or Adele Drew."

"I get the picture," Mason said, reaching over and touching my hand. "I'll see what I can find out." He squeezed my hand and let go. When I looked up, I was surprised to see the good humor had drained from his face.

"What's the matter?" I said. He started to say "Nothing," and then stopped himself.

"Old habits die hard," he said. "I'm still getting used to the idea of talking about things, instead of just dealing with them." He paused and took a breath. "It's the wedding disaster and my ex-wife." The words came out with a rush of air as though they'd escaped. He shook his head with dismay. "At least if she'd told me right away about the problem, I might have been able to do something." Now that he'd begun, the words flowed and the frustration was clear in his tone. "You don't know her, but it's her typical MO. She's going to take care of something, but only makes a mess of it. I can't trust her to do anything on her own."

"I know a little about event planning," I said. "Maybe I can help." Mason grinned at my comment and we both rolled our eyes. My events often ended up a little offbeat. They were always successful but there might be a police raid or the fire department could show up.

Not exactly what you'd want for a wedding.

"Thank you for listening—and for getting me to talk." His eyes were warm and I felt closer to him than I ever had. "All of this just reminds me of why we got a divorce. I think I'd rather talk about your murder," he said. "The robbery gone bad thing is a common cover-up. It probably was her husband, the Dollar King. So I don't think you have to worry about someone going after Dinah."

"Okay," I said, but I couldn't help wondering. What if it wasn't him? I thought back to the conversation of the two prop guys. They clearly knew Kelly and they certainly had access to her place. Could they have killed her? But why?

CHAPTER 10

"OH, DEAR," CEECEE SAID IN A DISTRESSED VOICE as she took her seat at the head of the worktable in the bookstore's yarn department. She had arrived late and Sheila, Rhoda, Elise, Eduardo, Dinah and I were already working on our crochet projects. We all followed CeeCee's gaze to see what had inspired her comment. Detective Heather and a uniform had just come into the bookstore.

"I'm afraid she's looking at you, Molly," CeeCee said. "That woman is relentless." CeeCee knew that firsthand from some past dealings she'd had with the attractive homicide detective.

"Try to ignore her," Elise said in her wispy voice. The small woman waved her hook at me to try to divert my attention as if not looking at the detective would make me invisible. Sure.

Dinah leaned in to me. "You could tell her you know North Adams," she said with a smile. My friend had heard all about my weird encounter with the TV star and was as curious as I was about the whole episode. But my son Peter had simply refused to answer any questions.

A few days had passed since Kelly's murder. The cops had finished processing the crime scene and had released the Donahue house, and allowed the *L.A. 911* production to get back to work. Though the delay had caused the production people to redo their shooting schedule. Under the circumstances, they'd decided to wait until after the funeral to shoot the scene in the Donahue's backyard. I hated to admit it, but all the information had come from Adele or as she had anointed herself—the new sleuth on the block. She insisted she'd been offering important insights on the case to her motor cop boyfriend who was still working security on the set. She was sure he'd been passing them on to the right people.

Not looking at Detective Heather didn't work and a few moments later I sensed someone standing next to my chair. "Mrs. Pink, I wonder if I could speak to you," she said in her formal police voice. Calling me Mrs. Pink bordered on the ridiculous. How many times had she questioned me? How many times had I ended up actually helping her? How many times had she hoped Barry would dump me and choose her? Well, she had a better shot at that part now. I was one hundred percent out of the way, even if he was still living at my house.

I got up from the table and we walked over to the corner. Detective Heather was a knitter, a very good knitter—I'd seen a pair of socks she'd made for Barry. Actually I'd even sold her the yarn. She implied that the real way to a man's heart was through his feet. As I stopped next to a bin of some new novelty yarn we'd gotten in, I began to wonder about Barry's feet and what they were wearing. I hadn't been paying any attention to them other than to notice when his cast came off his left leg. Had she knitted him a whole wardrobe of socks? Were they caressing his feet even as he sat there drinking tea and telling me about his cold cases?

I forced the thought from my mind. Barry and I were done, so what he wore on his feet was no concern of mine. Once he left, I'd never think about it again.

Detective Heather noticed the novelty yarn and picked up a skein that was in various shades of blue. It looked like a flat strip, but when you pulled it open and knitted along the edge you ended up with tiers of ruffles. When I explained what it was, she dropped it like it had cooties. "Ruffles and a revolver just don't go," she said.

"So, what do you want to know?" I asked. I just wanted to be done with the questions and get back to the group.

She seemed to deflate a little at my question. It probably caught her off guard. I'm sure she was hoping I'd feel intimidated, but after all the times I'd been questioned by her, I had gotten a bit of a thick skin.

"Just tell me about the other morning at the Donahue house." Detective Heather had taken out her pad and pen.

I figured why play games? Who knew what Adele had told Eric, who in turn had told Heather. I just gave her the whole story, explaining that Kelly had joined the Hookers, not that there was anything really official about it. All she had to do was give her information to CeeCee for our roster and she was in. Kelly had been all enthusiastic about the group and wanted to make things for our table at the Jungle Days Fair. But then she hadn't come to the regular gatherings and nobody had seen any real examples of her work.

"We just went over there to see if we could count on her donations," I said.

"And?" Detective Heather said.

"She gave us some pieces and we left," I said hoping it would be the end of it. But Detective Heather jumped right into asking about Kelly's husband Dan. Did I know if he was having money troubles with his store? Did they get along? Did he have an insurance policy on her? Poor guy, I wondered if he knew that Detective Heather was doing her best to close in on him.

After telling her that I didn't know anything about his finances, other than I wondered if there really was a market for Suckers jam, even if it was only a dollar a jar, I looked her in the eye. "Have you considered he might not be the guy?" I brought up the robbery scenario and Detective Heather glared in response.

"You're not going to do the amateur sleuth thing again, are you?" She said. When I didn't answer, she looked even more annoyed. "Let's see what I can arrest you for. Interfering with a police investigation, tampering with evidence, getting in my way," she said in a terse voice.

"I have helped you in the past. You've even thanked me," I said, but she stopped me.

"I was just humoring you. Barry said you were going through a tough time since you were getting close to being a half-century old."

I rolled my eyes. She was only in her late thirties and she knew how to rub it in.

I was relieved when she left and I went back to join the Hookers. Everyone wanted to know what Detective Heather had said and we all started discussing Kelly's business or what we knew of it.

"I think they were struggling," Elise said. "Her husband is still just starting out with that dollar store."

From across the bookstore, kids began filing out of the children's area and rejoining whoever had brought them.

Adele came out at the end and headed across the store toward us.

"I think Adele has outdone herself. Look what she's wearing," Rhoda said as we watched Adele approach. As usual, Adele had dressed for story time. Whatever she'd read must have been about plants because she was all in bright green, from the tights to the long tunic with crocheted leaves sewn on the long sleeves. When she got to the table, I saw that she had something on her head.

"What's that?" Rhoda barked, pointing at the tiny green top hat sitting toward the front of her head on an angle.

Adele set down her tote bag and touched the mini hat. "It's called a fascinator. Of course, I made it," she said.

"For you or Kermit the Frog?" Rhoda said punctuating her comment with a laugh.

"I'll have you know they're all the rage now," Adele said indignantly. "You people have no imagination, no oomph in the style department. I made several and Eric thinks they're adorable," she said, her voice brimming with pride.

Sheila had been watching it all while continuing to crochet. She swallowed a few times before she spoke up. "We got a couple of fascinators in the other day. They are one of a kind and fit in perfectly with the kind of things Luxe sells," she said. Though the ones in the lifestyle store were a little more elaborate than Adele's. Sheila said something about one looking like a red rose with a bit of red veil and that the other had a bunch of feathers on it. Adele appeared stricken that something might be more showy than her tiny top hat.

Now that the group seemed to be coming to order, Sheila set down the rectangular shawl she was making in her signature colors of greens, blues and lavenders. The large hook she was using gave it a lacy appearance. She rolled up the completed portion of the shawl around the yarn and put it in the large tote on the chair next to her. "We're working on things for Jungle Days, right?" she said looking through the contents of her bag.

"Yes, and we better get our hooks moving," CeeCee said. "The street fair is in a couple of weeks and last time I looked in the collection box, I had a pretty clear view of the bottom. Ladies, this is the Tarzana street fair and we are the Tarzana Hookers. We don't want to look bad to our fellow Tarzanians." CeeCee hadn't been hanging around the table as much as the rest of the group. Between the taping of *Making Amends*, and meetings she was having about a sequel to *Caught by a Kiss*, and thanks to the hum of Oscar buzz, she'd been pretty busy lately.

"What do you think of this look?" CeeCee said turning around so we could all see what her stylist had come up with now. The linen pants and long shirt were pale shades of peach. Rhoda shook her head. "It's better than the mint outfit you had on the other day, but it still looks kind of blah. I wish I could say the same for the makeup."

"What do you mean, dear?" CeeCee said, pulling out a small mirror. When she caught sight of herself, she looked a little stunned. "My, it is a little heavy isn't it." A little heavy was an understatement. What the outfit lacked in color had been more than made up by the makeup. The foundation made her face look too flawless, which didn't go with the color or condition of her neck. The eyeliner was too thick and the eye shadow too much for daytime. The red lipstick was the final blow. CeeCee pulled out a tissue and wiped off the lipstick. Then she thanked the group. "What would I do without this group to keep me real. Now to get back on topic, I suppose we could ask Kelly's husband for the things she made." She glanced over the rest of us. "Or would that be bad form under the circumstances?"

I looked at Dinah and we both turned toward Adele expecting her to jump into the middle of the conversation and insist she had it under control and already had Kelly's things. But Adele avoided our gazes and was strangely silent until Rhoda stepped in.

"Adele, you were making such a fuss about her being a crochet pretender. Didn't you go over to her house to see if she had really made anything?" All eyes turned to Adele. She set down the ring of apricot yarn she was working on, took out a stack of completed cotton cowls in a rainbow of colors, and pushed them across the table toward CeeCee.

"Don't worry about Kelly's pieces," Adele said. "I have more of these at home." Adele's response reminded me of a politician who ignored a question they didn't want to answer and simply spoke about something else.

Rhoda picked one up and tried it on. The ring of lacy stitches hung loosely around her neck. "It's August, Adele. Nobody is going to want to buy these. Who wants to put something around their neck in all this heat?" Rhoda pulled it off and added it back to the pile. Adele seemed unmoved and kept stitching.

"You should have asked me if you thought Kelly was a crochet pretender," Sheila said. She seemed a little surprised at her own voice. Sheila always got tense when she said something to the group. Her remedy was to pick up her hook and start to crochet. It didn't matter what it was or if she'd have to rip it later, the rhythmic movement helped her get over her tense moment. "I could have cleared that up right away." Sheila's finger kept moving as she spoke. "She saw that we were selling some of the things I make at Luxe and wanted

to know if we'd be interested in selling some of her crocheted items." Luxe was just down the street from the bookstore and was considered a lifestyle store, which meant
everything they sold was stylish.

"Kelly brought a piece in to give me an idea of what she
made," Sheila continued. "You should have seen it." Sheila
looked up at the group. "She'd crocheted a long tunic with
hand-dyed yarn. It was a one-of-a-kind item. I told her I'd
tell my boss about it. I think she was selling things some
other way, too."

"It sounds like she was looking for ways to bring in
money." Dinah said. "With the dollar store just starting out,
I suppose she was trying to help out. That's probably why
she rented out her yard to the production and signed her
house up to be used in the future."

Sheila's eyes darted around the group and she cleared her
throat. She seemed to hesitate, but finally she spoke up.
"When she came in the store, she bought a silver ruler."

"That doesn't sound like somebody who is trying to
bring in money to help her family," Rhoda said.

Eduardo had come in as Sheila was talking. He was a
stark contrast to the rest of us, towering over us with his
long raven hair pulled into a ponytail. He handed CeeCee
several bracelets he'd made using thread. He'd used a
granny square motif on all of them, but done them in different ways. One had the traditional several colors bordered
by black, another was done in a cream-colored thread with
an embellishment of pearls, and he'd made one all in black
with some crystals that reflected the light. It was hard to
imagine his large hands working with fine thread and a
slender steel hook, but he was a master at it. His Irish grandmother had taught him well.

"Are you talking about Kelly Donahue?" he asked as he

pulled out a chair. His handsome face appeared somber at the mention of her name. "It's hard to believe she was in my store just a few days ago." His gaze moved over the group. "She wasn't a fan of the merchandise her husband was selling. She told me he kept bringing all this off-brand stuff home and it was awful. She was into quality and bought bars of Penhalgion's Bluebell soap from my store. That's the fragrance Princess Diana favored."

Eduardo had all but given up his career as a cover model and sometime commercial spokesperson now that he'd bought the Crown Apothecary. It helped business that he spent time in the store and that everyone knew he owned it. People seemed to love to frequent stores and restaurants that had a celebrity connection.

He took some orbs of thread out of his bag along with a steel hook and laid them on the table. "I thought you all might want to try making the bracelets," he said before pulling out a stack of sheets that had the pattern and handing them out.

"I've been helping with the investigation," Adele said, taking out a little notepad. "Let me see now. You said Kelly told you she didn't like the stuff her husband sold. And she had expensive taste." Adele leaned closer to the group. "I'm going to pass these clues on through Eric. We already think it was her husband who did it. But what you just told me is the final corner in what we detectives call the golden triangle. One corner is for means. Dan had that. Eric said Dan owned a gun. The other corner is for opportunity. I bet Dan only claimed he discovered her body. He could easily have come by earlier, killed her and then acted all crazy and gone running to tell my boyfriend Eric." Adele let out a satisfied sigh. "And you just gave me the motive that fits into that last corner. Dan the dollar king probably didn't like it that she dissed his business." Adele's eyes grew brighter. "And that she was spending all their money on expensive soap and fancy yarn." She closed her little notebook. "With this information, they'll arrest Dan for sure."

"Golden triangle?" I said to Adele. "What detective exactly, used that term?"

Adele sputtered and threw me an angry glance. "Maybe it's my term, but I'm sure Eric will think it's brilliant and pass it on, along with the information."

"And what's this about Dan's gun?"

Adele sputtered again. "I know what you're doing, Pink. This is my case. And I just solved it. Who's the super sleuth now?"

CHAPTER 11

"I don't get it. If they found Dan's gun, why haven't they already arrested him?" I said.

"Because they were waiting for Adele's information to fill in the third corner of the golden triangle," Dinah said with a grin. We both shook our heads. Dinah and I had met up at the end of my workday. We'd decided to have a girls' night out, or in, really. The plan was we'd go to my house, order a pizza, watch some old classic movie and crochet.

"I wonder if Eric realizes what he's done by letting her in on his work," Dinah said. We'd gotten into the greenmobile and started on the short distance to my place.

"If he doesn't, he'll know soon when she starts wanting to do ride-alongs on his motorcycle.," I said as I pulled the car into my driveway. "And when she starts wanting to co-sign the traffic tickets." We both laughed as we got out and went across the backyard. As soon as I opened the back door, Cosmo ran outside followed by Blondie. Music was blaring from Samuel's room even with the door shut. I checked the cats' bowls next and when I saw they were empty, poured in some dry food.

Jeffrey came into the kitchen and greeted us before picking through the white paper bags of takeout food on the counter. I could tell by the smell it was burgers and fries.

"I don't think my dad has ever heard of salad," he said, his mouth twisted in disappointment.

I told him to check the vegetable drawer and help himself. I noticed voices coming from the living room and I asked Jeffrey who was there.

"I don't know. Some friend of my dad's," Jeffrey said before going to the refrigerator. Jeffrey took out some romaine lettuce, a cucumber, tomatoes and some green onions. He was rummaging for a cutting board and asked if he could borrow some olive oil.

"Maybe we should rethink the location of our girls' night," Dinah said. "My place might be a little more peaceful."

I nodded in agreement. "But let me check my yarn stash first. I'm sure I have a bunch of balls of the thread in different colors." We had both wanted to try Eduardo's pattern and make one of the bracelets using crochet thread. Dinah followed me into the living room. As we walked through it, the voices dropped to a whisper. I looked toward the couch and saw that Barry was talking to one of his cop friends. They looked in our direction and nodded in greeting before continuing their conversation.

"Maybe you can ask Barry why they haven't arrested Dan," Dinah said as we reached my side of the house. Once we entered the hall, it was blissfully quiet.

"I'll try later." I went over to the basket of yarn and started to rummage through it as Dinah looked around.

"I can see why you call this your haven—and why you

need it." She glanced back toward the other side of the house.

I replaced the yarn I'd pulled out and stood up. "The crochet thread isn't here. I must have packed it up with all the stuff I put in the storage locker." Since the room I'd given Barry was my former crochet room, I'd had to empty it. There was no place else in the house or the garage for all the stuff and I'd rented a storage unit nearby. They seemed to have popped up all over the place since everybody seemed to have so much excess stuff lately. "We can swing by the storage place on the way to your house," I said as we made our way back across the house. Barry and his company were standing at the front door talking in low voices as we passed.

"I think those thread bracelets would make great gifts," Dinah said. "We could make them holiday appropriate. A nice orange and black one would be great for Halloween." We got into my car and headed for the storage place.

"I rented one of the smaller units, so I can't pull the car in front of it," I explained as I parked in the lot at the edge of the rows of low buildings.

We passed the office on the end of one of the buildings. "I think that place must be open for an hour a day. The only time I've seen it open was when I came here to rent the space." We began down a walkway between twin buildings. The row of delft blue roll-up doors made it look like a row of mini garages, but then again, wasn't that what they were—extra garage space.

Twilight was beginning to morph into darkness and the place was deserted. Dinah seemed apprehensive as she looked over her shoulder. "This place is kind of creepy," she said. "Let's get the stuff and get out of here."

"If you think it's creepy now, just think of what it's like when it's completely dark." The lighting wasn't the best. Some kind of florescent floodlight did a better job of casting shadows than it did illuminating the place. I had the key to my lock in hand and was checking the numbers on the identical doors to find mine. "I heard that some people have actually been living in these kinds of places," I said.

Dinah looked at the long row of doors and shuddered. "Not for me. I wonder what people keep in these. Didn't I hear something about somebody keeping a body in a freezer in a storage unit?"

"I'm sure that wasn't at this place," I said. Now she'd gotten me nervous and I was looking around seeing bogeymen hanging in every shadow. "I bet all these just have old computers and boxes of baby clothes," I said. "Or at least I hope so."

We finally located mine and I undid the lock before rolling up the door. The air inside was hot and musty. To counteract the stuffiness and any bad smells that might be hanging around, I'd bought a bunch of dryer bags filled with lavender buds. I never used them in my dryer, but instead used them as sachets and often tucked one under my pillow since lavender was supposed to help you sleep. I had put the thin paper packets in all the containers of yarn I'd brought. It was also a good bug deterrent.

We moved inside the unit and Dinah began to look around. "If the door was shut it would be like a cave in here," she said with a little warble in her voice.

"Let's not talk about anymore scary stuff while we're in here," I said.

"Sorry. I was just trying to imagine people living in one of these," she said.

"If it makes you feel any better, I read that a family had worked out a way to get electricity with a bunch of extension cords and even had some kind of a chemical toilet."

"It doesn't," she said. "Let's hurry up."

I had left a flashlight in the unit for times like this. I used the light as I quickly began to sort through the bins of yarn. Dinah sat down in a folding chair I'd stashed along with some other odds and ends of furniture. "I was kind of surprised that CeeCee said we ought to all go to Kelly's funeral," Dinah said as I fumbled through a box of yarn. The actress-leader of the Hookers had said Kelly was one of our own and out of respect we should go.

"It figures that Adele would suggest that she go as our representative. I don't know what she thinks is going to happen. That Kelly will pop out of her casket and tell everybody that Adele is hiding the pieces she made for the sale because she doesn't want to admit that she can't do a bullion stitch."

"Knowing Adele, that's what she could be thinking," Dinah said. "But now that she's so busy playing detective, maybe she's forgotten." Dinah sat forward in the chair. "You know any day she's going to show up in a deerstalker hat a la Sherlock Holmes and start carrying a magnifying glass."

"And she'll probably crochet herself a badge. Maybe a big gold star with her name embroidered on it," I said and we both laughed. And we both knew Adele might really do it.

"I was already going to go to the funeral," Dinah said. "Kelly is a neighbor or was a neighbor." Dinah's good humor faded. "I hate to bring up scary things again, but do you really think Dan killed her?"

I stopped for a moment and straightened. It was a pleasure to be able to discuss it without Adele jumping in every second with something motor officer/security detail Eric had told her. Then I caught my friend's concerned expression and realized why she was asking.

Dinah lived down the street from Dan. And she lived alone.

"I'm sure even if he did it, he's not a serial killer. It had to be something between them. From what we've heard, they were kind of a mismatched pair. He with his boxes of Rice-A-Randy and she with her high-end English soap. Maybe he got mad that she was spending all their money. And remember, they were both married before. Maybe he got creamed on his last divorce and decided never again." I went back to combing the bins for the balls of thread. "And despite what Detective Adele said, it might be someone else entirely. There were lots of people coming and going since they were setting up the backyard for a scene." I told Dinah about the conversation I'd overheard between the prop guys and North Adams. "Fred and Zeke both knew Kelly from before. Think about it, they're prop guys on a cop show. They probably know all about weapons. And don't forget her neighbor. Miss PTA prez was very angry at Kelly. She seemed to think Kelly was ruining the neighborhood."

My best friend looked at me. "You're going to get involved in this aren't you?"

"Don't tell Adele. I'm already on it. I asked Mason to see what he could find out."

Dinah nodded and looked relieved. "I was hoping you'd say something like that."

I loaded up a tote bag with a bunch of orbs of thread in jewel-like colors along with several black ones. Then I searched through the box of hooks and found a selection of steel ones.

"Now how about we stop by the dollar store tomorrow and pick up some information along with the prize Dan promised you," I said as we stepped back into the walkway and I pulled down the door.

CHAPTER 12

"Look," Dinah said, pointing at a white banner reading "More Bang for Your Buck" that hung across the storefront. "Dan really did take my suggestion about the name." Dinah shook her head in disbelief. "I thought he was just being polite when we saw him in Le Grande Fromage. And it makes me have serious doubts whether he killed Kelly. If you were planning to kill your wife, would you really be worried about a new name for your store? But English teachers everywhere must be offering up a prayer of thanks."

I looked at the sign again and shuddered. "Yes, but if you were devastated because someone else killed your wife, would your store not only be open, but sporting a new name?"

We had waited until the next morning to make the trek to the store and were wearing the bracelets we'd made during the prior evening. The dollar store was located in one of the older storefronts in Tarzana and had previously housed an indoor play lot for kids.

"It looks like he made good use of the old decorations," I said looking through the large windows. The owners of the kids' place had decorated the walls with murals of stylized trees and hills with big flowers on them and a train full of animals chugging by. Dan had painted over the animals and replaced them with giant jars of Sucker's jam, Jerkmans hand cream and Tried detergent.

"And it looks like life has gone on," I said as we went inside. The store seemed to be bustling with aggressive shoppers and I almost got sideswiped by a woman racing her cart toward a display of cans of "krab" meat. We decided we should try to blend in and took one of the shopping carts to push while we walked around for a few minutes, checking out the merchandise. Dinah picked up a plastic bottle of Belcher's grape juice, made a face and put it back.

"Have you thought about what we're going to say to Dan?" Dinah said. "We could say 'Oh by the way, I heard that you have the golden triangle of means, motive and opportunity, and Detective Adele is closing in on you.'" Dinah saw a display of Leon's brand yarn and pushed the cart toward it.

"I'm sure the golden triangle line will get him to throw up his arms and confess to us," I joked, following along with her.

While we went through the bin of yarn, Dinah found some lightweight cotton in a pale yellow she thought would be perfect for one of the long scarves she favored. As she was dropping the skeins in the cart, she looked up at me. "I wonder if Kelly used any of this yarn."

I shook my head. "I don't think so. Everything I saw about Kelly makes me think she was purely a real-brand girl, and fancy brands at that." Once Dinah had gotten the yarn she wanted, we went back to discussing how to talk to Dan.

"We could bring up that we stopped by his house the day Kelly was shot," I said.

"And imply that we saw him there," Dinah said.

"Good idea," I said. I had been avoiding thinking about the visit because it made me feel like a jinx, but now that it was out in the open we talked back and forth about what time we'd gone there and agreed that it was right around midday.

"Remember, the prop guys were taking off for lunch when we got there," I added. I mentioned the visit had been very short thanks to Adele. Our conversation was interrupted by a noise coming over the loudspeaker in the store. A bell rang and was followed by a voice.

"Hello shoppers. Just five minutes until the dollar-of-the-hour special starts. The mystery boxes are already in the back of the store." At that, there was a rush of carts trying to get past ours. I heard several shoppers suggest that they should have just bumped my cart out of the way.

The sound of the bell triggered something in my mind. "Kelly's doorbell rang while we were there," I said.

Dinah nodded in recognition. "She said it was a real estate agent or something. And then she hustled us out of there."

"What if it wasn't just someone wanting to leave off an advertising brochure?"

The voice returned to the loudspeaker interrupting our conversation again. The frenzy toward the center of the store got wilder when the voice announced the boxes had been brought out and were being opened. Our curiosity won out and Dinah and I joined the stream of carts heading toward the center of the store. Though we ditched our cart when we hit a traffic jam and held on to each other as we threaded through the mess.

The stack of unmarked cardboard boxes was like an island in the middle of a sea of carts. I could have taken off all my clothes and jumped on one of the displays and started dancing and no one would have noticed.

A clerk was cutting open the boxes and unloading their contents while eyeing the encroaching crowd nervously. The area around where he was working was roped off. But as the carts kept jostling for a better position, the poles holding the ropes fell over. The carts moved in like sharks on a sea lion. He left his post with the boxes half-open and squirmed through the crowd. I didn't see where he went because there was a crowd of people squeezed around the barricade of carts. I just heard the sound of boxes being opened, the thud of something being thrown into the carts and a lot of angry voices, complaining the people in the front were getting everything.

A well-dressed woman with recently styled hair stopped next to Dinah and me. "They should put some kind of a limit on how many you can buy. The people in the front take everything."

"What is it?" I asked, and the woman shrugged.

"Who knows, or cares. All that matters is that it's a bargain."

Dinah and I held our ground far back from the fray. I noticed the crowd begin to disperse and the victors headed for the checkout, guarding the contents of the carts while being harassed by people who'd gotten there too late. Even so, a tussle broke out because someone snatched the sale item out of another person's cart and said it wasn't fair that she got to buy ten and some people hadn't gotten any.

"It's a free country," the woman with the cartful of merchandise said, trying to get back the snatched item.

Dinah stood on her tiptoes and tried to see what the fuss was about. Then she started to laugh and nudged me. "You won't believe what the dollar-of-the-hour item is." She knew how to use a pause to build up suspense. "Cotton candy makers."

When things went back to normal, I found the clerk who'd opened the boxes. He was half in an entryway that said "Employees Only." His eyes widened as we approached him and he put up his hands in a defensive manner. "There's no more in the back, ladies. No matter what you say to me or promise me, everything we had was in those boxes." He let out his breath. "And I know the store is called Hollar for, I mean More Bang for Your Buck, but the dollar-of-the-hour specials are five bucks."

"Really," Dinah said. "You know that's false advertising. It should be the five-dollar-of-the-hour special."

"I'll tell the boss." The clerk started to back away, but I stepped in and said we wanted to speak to Dan. The clerk had put more distance between us before he said that Dan wasn't there, while mumbling that even if it came with extra pay he wasn't going to be doing the dollar-of-the-hour item anymore. "He's in the middle of a family situation," the guy said, looking Dinah and me over carefully. "I'm the assistant manager. Anything I can do for you?"

I was tempted to bring up getting one of the bargain items as a joke, but he didn't look like he had a sense of humor. I told him we'd known Dan's wife and we'd stopped in to give him our condolences. The man's demeanor changed and he actually stepped closer to us. Now that he knew we weren't trying to squeeze more cotton candy makers out of him, he relaxed.

"So you knew her," he said with a sad movement of his head. "It's just terrible and so pointless. If somebody wanted to rob the place, why did they have to kill her," he said. "I only met her once. Dan kept hoping she'd work here and help out. It's not easy launching a store," he said gesturing toward the line at the registers. "It looks like the customers are buying a lot, but you've got to remember everything, but the special, is a dollar. Somebody can walk out with two bags of merchandise and only drop ten bucks."

After dealing with the crush of crazy customers, the man seemed relieved to talk to us. Or rather unload. He started telling us how until recently it had been hard to get the merchandise for the dollar-of-the-hour special, which it turned out was really the dollar-of-the-day special. "Dan wanted to call it the dollar-of-the-hour special because dollar and hour rhyme."

I saw Dinah reacting and he looked at her. "I know it's false advertising, but nobody else has complained." The man had a walkie-talkie stuck to his belt, and it began to squawk. "Sorry ladies, got to go." He took off toward the front of the store where it appeared some kind of fuss had broken out.

"Did you notice that the assistant manager is the only one who seems to think Kelly's death was really a robbery gone bad?" I said when we got outside.

"Can you blame him? Everyone who doesn't think it was a robbery, thinks his boss did it." Dinah looked around and then glanced back at the store. "We forgot about the yarn. Should we go back and find the cart?" We both looked at the chaos in the store and shook our heads in unison.

I was working the late shift at the bookstore and still had time before I was supposed to start. I turned to my friend. "I'd really like to hear Dan's side of things. What do you say we make a condolence call at his house?"

I noticed Dinah was smiling as we started down the street and I asked what was going on. "I'm just so happy to be your Watson again," she said. She had been the first person to be my sidekick in an investigation, but ever since she'd started the relationship with Commander Blaine, her time wasn't always her own. He claimed a lot of it. Commander ran the local Mail It Center and was a widower. He'd been lonely right after his wife died and instead of wallowing in it, had used his energy to help put on events for Tarzana seniors and other groups. Dinah with her bubbly personality was great at helping out and once she got used to being with a man who wasn't always trying to ditch her, she enjoyed it. But I was glad she'd worked out some kind of balance, because I missed my friend.

"Hands down you're my favorite wingman," I said.

We both agreed we shouldn't show up empty-handed for the condolence call and we didn't have time to make anything, so we stopped by the bookstore and I talked our barista cookie baker, Bob, out of a batch of his Hurry Up Chocolate Chip Cookie Bars made using my recipe.

The commotion of the *L.A. 911* production disappeared as soon as we started down Kelly's street. When we got closer, I saw that the production company truck was no longer in the driveway, but the prop guys had left trees and bushes in pots behind, because there was a scene they still had to shoot.

We walked up to the entrance and I rang the bell. When the door opened, I prepared to say hello to Dan with his dark hair and everyman sort of looks, but the person who answered the door was anything but ordinary looking. I couldn't see my face, but I had a feeling I had a goofy smile. All I could think was that he was gorgeous. I caught myself and laughed in embarrassment.

The adorable man looked from me to Dinah and his face

lit in a smile that only made him more adorable. When I saw the dimples that matched Kelly's, I knew he must be a relative.

"Molly Pink," I said extending my hand. "And this is Dinah Lyons. We were looking for Dan. We wanted to express our condolences."

"Were you friends of my sister?" he asked before introducing himself as Stone Thomasville. There was something golden about him. His hair was golden blond with lighter streaks and his skin had a golden cast as if he'd been kissed by the sun. He wore a red and white Aloha shirt over a pair of khaki shorts. A pair of sunglasses hung around his neck and he smelled of suntan stuff. Then I remembered the remark the prop guy had made. He'd said Kelly had a brother who was a surfer and it all made sense.

I said how sorry I was about Kelly. Dinah chimed in that we'd been over a few days ago and thought we'd left something in her workroom. I looked over at her in surprise then understood what she was doing and gave her an approving nod.

Dan came up behind him and peered out as us. It was obvious he was trying to place us. "The bookstore lady and my prize winner," he said, finally. "More Bang for Your Buck is a great name." He started to go on about the store until I interrupted him and explained we had come to pay our condolences. The brightness went out of his face and he mumbled something about how he was trying not to think about it, as he invited us in. As I followed Dan and Stone inside I was struck by how differently the two men moved. Dan thrust his head forward, as if he was in a hurry to get somewhere, and had a brusque walk. Stone moved with the energetic grace of an athlete.

"What is it that you left?" Stone asked when we reached the living room.

We were unprepared for the question and both began to talk over each other with impromptu answers. I said it was my sweater, which when I thought about it was absurd since it was in the nineties outside. Dinah said she'd left her reading glasses and then did too much explaining about why she'd taken them off in the first place.

Luckily, neither of the men picked up on our confusion. "The cops went through the room and they left me a list of what they took. I don't remember anything about a sweater or glasses, so they're probably still there," Dan said before inviting us to sit down. I handed him Bob's cookies and told him again how sorry I was about Kelly and reminded him that we'd known her through our crochet group.

"I don't know how she had time for a crochet group. Did she tell you we both have kids from previous marriages? Every week was different around here with her kids or my kids staying over." Before I could ask where all the kids were now, he explained under the circumstances both sets of kids were staying with their other parent.

I really wanted to ask him about the circumstances he was under. I assumed it was the fact that he was a person of interest to the cops. He seemed distracted and then found his manners and offered us something to drink. We both said we didn't want to trouble him, but he insisted.

Stone had positioned himself on the arm of the sofa and I noticed he was drinking something from a small plastic bottle. I looked to see if it was some weird brand from Dan's store and Stone caught me staring at it. "I'd offer you some but it's the last bottle." He explained it was a coconut water energy drink he was involved with marketing.

"Stone's a famous surfer," Dan said. He started to reel off a list of the championships Stone had won and explained what they were. It was all pretty much lost on me since I wasn't a fan of the sport myself and Stone seemed a little embarrassed by the fuss.

"The competing is all in the past. Now I just rest on my laurels," Stone said with a smile. He mentioned that he'd moved to Hawaii awhile ago. Even though I'm not competing anymore, we're hoping my name still means something," he said handing me the plastic drink bottle. It was sky blue and had an image of him on a surfboard. He explained they were making it in small batches in Hawaii, but were hoping to take it to a bigger level.

"That's why I'm here," he said. "I flew into Denver to meet with a drink company. I was going to stop here on the way back to Maui. . . ." His voice trailed off and he looked down. "I had no idea I'd be coming for a funeral."

I made mention that he'd said "we," and he got the dimpled smile again. "I'm afraid it's a bit of an affectation. There is no 'we' really. It's just me."

Dan excused himself to get the drinks and as soon as he left the room Stone's smile faded. "What is with the cops?" he muttered under his breath. He let out a heavy sigh. "It couldn't be more obvious. He killed my sister." His expression changed to frustration. "The cops claim they're working on it, but don't have the right kind of evidence yet." He looked toward the kitchen. "Don't say anything to Dan. I'm trying to make it look like I'm on his side. But I want to find the evidence they need to lock him up. I'm not going anywhere until that detective takes Dan into custody."

As Dan came back in the room Stone's demeanor changed back to friendly. Dan set down a tray of glasses and a large bottle of Mountain Dew. "This stuff is great," he said pouring the greenish carbonated drink over the ice in the glasses. We took a couple of polite sips and then said we both needed to be on our way.

"If we could look for our things," I said, purposely being vague this time. I got up and made a move toward the workroom. Dinah set down her glass and followed. Dan got in front of us and led the way. Stone took up the rear.

Dan opened the door with a certain amount of trepidation. "This was her special place. She never allowed any of us in here," he said as he stepped inside. His eyes swept the room. "You know how it is with kids. They knock everything around, and I suppose she was worried they'd start playing with her computer. She had an online business selling things she'd crocheted and I think she thought the kids would mess things up." He seemed a little hurt. "But I don't know why she kept me out."

I remembered hearing about an online business. Sheila had mentioned that Kelly was interested in selling things to Luxe, but apparently that was another avenue for Kelly's pieces. Now her yarn supply and the stash of shipping boxes made sense. I tried to get more details, but he shrugged. "It was strictly her business." He touched the computer table. "I think it was because she'd been married before and wanted something of her own. She had some trust issues."

It was eerie being in the room now, knowing that this is where Kelly had been shot. There was a faint smell of bleach and part of the carpet had been cut out. The room seemed shadowy and dim and I realized the line of poplar trees from the production company were still in front of the sliding glass door. Dan looked around for a light. He passed on the full-spectrum lamp next to the Mission-style chair and found an overhead light that illuminated the room. It seemed like someone had cleaned up after the cops had left, but not done a very good job of it. The plastic bins were stacked against the wall, but they were askew, as were the unfolded shipping boxes on the floor.

"Was the room ransacked?" Dinah asked.

"It was a mess when I came in." Dan swallowed hard and his voice became a monotone as he told us that he'd just stopped home that day for a few minutes and hadn't expected Kelly to be there. He'd seen the door to her workroom open. At that, he stopped. "I've told this story so many times, it should be easier," he said. "She was lying there on her back." He swallowed again and shook his head as if he couldn't describe it one more time. "The plastic bins were knocked around and there was yarn everywhere."

I said I'd heard Kelly had been shot and asked if he'd seen a gun. He appeared very uncomfortable as he acknowledged that she had been shot, but then shook his head and said he didn't know anything about a gun.

"Was there anything missing?" I asked as I glanced around the room trying to compare it to what I'd seen before.

"The cops asked the same question. All I can tell you is the truth. Like I said, I was almost never in here. I don't even know what she had in here." Dan didn't seem to care why I'd asked.

I looked at the library table that held her computer. "There was a lamp there," I said. "It had a leaded glass shade. . . ." I looked toward Dan, but he just shrugged and said he didn't know anything about it, and no it hadn't been one of the things the cops took.

It seemed like we'd found out all we were going to, and I started to go back toward the door, but Dinah was jerking her head, trying to get my attention. "Molly, your sweater," she said in a pointed tone. "And my reading glasses." I retraced my steps and as Dan and Stone watched, Dinah and I pretended to look for our stuff.

"I guess we were wrong," I said, finally as Dinah and I walked through the door and continued toward the front door.

Dan followed along behind us. "I know it sounds strange that I didn't know much about what Kelly was doing, but I've been consumed with trying to make my dollar store work," he said. "I'm hoping to have the stores all over the country. But first I have to make this one work. The dollar store business is very competitive now." His tone had changed and he sounded animated and excited as he brought up the dollar-of-the-hour special. I saw Dinah start to flinch and I hurried her out of there before she could bring up her issues with it. He called after us that he hadn't forgotten her prize and would give it to her next time she came in the store.

When we were back on the street, Dinah and I compared our thoughts. "You know sometimes a cigar is just a cigar," she said. "You saw how he said he didn't know anything about the gun, but thanks to Adele we know he owns one, and it's just unnatural the way he is so gung ho about his store when his wife has just died. Maybe this time, the obvious is the right answer. Maybe Dan really did kill Kelly?"

"But why would he take the leaded glass lamp?" I said.

CHAPTER 13

SHEDD & ROYAL BOOKS AND MORE WAS BUZZING when I walked in after leaving Dinah at her house. The production group must have been on some kind of break, because I recognized a number of them coming out of the café.

Mrs. Shedd was pointing out our selection of e-readers to a customer. My boss urged the woman to pick it up and try it out. No sooner had the woman taken Mrs. Shedd's suggestion, when an earsplitting wail started. All the activity in the bookstore stopped and everyone's eyes were on the table, the e-reader and the woman holding it. The customer dropped the small device like it was a hot tamale and made a fast exit while Mrs. Shedd put her hands over her ears and looked around, asking for help.

After the incident with the neighborhood shoplifters, Mr. Royal had decided we needed some security measures on the devices. Though he'd been everywhere and done everything, he still occasionally overestimated his abilities. It was certainly true when it came to the do-it-yourself alarm system he'd bought at the hardware store. There was a plastic leash on each of the e-readers now and you were supposed to be able to pick one up and move it around without a problem. The alarm was only supposed to go off if someone tried to pull it free. *Supposed to* was the operative phrase here. "Where's Joshua?" Mrs. Shedd said as the wail continued. "He knows how to shut this off." She looked at me. "Molly, help! Can't you do something?"

Suddenly Adele flounced through the gathered crowd and grabbed hold of the offending reader. She had something in her hand that she jammed into a little box on the leash and the awful noise stopped.

Adele turned toward all of us. "Look who saved the day—again." She pointed toward herself. "Could it be me? Yes, I think it is." She curtsied to the crowd and I rolled my eyes. With the noise stopped, the crowd went back to the café and browsing the bookstore.

"How did you do that?" Mrs. Shedd asked. Adele held up a key on an elaborate keychain with multiple pom-poms. "For some reason my house key fits into the slot," she said, demonstrating just as Joshua Royal joined us. When he heard that Adele's key fit in the alarm slot, he started trying to adjust it.

"Where have you been, Pink?" Adele said.

I was going to shrug off her question, but my evil twin took over. Between Eric giving her inside information about Kelly's murder and now her fixing the e-reader alarm, Adele was getting too big for the room and I couldn't take it any longer.

"You want to know where I was?" I said with a subtle touch of one-upmanship in my voice. "Dinah and I went to

Dan Donahue's store and we found out that Dan Donahue was upset that Kelly didn't help out in the store. We also went to the Donahue house and we met Kelly's brother." I took a breath. "You probably don't know anything about him. His name is Stone Thomasville and he's some kind of surfer champion." I went from there to telling her how Dinah and I had looked around the room where Kelly was shot. "And we found out that Kelly had an online business selling things she crocheted."

I couldn't stop myself. It was horrible. I was acting just like Adele.

"You're going to get yourself in trouble," Adele sputtered. "Eric told me that he'd get me all the info I needed, but that I could get in a lot of trouble if I started investigating on my own. Interfering with a police investigation or something." Joshua Royal stopped working on the alarm and looked up.

"You met Stone Thomasville?" he said with awe in his voice. He went over toward one of the bookshelves and came back a few minutes later holding a large coffee table picture book. He opened to a double page with a photograph of a man riding in the curl of a gigantic wave. He flipped the page and showed me the copy as he told me what it said.

"He won the Pipeline Master four times. Pipeline is a beach on Oahu's north shore. It has the world's deadliest waves. Surfers have died there, but Stone was like magic." Mr. Royal flipped the page and there was a shot of a huge wave forming a tube. A little figure was inside it and appeared to be upside down. "That's called a barrel roll. Body boarders do it a lot, but Stone is one of the only standing surfers to have mastered it."

It turned out that in addition to everything else Joshua Royal had done while he was traveling around the world adventuring, he'd been a surfer. He was awed to think Stone was staying right down the street. Adele had her storm cloud face. It was making her crazy that she was out of the loop.

"Do you think he'd be willing to come in and sign his photo in some books?" Then Mr. Royal considered what he was asking. "I suppose it might be in bad taste under the circumstances."

"I can ask him," I said. Mr. Royal brightened and said he'd check with the distributor to see if he could get in a stack of copies.

"What a wonderful idea, Joshua," Mrs. Shedd said, noticing the hefty price on the book's jacket. She'd joined us and overheard the plan.

I hadn't noticed that North Adams was carrying one of Bob's primo cappuccinos and was standing on the outskirts of our little group. The star of *L.A. 911* held the coffee drink up as if making a toast. "The cappuccinos here are the best." He took a satisfying sip and set the cup down on the table with the e-readers. "I couldn't help but overhear." He turned his attention to me. "You're investigating that woman's death? Are you some kind of amateur sleuth?" he asked.

Adele answered for me. "Pink likes to think she's a modern day Nancy Drew. But some of us are the real deal instead of just imitation fictional detectives. Adele Abrams, ad hoc PI, at your service," she said.

North looked like he didn't know whether to laugh or not, but then he seemed to figure out she wasn't joking. Ad hoc private investigator? What did that even mean? "Maybe I can help. Being a detective on this show for all these years has given me some investigative skills." His gaze went back and forth over both Adele and me.

Adele rolled her eyes, which luckily happened when North was looking at me. I thanked him for his offer and said I'd let him know when I heard anything new.

Later on Mrs. Shedd pulled me aside. "Good work, Molly," Mrs. Shedd said. "Our goal is to keep Mr. Adams coming in here. If he wants to play armchair detective with you, we don't want to stop him. But do what you can to control Adele."

As if I could!

CHAPTER 14

I WORKED UNTIL THE BOOKSTORE CLOSED AND evening was sliding into night when I headed for home. Even though it was August and the weather said summer, the daylight hours were dwindling. I drove home, thinking about a refreshing bath and an ice cream dinner. That plan died the moment I walked into my backyard.

The outdoor lights were on, illuminating Jeffrey and a group of his drama friends gathered around the umbrella table. They all had a bunch of stapled pages and I figured out they were doing a table read of some play. Jeffrey lifted a hand in greeting and then went back to hovering over his script.

Cosmo was enjoying all the activity, the small black mutt stretched out on the pavement watching. Having people around had the opposite effect on my other dog, Blondie, and without even looking I was sure she was holed up in my room. The cats were nowhere to be seen.

I walked into the kitchen and stopped short in the doorway. Barry was setting several pizza boxes on the counter. Next to him Detective Heather was counting out paper plates and napkins. She was still in her work suit and, when she moved, I saw her badge and her gun in a big belt around her waist. She flipped open the top pizza box and started putting slices on the plates. "I'll take them out to the kids," she said. As she turned and headed to the door she almost rammed into me.

"Oh," she said and looked toward Barry.

"Molly, I'm so sorry. I thought this would be over before you got home. The place the kids were supposed to do the read fell apart at the last minute. Jeffrey asked if they could come here."

Barry knew I had a soft spot for Jeffrey, or as his drama friends were probably calling him, Columbia. "Whatever. It's okay," I said. Detective Heather and I were still clogging up the doorway.

"I heard you were at the Donahue house today," Heather said.

"Don't go oiling your handcuffs," I said trying to get past her. "It was just a condolence call and I thought I'd forgotten something when I was there before." I should have left it at that, but I thought of Adele's golden triangle of guilt. "I heard you found Dan's gun."

Detective Heather looked at me as if I hadn't said anything.

Barry came toward us carrying a stack of paper plates with pizza slices. As we stepped aside to let him through, Heather touched his arm in a possessive manner. "Your leg bothering you, hon?" He said he was fine and went on outside.

"Don't worry, Jeffrey and I will take care of the cleanup," Heather said to me. "It'll be a bonding experience."

"Whatever," I said walking through my kitchen. The last thing I needed right now was to watch Detective Heather show off her mothering skills. More than ever I longed for my room. As I passed the hall, Samuel came out of his room. "You should do something. He's taking over the place." He pointed toward the closed door of his room. "I had to put the cats in there."

I was getting a little close to the edge. I didn't say anything, but I thought of how my other son Peter had complained when Samuel had moved back home. And now Samuel was complaining about Barry.

"There's too much commotion around here. I'm going over to Nell's," my son said. He'd started seeing CeeCee's niece. I wasn't sure if it was good or bad. Either way it was really none of my business. "She's got that great guesthouse. Too bad we couldn't build one here," he said. He went back in his room and came out holding his guitar case. "Got a gig later," he called as he went toward the front door.

I was already rethinking my plans as I entered my peaceful domain. No way could I relax in a bath, and did I really want to fill up a bowl with rich ice cream under Detective Heather's judgmental stare? How had I managed to lose control of my own house?

When Mason had first mentioned that his daughter was getting married—back when he simply referred to her as "my oldest"—I'd decided to make a wedding hankie for her because of how I felt about him. I'd found a white linen one with no edging and then added a lacy trim with white crochet thread. I'd always intended to give it to him so he could pass it on to her. Now seemed like a good time to take it

over there even though I'd be showing up unannounced. I
wrote a note and wrapped the hankie in some tissue paper
and put them in a rosy pink small shopping bag.

I took the back roads to get to Mason's. It was dark and
atmospheric as I passed the giant eucalyptus trees along
Wells Drive and turned onto Valley Vista, which twisted
through the rustically landscaped area of Encino. Mason's
house was on the other side of Ventura Boulevard and eventually, I turned onto a side street and headed north. It wasn't
quite the soothing bath I'd envisioned taking, but the ride
did a lot to smooth out the kinks.

I parked in front of his sprawling ranch-style house. Soft
lights illuminated the white-barked beech trees in the slop-
ing front yard. I rethought the idea of just ringing his doorbell, and was about to call him on my phone, but then
decided a call would make too big a production out of it. If
no one answered the door, I would just leave the package.

I loved the redbrick walkway that led to the small porch
in front of the door. I was pleased with how I packaged the
hankie in the deep pink shopping bag. I punched the bell
and, after a beat, bent down to leave the package. When I
felt the whoosh of the door opening, I grabbed the bag and
straightened.

"I thought you weren't home," I said expecting to see
Mason. Instead a blond woman stood in the doorway, looking me up and down.

I admit I was also eyeing her, wondering who she was. I
had a sudden desire to leave. I'd been the third wheel enough
today. "If you could give this to Mason. It's for his daughter," I said pushing the shopping bag on her. "I made her
something for her wedding, but I don't really know her." I
was babbling and I wanted to get out of there. She took the
bag and rustled through the tissue paper. She pulled out the

hankie and didn't seem to know what to do with it. Finally she dropped it back in the bag.

"Molly, don't go," Mason's voice called from inside. Mason's and my relationship had moved up a notch beyond just friends, but we didn't really have strings on each other. There was nothing to stop him from seeing other women. This was too embarrassing. Mason came through the doorway and grabbed my arm leading me back to the house.

He must have seen the uncomfortable expression on my face and realized what I was thinking. "Molly, this is my ex-wife, Jaimee," he said.

"Oh," I said regarding Jaimee with new interest. Oops, Mason's worlds had just collided. Mason might have wanted to take baby steps to let me in his life, but it looked like he'd just taken a giant step whether he wanted to or not.

"Come in, sunshine," Mason said to me again. I thought Jaimee's eyes would fall out of their sockets.

"Sunshine?" she said, stifling a laugh.

"Didn't you say you had to go?" Mason said to her, but she shook her head.

Mason ushered me in and I could feel Jaimee's eyes on me as we all walked back to the den. Since Mason had kept his family, which included Jaimee, separate from his social life, this was probably the first time she'd seen any woman in his life. We were both measuring ourselves against each other and I was pretty sure I came up short.

In the few minutes I'd seen her, I had already gotten a feeling about who she was. She reminded me of an older version of the women I'd met when I'd helped out at my sons' elementary school. They were married to doctors and lawyers, all drove similar cars, had some shade of blond hair, manicured nails and houses that were far neater than mine. Jaimee was dressed in the high-end jeans of the moment with heels—a look I would never understand. She wore a white tee shirt with some kind of gauzy overshirt on top of it. It seemed a little much considering the heat, but her look was less about comfort and more about style. I suspected the purpose of the overshirt was to flow over any little lumps and bumps.

I could just imagine what she was thinking about me. I had changed when I got home and left behind my usual work clothes of khaki pants and a white shirt. No double layers for me. I had put on cargo-style capri pants with just a tee shirt, lumps and bumps be darned.

Jaimee was still holding the pink gift bag and said it was something I'd made for their daughter's wedding. She tried to give it back to me, but Mason asked to see it. "This is awkward," Jaimee said to me as she handed it over to him. "It really doesn't go with Thursday's dress. Why don't you keep it for somebody else."

Mason took the hankie from her and laid it on the coffee table. "Doesn't go with Thursday's dress? They're both white." He turned to me. "It's beautiful, sunshine. I'm sure Thursday will treasure it."

To put it mildly there was an awkward silence. Mason tried to break it by telling Jaimee about the Tarzana Hookers. She didn't seem interested and began talking to Mason about the wedding present they needed to buy for Thursday.

"There's a wonderful design studio in Santa Barbara where all the celebrities go," she said. "They have all these fantastic pieces—the kinds of things that will make her living room look legendary." When Mason seemed unmoved, she said something about taking care of it herself.

"You might want to look at Luxe," I said, referring to the lifestyle store near the bookstore. "They have a lot of one-of-a-kind items."

Jaimee glared at me as if I'd just suggested she go look in the broom closet.

We had reached another awkward moment. Mason looked at his watch. "I didn't realize how late it was," Mason said to his ex. She glanced from him to me and back to him before checking her watch.

"Mark worries about me if I'm out too late," she said, explaining to me that he was her boyfriend. Mason just shook his head and rolled his eyes. Even so, she seemed reluctant to leave. Maybe she didn't want Mason anymore, but she didn't really want someone else to have him, either. Finally she made a move toward the door and Mason walked her out. I noticed she had knocked the shopping bag with the hankie onto the floor.

Mason returned a few moments later and when he saw I was still standing, he urged me to sit. I realized for the first time that Spike wasn't around and asked Mason where he was. "Spike and Jaimee don't get along," he said before going to the service porch to let the dog in. I heard the clatter of claws as Spike charged into the room. The toy fox terrier sniffed the floor, looking indignant. He then ran straight to where Jaimee had been standing and started to bark. It took a few minutes of Mason telling his dog Jaimee was gone before Spike would calm down.

Mason put the hankie back into the bag and thanked me again, saying he would make sure his daughter got it. Then he sat down next to me on the soft leather couch.

"So, that's your ex," I said. I left it hanging, hoping he'd explain why she was there. Mason picked up on it and said she'd claimed to have found a location for the wedding and wanted a check for the deposit.

"But I wanted to see the place and talk to the manager," he said, "so we both drove down in my car. Lucky that I did.

Jaimee made it all sound perfect until we got there. They're renovating the hotel. No wonder the room was available. It was stripped down to the studs." Mason started to laugh. "The manager promised me they'd hang white tarps over the ripped out walls for the reception." He shook his head a bunch of times like he was trying to make sense of something. "She argued all the way back here. Like somehow this mess is my fault."

He leaned next to me and put his arm around my shoulders. "She's nothing like you. You're fun, an adventure to be around. Believe me, I never had to get her out of jail."

"Is her boyfriend Mark coming to the wedding?" I asked.

I felt Mason stiffen. "We're discussing it." Before I could pry more, Mason reminded me that I'd asked him to find out anything he could about Dan Donahue.

"He's a pretty blah guy," Mason began. "No arrests or anything like that. The best I could find out was that he's struggling with the store, but . . ." Mason stopped and leaned in a little closer. "He just got an influx of money."

"How'd you learn that?" I asked.

Mason chuckled. "I've got contacts everywhere. I talked to the owner of the building. It seems Dan was consistently late on his rent until a month ago. He told the landlord he had a new investor." Mason let the information sink in and then glanced at the empty coffee table. "What kind of host am I? What can I get you?" He paused for a moment then got an impish grin.

"Coffee, tea or me?"

CHAPTER 15

I ENDED UP PASSING ON ALL THREE OF MASON'S offers. He'd wanted me to stay—overnight—but I put him off. I was not ready to walk in my house the next morning and have to pass Barry pouring a bowl of cereal, so I convinced Mason to wait until my house was my own again.

When I finally pulled into my driveway, I wasn't sure what to expect. I was relieved to find the backyard quiet and without so much as a stray paper plate to show what had gone on there before. The kitchen was empty when I walked in. The trash had been taken out and the counter wiped clean of pizza residue. No animals rushed out to greet me. I assumed they were all sacked out somewhere, worn out from all the earlier activity. I went to turn out the light and quietly go across the house. Okay, it was more like sneak across the house.

I had my hand on the light switch when I heard one of the bedroom doors open. "Oh, you're home," Barry said in what I'd call feigned surprise as he came into the kitchen. I did a little double take at his attire. He had on blue plaid pajama pants and a white tee shirt. I guess he was wearing clothes, but just barely. He noticed me noticing his outfit and smiled. "Hey, I see people at the grocery story like this, but it seems to be making you uncomfortable." He went out of the room and reappeared a moment later with jeans on.

"Jeffrey's asleep, but he wanted me to be sure to thank you for this evening. It meant a lot to him to have the drama group over." Barry leaned against the counter. "I'm sorry. I know I should have checked with you first. There isn't any excuse for it. It all happened at the last minute."

I could see that he really meant it and in the big scheme of things it wasn't that big a deal, so I told him it was okay. I watched the tension go out of his expression. "Are you going to have tea, again?" Before I could answer he was already taking out a couple of mugs and looking through my tea stash. "How about some Constant Comment?"

"The tea is a good idea," I said finally. "We need to talk about some things."

"Uh-oh," Barry said in a teasing voice. "I said I was sorry. It won't ever happen again." This time he made the tea. Not that it took much effort. All he had to do was drop a couple of tea bags in the mugs and fill them with water from the instant hot spigot. Immediately the air filled with the spicy orange scent.

Before I could even suggest we sit outside, he was on his way out the door carrying the mugs. "If what you want to talk about is Heather being here, I'm sorry for that, too. She realized how awkward it was."

"It's your life and you can do what you want," I said setting my mug on the little glass table. The yard was so still, it almost didn't feel like we were outside. I looked up at the night blue sky and saw some stars twinkling. Then I gathered my strength and turned toward him. "You seem okay and you're back to work. If you moved back home, whatever you did and with whoever wouldn't matter. What does your doctor say about you doing stairs?"

"I know you're probably curious what's going on with the investigation into your crochet friend's murder. Heather talked about it a lot." Barry let it hang in the air for a minute. I knew he was just trying to change the subject by dangling information in front of me. I wish I could say that I was strong and went right back to asking when he was going to leave, but all I could think about was sharing the information with the group the next day, and well, flaunting it in front of Adele. I'm not proud of it, but at least I was being honest.

"Did she say anything about finding the gun?" I said, doing my best not to notice that Barry's lips had curved into a triumphant little smile. I told myself I could get back to trying to pin down when he was leaving later.

"That's the problem, she hasn't found the murder weapon," Barry said. I didn't bring up Adele's golden triangle of guilt, but said I'd heard she'd found Dan Donahue's gun.

"Oh, that gun," Barry said. "Heather had it tested, and it hadn't been fired. Not only that, Dan's hands were swabbed and his clothing checked and there was no gunpowder residue, which should have been there if he'd fired a weapon. His gun is registered and legal, so she had to give it back to him. Even so, her gut tells her Dan killed his wife."

Well, at least now I understood why Dan hadn't been arrested. Adele wouldn't be happy to hear that her golden triangle had just lost one of its corners. I asked Barry if Heather knew that something was missing from Kelly's room. He said she had discounted it as being a robbery gone bad from the start. Then it was as if he realized exactly what I'd said.

"Are you saying you know something is missing from the room?" he said, and I nodded. This time it was my turn to have a little triumphant smile. "Well, are you going to tell me or what?" Barry said.

I explained our two trips to Kelly's before she was killed. "Adele just about knocked over a lamp with a leaded glass shade. But when I went back there today, it was gone. Dan said he didn't know anything about it." Barry asked for more details about the lamp and I described what I remembered about the colors of the shade.

"Did Heather talk to Kelly's brother, Stone?" I was going to mention that Stone thought Dan had done it, too, and might be able to help her, but Barry was already shaking his head.

"The surfer dude wasn't even in town when it happened. Heather checked out his story about going to Denver to meet someone about his coconut energy drink. She talked to the person he'd met with in Denver and even looked at his boarding pass from Kahului Airport in Maui to Denver."

"She thought he was a suspect?" I said surprised. "I don't suppose you saw him. He's adorable."

Barry's lips went into a straight line of consternation. "Adorable people can be murderers. Heather is very thorough. She thinks everybody is a suspect, including the neighbor woman who was trying to get Donahue to renege on letting the production use the backyard. Heather talked to the prop guys who'd been arranging all the plants, too. They said Kelly Donahue was alive when they left to go to lunch. Heather had no way to prove what they said was true, but she put them on the back burner of her suspect list. Where's a motive?"

"Did they tell Heather they knew Kelly from before? She was a production assistant on a show they worked on."

Barry appeared surprised. "They didn't tell Heather about that. I'll be sure and pass it along." I was amazed at how much information Barry had shared and how much attention he had paid to what I'd said. It had never been like this when we were a couple.

He leaned closer and checked my expression. "You sounded kind of gushy when you talked about the surfer. Is there something going on between you two?"

I laughed. "What if there was? It's none of your business. Remember we're over and done with."

"Somebody better tell Mason he's got competition. And what was with that fake detective from *L.A. 911*? What was he doing coming home with you?"

I just glared at Barry. "Right," he said. "It's none of my business."

"I know you were trying to change the subject when I asked when you'd be moving back home. If you can't give me an exact date, how about a rough time frame?" Barry drank some of his tea and set the mug down. There was no triumphant smile this time.

"My doctor thinks I should avoid stairs for a few more weeks. And since we're out of my place, it seemed like a good time to get the floors done, along with painting and a few odds and ends. You know workmen. They say it'll take a few days and it turns into a few months." I must have looked stricken because he said he was just joking. "I'm hoping we'll be good to go in two weeks. If that's okay."

How could I say it wasn't? So, I told him it was fine.

"This was very nice," he said as we walked inside. "Just

two friends having a cup of tea." He was right we were two friends. But then I blurted out. "So what's going on with you and Detective Heather?"

Barry laughed. "I'll give you the same response you gave me when I asked about surfer dude. None of your business."

CHAPTER 16

"WHY DON'T YOU SUGGEST HE MOVE INTO DETECtive Heather's place?" Dinah said. Though it was barely nine in the morning, it was already hot walking along Ventura Boulevard. Dinah and I had agreed to eat at Le Grande Fromage and I'd picked her up at her house and we were in the process of walking the couple of blocks to the neighborhood bistro.

I could have eaten at home, but now that Barry was back to work, it was just too weird to watch him come through the kitchen at 8:47 A.M. while I was nursing my morning coffee that he had made. Dressed in a suit and tie, he'd pour some of the coffee into a commuter mug, eat a bowl of cereal standing at the counter and head out.

I never knew how to act. Should I make conversation? Invite him to sit at the table? It was just awkward. He seemed to have adjusted to the situation and always wished me a good day on his way out. I wished him the same, but most of all I wished he was starting it from someplace else.

Jeffrey, like other boys his age, slept in. Barry had tried to talk him into going to day camp. Day camp for a fourteen-year-old? Instead, on his own, Jeffrey had found a summer acting program that he got to and from on his bicycle.

"I wouldn't do that to Jeffrey," I said in reference to Dinah's suggestion. Having Jeffrey at my place was no problem. I had liked the kid from the day I'd met him. Maybe after bringing up two sons, I had a weakness for boys. When the end had come for Barry and me, one of my regrets was losing Jeffrey in the process. Luckily, there was no awkwardness between us and he kept me posted on how much he missed his girlfriend Autumn, who was away at camp. "You should have seen Detective Heather trying to be motherly. If Barry and Heather do get together, I think Jeffrey is going to find that boarding school is in his future."

We'd reached the small café and it was pleasant to walk into the cool interior. It was bright and airy inside and filled with plants. Almost all the tables were full with a combination of people stopping in after their morning exercise walk and the people who used the tables as their office. Dinah placed our order and I found a table.

Imagine my shock when I realized Adele was at the table behind us. She had her back to the room and was bent over, focusing on something. A mug and plate with a residue of breakfast sat across from her and I guessed she must have been eating with Eric. I tried to see what she was doing, but she had herself positioned so that whatever it was was completely hidden.

Dinah came to the table a moment later and I gestured toward Adele. Dinah was still standing and tried to look over the top of Adele's head, but it didn't work and my friend sat down.

The door whooshed open and I automatically looked up. Stone Thomasville came in with three men who had the same streaked hair and tanned skin and followed him like disciples. I admit that I stared at Stone for a moment. He had the kind of looks that made you do that.

"Should we invite them to sit with us?" Dinah asked, noting that all the tables were full.

"I do have to ask him about something," I said. Adele heard us talking and turned around in her seat. She followed my gaze and saw who we were talking about, as Dinah went over to invite him to join us.

"What's going on? Who's he?" she asked quickly stuffing something in her tote bag. I told her he was Kelly's brother and then asked what she was being so secretive about.

Adele hesitated. "Can I trust you?' she asked, glancing around furtively.

"Adele, I had you over for French toast. Just you and no one else. You said after that I was your best friend. You can trust me."

Adele did another sweep of the room and then took out a skein of worsted weight acrylic yarn and a size K hook. She'd made a foundation row and on top of it she started another stitch. She wound the yarn around the hook a bunch of times and picked up another loop. "Watch this," she said. "She began to pull the hook through all the loops. For a moment it went okay, then the whole thing started to unravel. "It worked before," she said in a frustrated tone. "I almost have the bullion stitch."

"I promise I won't tell CeeCee you haven't mastered it yet, but you have to give her the things Kelly made. They

are Kelly's last creations and she meant them for the fair.
You can't leave them stuffed in one of the yarn cupboards."

"Just give me a little more time. Please."

I hadn't realized Dinah was standing right behind me
until I took a step back and almost fell over her. Stone
grabbed me just in time.

He thanked us for the offer of sharing our table, but said
he and his group were just picking up something to eat in
the car on the way to the beach. "Dan tried to push some
cereal on me. It probably tastes fine," Stone said rolling his
eyes. "But the name—Corporal Crack?" He gestured toward the group. "Some old surfing buddies and I are hitting
the waves."

"Ahem," Adele said and, when I didn't immediately
react, she poked my shoulder.

I introduced him to Adele and she threw her arms around
him. "I'm so sorry about your loss. We were like blood sisters, only it was yarn, but for we crocheters, yarn is even
thicker than blood." As soon as she started talking about her
cop boyfriend and that she knew who had really killed his
sister, I stepped in.

"This place is full of ears," I said to Adele in a pointed
tone.

"Pink, you're right." She narrowed her eyes as she surveyed
the customers in the restaurant, focusing on the two prop
guys eating breakfast sandwiches. She hugged a surprised-
looking Stone again. "I just want you to know that I'm working in adjunct with the police."

Maybe if she hadn't been wearing her hair in pigtails,
with a blue and white gingham pinafore over a white blouse
with puffy sleeves and her version of ruby slippers that were
red sneakers, he might have taken her more seriously. I
quickly explained that she was running the summer kids'

reading group and she was reading them *The Wizard of Oz.* He glanced around her and said she must have misplaced Toto.

Without missing a beat, Adele pulled out such a lifelike stuffed dog that I jumped.

Stone heard his order number called and made a move toward the counter. I stepped in front of him and apologized for Adele. "She means well," I said. He seemed a little doubtful and, when I didn't move out of the way, asked if there was something else.

"I apologize for this under the circumstances, but we were wondering if you'd be willing to do an informal book signing one night." I explained Mr. Royal had shown me the book, with the photograph and story about him, and was ordering a stack of them.

Stone barely took a moment to consider the request. "Sure. Why not? I can give out some brochures about the coconut water energy drink."

"You could even give out samples," I said. It was hard not to keep looking at his face. His blue eyes sparkled and had little crinkles around them when he smiled. And then there were those family dimples. All that and a great body. It was hard not to notice it since he was wearing just swimming shorts and an open shirt.

"Too bad they're all gone. I don't even have an empty bottle to show off. No way to get any more, either. The only place you can buy it now is in one store in Wailea, Maui." I asked him if he'd rather wait until after Kelly's funeral, but he said he'd be leaving right after. He leaned in close. "I hope I'm here when they finally arrest you know who. I told the cops he had a big insurance policy on my sister. How much evidence do they need?"

I tried to calm him and told him I knew for a fact the

cops had zeroed in on Dan, which seemed to make him feel a little better. It was a little bit of a segue, but I went back to the book signing and we agreed on a day and time. Finally, he picked up his breakfast sandwich and latte and headed out.

When Dinah and I finally sat down, I noticed Adele had moved to our table. I knew if I so much as mentioned Barry, she'd launch into her superior relationship with Eric "Cutchykins." She considered herself an expert now on relationships with cops and I didn't want her advice or even any comments. So the easiest subject to talk about was Kelly's murder.

"Ha," Adele said. "I don't know why Stone wasn't including me in what he said. I'm probably already ahead of you two in the figuring-it-out department. The problem here isn't figuring out who did it, it's getting some evidence. There have been lots of murder cases around here where everybody knows who did it, but there isn't enough evidence to convince a jury beyond reasonable doubt." Adele's comment surprised me for its rational quality, but then her tone became Miss Know It All. "Eric thinks I can find the evidence they need to nail Dan."

"He said that?" I said.

"Maybe not in those exact words," Adele said. "But that's what my cutchykins meant." She adjusted a pigtail that was about to be dipped in her drink. "He takes what I say very seriously."

"You do know that Dan's gun isn't the murder weapon." I said and Adele waved her arm broadly.

"Pink, that's such old news."

After breakfast the three of us walked outside. The sun was heating up the air and it promised to be another scorcher.

We headed up the street and stopped when we got in front
of the bookstore and Dinah said something about having a
faculty meeting later in the morning. The new semester now
started in August. Whatever happened to waiting until after
Labor Day?

"I'll see you in a while," I said to Adele motioning toward
the door of the bookstore as if I could will her to go inside.

"Where are you going?" Adele said with a whine in her
voice. I pointed toward the side street and said I was going
to walk Dinah home. Adele glanced at her bulging tote bag
with the stuffed Toto's head sticking out of it and started to
go in, but hesitated.

"I'm coming with," she said. "I'll just drop this off."

"I'll be back before you get out of the store," I said. "You
don't have to come." I motioned to Dinah and we began to
walk toward the corner.

Adele ditched her plan of leaving the tote bag and rushed
after us. "You know Molly had me over for French toast,"
Adele said to Dinah. "Just me." She let the words sink in before continuing. "Did she ever have just you over for French
toast?"

I saw that Dinah was stifling a chuckle before she said
no. Adele gave her a knowing nod.

"Maybe you're not the best friend you thought you were."
Adele threaded her arm through mine. "Pink and I are French
toast sisters." First it was yarn sisters, now French toast sisters,
what was next?

The street curved up ahead and at first all we could see
was Dinah's house on the next corner. Only when we got
closer, did the production come into view. Eric stood at the
curb next to his motorcycle.

They must have been planning to film a scene in the

street as all the trucks had been moved out of view. Several cars were parked at the curb, including a police car.

A group of people were congregated in front of a house, several down from Dinah's.

Without saying a word, the three of us stopped in front of Dinah's and watched, mesmerized. I knew there'd be no embarrassing interventions from me this time. Not only was I very aware that whatever was going on in front of me was fake, but now that Barry was out and about, I wasn't as sensitive anymore.

The scene in front of us did not look at all like what it would look like on television. All the audience would see was North Adams, in character, trying to console a distraught woman. The audience wouldn't see all the people standing around the pair, or the large reflectors bringing more light into the shot, or the camera and other equipment.

I stepped a little closer to get a better view and I had to laugh. It appeared that North had listened to Barry's advice and this time his dress shirt had a few well-placed wrinkles. But while he had the right amount of stubble on his face, his close-cropped dark hair was still a little too perfect to believe he'd been working all night.

They seemed to be rehearsing and then all the outer activity stopped as they began to actually film the scene. Suddenly an angry voice yelled "Cut!" and everything stopped. I recognized the tall jean-clad director from before.

Adele turned toward me. "Did you do something, Pink?"

I put up my arms in a sign of annoyance. The director motioned to Eric and a few moments later, the motor cop appeared holding the handlebars of a bicycle in one hand and someone's arm in the other.

Jeffrey? Again?

Eric walked the bicycle and Jeffrey toward us as the director joined them. Barry's son gave me a weak wave.

The director glared at me, clearly remembering me from before. "You know him?" he said with an annoyed shake of his head. "It figures." His gaze moved to Adele and her Dorothy from *The Wizard of Oz* outfit and he rolled his eyes. He stepped in front of Jeffrey. "Kid, stay out of the shot—now and forever." The director walked back to the setup.

"Don't tell my dad," Jeffrey said with a touch of panic in his voice. Eric with his duty done, had turned his attention to Adele. He winked and blew her a secret kiss.

"See you later, cutchykins," he said in a low voice before going back to his station.

We withdrew from our position and moved around the corner while Jeffrey explained about his reel, again.

"I was riding by Autumn's house," he said. "I was going to ask her mother when she's coming home from camp. But when I passed the street and saw they were shooting, it was like fate, or something. So I just drove my bicycle up the sidewalk."

He gestured around the corner. "I might as well go see if Autumn's mother knows anything. Some camp," he said with a groan. "No cell phones or e-mail."

I was prepared to let him go, but Dinah turned to me. "I think we should make sure he gets where he says he's going." All the years of dealing with unruly freshmen at Beasley Community College had given her an intuitive edge. "We want to make sure he doesn't just go back around the block and show up in their shot again."

I'm sure the last thing in the world Jeffrey wanted was three women escorting him to his girlfriend's house, but he was stuck with us.

"Where does Autumn live?" I said as we started down the block. I could tell he didn't want to answer and hoped we'd disappear, but he finally pointed and I nudged Dinah.

"What's Autumn's last name?" I said. Jeffrey let out a world-weary sigh, not unlike the way his father did.

"Silvers. That's her mother," he said, gesturing up ahead. We all stopped and watched as Nanci Silvers walked up her driveway with Dan Donahue. They were deep in conversation and her demeanor was totally different than when we'd seen her fussing about Kelly and the filming in the Dona- hue's yard. She appeared friendly toward him. Maybe even a little flirtatious.

There was no way all of us could get close enough to see what was going on without being noticed. Apparently, Jef- frey was just concerned with getting something for his reel and missing Autumn and had no idea what had gone on next door. When I told him about Kelly being murdered, his eyes grew big.

"You mean there's a killer on the loose." His eyes darted down the street toward his girlfriend's house. He was even more concerned when I told him that Detective Heather thought Autumn's next-door neighbor was the guy.

"You can help," I said. "Just cruise by on your bike and see what's going on. Just don't say anything to Autumn's mother."

"You mean stay invisible," he said with a nod. He had a baseball cap stuck in his back pocket and put it over his gelled into spiky splendor hair. "Easy peasy."

"And don't mention this to your dad or Heather, okay?"

"No problem," he said as he drove his bike into the street. We watched as he rode by several times and then he came back to where we were standing.

"So?" I said as he stepped on the ground to stop his bike.

"They were doing something in the Silvers's garage. Something with boxes. They were looking inside of them and then—" Jeffrey got a look of discomfort. "And then they hugged each other and I heard him say, 'You're the best.'"

CHAPTER 17

"I DIDN'T THINK I'D BE ABLE TO MAKE IT, BUT here I am," CeeCee said in a happy, though slightly rushed, voice. She put her tote bag on the worktable in the yarn department and pulled out her chair. It was late in the day for the Hookers to get together, but everyone had schedule issues. The dinner hour was the slowest time in the bookstore and a good time for us to meet as far as I was concerned. Mrs. Shedd never objected to me joining the group when things were quiet.

CeeCee looked down the table. "I hate to sound like a broken record, but I checked the donation box for the Jungle Days booth, and it's still looking pretty slim." She turned to Adele. "Dear, I think we're going to have to include the items Kelly made. At least let me have a look at them."

Not missing a beat, and still wearing her Dorothy outfit, Adele rummaged in her tote bag and brought out some more of the cowls. "These are much better."

The whole group groaned in unison. "Adele, have you lost your mind? Not those cowls again. It's August, it's hot. September is often even hotter around here. Nobody wants something around their neck," Rhoda said.

Elise tried to soften it a bit, but said pretty much the same thing in her birdlike voice. Sheila got tense just looking at them. Dinah said she was sticking to making washcloths which she could put together with some nice soap.

Eduardo brought out several pairs of earrings made in silvery thread. CeeCee looked at them and smiled. "That's more like it." She turned to the whole group. "With things heating up with my career, I haven't had enough time to work on things myself." She sighed and brought up Kelly's funeral. "Even with my schedule, I'm planning to attend." She looked to the rest of us and went around the group getting a yes from everyone. When she got to me, she asked if there was any news on Kelly's killer. I heard Adele having a sputtering fit before she jumped out of her chair.

"You should be asking me," she said. "I'm way ahead of Pink in the investigating department." She let her gaze move over the whole table. "Here's the crux of the whole case. There's a chink in the golden triangle of guilt. We need to find the murder weapon and a little more direct evidence to tie . . ." Adele's voice trailed off as she checked the area then dropped her voice. "We're all sure Dan did it, but we need something more before we can charge him." Adele adjusted her pigtail as her lips curved in a self-satisfied smile. "And there's something else. After story time, I met with Eric. You know he's a motor officer and was the first responder."

"We know," Rhoda said in her nasally voice. "Get to the point."

"The point is, I told Eric about something I found out

this morning. There's something going on with Dan Donahue and his neighbor."

Dinah and I looked at each other. Adele was out of
control.

Thankfully, CeeCee changed the subject back to the crochet pieces for our booth at the fair. She knew it was hopeless to get Adele to stop making the cowls, but said it would
be nice to have more of Eduardo's bracelets from the rest of
us. When the group broke up, Dinah and I walked to the
front of the store.

"I'm not competing with Adele to solve this case," I said
to Dinah.

"Of course, you're not." Dinah said. "It's just that if Adele
does beat you to the punch, we'll never hear the end of it."

"We should really see what we can find out about Nanci
Silvers," I said, but I'd already lost Dinah's attention. Commander Blaine had just come through the door. Dinah had
no problem with his longish thick white hair, but she was
still adjusting to his clothing choices. The wrinkle-free dress
shirt tucked into the khaki slacks with sharp creases was a
little too perfect for her taste.

As soon as he caught sight of Dinah, Commander's eyes
lit up. Sadly, Dinah was even having trouble with that part.
After an ex-husband who was a jerk and several boyfriends
who were about the same, she was having a hard time getting used to someone who actually wanted to spend time
with her, and didn't have a line of ladies on the side. But
Commander was a gentleman through and through.

"Ready?" he said linking arms with Dinah after giving
her a welcoming hug. "You're welcome to join us," he said to
me. We're putting on game night at the senior center. Cha-
rades, Monopoly, Parcheesi, and more. You'll have fun."

I thanked him, but declined and went back to work as they left. Not that there was much to do.

Mrs. Shedd and Mr. Royal were busy conferring over the e-reader display. Even the table in the yarn department was empty for the moment. I walked around the bookstore picking up stray books and putting them back where they belonged.

Mason came in as I was doing a little housekeeping in the yarn department. "I thought I would just come by instead of calling," he said giving me a hug. "Can you leave?" He glanced around the empty store. "I thought we could get dinner or something."

He was still in his work clothes, a tan-colored suit and a cream-colored shirt with the collar open. Despite his smile and the lightness of his comments, I sensed something was wrong. He usually appeared untarnished by the day, but not this time. I'd never seen him look quite this way. Exhausted? Strained? I wasn't sure what it was.

I suggested he sit down while I finished putting all the skeins of yarn in their correct bins. "There's something wrong, isn't there?" I said as he took a seat.

He smiled briefly and then his expression dimmed and he looked away. "You caught that, huh," he said in a low voice. "Run away to the beach with me and I'll tell you all about it. We can still make the sunset."

I checked with Mrs. Shedd and she was fine with me taking off. Mason was waiting by the door when I came to the front with my things.

"Okay, what's up?" I said once we were in the black Mercedes sedan and on the freeway.

He sighed deeply. "I have been spending too much time with my ex-wife. I can't trust her to do anything on her own with this wedding. I spent the afternoon tasting appetizers and looking at flowers. Jaimee can't seem to get it through her head that we need someplace for the flowers to be delivered to first. If she would just let me handle it, it would be better, but she's insisting on being in the middle of everything. When I told you my ex and I had a civil relationship that was because we barely saw each other when there wasn't other family around."

I had never seen Mason like this. He was usually jovial and fun. And yet I liked it because he was opening up to me.

"By the way, I gave my daughter the hankie you crocheted. She thought it was lovely."

"I'm just curious. Who did you tell her it was from?"

"I said you were a special friend," he said starting to get back to the Mason I was used to.

"And she probably thinks I'm the sweet little old lady who lives down the block, right?" I looked over at Mason and he was grinning.

"Maybe," he said in a teasing tone. He'd gotten on the 101 Freeway and transitioned onto the 405. Traffic wasn't bad and we flew past the mountains in the Sepulveda Pass and then through the Westside. I had expected him to turn off someplace, but he kept driving. I wondered if he was so distracted by everything with Jaimee that he'd forgotten where we were going—wherever that was. All he'd said to me was the beach. Should I say something?

As I watched the connection to the Santa Monica Freeway go by, I decided to speak up. "Are we headed any place in particular?" I said gingerly. "I thought I better say something before we ended up in Tijuana."

"Sunshine, I assure you, I'm never so distracted that I'd drive through the border crossing without noticing," he said with a good-humored laugh. He let out a deep breath and his shoulders relaxed. "I have a plan. I need the ocean, but not the usual Malibu or Santa Monica."

He finally turned off the freeway and took surface streets going toward the sun that was hanging low in the sky. I was glad he knew where he was going, because I hadn't a clue. He pulled into a parking structure and we got out. When we reached the street, he made a grand gesture with his arm. "Manhattan Beach."

It had to be at least twenty degrees cooler than the Valley, which was a welcome relief. He took my hand and we crossed the street to a coffee place. "Cappuccinos are a perfect complement to the sunset," he said before ordering one for each of us. Carrying our drinks we headed down the street of interesting shops and restaurants that sloped toward the water. Ahead the ocean caught the orange sun and a pier jutted out into the water. Just before the beach, a paved walkway went off in both directions. Being a weekday, it wasn't crowded. The stragglers were carrying their folding chairs and brightly colored towels as they left the beach. A few joggers went past and, on the separate bike trail, some riders rode by. Mason suggested we go to the right.

"Take a deep breath, sunshine. Smell that cool breeze," he said as we strolled down the path, sipping our drinks. A gull was almost eye level as it rode on the wind, before it flapped it wings and changed directions. The sky was apricot and pink as the sun hovered over the water.

On one side was the beach and on the other, houses that were so close to the walkway, we could have stepped right onto any patio and plopped on their lawn furniture. We found a bench and sat facing the water.

"Uh-oh," he said with his trademark grin. "I'm starting

to think about my ex and the wedding again. Quick, distract me with something in your life. What's going on with the murder investigation?"

"You asked for it," I said, with a laugh. I started to download everything that had happened. "Dan Donahue still seems to be the number one suspect." I listed the motives, from insurance money to help his business, to it being the no-pay way to get a divorce. "But the trouble is the absence of a murder weapon," I said. Then I told him about all the swabbing and testing that had been done on Dan's gun and how none of it came back incriminating Dan. "They need the murder weapon. They need some solid evidence so they can arrest him."

"You seem to have a lot of inside information," he said. "Barry?"

I rolled my eyes and rocked my head. "Mostly as a stall when I asked him about when he'd be moving out."

Mason's expression faded and he asked if Barry and I were spending a lot of time together. Before I could say anything, he asked if I'd gotten anything specific about when Barry was moving out. Mason shook his head when I told him about the work being done on Barry's place.

"That could go on for a year," Mason said. "You've made it entirely too comfortable for him and his son." Mason realized his tone sounded a little harsh and put his hand over mine. "I know. It all started when he was injured and vulnerable. You are too kind. But that's what I lov—like about you so much. And you're fun besides. And I want more time with you."

This seemed like the perfect time to bring it up and I asked him about my coming to the wedding.

"I don't know. My daughters have never met anyone I—"

He interrupted himself. "What is it you were telling me about your day?"

At least I could tell he was thinking about inviting me. It wasn't so much about the wedding itself, it was about letting me have full access to his world. He certainly had access to mine.

But I let the subject go and told him about Adele in her *Wizard of Oz* outfit and Jeffrey trying to get into the *L.A. 911* shot and how weird it was that Jeffrey's girlfriend's mother was the Donahue's next-door neighbor. When I got to the part about sending Jeffrey down to check out the action, Mason seemed concerned again.

"You're really attached to that kid, aren't you?"

I sighed. "Yes, I can't help it. No matter that its over between Barry and me, I don't want to let go of Jeffrey."

Mason didn't look happy.

By now the sun had slipped into the water like a coin into a piggy bank. The last of the pink and orange glow hung above the water while the sky had turned a soft blue. The breeze felt cold now and Mason took off his suit jacket and draped it around my shoulders. I covered the silence by going on about Adele and Eric and how she kept flaunting all her inside information. Finally Mason chuckled.

"You're worried she's going to solve this one before you do," he said. I hung my head and nodded.

"Do you have any idea of what it would be like if she did?" I said and Mason chuckled again.

"I think I have a pretty good idea. But Molly, you've solved mysteries without inside information. You always said all Barry ever said to you was to keep out of it. You've done it with this," he said touching the side of my head to indicate my brains. "And maybe a little help from me on occasion."

Twilight was slowly deepening and the sand, water and sky were all blending together. Mason let out a little shiver. "I don't know about you, but a nice cozy restaurant and some food sounds good."

We retraced our steps up the hill and went back to the car. Mason had a restaurant in mind in Palos Verdes. He pulled into a parking lot on a cliff high above the water. The restaurant had a wall of windows and outside the twilight had almost turned into night.

"Maybe I can help you. Tell me everything you know about the case."

I began to throw out things I remembered or had heard. "Kelly had an online business according to Dan. She sold things she crocheted. Dan is obsessed with his store. He would talk about Kelly for a moment and then go back to talking about his plans to have a nationwide chain." I stopped and sighed. "I don't think this is getting anywhere."

"How about talking about the last time you saw her?" Mason said. He even suggested I close my eyes and describe what I saw.

"It was a treat to see Kelly's workroom again." I sighed. "When Barry goes and I get all my stuff out of the storage locker, I'm going to get my room organized." I heard Mason laugh and then he encouraged me to go on.

"The lamp," I said. "How could I have forgotten to tell the group and you about that. It was there the first two times I went to Kelly's but when we went afterward, it wasn't there. Dan didn't know anything about it, or so he said. I told Barry about it, but I don't know what he'll do with the information." I had opened my eyes and Mason urged me to close them again.

No sooner had I shut them when out of nowhere, I remembered Kelly going to answer the door. "Kelly said it was a real estate agent handing out brochures. Wait," I said in an excited voice. "Kelly had us go out through the yard. I bet she didn't want us to see who it was." I laughed out loud. "And Adele, super detective that she claims to be, never even noticed." I put my hands up in a triumphant Rocky pose. "I've got an important clue and she doesn't." Maybe I sounded a little childish, but then she'd sounded that way first.

"You're a genius," I said to Mason throwing my arms around him. "All I have to do now is figure out who came over."

CHAPTER 18

As soon as I walked through the door of my house, I called Dinah and told her about my recollection of the last time we'd seen Kelly.

"It never occurred to me that Kelly didn't want us to see who came to the door," Dinah said. She reminded me that we'd thought of Kelly answering the door while on our trip to the dollar store, but in all the commotion over the dollar-of-the-hour special, we'd gotten distracted and dropped it. I'd hoped she could add some new observation, but she seemed a little distracted and I could hear Commander in the background. "Let me sleep on it," she said. I would have liked to talk about it longer, but I certainly understood.

Since I didn't have Dinah to talk to, I began to replay the evening in my mind. Dinner with Mason had been fun. Once we stopped talking about weddings and murders, we told each other funny stories and laughed a lot. Afterward, he'd driven me back to the bookstore to get my car and then followed me home to make sure I got inside safely.

I'd pulled into my driveway and expected him to drive on, but instead, he parked at the curb and walked to where I was standing. "This is so sweet and romantic," he said taking me in his arms and kissing me good night. "I feel like I'm in high school all over again." As he said that the motion sensor light came on. Mason laughed and said it was like in the old days when someone's parents ended a make-out session by turning on the porch light. He gave me another quick kiss and bid me good night.

BUT NOW THAT I WAS HOME I STILL FELT WIRED. I went into the kitchen to make a large cup of tea, figuring I would take it to my room and spend some time crocheting. There was nothing like the repetitive motion of the craft to iron out the kinks and get me to relax.

"Having tea again," Barry said and I jumped. I hadn't realized he'd come in the kitchen. "Just to let you know, the trash has been taken out, and I let the dogs out in the yard for a last hurrah before bedtime. The cats have been fed and their box attended to." This time he didn't even ask if he could join me and just took out two mugs. He checked the basket that held my assortment of teas. "What shall we have tonight?" He held up a box of Earl Grey and I nodded. He filled the mugs from the hot water dispenser. The air filled with the unique fragrance of the tea laced with oil of bergamot.

"Go on outside. I'll bring it," Barry said. When I looked up, Jeffrey had come in the room and was standing behind his dad. When we made eye contact, he started doing elaborate hand gestures and there was a touch of panic to his expression. I answered with a knowing nod. He didn't have to worry. I wouldn't tell Barry about him getting caught trying to sneak in the *L.A. 911* scene.

Jeffrey smiled with relief and then announced that he was going to bed. I went on outside and sat down. I heard the door open and click close and a moment later Barry set the mugs on the small round glass table. He settled into the chair next to me, pushing his legs out in front of him before stretching and flexing the leg that had been injured.

"It's still stiff," he said in a dispirited tone. He lifted the mug. "It's so strange keeping regular hours. I don't know what to do with myself." He gestured toward the fence. I fixed your gate. It was dragging." He mentioned a few other repairs he'd done. Barry could fix anything and one of my concerns when we broke up was that my house would fall apart. He drank some of the tea and commented on the interesting flavor before setting the mug down and turning to face me. "I just want to let you know I understand about the condo in Simi." I was going to say something, but he continued. "I learned my lesson for next time. It was wrong to try to force that condo on you."

An image came to mind as he was talking. A few months ago, Barry had this idea we should make a fresh start if we got married. Unilaterally he'd picked out a condo in Simi Valley he thought would be perfect for us. Thank heavens he hadn't put a deposit on it because I wasn't interested in moving so far away from my job and my friends. It had turned out to be the beginning of the end for us, anyway.

"You mean for you and Heather?"

"For me and whoever," he said.

"Whatever," I said, trying to dismiss it. I didn't want to

get into a discussion about his future romances or reopen talking about that condo. It was a little awkward, but I turned the subject to Kelly. "I remembered something that happened when I went over to Kelly's that last time." I told him about the doorbell and that I thought she'd said it was a real estate agent handing out something. "I was thinking that maybe it was somebody she didn't want us to see, so that's why she hustled us out of there so fast."

"You said Adele was with you," Barry said beginning to smile. "Maybe Kelly just wanted to get rid of you guys."

"Maybe so," I said. "But if there really was a real estate agent, they might have seen something." I was thinking out loud. "The ones who have come by my house always leave a notepad of paper with their picture and information." I thought about it for a moment. "I bet Kelly's brother would help me look around their place."

"The adorable surfer," Barry said with distaste. His face slipped into cop mode and he seemed to be considering something. "Heather would probably dismiss your real estate agent tip because it came from you. . . ." His voice trailed off and he seemed to be battling with himself. "I need to get these cold cases taken care of and get back to my real job," he said, shaking his head. "You didn't hear this from me, but here's something to think about. If a real estate agent stopped at the Donahue's, they probably worked the whole area."

I got his point. "Then they might have stopped at Dinah's and the Donahue's next-door neighbor." I smiled at Barry. "Good thinking. Thanks for the help."

"Don't mention it," Barry said. Then he rolled his eyes. "And I really mean don't mention it. I don't want it to get back to Heather that I helped you." Barry yawned and mentioned his early morning. We got up to go inside. The tea and conversation had gotten rid of my wired feeling and sleep sounded good.

As I headed across the living room to my side of the house, Barry called after me. "By the way, I know all about Jeffrey," he said. "I'm a detective, remember."

Uh-oh.

I CALLED DINAH FIRST THING IN THE MORNING and asked her if she'd found a notepad or anything from a real estate agent left at her front door the day of the murder. While she was trying to remember, I told her why and who had suggested the line of thinking.

"Barry's helping you now?" she laughed.

"I think it's all about him missing his regular detective job, and he can't resist getting involved."

"And an excuse to spend time with you," Dinah said. While we talked, Dinah checked various places in her house. "I don't remember getting anything, but I could have just picked it up off the porch without thinking." She said she would have tossed a brochure, but would have kept the pad of paper. "They come in handy for phone calls and writing down notes on crochet projects. I could have just stuck it somewhere." I heard the clang of hooks hitting the floor. "Nope, not in my crochet bag."

"The person might not have gotten as far as your house," I said. "I was thinking about stopping by Kelly's."

"I'm in," Dinah said. "Just give me a moment to throw on a scarf."

I parked the greenmobile in the bookstore parking lot and walked over to Dinah's. She was standing on her tiny porch, with a long, white gauzy scarf flapping in the breeze over an outfit in shades of olive green. Her salt-and-pepper hair looked perky with all the uneven spikes. She was down the steps before I opened the gate to her yard.

"Are we climbing in any windows?" my friend asked with a sparkle in her eye. "It's so good to be sleuthing along with you again."

"I was thinking we could just knock at the door and ask?" I said. "I'd rather go there when Dan isn't home."

Dinah nodded. "Right, we don't want him to know we're investigating." As we walked around the corner and down the street we talked about Dan.

"Maybe he has two guns. The legal one he showed Detective Heather and another one he used to shoot Kelly. I'm betting that one isn't legal. But what did he do with it and how did he manage not to have residue on his hands and clothes?"

"Maybe it won't matter. If the real estate agent saw him and can place him there a while before he went running for Eric—"

"He'd certainly have some explaining to do," I said interrupting Dinah. "But we don't even know for sure there was really a real estate agent at the door." By now we were in front of the Donahue house.

"What if nobody is home?" my friend said.

"We come back," I said.

"Or we climb in a window," Dinah said with a naughty look.

Before we walked down the short path to the Donahue's door, I glanced next door at the Silvers'. The house was quiet for now and the driveway empty. A SUV was sitting in the Donahue's driveway with a surfboard attached to the top. Stone opened the door before we could ring the bell, apparently on the way out. He was carrying a wet suit and a towel.

His sunglasses hung from a cord around his neck and, as usual, he smelled like coconut suntan lotion. He seemed surprised to see us.

I broke the ice by telling him how pleased my bosses were that he'd agreed to the book signing. "I'm sure it will bring in a big crowd," I said. Then I got down to why we were there and told him the story about the mysterious real estate agent and how they might be able to place Dan at the house before he'd said he'd arrived."

"By all means come in and look around. I don't recall seeing a pad of paper with a photo on it, but that doesn't mean anything." He led us inside and we looked around the living room and came up empty. "Maybe my sister took it into her workroom," Stone suggested. "Anything to help nail Dan."

I felt a little less unsettled going into Kelly's workroom this time. The room looked different. There were things on the computer table I didn't recognize from before. Stone explained that Dan was using the computer.

"Is he handling her online business?" I asked, but Stone shook his head. "All he cares about is his own business." Stone helped us check every surface for one of those dollar-shaped pads all the real estate agents used as advertising. I even opened one of the plastic bins. I'd expected to see the neat skeins of yarn, but it was a jumble of twisted yarn, hooks and other paraphernalia. Stone noticed my expression. "It's kind of a mess. Dan's been going through all the bins like he's looking for something."

We did one more look around and then Dinah and I admitted defeat. Before we left, Stone pulled out a box from the closet. "I left some stuff with my sister when I moved to Hawaii. This might come in handy," he said, handing me a publicity photo of him surfing. Stone walked us out and thanked us for trying to help before he climbed into Kelly's SUV and headed for the beach.

I noticed a car was in the Silvers's driveway now. "Maybe all isn't lost. How about we pay her a visit."

Nanci Silvers seemed surprised to see us and hesitantly invited us in. I nudged Dinah when I saw the box of Orioles chocolate sandwich cookies by the door. She certainly dressed the part of PTA president. The beige linen shift and sandals with a heel gave her an air of authority. We all sat staring at each other for a moment and finally Nanci asked if there was a purpose to our visit. Dinah and I'd had no chance to discuss our strategy. I was hoping to somehow naturally bring up the wandering real estate agent. I was winging it and remembered her fuss about the Donahue house being registered as a location. "Dinah wanted to know if you're still collecting signatures for your petition."

Nanci's sharp expression grew a little vague. "Signatures for what?" I reminded her about her previous concern and a look of recognition came over her face.

"It's not an issue anymore. Once they shoot the one scene in the yard, the house won't be used again. Dan took it off the list."

"I guess you know him pretty well," I said, pointing at the case of Orioles cookies. Nanci suddenly got that deer-in-the-headlights look. "Ah, it's a donation for the first bake sale of the season."

"Bake sale? Whatever happened to homemade baked items?" I said remembering all the platters of chocolate chip cookie bars I had made for the bake sales when my sons went to Wilbur Elementary.

Nanci flicked something off one of her nails and leveled her gaze at me. "Nobody bakes anymore, or cooks, either. I know I certainly don't have time." She seemed to be getting impatient with us and I was afraid she was going to show us the door, but we were saved by the bell. Her cell phone rang. As soon as she answered, she made an apology and went into the other room.

"This is our chance to look around," I whispered to Dinah. We began to check the various surfaces in the living room. There was a stack of mail on a stand by the door. I went through it quickly, thinking the pad could have gotten mixed in with it. "Dinah, look at this," I said in a loud whisper. I held up an advertisement that pictured some fancy guns with the headline "Life Is Too Short for an Ugly Gun."

Dinah's eyes got wide when she read it, but then she took me over to the wall and pointed out a photo of Nanci and a man, both holding rifles and smiling. There was some kind of certificate below it for skeet shooting.

Both of us noticed the cream-colored crocheted wrap sitting on the edge of the sofa.

"Sorry, for the interruption," Nanci said as she came back in the room. Dinah and I dropped back into our chairs with a thud. "Was there anything else?" Nanci asked. I noticed that she didn't sit down, a definite sign she was looking to end our visit.

"Dinah was just saying that here she lives barely a half block from you and doesn't know anything about you." I smiled innocently. "So, are you married, divorced or what?"

"I'm married, but you probably haven't seen my husband," she said directing her comment at Dinah." He's the sales manager for a manufacturer up in Chatsworth and he's on the road most of the time."

"What do they manufacture?" Dinah said. I knew she was trying to keep the conversation going until I brought up the real estate agent.

"This and that," she said. She stared directly at us. "What is it exactly that you're here for?"

I picked up the wrap. "Do you crochet? We're always looking for more Hookers," I said.

It took a moment for it to compute. "You mean your crochet group that meets at the bookstore." She punctuated it with a laugh as if it was an absurd idea. "I certainly have no time for handicrafts. I bought that from Kelly."

"Then you were familiar with her online business," I said. Nanci answered with an impatient sigh.

"No. She just showed me what she was selling. I just bought a few things—most of it was too expensive for me. She made a point that she used only very expensive yarn and made one-of-a-kind items." Nanci picked up the wrap and showed us how there were beads spaced through it and the yarn, though the same color, changed texture. There was a moment of silence and I saw Nanci glance toward the door. Any second she was going to push us out.

I struggled for a topic that would grab her interest and buy me some more time. "It's about Autumn," I said. At the mention of her daughter's name, Nanci snapped to attention.

"How do you know my daughter?"

"I don't really know her very well. It's more her boy-friend."

"Boyfriend?" Nanci was really alert now.

"Yes, Jeffrey Greenberg or maybe you know him by his stage name Columbia."

Nanci appeared dumbfounded. "The kid on the bicycle? He's like a baby."

"Isn't that the truth. Girls mature so much faster. I just wanted you to know that he's a really good kid and Autumn couldn't do any better."

Apparently Nanci didn't agree. She went into a whole

rant about how Autumn had no time for boyfriends now. She had school, her dance lessons, the soccer team, show choir and of course, preparing for her future, which Nanci was confident was going to include an Ivy League college and a big career. "She's going to use her talents for more than running the PTA."

Nanci must have given up her concern about being rude, because she started walking toward the door. "You must have some important appointments to get to."

Dinah and I looked at each other. It was our last chance. *The Average Joe's Guide to Criminal Investigation* said if time for questioning was limited, go right for the throat.

"Here's the thing," I said as we reached the front door and she opened it. I quickly told her how Dinah and I had been next door the day Kelly was shot. "We're pretty sure a real estate agent stopped by while we were there." I told her I was trying to find out their identity and wondered if they'd left information at her house.

Nanci paused. "Nobody left anything here."

"Were you home that day?" I asked.

She looked me directly in the eye. "I heard about you two. Someone at the PTA called you Sherlockette and Watson. Not that I have to tell you anything, but I wasn't home."

"Where were you?" Dinah said.

"Don't be ridiculous," Nanci said as she ushered us out. "I don't have to give you an alibi."

CHAPTER 19

"YOU BETTER NOT TELL JEFFREY WHAT AUTUMN'S mother said," Dinah said as we walked into the bookstore through the café. The smell of baking chocolate chip cookie bars was so delicious, it practically put me into a stupor. So, nobody baked anymore, huh. True it was for the café, but Bob was using my recipe, which I used all the time. I pinched a little excess on my hip—maybe too much of the time.

"I would never tell Jeffrey what she said. But at least we got our answer about the real estate agent. I'm pretty sure he or she doesn't exist. So for whatever reason, Kelly didn't want us to know who'd come over," I said.

"It could have been Nanci," Dinah said. "You notice that she got her way. After *L.A. 911* uses the yard, that will be it."

"It seems crazy, but she was pretty upset about the idea of filming on her street. And we know she knows how to shoot a gun." I reached out to take the red eye Bob had made for me. He handed Dinah her café au lait.

"Do you think she has a gun?" Dinah asked.

I nodded. "And I bet it's a pretty one." I reminded Dinah of the brochure showing off fancy guns.

"Too bad we didn't ask to see it. Not that I have any idea how to tell if it had been fired recently. I suppose the cops must have found bullet casings and can match them up with a gun. Do you think Detective Heather knows about Nanci's gun?"

I put up my hands in ignorance. "I'm not going to be the one to tell her, either, unless I'm sure it's the murder weapon." We took our drinks and went on into the bookstore while trying to figure out a way to get a look at Nanci's gun or trick her into admitting that she'd killed Kelly.

The production company must have been filming a scene because none of them were hanging around. Rayaad was even reading a magazine at the cashier stand. She looked up and said Mrs. Shedd and Mr. Royal were unloading books for the signing.

We found my bosses setting up a display of the books with Stone's photo and story. They had moved one of the signs promoting the event to stand next to the table. Once Stone had agreed to sign his picture in the surfing book, I'd put up signs around the bookstore and was trying to spread the news by word of mouth. It was all kind of last minute and I was hoping for the best.

I gave Mr. Royal the photo Stone had given me. It was an amazing shot of him walking on the beach holding a surfboard. "If he wants to put out anything about his energy drink, there will be room on the table," Mr. Royal said. He stared at the photo and spent a few minutes raving on about Stone's surfing prowess.

"I wonder where Adele is," I said, doing a three sixty around the bookstore. "It's too quiet in here." Dinah followed me as we headed toward the kids' section. But when we walked into the area with cows jumping over the moon on the carpets and kid-size tables and chairs, there was no Adele.

"Her stuff is here," Dinah said touching Adele's tote bag sitting next to a notebook on the counter against the wall. Dinah's elbow brushed the tote bag and it toppled off the counter and fell bottom up on the floor.

"We better pick this up before Adele comes in," I said grabbing a runaway ball of yarn. I noticed a hook had fallen free. "Did you see where this came from?" I asked Dinah as I rummaged through the stuff on the floor. I finally found a swatch of yarn missing a hook and figured they belonged together. Before I slipped the hook back into a loop, I examined the cream-colored yarn. I held it up to show Dinah.

"Poor Adele," I said. "These are supposed to be bullion stitches." I handed them to Dinah and she shook her head in dismay.

"I see what she means about it being her Achilles' heel. These are terrible." We'd both seen photos of properly done bullion stitches and they were tight coils with a slightly crescent shape. Adele's coils were anything but tight or neat and appeared to be coming undone. We put everything back in the bag and set it back where it was.

"What's in the notebook?" Dinah asked.

"It is just sitting here," I said as if that made snooping in it okay. As soon as I opened it, I almost dropped it.

"Look." I pointed to the title "Adele Abrams, Very Private Detective" on the first page. Underneath it said "Case Book." There was no way I was putting it down now. I flipped to the next page and saw "Case #1—The Murder of Kelly Donahue." Beyond that she had a page titled "Suspects" and below that had headings for "Who Gained From Her Death," "Alibis," and "Adele's Golden Triangle of Guilt." A whole separate sheet was called "What to Wear to an Investigation."

"Wow, she sure has a long list of suspects." I did a double take as I got lower on the list. "Including you and me."

"Geez, is she crazy?" Dinah said looking over my shoulder.

"She put an '*LOL*' next to us," I said going through the list. "She's got Dan at the top with an asterisk. Nanci Silvers is right under him. Look at all the production people she listed. The only names I recognized were Fred and Zeke, the two prop guys I'd overheard and North Adams." It seemed like she'd listed everyone on the cast and crew except Eric. "She ought to put herself on the list. She could be trying to kill everyone who knows how to do the bullion stitch, so she won't look bad." I was just joking about that and we both started to laugh. Neither of us heard Adele come in until it was too late.

"What are you doing?" she demanded pulling the binder from my hands. She stuffed it into her tote bag. As she did, she noticed that things weren't quite as she'd left them. "CeeCee knows, doesn't she?" She pulled out the little swatch of bullion stitches and she started to cry and pull out the stitches at the same time. Adele cried like everything else she did, loudly and with a lot of drama.

Dinah and I surrounded her and gave her a group hug. She seemed so heartbroken over her crochet disability as she called it, we both reassured her that we were sure she'd master the stitch in no time and once again promised not to mention it to CeeCee.

I was hoping the fuss would make her forget we'd been looking at her detective book. Of course it didn't. "A lot you know. Eric was helping me with it. Maybe you don't know, Pink, but homicide detectives make up a murder book for each of their cases. Us serious freelancers do, too." She pulled the notebook back out. "When you see this you'll understand how on top of things I am. I couldn't get any crime-scene photos of the body so I had to improvise." She turned to a page I hadn't seen and showed how she'd drawn Kelly's workroom with a stick figure sprawled face up with a large red mark in the middle of her chest in front of the sliding glass door. She had used red curlicues going from the stick figure to areas all around it to show the blood spatter. "Eric told me where the body was."

"I've seen a real murder book," I said to Adele. "Just the other night, Barry showed me the one from a case he's working on." I was going to tell Adele more about it, but she cut me off.

"Mine is almost as good as the real thing," she said, holding the picture page open.

"I drew it all based on what Eric told me, like they could tell that Kelly was shot at close range and was facing her assailant."

"So then this is accurate? She was on her back?" I asked, and Adele nodded. "It means she was facing her killer."

Adele snapped the book shut. "All of it points toward the culprit being Dan Donahue. Except they haven't found the murder weapon and they don't have any other hard evidence that he did it. At least, not yet," Adele said, giving us a knowing look.

ALTHOUGH MASON AND I HAD BEEN HAVING DIN-ner together most nights, that night we didn't. He called to tell me they were having some kind of family powwow about the wedding situation. I realized I had no place in it, but I still felt left out.

I was surprised to come home to an empty house. For so long Barry had been there every night, mostly Jeffrey, too. But now that Barry was back on his feet, literally, it made sense they wouldn't just be staying put. I could tell by the trash, they'd had dinner before they went wherever. The takeout food containers gave it away. And the number of dishes in the dishwasher.

I laughed at myself. I was becoming quite the detective. Figuring out Samuel was out was easy. The light was off in his room and the door was shut. I had the house all to myself, finally. It was still balmy outside due to the fact it had been over one hundred degrees during the day. It seemed like a perfect night for an ice cream dinner. The only problem was no ice cream.

I brought the dogs inside and grabbed my purse. Gelson's and Whole Foods were closing for the night, so I headed toward Ralphs. The hot weather seemed to have made lots of people put off their grocery shopping because even though it was almost ten, the parking lot was crowded.

Once I got inside the store, I remembered other things I needed and, before I realized it, had a cart full of things like paper towels and cat food. I was ready to pick up the ice cream and check out, when I almost crashed carts with Dan Donahue. I had assumed by what I'd seen at their house that Dan brought everything they needed from his store, but apparently I was wrong. His cart had a whole selection of merchandise.

When he looked up to apologize for the cart crash, I said "Hello."

"Molly Pink, the bookstore lady, right?" he said. I nodded and he started to back his cart away. I wasn't about to let go of the opportunity to ask him a few questions, so I grabbed the side of it and stopped his escape.

I wished Dinah was there. We could do a good cop, bad cop thing and get information out of him without him even realizing he was giving it. But with no Dinah, my options were limited. You couldn't do just bad cop.

"I'm surprised to see you shopping here," I said. I studied his face. He looked tired and his smile seemed a little wan.

He glanced at his cart with a sheepish expression. "Bang for a Buck doesn't carry everything. I'm going to have the reception for Kelly's funeral at the house and I needed some things." He paused with a long sigh. "I wanted to have what she particularly liked."

"How are you holding up?" I said. This was the hard part. How to figure out if Detective Heather and Stone, along with everybody else, were right and he was a cold-blooded killer, or was he a grieving husband. He sighed again as he moved a loaf of cocktail rye bread so it wouldn't get squished by a bottle of Kalamata olives.

"Thanks for asking." I thought he was going to leave it at that, but then he continued on. I wasn't sure if he needed to vent or he was trying to work up sympathy. He began by talking about the shock of coming home to find Kelly. I noticed he seemed a little weak-kneed and I suggested we sit down by the closed coffee kiosk.

I started by saying it seemed like too much of a burden for him to have to arrange the reception after the funeral. "I'd be glad to handle it. I'm sure I can get your neighbor Dinah Lyons and her friend Commander Blaine to help." He gratefully accepted.

"And then to have the cops all over me." He was leaning

on his knees, clasping his hands. He lifted his head and looked at me directly. "You don't think I killed my wife, do you?"

This is where I started to play stupid cop. "The cops think *you* killed Kelly?" I tried to sound shocked at the thought. He reacted with relief.

"Good. I was afraid the word on the street was that I did it. It's crazy. Why would I want to kill Kelly?"

The list of reasons clicked off in my head. There was the big insurance payment I heard he was getting. There was the fact that they weren't getting along and another divorce would break him. Then there was what the assistant manager of Dan's store said about him being upset that Kelly wouldn't help out at the store. And what about whatever was going on between him and Nanci Silvers. I just gave him a sympathetic smile.

"I thought at least my kids would be here, but under the circumstances my ex is keeping them. Kelly's kids are staying with her ex. I don't know what to do." He seemed like he might cry. He was seeming less and less like a cold-blooded murderer and more and more like someone Detective Heather had just latched onto. It certainly wouldn't be the first time.

"I'm just curious. When you came home that day, did you ring the doorbell?"

"That's a strange question," he said. "Why do you ask?"

I hate it when people answer a question with a question. It comes across like they are trying to avoid something. I started viewing him as the cold-blooded killer again. Maybe I'd catch him off guard by seeming sympathetic.

"I'm sure the cops will drop it. What evidence do they even have?" I said.

He took a breath and nodded. "Exactly. They tested my

hands, no residue of gunpowder. Just because I'm the one who found her doesn't mean anything."

"Then the obvious question is who did kill her?" I waited a beat before continuing. "What about your neighbor, Nanci Silvers? How well do you know her?"

He stood up and prepared to leave. "I don't know her at all."

I checked his eyes. No surprise he was looking away.

Even though it was late by the time I finally got home with my ice cream, I called Dinah. Commander was with her and they both were enthusiastic about putting on the reception, but for different reasons. Commander liked to arrange any kind of gathering, particularly if it helped someone out during a tough time. On the other hand, after hearing that Dan claimed not to know Nanci, Dinah saw it as an investigation opportunity. While I was on the phone, Barry and Jeffrey walked in, arguing.

"But Dad, I don't see why I can't just ride over to our place. I can go up stairs."

Barry's face looked stormy. "There's no discussion. Give me your key."

I had to stick my finger in my free ear to be able to hear Dinah. She picked up on their fussing.

"Barry seems to be having a hard time letting Jeffrey be independent," she said. I just murmured an uh-huh in response. Dinah and I finished her call and I finally sat down to my ice cream dinner. I had the kitchen to myself for only a moment before Barry popped in.

"I thought I'd have some tea." He opened the cupboard I had given over to them and took out several boxes. "I owe you some tea bags." He undid the cellophane and started to take some out. I told him to forget it, but he insisted on at least making me a cup.

He saw the dish of strawberry ice cream. "Having one of your ice cream dinners, huh? What happened to Mason?" There was a subtle dig in his tone.

I explained the wedding mess and his confab with his family. "And he didn't include you?" Barry said. "Since your job is to put on events, you'd think he'd want your help." Even though I'd never exactly told Barry that Mason kept me separate from his family, detective Barry had figured it out and knew it bothered me.

Barry brought the two cups of tea to the table and pulled out the bench and sat down. I didn't want to get into a discussion of Mason, so I changed the subject. The segue was easy. Barry had brought up that I planned events and so I told him about the latest one at the bookstore.

"It's kind of last minute, but Mr. Royal thought it would be a good idea to have Kelly's brother sign a book that has a segment on him. Stone Thomasville is a world-class surfer. I guess that's why he moved to Hawaii."

"All that and adorable, too," Barry said with distaste. Then he changed subjects. "How'd it go with your search for the real estate agent?"

"It didn't. Nobody had any notepads. I don't think there was any real estate agent." There was something on my mind that had been bothering me. I shouldn't have said anything, but I couldn't seem to stop myself. "Eric is giving Adele all kinds of inside information on Kelly's murder, like where the body was. You always said you couldn't tell me anything." I looked at him directly. "So what gives?"

Barry used taking a sip of the tea to pause, then he blew out his breath. "I only had the best of intentions. I wanted to keep you out of trouble." He chuckled. "Not that it did much good." He paused while something computed in his head. "Hey, I made the suggestion about the real estate agent and I told you Heather was looking for the murder weapon."

"Do you know anything else?"

Barry's eyes went skyward. "No, and I don't want to discuss it anymore." I made a face at him, which he found highly amusing.

"Too bad because I was going to tell you something I found out."

"That's different," Barry said. "You'd be withholding information. Maybe you'd even be interfering with a police investigation. I think you better tell me what you know." His smile had faded, but I was pretty sure he was just teasing with the threats. At least I certainly hoped so, but I told him that both Dan and his neighbor claimed to barely know each other and I knew it wasn't true.

"And how is it that you know that?" he asked. "Any breaking and entering involved?"

"No," I said indignantly. "It was all out in the open. You can ask Jeffrey." I regretted saying his name as soon as it was out of my mouth.

Barry's eyes narrowed. "What does Jeffrey have to do with it?" He stopped and his expression got a little pointed. "You didn't get him tangled up in your crazy investigations, did you?" Barry had his eagle eyes trained on me as he went into interrogation mode. I tried looking away, but quickly swiveled my head back toward him. Looking away was a sure sign you intended to lie. I didn't intend to lie, I just intended to give out as few details as possible.

I started out by trying to say nothing, but he saw right through that.

"I've got all night, Molly," he said. "I just live down the

hall." He pointed toward his room as a reminder. "I already heard from Eric that Jeffrey tried to get in the scene they were shooting. I suppose you helped him with that."

I rolled my eyes in response. "Jeffrey just happened to be riding his bike past the Donahue house and he saw Dan and his neighbor Nanci Silvers acting kind of friendly in her garage."

Barry narrowed his eyes. "You're leaving something out. Why does Jeffrey even know who these people are or where they live?"

The question hung in the air. I didn't want to get Jeffrey in trouble, but Barry had me in a corner. I mentioned that Nanci was Autumn's mother. I tried to leave it at that, but Barry was unrelenting. No wonder he got so many confessions.

"Okay, Jeffrey wanted to ask her when Autumn was coming home from camp." I took a sip of my tea, which by now was cold. "I know you're upset about Jeffrey having a girlfriend, but you don't have to worry. Nanci is just as upset with her daughter having Jeffrey as a boyfriend."

"And how is it that you know this?" Barry asked. He was leaning forward in his chair, watching me intently.

"I know that and more. How about Nanci probably has a fancy gun and likes to shoot skeets." I told Barry I'd found it all out when I stopped by to see if she had a notepad from a real estate agent. He ignored my investigating and only focused on what Nanci had said. Apparently while he wasn't happy with his son having a girlfriend, he was more upset that her mother implied Jeffrey might not be quite up to her standards.

I finally got up to go across the house.

"Good night, bab—I mean, Molly," he said. He came up

behind me and stopped. I could feel his breath on the back of my neck. He paused for a moment and then he put his hand gently on my shoulder. "You know Jeffrey really likes you and . . ." I wasn't sure what was coming next and I didn't hang around to find out.

CHAPTER 20

Despite what I had said, I was really concerned about the turnout for Stone's picture signing. Mr. Royal was a fan and apparently thought that all of Tarzana was, too, because he'd ordered fifty copies of the book. There were only two pages devoted to Stone and the book was expensive. I'd asked all the Hookers to come, so at least there'd be some bodies in the chairs.

But it turned out to be unnecessary. Even before Stone got there, people started to show up. They were mostly men and they all looked like Stone with the shaggy sun-streaked hair and deep tans. I recognized a few of them from the group I'd seen him with at Le Grande Fromage. They appeared to think he was a god and were honored to be able to go surfing with him.

Since I wasn't interested in surfing, it was hard to understand how they felt. I tried to put it in terms that made sense to me and guessed it was like getting a chance to go yarn shopping with Vanna White.

Mr. Royal had tried to give the bookstore a Hawaiian feel by hanging brightly colored paper leis off the bookcases. He'd found a fake palm tree somewhere and brought it into the middle of the store. Next to it, I'd set up a table with some of the books. Mr. Royal had found a documentary that featured Stone and some other surfers, traveling the world's best surfing beaches. He'd brought in some DVDs of it to sell and placed them next to the books. We'd set up chairs and Stone had agreed to tell some surfing stories to try to make it more of an event.

Rhoda and Elise were in the front row, crocheting as they waited. Dinah and Commander found me and we discussed my offer of our help with the reception after Kelly's funeral.

"I'm glad to help out," Commander said. "You know Kelly had a post office box at my place and she dropped off packages all the time for UPS or FedEx to pick up."

"Really?" I said, surprised, but then it made sense. For privacy reasons, a lot of people who worked from their homes didn't want to use their address as a return address. Commander Blaine had said what made his place special was that he gave his customers a real address to use instead of just a post office box number. I asked how well he knew her and if he'd seen any examples of what she sold.

Commander smoothed back his thick shock of white hair. "She was always in a hurry so I never really got to talk to her, and her packages were always sealed and ready to go. You know I view everybody who uses my services like family. She was just a little more distant than the rest of them."

"Sit with us," Rhoda called, waving at Commander and Dinah. As they went to take their seats, I noticed that some of the production people had come in. I recognized Fred and Zeke, the two prop guys who'd been placing the plants in Kelly's backyard.

I'd overheard their conversation with North Adams, but never talked to them myself. It was always a little awkward just going up to people cold and starting to grill them. This is where Detective Heather had a distinct advantage. All she had to do was show her badge.

I didn't have a badge, but I had cookies. Bob had made passion fruit ice tea and butter cookies in the shape of pineapples. I picked up a couple of the cookies and offered the two men each a free sample. I doubted Detective Heather got the smiles and happy response I did.

Now that I was closer I could see both men looked older. They both had brown hair and leathery tanned skin. I introduced myself, went into Stone's appearance, and then asked if they were surfers.

"Heck, not like him." The first man stuck out his non-cookie-holding hand. "Fred Robinson. Pleased to meet you." He jerked his thumb toward his companion. "Zeke Nichols." They almost looked like brothers, but Fred seemed to be the older of the two.

"I see so many people in the bookstore," I began. "But you two look familiar." I left it open-ended hoping they'd say what they did and give me an opening to ask about Kelly. Doing anything in the entertainment business had a certain cachet to it, so they were only too happy to bring up what they did.

"People don't realize how important props are. Any kind of obscure item a director wants, we find it or make it. You know the perfect blue needle pine that Sandra Bullock carried in *Secret Santa*?" He pointed at his chest. "I did it. Nobody realized it was a fake. I made it out of wire and a lot of bottle brushes I spray-painted."

I nodded in interest. "So, then you two are the ones who put all the trees in Kelly Donahue's yard." Both men's expressions faded. "And you were in the yard the day she was killed, weren't you?"

Fred seemed to be the spokesperson. "We kept having to bring in more pots. The director wanted the look of total green and we had to block out the house." He stopped talking and swallowed hard. "If we hadn't gone around the corner to pick up our lunch at catering, we might have been there. . . ." He swallowed again. "Maybe we could have done something to save her."

Zeke nodded. "I understand it's just a matter of time before they arrest her husband."

Instead of discussing Dan's possible guilt, I wanted to see what they knew. "Did you see anyone around the front of the house when you left?" I asked.

"Naw, nobody," Fred said.

"The street was dead," Zeke added.

Their answers troubled me. Were they lying or did they just have bad memories? I didn't consider Dinah, Adele and me as nobody, and we were there as they left for lunch. I also noticed they didn't say anything about knowing Kelly from before. I tried to draw them out by asking what they knew about her. Fred spoke up first.

"She was very accommodating about us using her yard. She gave us full access, no problems." Fred stopped and looked at his coworker. Zeke gave him a go-ahead gesture. "I knew Kelly, a little anyway. We worked on the same show a while back. Her father was in the business and she helped him out." I waited to see if he was going to say more, but he quickly changed the subject.

"That neighbor of Kelly's was nothing but trouble. Kind of a tough-looking woman with blond hair cut like knife blades. Every time we'd pull into the driveway, she'd come out and start fussing at us. She said Kelly was going to ruin the peaceful quality of the street by letting productions use her house. She fussed when we parked too close to the edge and another time when some leaves fell off one of the bushes and blew onto her sidewalk. She complained to me about the cars the production had parked on her street." Fred said he'd tried to explain to her that he had nothing to do with that.

"If you want my opinion. I think she was jealous. She wanted the production to use her yard." Zeke said, joining the conversation again.

"Did you ever see Kelly and the neighbor talking together?" I asked. The two men looked at each other and seemed to be considering what to say.

"Let's just say, I think Ms. Donahue should have thought twice before borrowing any sugar from her neighbor." Fred glanced toward the entrance of the café. "What's he doing here?" The two men nodded a greeting as North Adams approached, carrying an ice tea. Fred and Zeke thanked me for the cookies and went to find seats.

North was out of costume in the fancy jeans again—the kind that had gone through a bunch of processes to look soft and worn. This time he'd paired them with a pale blue dress shirt, worn out, and soft leather loafers with no socks.

It was hard not to be struck by his dark hair and rugged features. Several women recognized him and seemed to get all flirty. He knew how to play the game and flirted right back. It was fun watching their expressions as they walked away. They were giggling and talking and seemed awestruck. Had he come to see Stone? North didn't look like a surfer, but then who knew.

Stone had come in and joined me at the edge of the crowd. He looked every bit the surfer with the khaki shorts, blue and white silk Hawaiian shirt and sandals. I had the feeling that was the way he dressed for every occasion. He had a backpack slung on his shoulder and took out a stack of brochures touting the coconut energy drink.

"Okay if I put these out," he said, holding onto a handful. I said I'd put them out on the front table. We decided it would be more dramatic if he made an entrance after I did a few minutes on who he was. I noticed that North was staring at me. He waved me over.

"Now that you know, I need your help again."

"Know what?" I said. Instead of an answer he pushed his cell phone in my hand and gestured for me to listen.

"Hello?" I said tentatively. As soon as I heard the "Mo—" of "Mother" I knew it was my son Peter. Not that I got a chance to greet him because he launched into a bunch of commands.

"You need to do the same thing with North. Take him home with you. Remember take Wells Drive. And don't ask him any questions."

Peter finally stopped to breathe and I said I couldn't leave the bookstore. "I'm in the middle of an event."

My son made a bunch of unhappy sounds and then asked to talk to the actor again. North listened and didn't look pleased with what he was hearing. "You should really take better care of things," North said. "This is the second time. There better not be a third."

I didn't want to be in the middle of any disagreement between my son and his client.

Peter and I had our differences, but I would still always take his side no matter what. North handed the phone back to me. Peter sounded tense and tired. "Mother, just do the best you can to keep him happy until I can get there. Please."

North looked around at the decorations and chairs and asked what was going on. I told him about the book signing and surreptitiously waved Dinah over. Another fan approached North and I took the opportunity to tell Dinah the situation. She got Commander to join her and then they took over the care of North Adams. Commander was so good at handling people, I don't think North realized I'd passed him off.

I was surprised to see Kelly's husband Dan join the crowd. He stopped by to say hello to me, gesturing with his free arm toward the table setup. "I came to support Stone," he said before taking a chair on the end of one of the rows. Did Dan have any idea a lot of people there were convinced he'd murdered his wife and was getting away with it? Or did he think this was a way to convince them that he didn't kill her? Personally, I wasn't so sure anymore.

The seats were really filling up. Mr. Royal watched with a pleased expression and nodded to Mrs. Shedd.

Sheila, our nervous Hooker, came up to me and greeted me with a hug. She glanced shyly to the side at the man with her.

"Nicholas," I said in surprise. He owned Luxe where Sheila worked, but due to his successful writing career, was away a lot. He said something about being glad to support a fellow store before he and Sheila found seats. The way he touched Sheila's back to guide her into the chair made me think there was more to this than just employee-boss. I hoped so because we all knew Sheila got gooey-eyed whenever she talked about him.

Our resident actress, CeeCee, had told me she couldn't

make it. I'd thought Adele was going to come, but so far, she was a no-show. I was about to give up on her and start the festivities when Adele and Eric came in the door. It was more accurate to say the couple made an entrance.

I should have known she would dress for the occasion. Her costume consisted of white capri pants topped with a brick red Hawaiian shirt and a whole tube of self tanner that had left her skin with an orangy tan. I'd never seen Eric out of uniform and was surprised to see that she'd played dress up with him and gotten him to wear a matching outfit—only his pants went all the way down to his shoe tops. He seemed a little self-conscious. Who could blame him. He looked like he'd eaten too many carrots and they'd turned his skin orange. "I thought you said everyone would be dressed this way," he said as they walked toward the front row.

Welcome to Adele's world.

Mr. Royal gave me a nod and a wave, which meant he was impatient for me to start. I stepped to the front of the group and started to talk about Stone. Mr. Royal had written the introduction. The gist was that Stone had conquered what was considered the most dangerous beach in Hawaii and had stopped competing while he was still on top.

There was a hardy round of applause as Stone stepped from behind the bookcases that surrounded the area we'd set aside for the event. He leaned against the table and smiled at the crowd, displaying his dimples.

I was surprised to see Barry standing at the back. I guessed he'd heard enough about Stone and wanted to see what Mr. Adorable looked like.

"Thank you all for coming. You're too kind to an old surfer dude past his prime." His self-effacing comment won over the crowd and they said "aw" in unison. He began the talk by describing the thrill of surfing and was segueing into the energy drink when there was the sound of an alarm going off. A whirr of running figures flew by the outskirts of the chairs. Before Mr. Royal could respond, Eric in all his orange glory jumped out of his seat and took off after them.

Stone instinctively stopped, but I encouraged him to continue, and then I followed Mr. Royal to find out what was going on.

Eric came back inside after a few minutes. He was out of breath and leaned against the counter. "They disappeared into the darkness," he said. "Sorry." Mr. Royal thanked him for his efforts and then Mrs. Shedd, Mr. Royal and I made the rounds to see if anything was missing. One of the e-readers had been pulled free from its leash and was gone. The chocolate rack was missing some bars and when we walked back to the yarn area, skeins were laying all over the floor and the cabinet was open and the plastic bin that had held Kelly's crochet pieces was on the floor. It was empty except for a few stray strands of yarn.

"Those kids again," Mrs. Shedd said, shaking her head with dismay.

Adele checked out the mess in the yarn department while making some comment about how terrible it was that all of Kelly's donations were gone. I looked intently at Adele. "No chance of CeeCee seeing all those bullion stitch flowers now, is there?" I said, waiting to see her reaction. She let out an annoyed huff at my implied accusation.

The other thing—actually the other person—missing, was Barry. When I asked Eric, he said that as he was chasing the shoplifters he'd spotted Barry getting in his Tahoe. Very strange.

CHAPTER 21

"I MISSED ALL THE EXCITEMENT," CEECEE SAID IN a disappointed tone. It was the next day and the Hookers were assembled at the worktable in the yarn department. I'd just finished fixing the last of the mess from the night before. CeeCee glanced over the wall with the cubbies of yarn and the cabinets beneath. "Did they take anything or just make a mess?"

I looked at Adele, who's eyes had suddenly become big with fear. She made eye contact with me and even put her hands together in a prayer posture as she threw me a silent plea.

She didn't have to worry. I wasn't going to bring up the fact that the crochet pieces Kelly had given us for the street fair were missing. It would only open a bunch of problems. CeeCee would want to know why she hadn't been told about the pieces in the first place and then she would be upset with all of us for keeping them from her. It was better to just avoid the subject all together.

"The biggest thing they took was the e-reader even with the do-it-yourself alarm Mr. Royal installed." I said that Eric had called in the robbery, and a whole contingent of cops had shown up, although there was nothing to do but take a report. Well, there was something else they'd done. They'd chuckled at Eric who looked like a giant carrot.

"What happened to the surfer?" CeeCee asked. "You said he was such a charming man. I'd hate to think his moment in the spotlight was ruined."

I laughed inside. As with my other mini disaster book signings, this one had turned out okay, too. Once the cops had talked to Mrs. Shedd, Mr. Royal and me, and we'd all come to the same conclusion that it was the neighborhood kids out for a thrill, they'd noticed Stone. A couple of the cops were surfers and knew who he was. They told their fellow cops and they all stayed while he finished talking about what it was like to surf some place called Banzai Pipeline. He said something about thick curls of waves that he was able to tube ride. It didn't mean a lot to me, but the crowd seemed fascinated. They all seemed interested in the coconut energy drink, but were sorry to hear there wasn't even a bottle of it to see. He'd won the crowd over and thirty of the books sold, along with some of the DVDs.

CeeCee was relieved to hear it was a success. She looked over at Adele who was working on a purple cowl. "Adele, you're such a good crocheter. I can't believe you're working on something so simple. And, dear, I can't see the cowls being a success at this time of year."

Adele sputtered a few times. "A lot you know. I have been working on some very complicated things. I stand by my decision to make cowls for the sale. You'll see, they'll be a big success."

Elise produced her vampire version and said she thought hers would be even more in demand. Dinah knew better than to say anything. Sheila avoided the fuss and kept her eyes on her crocheting. She was churning out pot holders and other small items.

"I can't wait for this foofie vampire trend to be over," Rhoda Klein said with a harrumph. "Dracula would never wear one of those."

Eduardo just chuckled and showed off the water bottle holder he was making for the sale.

"Now that is seasonally correct," CeeCee said. "Someone should bring a cooler full of bottled water." CeeCee looked over the group for a volunteer and Rhoda waved her hand.

"I forgot to mention that North Adams was there for the whole event," I said. CeeCee seemed surprised.

"He must be a big surfing fan. He'd probably been on the set since eight in the morning. I know when my day on the set of *Making Amends* wraps, all I want to do is go home," she said.

I just nodded in agreement. My son Peter had sworn me to secrecy about the rest of last night, so I made no mention that when Peter didn't get there in time I'd taken North to my house, via the side streets. Or that he had acted as if he was smitten with me. He'd even kept up the charade once we were back inside my place, which was very awkward when we walked into the kitchen and saw Barry was hanging around, hoping he and I would have tea together. I didn't have to be a mind reader to see he had something on his mind and to figure it had something to do with his sudden departure from the bookstore.

"What's he doing here?" Barry said to me, when North went on into the living room. I was saved from answering by the sound of my front door opening, followed by male voices. A moment later Mason and Samuel came into the kitchen asking why North Adams was sitting in my living room.

While I was trying to answer without really saying anything, Peter finally showed up and took North with him. When the door clicked shut, all eyes were back on me. I went the politician way and simply turned the questions back on them, asking what Samuel and Mason were doing there together.

Mason let out a sigh. "Would you believe I'm trying to round up musicians for Thursday's wedding?"

Samuel had touched him on the shoulder. "You won't be disappointed. My guys can do anything you want."

Barry had moved to the edge of the group. Usually he was able to hide his emotions under the mask of his cop face, but not tonight. He appeared distracted and distressed. He glanced in my direction and there was worry in his dark eyes as he muttered "good night" and headed up the hall. Probably he was embarrassed about driving away instead of helping Eric chase down the shoplifters. Poor Barry. Would he ever get his mojo back?

CHAPTER 22

"Sunshine, I'm going to have to back out of our plans," Mason said. It was the next day and I was just getting ready to leave the bookstore. We'd talked several times during the day and had planned on barbecuing at his house. I could almost hear Mason shaking his head with frustration as he told me there was another family wedding meeting.

"Whatever," I said, trying to hide my disappointment. It was ridiculous for me to feel left out—it was his family—but I did.

"I'm sorry," he said and I knew by his tone he really meant it. "I'll make it up to you."

"An invitation to the wedding would do," I said, trying to sound like I was joking. There was a long silence on his end and for a moment I thought we'd been cut off.

"I'm working on it, sunshine," he responded finally before we said our good-byes and hung up.

Working on it? How much work was involved with say-ing "Hey, Molly, come to my daughter's wedding." I knew it wasn't quite that easy for him. I gathered there was some agreement with his ex about keeping family things separate from their new social lives. Maybe I was being silly, but in my mind unless Mason acted like I was a fixture in his life, our relationship wouldn't go any further. We'd stay friends, but friends without benefits.

After that I went directly home wondering what was waiting for me this time. I came in through the kitchen door and was relieved to find quiet. But I'd barely closed the door when Barry walked in. Was it my imagination or did it seem like he'd been listening for me to come home?

He acted surprised to see me, but he could have been faking it. Then he made a move toward the cabinet with the dishes. "I was just coming in for a cup of tea." He reached for a stoneware mug. "You really started something with the tea drinking. It's a nice way to cap off the evening. He looked at the area around me. "No entourage?" I knew he was refer-ring to the previous evening when North had been with me and Mason showed up right after.

Whatever distress he'd shown the previous night had been filed far inside and he was back to his usual self.

"Not tonight," I said.

"Where's the counselor?" Barry asked. I explained about Mason's daughter's wedding and his efforts to try to put it together.

"Hmm, so the lawyer finally found something he couldn't fix so easily. It must be a shock." He went to reach for an-other mug. "Want to join me?"

Having tea at night had become a nice habit and I nod-ded in agreement. He took out another mug and set up both drinks. As we went outside, Cosmo came in the kitchen to see what was going on and the small black mutt followed us out.

I LEANED BACK IN THE CHAIR AND TOOK A DEEP breath of the night air. The crickets were chirping and all the night birds were talking to each other.

"Isn't this nice how we can just sit together, have tea and talk." I smiled at him. "See, no matter what you thought, we *can* still be friends."

Barry flinched at the comment. I asked where Jeffrey was and he said he was spending the night at one of his drama friends. They were camping out in his backyard. I glanced toward the house. "What about Samuel?"

"He's off somewhere. He doesn't keep me in the loop," Barry said. "So, it looks like it's just you and me."

There was no reason for me to feel awkward, but I did. Although there had been a time when having the place to ourselves would have meant something, that was long past. Barry let out a noise that sounded like a wistful sigh. I knew he was thinking the same thing I was.

For a few moments we just sat there drinking our tea. I didn't know about him, but I was feeling this vibe in the air that seemed to be getting more intense. Barry leaned forward slightly and I saw his hand coming toward my arm.

There was nothing to do but throw cold water on the situation. So I started talking about Kelly's murder. "I know that Detective Heather has zeroed in on Dan as the killer and dismissed the other suspects, but I'm not so sure she's right."

My comment had the desired effect. Barry had pulled his

hand back to his armrest as if he'd just hit a hot coal and then he laughed. "As if it's anything new that you think Heather has it wrong. I suppose you've come up with your own list of suspects."

"Maybe I have," I said.

Barry sat up in his chair. "Okay, let's hear it." His lips were curved in an indulgent smile.

"To start with there's Nanci Silvers." Barry's eyes flickered in response to the name before I went through the reasons why, which were adding up. She lived next door and had no alibi, which gave her opportunity. I had a pretty good idea she knew how to use a gun and probably had one. And as for motive—it appeared there was something going on between her and Dan, along with the fact Nanci seemed determined to keep the Donahue house from being used in future productions. If Adele had been there, she would have said Nanci had the golden triangle of guilt.

"Autumn's mother?" he said.

"You'd love it to be her, wouldn't you? Then you could tell Jeffrey his girlfriend's mother was a murderer. That would break them up for sure."

Barry rolled his eyes. "I'm not that bad. I just worry about Jeffrey getting in over his head." He picked up his mug. "Is that it, or do you have more suspects?"

I mentioned that the two prop guys had said they knew Kelly from before.

"I saw them go to lunch, but they could have easily come back. As for means, there are lots of guns in *L.A. 911*."

Barry stopped me. "They're prop guns."

"But what if they mixed a real one in with the prop ones? It would be a great way to hide it in plain sight." Barry explained that fake guns were all supposed to have an orange plug in the barrel.

"And what's their motive?" he said.

"I don't know." I gazed upward and began to improvise. "Maybe it had something to do with the disappearing lamp." Barry seemed unimpressed and I brought up Kelly's online business. "Maybe it was a disgruntled customer or someone random," I offered. "But one thing I'm sure of."

I reminded Barry that Dinah and I had been there that day and someone, which we now knew probably hadn't been a real estate agent, had come to the door. "Don't you think that person probably is the killer?"

Barry nodded with approval. "That sounds reasonable. Why don't you try to think back to what you saw in the street when you left Kelly's." He suggested I close my eyes and try to picture the scene. I was surprised how well it worked. After noting that the sidewalk was empty, I began to see a line of cars and commercial vehicles parked along the street.

"Let's see, there was a plumber's van, several cars, a cab, the truck with the wooden slates that the prop guys used and the Crown Victoria, North Adams drove. But they were all just parked there for the production."

When I opened my eyes Barry's face was lit up in a smile.

"It doesn't sound like your remembrance changes anything. And who would be more likely to show up at her house than her husband? Ah, we're back to what Heather thinks." He rolled his eyes, while shaking his head in good-natured disbelief. "I can't believe you got me to play clue with you," he said as we both got up to go inside.

I NEVER KNEW QUITE HOW TO DRESS FOR A FU-neral. The day of everybody wearing black dresses and veils was long over with, if it ever really existed anywhere but in my imagination. Besides, with the temperature in the high nineties, long sleeves and heavy clothes were even less appealing. Couple that with my helping at the house afterward, and I felt even more confused about what to wear. Who would have thought Barry would have ended up helping me?

As a homicide detective he'd been at far more funerals than I had and when we went inside after our tea, I made a comment about my clothing dilemma. He took both our mugs and put them in the dishwasher and offered his assistance.

It was weird showing him my closet, but then we were just housemates now, right? He stood next to me as I pushed clothes down the rack. Close enough that I could feel the heat coming off his body.

"How about that," he said when I got to a linen dress that had tiny black-and-white checks. From a distance it appeared gray. It was sleeveless and loose fitting. "Do you need help with shoes?" he said with a teasing smile. "I've become quite an expert thanks to Heather. Those heels sure do something with the way a woman walks."

I pulled him out of my closet and said I could handle the shoes myself. I should have left it at that, but the whole heels comment had annoyed me. "Sorry I didn't have that tart walk going when we were together," I said.

Barry stifled a laugh and I asked how the work was coming at his apartment.

"Huh?" he said as I walked him back toward his side of the house. I repeated the question and he threw up his hands. "You know workmen. It was too hot to paint, so there's a delay. They brought the wrong carpet. The one I wanted had to be special ordered so there's another delay. If it's such a burden having us here, I could find someplace else to stay. Heather's building has an elevator."

"It's okay if you stay here until your place is decorated," I said. I knew the comment about Heather was a setup, but I fell for it anyway. Frustrated with myself I shut the door to my wing of the house and called it a night.

Barry's clothes choice for me turned out to be perfect. Kelly's funeral was held at a small chapel at Forest Lawn. The cemetery was set on an expanse of green hillside with a view of the eastern Valley and there was no shade to soften the blinding sun. Dinah and I arrived together. Commander was off getting the things for the reception in order.

Inside, we found CeeCee. She was the only one decked out in a black sheath dress and a wide-brimmed black hat with a veil. In her mind there might be paparazzi anywhere and she was always ready for her close-up. Rhoda and Elise were next to her. Both of them had a small crochet project in their laps. I think just like some people always carry a book, they carried crochet.

Eduardo hadn't been able to make it. Then Sheila came in and took the seat next to Dinah. "Funerals make me nervous," she said in a breathy voice. Adele plopped into the seat next to Sheila and launched into the benefits of them sharing an apartment, which Adele was pushing for.

"If we get a place together, I'll throw in confidence lessons. In no time you'll own every room you enter, just like me," Adele said as she adjusted her hat. I didn't say anything, but I thought Adele's concept of owning a room was really more like kidnapping it.

No surprise, Adele didn't wear black. All I could think of was that she looked like a block of butter. She wore a long yellow dress that appeared to be cotton, but had a sheen to it. She had added a scarf of crocheted flowers, all creamy yellow as well. No big hat for Adele this time, she'd worn another tiny yellow fascinator on the front of her head. It had a snippet of yellow veil and seemed to be erupting tiny flowers on long wire stems. Every time she moved, the flowers bobbed. Adele was big on wearing things with moveable parts.

The Hookers began to talk among themselves while Dinah and I checked out the rest of the crowd. I noticed Detective Heather slip into the last row. What did she think—that Dan was going to jump up and confess in the middle of the service?

Dinah and I turned our attention to the first row. Dan was already seated in the first seat on the end.

"I bet that's Kelly's mother," Dinah said as a slender woman in a classic black dress walked along the front row. I could just make out her expression as she approached Dan.

"It looks like she's on the same page as Detective Heather and thinks Dan killed her daughter," I said. She scowled at Dan as she offered him a cursory greeting before she took a seat at the opposite end of the row.

"I'm actually beginning to feel sorry for him," Dinah said. "It's not like he's been convicted. What happened to innocent until proven guilty?"

"What happened is everyone thinks he did it and is getting away with it. Detective Heather will keep investigating and trying to get him to confess, but if he doesn't, it'll be shelved like the cases Barry's working on. He said in one of the cases they knew the maid did it, but could never get enough evidence to charge her. There's no statute on murder, so Dan will forever be in limbo unless they get evidence that he did it, or evidence that he didn't do it. In the meantime, they might be treating him like he's guilty, but he's still a free man."

"But the important thing is, are we convinced he's the guy?" Dinah asked.

"I keep going back and forth. With no real evidence, I'm not sure who did it," I said as we went back to watching the first row. Even from a distance I recognized the family dimples of the two little girls who walked in with their father. The girls seemed confused and unhappy and the man with them seemed distraught. "He must be Kelly's first husband," I said. His greeting to Dan consisted of an angry head shake as he kept his arms protectively around his daughters.

"How about him for a suspect?" Dinah said.

"No motive. Even Dan said there was no problem between her first husband and Kelly. The divorce has been settled for a while and there weren't any custody issues." I continued to watch the family drama in the first row. An older man had joined the group. He had the trademark dimples and I was sure he was Kelly's father. He was a little wooden in greeting his granddaughters. It might have had something to do with the young woman with him. By the rock on her finger and the way she was hanging on to him, I was guessing she was his wife and also guessed he probably didn't like being called "Gramps."

Stone came in last. I was glad to see he'd worn long pants and a dress shirt instead of his usual shorts and Aloha shirt. He'd even replaced his sandals with loafers. He moved down the row talking to his father and then his mother. The only seat left was next to Dan.

A few more people came into the chapel. I noticed Nanci Silvers take a seat in the back. The service was short and referred to a life cut off in the middle, but made no mention of her death being murder. I wondered who'd planned it.

Dinah and I left early to meet up with Commander who had picked up the food. We'd just pulled up in front of the Donahue house when Dan drove into the driveway.

He seemed distracted as he let us in. More cars arrived and the living room filled up with neighbors, the Hookers, Dan's store employees and some of Kelly's family. I had wondered if they would even come, but I suppose it was more out of respect for her than sympathy for Dan. Dan sat on the couch staring off into space and didn't act as the host. Commander was particularly good at playing host and worked the room to make sure everyone went into the dining room and helped themselves.

I had hoped to get a chance to talk to Kelly's family, but they stayed only long enough to make an appearance and then left en masse.

I looked around the living room and wondered if anyone would notice if I took a little side trip. I had never been alone in Kelly's crochet room and I wanted to poke around in it without watchful eyes.

The room seemed dimmer than I remembered and I realized the sheer curtains had been drawn across the sliding glass door. It seemed eerie and still and I suddenly wished Dinah had come with me. The computer was sitting on the library table and when I hit the power button, it came on. I didn't know what I was looking for, but I was curious about her business. Nobody seemed to know the name of it. I sorted through the folders and came across one called online store. When I clicked on it, two folders appeared. I clicked on the one labeled "Crochet." There was a long list of files with unintelligible names. I clicked on a few and saw that each had a picture of a crocheted item and a brief description and whether she'd sold it, and for how much, along with how long it had taken her to make it and how much the yarn had cost.

She had spent a lot on yarn, but she'd also sold the pieces for a lot. The fact that they were one of kind and almost art pieces was probably why she got her price. I wondered about the other folder under the "Online Store" heading and backtracked until I got there. It was marked "Non-Crochet Items." Kelly must have been selling more than just things she made. I clicked on the folder and a list of files with numbers instead of names showed up.

I was about to open the first one, when Adele sashayed in. "Pink, I thought I'd find you in here. What are you doing?"

I took it as a rhetorical question and didn't answer it. "Did you find anything else made with the bull—" Adele looked around to see if anyone was listening. "You know that special stitch."

Adele moved further into the room and began looking around. She noticed a pillow that had fallen off the couch. It had a three-dimensional design with rows and rows of different-size bullion stitches.

She picked it up and was touching the stitches as if they could impart the magic of how to make them.

Suddenly CeeCee swept into the room. "There you two are. I'm going to have to leave. The atmosphere in there is terrible. All those people staring at Dan. He finally got up and went outside." CeeCee saw Adele clutching the pillow and took it from her to examine it.

"Dear, those bullion stitches are lovely." She commented further on how perfectly the stitches laid next to each other before turning to Adele. "The Hookers should make something using that stitch. Of course, we'd probably have to teach almost everybody how to do it." She looked at Adele again. "What do you think, dear?"

Adele squirmed and looked to me for help. I shrugged as an answer. CeeCee was busy looking at the pillow and around the room and didn't notice Adele's look of panic.

"I had no idea that Kelly was such a fine crocheter," CeeCee said. Adele had plastered herself against the back of the couch with the terrified expression as if any second CeeCee was going to make her prove she knew how to do the tricky stitch. CeeCee apparently had other things on her mind, because she didn't seem to notice that Adele had never answered her comment. She checked her watch.

"I have to get across the Valley to a meeting," she said moving toward the door. "Success has its drawbacks," she said in a feigned upset tone. "Everybody wants you in their project." She waved her hand toward the yard. "I'm surprised the *L.A. 911* people haven't asked me to do a guest spot."

When she was gone, Adele let out her breath. In panic mode she grabbed a hook. She made a foundation chain and the next thing I knew she was wrapping the yarn around the hook and then trying to pull the hook through it with no luck. I thought Adele was going to cry and did my best to console her as I pulled her out of the room and shut the door.

"Pink, you really are the best friend I've ever had," Adele said. She had lost her usual look of bravado and appeared vulnerable as she hugged me. But typical Adele, she was back to her usual self by the time we reached the living room and she made her way through the people standing around. I didn't see Dan anywhere.

I picked up some used dishes and carried them into the

kitchen. The window over the sink faced the driveway. Dan was standing there having an animated conversation with Nanci Silvers. Abruptly she put her arms around him and hugged him tight.

Not exactly the sign of a grieving husband.

CHAPTER 23

"YOU'RE DRINKING TEA WITH THE DETECTIVE every night now?" Mason said. "What happened to the idea that he was just a boarder? The whole ships passing in the kitchen thing." Mason didn't sound happy.

"It's nothing. We don't talk about anything personal." I noticed that there was suddenly a furrow of worry in Mason's brow. "Don't worry, he's not trying to start things up between us. From what I gather, Detective Heather has been a frequent visitor."

Mason's face relaxed and he laughed. "I'd like to see you call her that to her face."

"Not unless I want her to handcuff me and throw away the key." I brought up the little pizza party and how she'd been trying to relate to Jeffrey's drama friends.

"How'd that go?" he said.

"I don't think she could help it. You know how cops have that air of authority. That and she had a way of looking at them as if she thought they were all guilty of something. The topper was when I heard her call one of the girls 'ma'am' as she handed her a slice of pizza."

Apparently that image tickled Mason and he did a full belly laugh in response. He was good at seeing the humor in most things.

Mason had come in just as the bookstore was about to close to intercept me before I went home. He'd waited while I got my things and we'd headed down the street for dinner. Mason took my hand as we walked and said how nice it was to be just the two of us. But when I glanced toward him, his brows were furrowed in concern. He suggested we go to the Italian place down the street again. It was a Tarzana fixture and the fragrance of garlic and tomato sauce was comforting, even if Mason's demeanor wasn't.

Since it was late, the place was almost empty and we took a table by the window that looked out on Ventura Boulevard. The sidewalk was deserted and the street had only thin traffic. We ordered a Margherita pizza to share along with a Caesar salad.

"Okay, what is it?" I said when the waiter left after taking our order.

Mason smiled. "Am I that transparent?" He put his hand on mine. "Sunshine, I need to ask you a favor." I looked at him expectantly. "Would you come to Santa Barbara with me?"

"That's it?" I said. I hadn't meant to, but there was a squeak in my voice. Even though Mason and I had been more or less dating since the big break up with Barry, we hadn't spent a night together. There seemed to be one excuse after another—on my part, anyway. The plan, at least in my head, was to wait until Barry moved back home. But a trip out of town, even to Santa Barbara, which was only a little over an hour's drive, seemed to be pushing up the moment. Mason picked up on my hesitation.

"It's not what you're thinking. I have to go up there about the wedding and I'm afraid if I go alone with my wife, I might kill her." He sounded weary as the whole story came out.

"Jaimee heard about a hotel up there with a cancellation. After all that's gone on, I'm not committing to anything without seeing it. I certainly can't trust her to handle it, and she won't let me handle it alone." There was pleading in his eyes as he looked at me. "So, will you come?"

Mason had come through for me on numerous occasions and even though playing referee between him and his ex didn't sound very appealing, I agreed to go. Hmm, I noticed that he referred to her as his wife. I guess that was the thing with divorce, it didn't erase the relationship.

"Good," he said as relief spread over his face and the usual Mason came back. "And I promise there will be a stop at the McConnell's ice cream store," he added with a grin.

McConnell's of Santa Barbara was my ice cream of choice. The grocery stores that sold it locally only had the basic flavors, but the shop in Santa Barbara had a whole array of choices.

"You know my weak spot," I teased.

"It's the least I can do in exchange for keeping me from strangling Jaimee. With that out of the way, Mason leaned back in his chair and turned into the fun person I was used to.

Mason knew I'd gone to Kelly's funeral and asked if I'd found anything more about her murder.

"I saw some of the crochet pieces she was selling online, but I don't think they had anything to do with her death. I did see something strange outside though." I mentioned seeing Dan hugging the neighbor he told me he barely knew.

"So he is still the number one suspect?" Mason said.

The waiter dropped off our salads and I waited to answer. "Apparently for Detective Heather he is, even though she doesn't have any evidence and his hands were swabbed and there was no gunpowder residue on them or his clothes. And his gun hadn't been fired."

"Well, there are explanations for that. He could have worn gloves and he could have changed his clothes. As for the gun, maybe he had two. One to shoot her with and get rid of, and one that hadn't been fired to show the cops." Mason didn't say anything, but I had a feeling he knew that from past experience with a client. "Did anybody swab the neighbor's hands?"

"I don't think so and it's too late now."

We finished dinner and before we parted company, Mason mentioned the time frame of the trip to Santa Barbara. He certainly wasn't one to put things off. He wanted to go the next day.

Luckily, I had the next day off, so it was no problem. The following morning Mason picked me up and we made a fast stop at the bookstore café to get drinks for the road. I looked in to say hello to my bosses. They were busy rearranging a display, adding a sign that read "Serenity" over a table that featured candles with soothing scents, books on meditation, soothing teas and lavender sachets. Mr. Royal showed me a beaten up e-reader he said he'd found in front of the store when they opened. "I guess the shoplifter had a guilty conscience," he said. But apparently not about all the crochet pieces.

When I returned to Mason's black Mercedes, I set a cup

of estate-grown Kenyan coffee in the drink holder for him and a red eye for me. "I don't know what Jaimee drinks," I said with a shrug before pulling out a bottle of a premade sweetened coffee drink. "So I got her this so she won't feel left out."

Mason chuckled and shook his head as he steered the car onto the street. "Nice thought, but she probably won't drink it."

"Oh," I said sinking back into the soft leather seat.

Jaimee lived in a house in a gated community at the top of the mountains, along Mulholland Drive. According to Mason she counted a number of A-list celebrities as her neighbors. As we pulled in front of her huge house, a tan well-built man stood in the front door with one arm around Jaimee and the other holding a bag with a tennis racket sticking out. He was clearly a lot younger than she was.

Mason gave the guy a distasteful curl of his mouth. "That's Mark. You'd think she could be a little more original than getting involved with her tennis instructor."

The guy headed toward his silver sports car and Mason muttered something about how it figured he'd drive something like that and he wondered if it had been a gift from her. I took a sip of my red eye and wondered what I'd gotten myself into.

With her boy toy gone, Jaimee shut the front door and walked to the car. She pulled open the door on the passenger side and yelped in surprise when she saw me. As soon as she recovered she asked if I'd take the backseat because she had car sickness issues and could only sit in the front.

Mason touched my arm as I retrieved my coffee. "Sorry, sunshine, it must be something new." He rolled his eyes and sighed.

I offered the coffee drink to Jaimee as we headed down

the mountain toward the 101 Freeway. She turned and gave me an uncomfortable smile. "It has sugar," she said in a reproachful tone as if I'd just offered her a shot of poison.

We headed west on the freeway and the San Fernando Valley gave way to golden brown hills dotted with squat California oak trees. I looked out the window as we whizzed through Westlake, Thousand Oaks and went down the steep grade between jagged mountains toward Camarillo. Jaimee talked on, excited because she was being considered for a new reality show *The Housewives of Mulholland Drive*. I tuned it all out and took in the panoramic view of farmland and the shimmer of sun off the distant ocean.

By the time we'd gotten past the city of Ventura and were on the thread of highway between the Pacific Ocean and the green scrub-covered mountains, I understood why Mason had convinced me to come along. I wanted to kill Jaimee. It was the tone of her voice, the clack of her long manicured nails against the console and the way she kept insisting that they had to stop at some design studio to pick out something for Thursday's home. "I know you don't care," Jaimee said in her abrasive voice, "but they need to have a center to the room. Something unique that sets them apart and brings the room together."

No chuckles from Mason this time, except when he mentioned the proposed stop at McConnell's. You'd think he was proposing we stop for arsenic. Jaimee looked back over the front seat and gave me the once-over. I felt very self-conscious and tried to suck everything in. "You're going to eat ice cream?" she said making a tsk-tsk sound. "Mason, I guess your taste in women has changed."

I said nothing and took in the view of Santa Barbara from the window. The small city was draped over the hills at the base of the tall green Santa Ynez Mountains. The hills sloped down to a sparkling bay. I could see why people called it the "American Riviera."

Mason pulled off the highway and parked by the beach. I looked out at the water while the two of them headed across the street to the hotel they'd come to check out. It was a classic white stucco building with a red-tiled roof, surrounded by lush landscaping.

When they returned I could tell by their expressions that it hadn't gone well. The mood in the car was tense. Jaimee insisted if Mason had let her handle it, they would have been offered a better space. Mason looked like a pressure cooker about to explode.

"How about we go for that ice cream," I said, hoping to lighten the mood. Mason pulled away from the curb and headed into the city. We parked in front of a cat hotel.

While Mason and I crossed the street to the small ice cream store, Jaimee went in the other direction to a health food emporium and said she was getting a shot of wheat grass juice. Mason and I surveyed the ice cream offerings. To make up for everything, he insisted I get two scoops and I chose strawberry cheesecake and he got Vermont blueberry. We took our ice cream and sat at one of the wire tables outside.

"I'm sorry for her and thank you again for coming," he said. "You said you wanted to be included in my family," he joked. I took a spoonful of the ice cream and at last savored the creamy flavor. There were just inches between our arms and I moved mine against his and leaned my head on his shoulder.

"At least I understand why you got a divorce," I said. He settled his free arm around my shoulder.

"Who knew all those years I was so busy working what she was really like." He paused. "Or maybe she became this way." He shook his head and grumbled about the situation of the wedding. "We've got two hundred people and still no place to put them."

"Would it be so hard to make it two hundred and one?" I said. I hadn't meant to, but it slipped out.

Mason hung his head. "You really want to come?"

"If Samuel was getting married, I'd invite you. It makes me feel like I'm in the shadows of your life," I said. Jaimee showed up at that moment with a tiny cup of bright green liquid and the conversation ended. I caught the scent of her drink and it reminded me of newly mown grass.

"Cheers," she said lifting the cup as she gave our ice cream a disgusted look, and then she chugged it.

We made another stop at a hotel under renovation. They said they could do it outside, but the Amtrak tracks ran right through the property. "So it's not a wasted trip, let's go to that design studio," Jaimee said as we walked back to the car.

We drove up State Street, which was the main drag in town. It was lined with attractive stores and eateries, and was crowded with people. Jaimee directed Mason to turn on a side street and park. I think Jaimee was hoping I'd stay in the car, but I followed them into a low building around a courtyard filled with plants and a fountain. The moisture in the air here mixed with the sunlight and gave it an iridescent sheen.

I was surprised to see the proprietor of the design studio was a familiar figure. "Rexford Thomasville," I muttered recognizing Kelly and Stone's father.

"How do you know him?" Jaimee snapped.

"Allow me," Mason said with a grin. "Molly is investigating the murder of his daughter." Jaimee flashed a surprised expression and suggested I keep my Nancy Drew act on hold. "We're here to shop, not play detective. I want to get a good piece from him, not antagonize him." She waved her hand toward the courtyard. "Why don't you go wait outside."

I'd had enough being pushed aside by her. The day was almost over and by now I didn't care if Mason killed her or not. I might have even helped. "No way am I turning down a chance like this."

Jaimee's mouth fell open and she turned to Mason and said, "Do something before she makes a scene." Mason shrugged and chuckled and, with a brush of his hand, urged me on.

Jaimee got in front of me and reached the proprietor first. She threw her arms around the gray-haired man and said how good it was to see him again and that she needed the perfect focal spot for her soon-to-be married daughter's home. I noticed his wife in an office and Jaimee gave me a shove in her direction saying, "Why don't you talk to her." Then she started in on Rexford, letting him know he was dealing with a soon to be member of *The Housewives of Mulholland Drive* show.

I didn't take Jaimee's suggestion and while she monopolized Rexford's attention, I tried to remember what I knew about him. He had only made an appearance at Kelly's funeral and no one had said much about him. All I could remember was what the prop guy had said, that Rexford Thomasville had been a set director before opening this place. I got why they called it a studio instead of a store. There weren't price tags on anything and the idea was that people shopping here weren't looking for a bargain.

I surveyed the room and quickly figured out that the theme here was unique. A suit of armor stood guard just inside the door. A gazelle head, which I hoped was just an artist's rendition, hung from the wall. Below it, a wooden horse displayed a bar setup on a trapdoor on its side. A graceful purple velvet divan was covered with pillows made out of old fabric. The walls were decorated with interesting pieces. There were collages made using old jewelry and coins, along with framed stamp collections. There were tall cabinets made out of interesting old doors. Lots of unusual lamps and something I particularly liked—a tree trunk that had been sandblasted smooth and turned into a coat-rack.

Rexford glanced in my direction several times while Jaimee went on describing what she was looking for. Basically it was something everyone would notice and wish they owned.

When she'd finished, he pointed out some items and then left her to look around on her own. He approached me. "Do I know you?"

I explained who I was and that I'd been at Kelly's funeral and his face lit with recognition. The small sad smile was enough to bring out his dimples and I could see both Kelly's and Stone's face in his. I mentioned that I was a bit of an amateur sleuth and had been investigating Kelly's death.

"I'm glad somebody is," he said with annoyance. "I don't understand why they haven't charged her husband."

I explained that the evidence they had against him wasn't very good and that they were probably hoping he'd have a guilty conscience and it would get him to confess. "And there is the possibility he didn't do it," I said.

Rexford's mouth gathered in disapproval. "What are the chances of that? Is anybody going to believe that story of his that it was some kind of robbery?"

I asked about Kelly's ex-husband.

"I thought about him myself. I don't think there was any problems between them, and he was at Disneyland with her kids that day."

I asked him if he'd been close to Kelly. I was surprised when he glared at me.

"Did Stone say something to you? I tried to mend fences with him, but all he seemed to care about was investing in the energy drink business. I hope it works out for him. I tried to give him some advice." He sighed. "But I guess it's a little too late for that." He looked at me directly. "I wasn't the best father or husband." He ran his hand along the wood trim on the purple divan. "I tried to smooth things over with my ex, too, but we just had a few minutes at the funeral. She lives on the East Coast now."

Out of the corner of my eye, I could see Jaimee standing near us with her arms crossed. She was actually tapping her foot with impatience. She snagged Mason away from checking his BlackBerry and ordered him to do something because they were real customers. Mason suggested she keep looking around on her own.

Rexford seemed unaware of what was going on around him. I gathered all this had been playing on his mind and he wanted to vent his feelings.

"It's not as though I didn't try. When Kelly got in touch with me and said she wanted to be in the business, I got her a production assistant job on a show I was working on. I helped Stone get a job, too." He shook his head with regret. "I thought Kelly would know on her own that it was a no-no to get involved with the talent. She didn't get that she was expendable, and as soon as North Adams was finished with their fling, she was gone."

"North Adams?" I repeated. "She had a relationship with him?" Rexford seemed surprised by my reaction and before

I had a chance to explain, Jaimee took the situation in her own hands and simply interrupted by walking in front of me. She pointed toward several items and wanted him to tell her about them. "The story is everything," she said to him as she physically took his hand and led him away from me.

I barely noticed; all I could think about was that North Adams had known Kelly and never said a word.

CHAPTER 24

"I've got another suspect. You have to tell Heather to check him out," I said as I rushed into the room. I was intent on grabbing my jacket since Mason was waiting for me outside in the car, but when I saw Barry I couldn't resist blurting out my new finding. Barry was sitting in the den watching some sports game and it took a moment for what I'd said to register. He turned down the volume and asked me to repeat myself.

"Heather has to talk to North Adams." I told him how all along Adams had known Kelly. "Isn't it suspicious that Adams never admitted to knowing her?"

Barry put his hand up. "Do you think Heather is really going to go after some A-list actor on your say-so? Molly, she's got her person of interest."

"Fine, I'll just have to take care of it myself." I started to leave the room and saw that Barry was right behind me.

"Where were you?" he said. "I stopped by the bookstore—Jeffrey needed something," he added a little too quickly. "No one seemed to know where you were."

I hesitated. We were just ships passing in the kitchen or in this case the den and I didn't need to explain to Barry, but then I didn't need to keep it from him, either. "I was in Santa Barbara with Mason." I moved down the hall toward my closet with Barry on my tail. I noticed there was just the slightest hint of a limp. Was it real or for sympathy? "I just stopped home to get a jacket. Mason's waiting for me outside. We're going to grab a bite."

"Then you don't have time for tea now? Maybe later," he said expectantly.

"No. And you better not wait for me. I'm not sure when I'll be back," I said. I couldn't believe it, but as soon as the words were out of my mouth Barry's blank cop face crumbled.

"I hate working regular hours," he grumbled as he went back to the TV.

Once I got back outside, Mason leaned over and opened the passenger door. The hot day had turned into a cool evening and I was glad to have the cotton shawl to wrap around my shoulders. After the day with Jaimee, both of us needed some peace. A noisy restaurant didn't sound appealing. As usual, Mason had come up with a perfect solution. Le Grande Fromage had been closing up for the night and we'd gotten the last croissants, some slices of cheese, fruit salad and their trademark chopped lettuce salad. Mason had picked out some bottled drinks from their cooler and we'd gotten utensils and plenty of napkins.

"Who said you can only have picnics during the day?" Mason said. He turned onto Reseda toward the mountains.

A short drive later he pulled into the empty parking lot for the Marvin Braude Mulholland Gateway Park. Mason had picked up a couple of lawn chairs and a small table from his house and he unloaded them and set them up. I brought out the food and drinks. Behind us the Santa Monica Mountains loomed in the darkness and a panoramic view of the twinkling lights of the San Fernando Valley spread before us. In the far distance the massive San Gabriel Mountains marked the end of the open area.

Jaimee hadn't been happy with either of us by the time we dropped her off. They still didn't have a location for Thursday's wedding and they hadn't been able to agree on anything at Rexford's studio as a gift. Mason had voted for the suit of armor and Jaimee wanted to get an armoire using a door from a monastery. She was irritated at me for just being there.

Mason held up his bottle of soda to make a toast. "To the end of an exhausting day."

A breeze glided along the ground with a hint of ocean. It was amazing how the wind could wind its way through the mountains and surprise you with some cool damp air. The crickets chirped and a distant cry of a coyote reminded us we were in the wild. Mason tapped me and pointed up. Something with a big wing span sailed above us.

"An owl," Mason said. It was soundless as it landed on a tree, waiting for its dinner to show up.

All the kinks of the day began to unravel as we ate and enjoyed the view.

"Did you see the detective when you stopped home?" Mason asked. I told him about Barry's reaction to telling Detective Heather about North Adams.

"I was hoping she'd take over," I said. Mason nodded. He

knew why. North Adams was represented by my son. Peter would have a fit if he thought I was harassing his client. I was afraid he'd rather a murderer go free than upset such a big moneymaker for the talent agency.

For a moment there was silence and Mason turned toward me, appearing uncomfortable. "I'm sorry, sunshine, but I can't help you with Adams. He's a client of the law firm and I don't think the partners would be too happy if I was investigating him."

I told Mason I understood.

"What are you going to do?" Mason asked.

"I'll think of something," I said and Mason chuckled.

"I figured you would say that."

THE NEXT AFTERNOON, DINAH AND I MET IN THE yarn department of the bookstore. It wasn't an organized meeting time for the Hookers. It was our personal meet up to talk and work on our projects for the street fair booth. I had already told her about North and my dilemma and we'd come up with a plan.

I had hoped that Adele would be there and she didn't disappoint. Lately, it seemed she was always hunched in the corner, working on perfecting the bullion stitch.

Beyond us the bookstore was slow, and I assumed the production company people were all busy working. Even the café was quiet, and I hadn't had to wait for my red eye.

I asked Adele how it was going. She moved her arm so I could see her work. She was still struggling to get her hook through the multiwraps of yarn. "You can't tell anyone how much trouble I'm having with this stitch. I'm supposed to be the expert, the go-to person for anything crochet." She dropped her work in disgust. Then she pulled out a bright orange cowl and began working on it. Crocheting something she could handle easily made a huge difference in her demeanor.

"So how's your investigation going?" I asked. I was surprised to see Adele's expression falter.

"Eric thinks I shouldn't pursue being a sleuth. He says one coplike person in a couple is enough."

"What do you think about it?" Dinah said. "I have never thought of you as being a give-in-to-your-man type."

Adele sat a little straighter. "You know that's what I was thinking." She turned to me. "You're lucky, nobody cares what you do. I guess that's how it goes when you don't have a boyfriend in law enforcement."

"Do you ever think about what you're saying?" Dinah asked. Adele gave Dinah a blank look.

"Did I say something wrong?" Adele looked at Dinah, waiting for an answer. Dinah did her best to explain tact and thinking about how other people might have interpreted what Adele said. Adele listened but didn't seem to understand. She turned back to me. "So, Pink, what's up with your investigating?"

"I don't think I should tell you about it since you're stepping down. I wouldn't want to get you in trouble with Eric." Adele fell for it and begged me to tell her what was up. Finally I told her what I'd found out about North Adams, and my dilemma.

"No problem for *moi*," she said pointing at herself in a theatrical manner. "I don't have any connection to North to mess up." She knit her brows and jiggled her head as if she was having an inner conversation. "I don't care what Eric said. I have to take over—in the name of justice."

I was hoping she'd say something like that. "All you'd have to do is question him, but make it seem like you're just talking to him," I said.

"I know what to do, Pink. I have my ways to get a man to talk." She waved her hands in a way I think was meant to demonstrate a flirtatious move, but it came off like she was doing some kind of weird hand dance. I rolled my eyes. What choice did I have?

Dinah had taken out some soft pink organic cotton yarn. Despite Adele's efforts to get everyone to make cowls for the sale, Dinah was sticking to washcloths and making them in all different patterns. In the end, she was going to wrap each one around a small bar of scented soap and tie it with a lavender flower.

I had brought out the off-white cowl I kept there and started to work on it.

Adele was happily working on her cowl now and I had to nudge her to get her to tell me her plan.

"I don't know why you want to talk to him. Why not take some kind of action?" she said.

"All you have to do is ask him if it's true that he and Kelly had an affair. If he says no, you tell him you have it on good authority that they did and then ask him why he's not admitting he knows her," I said.

Adele snorted. "I don't need you to tell me what to say, or do. They're doing a night shoot tomorrow. I'll just go hang out with Eric and then say I want to watch. He doesn't mind because, unlike some people, I've never made a scene. Then when there's a break in shooting, I'll move in on North." The plan was, as soon as she talked to North, she'd come to Dinah's and fill us in, and we'd decide how to proceed.

Her last words were, "So I should stay out of the crime

fighting business, huh? I don't think so." She picked up her things and went to the children's department.

"I never thought I'd be grateful for Adele's help," I said to Dinah.

"Maybe you better wait until it's mission accomplished before you speak," Dinah said, giving me a knowing nod.

CHAPTER 25

BEFORE ADELE COULD DO HER DETECTIVE WORK, we had to take care of some Hookers' stuff. CeeCee had called a meeting at her house the next evening. The plan was we'd all look over what we'd accumulated for the street fair. "This way, if everyone can see what we have, then I don't have to be the bad guy all the time, telling the rest of you we don't have enough things," CeeCee told everybody when she gave them the details. Due to everybody's busy schedules the only time we could meet was at dinner hour. And Dinah and I, nice folks that we are, had volunteered to bring dinner for everyone. At CeeCee's request, I'd promised to bring a pan of my "Mac, Cheese and More."

Dinah helped me shop and cook, and after leaving the extra mac and cheese for Barry and Jeffrey, we headed over to CeeCee's. She hailed our arrival with great excitement. CeeCee might not cook, but she loved to eat. She sniffed the casserole dish of macaroni and cheese as I carried it in the kitchen. I popped the pan in the oven while I poured the dressing on the salad I'd brought, too. It hadn't inspired the same excitement from CeeCee.

"Thank heavens," Rhoda said. She held up a glass of water. "This was all CeeCee could manage."

Sheila nodded with approval at the food scents and said something about being so busy at Luxe she hadn't had lunch. She put down the cowl she was working on and started to help clear the table of yarn and crochet tools. Elise seemed off in dreamland as she added a red tassel to the vampire cowl she'd made. Adele rolled her eyes at the black-and-white stripes done in half double crochet, which Elise insisted resembled fangs. Eduardo let out a tired sigh as he set down the white thread cowl he was making. He'd added an Irish crochet flower motif as decoration. Between all of this, Adele kept giving me knowing looks and dropping little hints like the mission was a go. I was so close to telling her to forget it, but I knew that even if I did, she'd go ahead with her plan anyway.

Adele wasn't happy with the cowls everyone was making. She thought they ought to be all the same design, but done in different colors. CeeCee cut in and said at this point, she was just glad everybody was making something. After dinner she brought out the collection box and it did still look a little thin. "What happened to Kelly's pieces, again?" CeeCee said. Dinah, Adele and I all started to talk at once, reminding her the shoplifter hooligans had taken them.

"It was just vandalism," I said with disgust. "They probably threw all the stuff in a trash can somewhere. After all, the e-reader turned up again. They were really just out for the thrill, not the actual goods."

CeeCee asked what we were going to do about packing up the items we sold. Dinah said Commander agreed to donate small shopping bags with stickers that said Tarzana Hookers on them.

"I love it," CeeCee said and wanted to know when she could see them. I explained we still had to pick them up.

The meeting ended quickly, mostly because Adele kept saying there was something important she had to do. Adele, Dinah and I walked out last. As soon as we were outside, Adele pulled off the pink fuzzy vest she'd been wearing and I saw she was dressed in all black. She pulled out a black hat and put it on. Somehow Adele had confused the detective look with a ninja look. She pointed her foot, displaying her black cloth shoes and demonstrated a few karate kicks.

"Wish me luck," she said as she got into her Matrix and headed to the location.

An hour later, when Adele hadn't shown up, I couldn't help myself. I started pacing across Dinah's living room. What was taking Adele so long? Even though she'd objected, I'd coached her on what to say. All she really had to do, was start talking with North about Kelly and say she knew about their thing. And then ask why he hadn't mentioned it to anybody. If she got the kind of reaction I thought she would, I was going to find a way to tell Detective Heather.

At last we heard footsteps coming toward the house and then someone rushing up the front stairs, followed by pounding on the door.

I was at the door before Dinah could even get out of her chair. "Well?" I said as I pulled it open. When I looked at Adele, I sucked in my breath so fast I almost choked on it. She was holding a gun on a chopstick.

The "Well?" turned into a "What?"

"Shut the door, shut the door," Adele said as she rushed inside. Dinah had joined me at the doorway by now and we both stood back giving Adele wide berth with the gun. She looked around the room hurriedly and finally deposited the gun on the coffee table with a loud clatter. I held my breath afraid it would go off, but thankfully it didn't.

Adele threw herself into the new chair Dinah had recently added. It was leather on a wood frame and had a slight capacity to rock. Adele made it rock for all it was worth, while fluttering her eyes and fanning herself with her hand.

"What happened?" I demanded. "What did you do this time?"

Adele sat forward and leveled her eyes at me. "I took care of things for you, Pink. The sign of a good freelance detective is that you improvise. I didn't need that silly average Joe Shmoe book to figure that out."

Adele knew she had the spotlight and she was going to milk it for all it was worth. She made a pretense of removing her hat and smoothing her hair and adjusting her clothes as she prepared to speak.

"I did just as I said I would. I hung out with Eric for a few minutes and then said I was curious about the scene they were shooting. He had to stay at his post because the crew was wetting down the street." Adele's tone changed as she explained they did that to add more contrast to the shot. I waved my hand impatiently at her to get back to the story.

"I just thought you two would like a little inside info," she said disgruntled at our disinterest. "I waited until they broke for a few minutes and then I went up to North. Of course, by now he knows me," she said with an air of self-importance we had all come to know and be annoyed by. "I put what you said to ask him into my own words. Something along the lines of how old was Kelly when you started the affair with her?" Adele seemed proud of her word choice and explained she didn't give him the option of denying it and it implied that maybe she was underage. "I thought that would shake him up." She just looked at us for a moment.

The silence hung in the air and I couldn't take it anymore. "Well, did it? What did he say? Just get on with the story without all the theatrical pauses," I said, wishing I'd never gotten her involved.

"Pink, this is where you miss the boat. It's not the story so much as how you tell it. I could just dump the facts on you and it would be pretty blah. But by throwing in a little suspense, it's much better." She actually nodded at us as if she was expecting us to agree. Dinah and I both jumped on her and said we didn't care about the story quality, we just wanted the facts, and now.

"You two are no fun." Adele took a mirror out of her pocket and checked her makeup. "Would you believe that he just looked at me and said he didn't know what I was talking about. He claimed he didn't know who Kelly was. I pointed toward her house and said she was the woman who'd been shot. You better believe I left a long silence after I said that. And I gave him my best knowing look." Adele gave us a re-creation of the moment and like everything else, it was over the top and looked comical instead of intimidating. She started to do the pause again, but Dinah's and my expression kept her going forward. North had continued to deny knowing what Adele was talking about.

"I told you I was more about action," she said. "Your idea of talking to him was getting nowhere. I remembered that the gun that killed Kelly still hadn't been found. I started thinking where I'd hide a gun if I was him and had just shot Kelly." Adele started to do another of her dramatic pauses, but our glares got her to stop playing storyteller and get to the point.

"If it was me and I had one of those nice RV dressing

rooms all to myself, that's where I'd put it. Everybody was busy on set and I remembered that Eric had been complaining that the locks on the trailers could be opened with a plastic card." Adele pulled out a plastic card from her pocket. It was the kind they used for hotel keys these days. She held it like a saw and demonstrated how she'd pushed it back and forth and it had freed the lock. She shook her head with disbelief. "It wasn't even hidden that well, but then as long as they're filming here, nobody would go in there, but North, so I guess he felt safe." She looked at the gun on the table. "So, I took care of it for you, Pink. I got the murder weapon. I didn't touch it, so the prints are all intact. It's up to you to get it to the cops."

"Why didn't you just give it to Eric?" I said. "He was right there and he is a cop."

Adele hung her head and all her bravado disappeared. She didn't want to talk, but I repeated the question. "I told you cutchykins said he thought one crime fighter in a couple was enough. He said he didn't want me sleuthing anymore. Besides which, I kind of broke in to the trailer." She didn't have to say more, we got it.

The three of us sat looking at the gun. "Adele, you got it from his trailer? Sorry to deflate your balloon, but it's got to be a prop gun." I explained what Barry had said about fake guns having an orange plug on the front. Adele got a stormy expression on her face as the three of us looked at the barrel of the gun. But then her face broke out into a triumphant smile. There was nothing orange or otherwise on the barrel of the gun.

Adele started doing a happy dance and singing her own praises as a superdetective.

Dinah and I continued to look at the gun, realizing it might very well be the murder weapon. "It has to have his fingerprints and they can match it up to the bullet casings," I said. "We did it. We found the evidence to solve the case."

"We?" Adele said getting back to her usual self-importance.

"Okay, you did, but it was a group plan," I said.

"Now, what?" Dinah said. "It's great that we have the evidence, but we can't do anything with it."

"I have an idea," I said.

CHAPTER 26

NEITHER DINAH NOR I KNEW ANYTHING ABOUT guns, and even though Adele claimed to be good at the shooting galleries in amusement parks, she was clueless about the real thing. Since we had no way of telling if it was loaded, no one wanted to touch it. Carrying it with the chopstick seemed a little risky because the chopstick was one of those disposable kinds you get at the grocery store and seemed like it might break at any moment.

"The Pinchy-Winchy might work," I said. Dinah had borrowed the device to pick up some icky stuff in the corner of her garage and still had it. She went off to fetch it.

I had thought of calling Detective Heather, but nixed the idea. Instead of thinking we'd helped her, she might consider our having the gun as tampering with evidence.

"This ought to be better than the chopstick," I said when Dinah returned with the Pinchy-Winchy. I positioned the open claw over the trigger guard and let the claw hand shut.

Carefully, carefully I lifted the Pinchy-Winchy and the gun dangled from it as I held my arms out so that the gun was as far away from me as possible. Slowly, the three of us headed for the greenmobile. Nobody wanted to take over holding the gun, so I got in the backseat and Dinah drove. Adele had gone from freelance detective to CSI expert and kept looking back to make sure I was dangling the gun, so it wouldn't hit the seat and smudge the prints.

By the time we pulled into my driveway, I was sweating. Dinah and Adele got out first and then I slid out holding the Pinchy-Winchy in front of me with the claw gripping the gun. Dinah led the way to the house, opening the gate to the backyard and then the kitchen door. Adele took up the rear.

"Barry," I called loudly as soon as I was in the door. I yelled his name again, and said I needed him. I heard footsteps and then he was in the kitchen. He started to take in the scene, but his eye went right to the gun. I guess even though it was hanging upside down, it looked like it was pointed at him and his face went pale.

I realized he was having an automatic reaction that stemmed from his incident with the shoplifter so I quickly moved the Pinchy-Winchy so the gun wasn't pointing at him anymore. Before I could explain, Adele stepped in. "I found the gun that killed Kelly Donahue."

"I thought you'd know what to do with it," I said. Barry's color had returned and while shaking his head with disbelief, he told me to lay the gun carefully on the floor.

While he moved closer and crouched next to it, Adele poured out her story of how she'd figured it all out and then checked North's trailer, not mentioning that she'd broken in.

Barry sat back on his heels and asked me to hand him a

knife. He used it to pick up the gun without touching it as he continued to examine it. The head shaking started again and this time it was accompanied by a laugh.

"North Adams might have killed Kelly, but he didn't do it with this. Sorry ladies, but this isn't the murder weapon. This is Jake Blake's gun from the show."

"What?" I said. "I thought you told me fake guns always had an orange plug in them. And how do you know what Jake Blake's gun looks like?" I said. Barry suddenly appeared sheepish.

"Okay, I admit it. I watch *L.A. 911*." He looked up at the three of us. "Just to see what they get wrong—which is just about everything." Barry pointed out the gun was a .357 Magnum six-inch barrel. "Everybody knows his initials are engraved on the handle," he said, showing us the engraved *JB*. "I said fake guns have a plug in them, but they can't very well film them with a bright orange thing on the end."

He got a bamboo skewer from the kitchen and poked it inside the gun barrel. When he pulled it out, an orange plastic plug was hanging off of it. He stared at the three of us. We got more head shakes. And then Barry's gaze rested on me. "How do you manage to get in so much trouble?" I was relieved to see he said it with a smile. "I'm going to miss all the comic relief." He looked at the gun still lying on the floor with the red and yellow handled Pinchy-Winchy next to it. "I hope you have a plan for getting it back where it belongs." He started to leave the room. "Don't worry. I didn't see anything."

I didn't want my fingerprints on the prop gun, so I picked it up with a pencil and dropped it in a plastic bag. Adele was already backing toward the door. "I can't go back there." It wasn't until she was outside in the yard that she realized her car was parked back by Dinah's house and she couldn't make a hasty exit.

"Cutchykins can't know I had anything to do with this," Adele said with a worried tone. "I'm not giving up my detective career, no matter what he says, but he can't know about this."

I drove us back to Dinah's and as soon as I pulled in front of her house, Adele had the door open. She started to walk toward her Matrix, but then stopped and appeared to have a soul-searching moment before she turned back and rejoined us. "I can't bail on you. We're the three musketeers."

As we looked down the dark street, we could see the night filming was still going on. It was hard to miss the tall crane with the bright light illuminating the area. I imagined Nanci Silvers grumbling in her house since the light probably was shining in her back windows as well. Eric was sitting atop his motorcycle facing away from us.

Adele had a plan. I didn't really trust her plans, but we had limited time and she was the one who knew the lay of things and where exactly the gun had come from. It seemed that while Eric was guarding the north end of the street, no one was really watching the south end. We walked around the block past the Donahue house and Nanci Silvers' and came around the other way. Just as Adele had said, it was all quiet on that end of the production. North's trailer was parked away from the action in front of the middle school.

"This should be easy," I whispered as we looked ahead toward the luxury RV dressing room. Adele pushed the plastic card toward me.

"I can't go back in there," she said sounding panicky. "If anything happens and I get caught, I'll lose cutchykins."

"Well, I can't go in there," I said. "If anything happens and I get caught, my son will lose a big client."

Dinah grabbed the plastic card. "I'll do it," she said, wrapping her long scarf around her neck several times so it wouldn't trail her. Adele gave her the details of how to open the door and where to put the gun and I handed my friend the plastic bag. Adele and I went back into the shadows and Dinah slipped quickly toward the door. I could barely make out her figure as she worked on the door. Then the shiny metal caught the reflection of a streetlamp as the door opened and closed.

I could feel my fast pulse throbbing in my neck and my mouth went dry. I kept my eye trained on the door, waiting for it to open and for Dinah to come out. Seconds turned to minutes and still the door stayed shut. Something was wrong.

"You can't leave," I said in a loud whisper. Adele had come out of the shadows and was looking down the street toward the filming zone. The lights were still illuminating the area, but the way everyone was milling around, it was obvious they were taking some kind of break. A catering truck had pulled up to the curb and was dispensing food. "Dinah has been in North's trailer too long. We have to do something."

"Not me." She edged away, but I grabbed her arm.

"You just stay put and keep your eyes open, if somebody comes down this way, stop them. I don't care what you have to do," I said. She groaned with unhappiness, but followed my order.

"Pink, what are you going to do?"

"I don't know, but I'm not going to leave her in there." I started walking toward the trailer. I couldn't worry about Peter and his client. Whatever happened happened, even if he never spoke to me again. I had to help Dinah.

I used a plastic coffee card to unlock the door and opened it slowly. It was dark inside. I stepped in and pulled the door behind me without making a sound. I heard Dinah making psst sounds, then her hand grabbed my ankle. She was sitting under a table, still holding the plastic bag. I got on my knees next to her.

"What's—" Dinah's hand clamped over my mouth as she used the other to point toward the back. I could see a line of light coming from underneath a door and there was noise coming from inside. I took the plastic bag and pointed her toward the exit. I stood up and dumped the gun on the first surface I felt. Dinah was already out of the RV and I was about to follow when the door in the back opened and I was caught in a flood of light. North was standing wrapped in a towel.

"Hey there, stop," he said as I tried to make a run for it. Here goes nothing, I thought turning back toward him. What could I possibly say? I opened my mouth, hoping something smart would come out.

North didn't seem the slightest concerned that he was standing there almost naked. He looked me over and smiled. "I had a break and I thought I'd take a shower and freshen up," he said gesturing toward the towel. He lowered his lids into his smoldering-eyes look and added a sexy smile. "I knew you had the hots for me. I knew it that first time you gave me the ride." He pointed toward himself. "North is never wrong about women. Though I have to say, most women your age—well, they're past sneaking in trailers. But no problem." He gestured toward the couch.

Was he really talking about himself in the third person? I smiled demurely as I backed away. "You're right. That's it. I'm here because I think you're so hot. But I really can't stay. I shouldn't have come. It's so wrong." I was babbling now as I moved closer and closer to the exit. He followed me and urged me to stay, but I was out of there in a flash.

Dinah and Adele were waiting for me and the three of us clasped hands and ran back the way we'd come. We were laughing and talking, all a product of our nerves. By the time we were passing the Donahue house, I had a pain in my side and we stopped to catch our breath. We just missed getting hit by a car pulling into the driveway. Dinah pulled Adele and me into the shadows as Dan got out of the driver's side. He opened the trunk and took out a box. I was going to say something to him, but instead of walking toward his house, he headed for Nanci Silvers'.

The three of us watched as she opened the door and he went inside.

What was that about?

CHAPTER 27

WHEN I FINALLY CHECKED MY BLACKBERRY, THERE were a bunch of messages from Mason. Needless to say I was pretty wired after all the business with the gun and then the run-in with North in his trailer. I was pretty sure having North think I was some kind of aging groupie wouldn't cause him to fire my son as his agent. At least I hoped so.

All it took was a call to Mason and he was ready to help me unwind. "I was just going for a late-night swim. It sounds like just what you need," he said.

It sounded perfect and I agreed. He was waiting with his front door open as soon as I pulled in front of his house and greeted me with a warm hug. "I'm so glad to see you." He was already wearing his red trunks. "But we could always go skinny-dipping," he joked, well, sort of joked. Maybe there was some wishful thinking going on.

I changed into the bathing suit I kept at his house and we went out into the dark yard. Spike looked at us like we were nuts and climbed up on the leather couch and went to sleep. Mason's backyard was dotted with little lights and was magical at night. The water was warm from the sun and felt refreshing as we slipped in. For a few minutes we swam back and forth and then hung by the side talking.

I began to tell Mason about my evening. He started laughing when he heard the story about the gun. "I wish I could have seen the detective's face when you walked in holding the gun with the Pinchy-Winchy. I hope he at least cracked a smile. He's usually so serious."

"Don't worry, he laughed," I said. "He seems to be loosening up a bit. I think the whole experience of being shot and being off work has affected him. He never would have sat outside drinking tea and talking before. Or if he had, he would have gotten a call in the middle and had to leave."

"Don't get your hopes up, it's probably not permanent," Mason said.

"I wasn't thinking about that. We're done. Once he moves back home, I'll probably never see him. If nothing else, Detective Heather will make sure of that."

"I'm glad to hear it," Mason said with a little shiver. "Let's move over to the whirlpool." He helped me out of the pool and we walked over to the tub of churning hot water. It was surrounded by jasmine and gardenia plants and the air was filled with fragrance. I noticed that Mason had started rubbing his temple and I asked if he had a headache.

"Yes, and her name is Jaimee," he said. He climbed into the tub and helped me in. "We're running out of time. We still don't have a location for the wedding. She is impossible. Pretty soon, it will end up being a weenie roast at the beach." He looked at me with a tired smile. "I'd rather hear about your sleuthing."

I finished the story about the gun and Mason got a good laugh about the episode in North's trailer.

"Maybe the gun wasn't the murder weapon, but he's still lying. Why wouldn't he admit to knowing Kelly?" I said.

"Just a guess, but it sounds to me as if he's trying to keep himself from being a suspect. If he doesn't admit to knowing her, how can he be accused of killing her," Mason offered.

"Barry's right. Detective Heather would never check out North based on anything I said. Besides, she still only has eyes for Dan. She ought to check out Nanci's house. Maybe the murder weapon is there."

"You should tell her," Mason said.

"Right," I said with a laugh. I told him it looked like there was trouble in cutchykins land because Adele's motor cop boyfriend didn't want her playing detective. "Good luck on that one, Eric," I said with a knowing shrug. "Nobody tells Adele what she can't do. I know that firsthand."

"I love hearing about your life." Mason grinned and then pulled his hand out of the water. "I don't know about you, but I'm turning into a human prune." We got out of the water, went inside and changed back into our clothes.

"Since you seem to like tea so much," Mason said when I came back into his den. He gestured toward the elaborate tea setup he had put out. No tea bags for him or grocery store tea. Instead, a cast-iron pot brewing a special oolong tea sat over a warming candle. There were handleless cups from Japan and a plate of bakery cookies. When the tea was brewed, he poured us each a cup and we sat together on the couch.

There was a certain amount of tension, for me, at least, as we sat next to each other. We were two consenting adults, both free and clear, but still something was holding me back from giving myself fully to our togetherness. There was nothing like a little crochet to get past a nervous moment. I rummaged around in the tote bag I was still using for a carryall and pulled out a hook. I went back in for something to use with the hook and a plastic bag stuck to my hand. I recognized it as the bag Adele had pushed on me when she found it in the bin of Kelly's crochet pieces. I noticed there was a small ball of yarn in the bag and went to take it out. There were some folded sheets of paper that came out with it. I gathered them up, unfolding them as I did. Several of the papers were from a yellow legal pad and had some notes and diagrams on them. Another piece of paper floated free. I laid it on my lap and recognized what it was right away. I had one just like it. It was an invoice for a storage locker. A small plastic bag with a key inside was stapled to the back.

I showed it to Mason and explained what it was. "I wonder why Kelly had a storage locker?" I said.

"Probably for the same reason you do," he said.

"I got mine when Barry moved in and I had to clear out the space."

"Right," Mason said. "She probably had stuff she didn't have room for in her house." I pointed out that both the locker number and the key were there.

"Are you saying you want to see what's in it?"

"She did give the bin this was in to us. So, it isn't like it would be breaking in or anything."

"Do you want to go now, tonight?" Mason said.

"There's twenty-four hour access."

"Sure. Let's go. I've missed not being part of your investigation," Mason said, looking enthused. "It's certainly more fun than finding wedding locations for Jaimee to nix."

Mason took Ventura Boulevard instead of the freeway. We had the street to ourselves as we passed closed businesses and dark apartments. It seemed like the whole Valley

was set on mute. Mason pulled his black Mercedes into the
parking lot of the storage place. I was glad that he parked
far away from the only other car in the parking lot. Could it
belong to someone living in one of the units?

Basically, there were four rows of low buildings with
identical blue garage-type pull-up doors. There were lights
on the end of each building, which made for lots of shadows,
but not much help in seeing. I regretted not having a flashlight. Mason had a small one on his key chain.

The buildings all looked the same and we finally realized
there was a sign on the end of each with the locker numbers on it. We found the row hers was in and went down
the wide walkway between the buildings. There were lots of
dark shadows and I was glad I hadn't come there alone.

Mason pointed the tiny pool of light from his flashlight
at each of the numbers next to the metal roll-up doors.
"Here it is," I said pointing to one in the middle of the row.
I had him put the light on the padlock. The light caught on
a spot of reflective paint as I felt for the key.

"Well, this is it." I put the key in the lock and when it
came free, Mason lifted the door. The only light source we
had was his small flashlight and little ambient light from the
fixture at the end of the row. It smelled a little musty as we
stepped inside and a herd of large black shiny bugs skittered
through the light beam.

Mason flashed the small light around the inside of the
locker. There were some odds and ends of furniture. I noticed a wood headboard and a dresser, along with several
chairs stacked on each other. There was a small round table
with a box on top. I reached for it, but Mason stopped me.
"Fingerprints," he cautioned, handing me a pen. I used it to
open the flaps as Mason put the light on it. I yelped when I
saw the contents.

"More of the bugs?" Mason said, lifting his free hand, prepared to do battle.

"No creepy crawlers," I said showing him the inside of the box. "But those are the pins and little toys Kelly gave us for the sale. Well, they were almost pins. She hadn't put the pin backs on. But that's not the point. They were in the cabinet at the bookstore and stolen by the shoplifters." I used the pen to ruffle through the flower pins. "The felt backs seem to be coming apart. I don't remember that from the first time I saw them."

Mason examined one. "More vandalism or do you think there was something hidden inside of them?"

"What would she have hidden in them? I guess we'll never know, but the point is, how did they get here?" I used the pen to open the top of a large box sitting on the ground. Mason trained the light where I was looking. I saw the top of a leaded glass shade and stared at the pieces of blue and green glass for a long time, wishing I could see the whole thing. "I'm almost positive this lamp was in Kelly's room. The lamp I'd noticed was missing after her murder."

I checked through more of the cardboard containers and found an assortment of bric-a-brac. It all appeared to be nice stuff. When I opened the last box, my breath caught. There was more bric-a-brac, but in the center I noticed a gun handle. Mason saw it, too.

Both Mason and I knew better than to touch it and we both began to back away toward the entrance.

"Who else do you think has access to the locker?" Mason said.

"There was only one key in the bag. You always get two with a lock. The obvious answer is Dan," I said.

CHAPTER 28

IT WAS VERY LATE WHEN WE LEFT THE STORAGE place and headed back to Mason's house. My car was still parked in front. "You look pretty tired. You're welcome to the couch, or any of the bedrooms in the house," Mason said as he pulled into his garage. He turned toward me with a good-natured smile. "No pressure."

"Thanks," I said. I opened the door to his car and got out. "But I think I'll go home."

Mason walked me to my car and gave me a last chance to change my mind. He leaned in the open window and kissed me. I guess he was hoping to sway me and he almost did, but I started the car and he stepped away.

I automatically turned off Ventura Boulevard as I passed the bookstore. I thought I would just drive past the Donahue house, but I didn't get that far. Late as it was, I noticed the lights were still on at Dinah's. I didn't want to scare her by just knocking at the door, so called her on my cell. Even so, the middle of the night phone call jangled her nerves, but she recovered fast and told me to come in.

"I was just watching television and crocheting. I couldn't sleep after our trip into North's trailer," she said.

"Ha, if you think that's keeping you awake, wait until I tell you where I've been." I told her about the storage locker and finding the gun. "I'm betting it really is the murder weapon. What a clever place for Dan to put it."

"You went without me?" she said with disappointment in her voice.

"Be glad I did. Remember how we said that place was probably creepy at night, well it is," I said and told her about the shadows and the herd of black bugs on the floor.

"So what's our next step?"

I felt my mouth slide into a smile. I liked the way she said "we." Dinah was a true-blue friend who had never let me down. Even with her relationship with Commander she found time for us. Everybody in the world should have one friend like her.

"Right now, I need some chamomile tea or I'm going to jump out of my skin," I said. Dinah apologized for not having any. When I looked out her window, I saw that the night sky was getting lighter and suggested we go up the street to Le Grande Fromage, which opened when they started baking their day's pastries.

The sky was still mostly dark as we walked up the street and the air felt cool with a touch of damp. I never saw this time of day and was surprised there was traffic on Ventura and people already on the street doing their early morning jogs. Le Grande Fromage wasn't crowded, but had more people than I would have expected. Stone and his surfer posse joined some of the production crew in line at the counter and I overheard them all talking about getting an early start.

I found a table and Dinah got the drinks. The effects of staying up all night were beginning to hit me. I was leaning on my arm when she handed me the tea. "Do you remember that lamp that was in Kelly's room? It had a pretty glass shade. The one I said was missing."

Dinah finally nodded with recognition and I told her it was in the storage locker, too. "I wonder why Dan put that in there?" I was going to say more, but Dinah gave me a loud psst and pointed while hiding her finger with her hand. When I looked up, Dan had just gone up to the counter. I slunk low in the seat.

He was clean shaven and dressed for a day at the store. He seemed in good humor as he ordered his coffee and said something about opening the store early. He certainly had tunnel vision when it came to his business. I wondered what he would do if I dangled Kelly's key in front of him.

I held my breath as he walked past our table and was relieved when he just waved a greeting before heading for the door.

When he was gone, we went back to talking.

"Why don't you talk to Barry?" Dinah said.

"Are you kidding, after the episode with the Pinchy-Winchy. Do you think there's a chance he'd take me seriously?"

"No, you're probably right," Dinah said.

"I have to get to Detective Heather. It is exactly what she needs."

As the tea began to relax my nervous energy, my whole body began to ache for sleep. I told Dinah I'd call her later and used the last of my energy to walk to the greenmobile and drive home.

I walked in through the kitchen door, hoping I could make it to bed without falling asleep first. Barry was freshly dressed for work and making coffee. He looked up when I passed him.

"Mason called a few minutes ago. He said to tell you that you left your shirt at his place." Barry scowled as he looked at my day-old clothes. I was too tired to even ask why he'd answered the phone. I responded with a shrug before dragging myself across the house and flopping on my bed.

I fell into a dead sleep for a couple of hours then forced myself up, showered and put on my work clothes before going to the bookstore. Bob took one look at me and automatically made me a black eye. He was right it was a two shots of espresso day for sure.

The jolt of caffeine went right to my brain and I was able to function. As I went through my tasks at the bookstore I considered how to approach Detective Heather. What was I going to do, call her and say, "By the way, last night I happened to be looking in Kelly Donahue's storage locker and I noticed there was a gun, which probably is the murder weapon." What if Barry mentioned the Pinchy-Winchy episode? After the look he'd given me when he'd seen me in the morning, anything was possible. Would it have made any difference if I'd explained to him where I'd been? Would he have believed me? I didn't owe him an explanation anyway. We were just ships passing in the kitchen, I reminded myself.

IT TURNED OUT I DIDN'T HAVE TO WORRY ABOUT contacting her, Detective Heather showed up at the bookstore. I saw her head back to the yarn department. On top of being hot looking, smart and a detective, Heather was an accomplished knitter and gave us a lot of her yarn business. She was dressed for work in a fitted navy blue suit and white blouse. I went back there and found her looking through our supply of circular knitting needles, which Adele kept trying to hide. I asked her if she needed help.

Detective Heather turned at the sound of my voice and then gave me a little laugh. "You could help me with something knitting related?"

"As a matter of a fact, I could." I pointed to the knitted swatches hanging on the bins of yarn. "I did those," I reminded her. Mrs. Shedd didn't want to lose any business, so she'd convinced me that we needed to have knitted and crocheted swatches of all of our yarns. Adele wanted no part of anything that had to do with knitting, so I'd done the knitted ones with my limited skill.

I picked up a set of high-end circs, as people in the know called circular needles, and said they were the best and everyone said they were worth the added cost. Detective Heather took them from me and began to look them over. I suggested she take them out and try them.

I got a ball of worsted yarn we kept for such a purpose and laid it on the table. We both sat down together. She began to cast on some stitches while I tried to turn the conversation to the storage locker. There was no easy segue, so I finally just went at it straight on.

"I know where the gun that killed Kelly Donahue is," I said and told her about the storage locker.

"The key was given to you?" she said with interest. "This could be good. If you let me in I wouldn't need a warrant." She wanted to go immediately. She talked to Mrs. Shedd and said she needed me on official police business.

It felt odd getting into her black Crown Victoria detective car and she was silent as I directed her to the storage facility. Even so, I could see a hint of excitement in her expression. The gun was just what she needed to tie the case up and get charges brought against Dan and prove she was right all along.

The storage place wasn't nearly as creepy looking during the day. Though there still didn't seem to be anyone around there. I had the invoice with the locker number and the key at the ready as we navigated through the low buildings. When I found the row Kelly's was in, I felt my heart rate kick up. Detective Heather would have to say something like a thank-you when I handed her the missing clue in her case.

"What number did you say it was?" she asked as we walked past the row of blue metal doors. She was a few steps ahead and was clearly excited. I repeated the number and she stopped in front of a unit.

"Here it is," she said. She motioned for me to open it. I held out the key and then noticed something alarming. There was no lock on it. Had I forgotten to replace it the night before? I swallowed hard and pulled up the metal door. And then we both looked in.

The locker was empty.

CHAPTER 29

LATE IN THE DAY, THE HOOKERS GATHERED AT THE back table for a group session. Whatever benefit I'd gotten from the few hours of sleep had worn off. The episode with Detective Heather hadn't helped, either. I was on my third black eye of the day. Since it wasn't exactly our finest hour, Adele, Dinah and I had agreed there was no reason to bring up our fiasco with North's gun, but I told the group about Kelly's storage locker.

"Are you sure you went to the right one?" Rhoda said. I nodded and said I'd checked over and over.

"That's horrible. How'd Detective Heather take it?" Dinah asked, looking up from her work. I choked on a laugh.

"Not well. She said she should have known better than to get sucked into one of my schemes. She rushed off and I had to run to catch up with her or she would have just left me there without a ride."

"What about getting Mason to back you up?" Sheila suggested.

"Like a cop is going to believe a lawyer," Adele said with a snort. "Face it, Pink, there's nothing you can do. You might as well just drop the whole thing and give up the amateur detective act. You're not going to be able to solve this one. And I'm sorry, but I can't help you. I've decided Eric is right after all. There is only room for one crime fighter in a couple."

CeeCee interrupted and handed out some sheets of paper. "Since some people in the group seem determined to make cowls, I came up with a faster pattern." She held up a sample she'd made before passing it around. Adele's cowls were made of dense stitches, while CeeCee's had lots of spaces. Adele seemed miffed when Rhoda said it seemed a lot more appropriate for summer.

When my workday ended, I practically crawled home from the bookstore. It wasn't like the days when I was in college, when I could pull an all-nighter and still get through the day. I was walking across my yard, grateful that home was in sight when Peter called on my cell. My son wanted to know if I really did have the hots for North Adams. I could hear the relief in his voice when I told him I didn't.

"But you won't tell him that, will you?" Peter said with some discomfort in his tone. I assured my older son that I would be happy to play along with North's fantasy just like I'd given him the rides, no questions asked.

"Just be nice to him, nothing more," Peter warned before he hung up.

"No problem on that one," I said out loud to myself as I walked into the kitchen.

I flinched when I heard a voice.

"Who are you talking to?" Barry asked. He was unloading white containers of Chinese food on the counter and had taken out a couple of plates.

"Just to myself," I said. Jeffrey came in the room looking glum. He glared at his father with a hopeless expression and turned to me. I asked him if something was wrong. Out of the corner of my eye, I saw Barry rocking his head and rolling his eyes.

"Autumn came back from camp, but she started hanging out with some other kids. Well, some other guy," he added sadly.

Barry doled out a plate of food for him and said they could eat together in the dining room. Jeffrey sighed dramatically and said he'd eat in his room, that he wanted to be alone.

Barry sighed. "I'm trying to be understanding. I don't know what to do with his moping around." He gestured toward the containers. "There's plenty. Help yourself." He started to leave it at that, but then added with an edge. "I'm sure after being out all night you don't feel like cooking."

For a moment I thought of explaining, but then thought why should I? It was bad enough being judged by my sons, but now by Barry, too. We were just supposed to be like roommates. I gave him a "no thank you" on the chow mein and marched out of the kitchen with the last of my energy.

I was more tired than hungry, anyway, and just fell on my bed in my clothes. Mason called and I awoke long enough to talk to him. He was shocked to hear about the storage locker but I was so tired I was beyond sharing in his disbelief. Two seconds after we hung up I was out for the night.

In the morning I felt like a new person. I bounced out of bed, showered and got dressed. It was only as I was walking across the house that I thought about Barry. I hoped he was gone. I couldn't handle another reproachful stare. No such luck. He was in the kitchen, sitting at the table, drinking coffee and eating some cereal while he checked the screen on his smart phone.

I was relieved when my house phone rang and it was Dinah. She said it had been bugging her about the lamp I'd seen. She couldn't remember what it looked like.

"I didn't take it out of the box and there wasn't much light so I couldn't make out the pattern in the leaded glass. But when I saw it at Kelly's it had some kind of blue and green pattern. Flowers maybe. I don't know." We arranged to meet later and I hung up.

Barry looked up with a question in his eyes. I just cut to the chase. "Dinah wanted to know about a lamp I saw in Kelly's storage locker. I suppose Detective Heather has told you all about it by now. How I took her on a wild-goose chase and led her to an empty storage unit. Well, when I went there the first time, it wasn't empty." I let out my breath in a huff. "How's that decorating coming at your place? Will they be done soon?"

Barry had on his inscrutable cop face. "No, Heather didn't tell me. It will just be a little longer until I can leave."

I spent the day at the bookstore immersed in work. I didn't want to think about anything else. Dinah came in just as I was finishing up.

"Let's get far away from here." She stuck her fingers in her ears. "It's even noiser at my place." The production crew was shooting a scene that had a helicopter landing up the street in the yard of the middle school. The thwack of the rotor was annoyingly loud even inside.

They weren't actually filming any scenes with actors until later. Most of them had some time off and when we left the bookstore, they were hanging around the café. North was among them. He looked over at me and gave me what he must have considered his special wink. I offered a weak smile in return.

I still wondered why he had lied about knowing Kelly. Was there any way I could question him without him taking it the wrong way? No.

To say I was bummed out was an understatement. I'd lost the last shred of credibility I had with Detective Heather. And what had happened to the locker's contents?

Dinah tried to cheer me up and said we might as well fulfill our promise to CeeCee to stop at Commander's Mail It Center and pick up the packing supplies he was donating to our booth.

"It looks so much nicer if you get a cute little shopping bag with your purchase, and with a Tarzana Hooker sticker, no less," Dinah said trying to sound cheery as I pulled the greenmobile in front of the Mail It Center. It was in a strip mall off Ventura Boulevard between a cell phone store and a nail salon. As we approached the small storefront, Commander saw us from inside and waved. More than waved. The minute he saw Dinah, his face lit up like a kid on Christmas morning. I was so happy for my friend.

As we passed the post office boxes in the front part of the small storefront, I remembered that Commander had said Kelly had one, for her online business.

"What happens with Kelly's box now that she's gone?" I said.

"Interesting that you should bring that up. She was paid up through last week. I'm trying to decide what to do with the contents of her box. For now I just put it over there"—he gestured toward a small bin in the corner.

"Mind if I have a look?" I asked. He seemed uncomfortable with the idea, but finally agreed. There were some pieces of junk mail, several catalogs for yarn and a small box. I picked it up and examined it. Commander saw what I was doing and pointed out "Return to sender, No such address" was stamped on the front.

"Kelly dropped off packages for pick up all the time. She must have made some kind of mistake on this one."

I held it up and shook it; something clunked inside. Yarn things didn't clunk and I was suddenly curious about the contents of the box. Commander nixed the idea of opening it.

"But you said the rent on her post office box ran out," I protested. He still seemed uneasy and said usually when someone stopped paying for a box, he just refused any packages, but he couldn't refuse a box being returned. Dinah started to work on him, too.

Finally he put up his hands in capitulation. "I'm going to get the packet of shopping bags and tissue paper for your booth. You two watch the front while I'm in the back where I can't see what's going on up here," he said in a knowing tone. "And make sure you put everything back the way it was." He paused. "That is if anything were to just happen to open."

As soon as he went to the back, Dinah pulled out a long letter opener and we used it to slide under the flap of the box and release the adhesive. "He must really love you," I said. Commander wasn't one to bend the rules and looking the other way was a big deal for him.

I don't know why my heart rate had kicked up when it took some doing to get the box open. It wasn't like he was trying to catch us. I suppose it was from the anticipation of finding out what was inside. Finally a small taped-up packet slid out. Dinah took what Commander had said seriously and used the knifelike letter opener to open the inner wrapping without tearing in. She handed it to me and I unfolded the bubble wrap, revealing two small green crocheted bags with drawstrings. I poked my finger into one of the bags to open it and emptied the contents on the counter. Two quarters fell out and pinged against the Formica.

"What's that about?" I said, picking up one of them.

"Maybe she just wanted to put something in the crocheted bag to weigh it down," Dinah said as I handed her the other one to look over.

"All the items she sold were pricey. How much could she make on a couple little bags? I quickly took a photo of the small bags and the coins with my BlackBerry before we put everything back. "That's certainly not what I expected," I said as I resealed the small cardboard box and dropped it back into the bin with Kelly's other mail. Dinah called to Commander and let him know we were done without saying it exactly and he reappeared carrying a brown shopping bag loaded with smaller shopping bags and tissue paper.

He avoided looking at the bin of Kelly's mail. "Did she send out a lot of little boxes like that?" I asked.

"Not at first, but then she'd started bringing one in every now and then. She never said anything about the contents. I tried to engage her in conversation, but she was always in a hurry." He seemed a little disappointed. "I like my customers to feel like family, but she didn't seem to have time to be friendly."

He pulled out one of the shopping bags and showed off the Tarzana Hooker stickers he'd had made. We both gushed over them and thanked him a bunch of times before we went back to my car. "We need to go someplace and figure out what's going on with that package," I said.

"I'd suggest my place," Dinah said as I pulled out of the parking lot, "but the helicopter cowboys are probably still buzzing my house."

Since I was never sure who or what I was going to find at my place anymore, my house wouldn't work, either. "How about dinner at Doc Hogan's Burgerama?" I said. Dinah thought it was a great idea.

The place featured a play yard for the kids and old-fashioned fast food with no pretense of being heart healthy. It was dinnertime and the place was crowded and noisy. Someone had some sense and had set aside a no kids zone.

We sat down at one of the yellow striped red tables. Their fries were made from fresh-cut potatoes cooked in some kind of good-tasting oil and then served in brown paper bags that were immediately dotted with grease stains. No fancy dipping sauce here, just oodles of catsup.

We'd gotten a jumbo order, which was okay because we were sharing it. Besides, the motion of dipping fries in catsup and then transporting them to my mouth always helped me think.

"So what do we have?" I said to Dinah as she ripped open the paper bag making the hot fries more accessible.

"French fries and catsup," she said giving me a puzzled look.

"I know that," I said. "I mean what information do we have and what does it all mean?" We'd gotten colas to go with the fries, and not diet, either. Not even American ones. We'd gotten the Mexican version that was made with real sugar instead of the high fructose syrup stuff.

"Worth every calorie," I said savoring the crispy fry with just the right amount of catsup. "Let's recap what we know about the whole Kelly business. I'll begin," I said. Even with the no kid zone, it was still pretty noisy and we had to talk loud. "We know North lied about knowing her. And we know that there was a gun in the storage locker." I wiped a dab of catsup off my knuckle. "But now it's gone." I groaned reliving the ride back with Detective Heather where she suggested maybe it had all been a dream. I assured Dinah I'd really seen the gun.

"I never doubted that you did," my friend said. "We just have to figure out what happened."

"Somehow Dan must have figured out that someone had been in the storage locker and realized he had to move the gun," I said.

"And he took everything because then there was no chance any of it could be traced back to him," Dinah added. She was curious about what else had been in there.

She already knew about the lamp. I chewed on a french fry. "That's right," I said amazed that I could have forgotten. "The crochet pieces we picked up. The ones with the bullion stitch that made Adele go nuts. They were in there."

"So it wasn't the junior shoplifters who took them from the bookstore. It must have been Dan," Dinah said incredulous. "Remember he came late. He could have taken them while everyone was gathering in the event area. Now that I think about it, he had a plastic bag, but I thought it was just stuff from his store. But why would he have taken them?"

"I don't know. When I saw them in the storage locker, the felt backing had been pulled apart." I took a slug of my cola drink. "It's just weird. And what's with the package at Commander Blaine's? I thought Kelly was selling gorgeous crocheted shawls in some pricey yarn, not little bags with quarters." I paused for a moment, looking down at the table. In my mind's eye I was seeing the bin of bullion flowers when Adele had first let me see them. I had assumed that Kelly meant to add pin findings to the felt discs she'd used as backing. But now I was seeing them in a different light. The pieces were round and not much bigger than the coins. Even the name of the stitch. I mentioned it to Dinah. "When you hear the word bullion what do you think of?"

"Clear soup?" Dinah said. I rolled my eyes.

"What else?"

"Okay, I think of gold, which is money."

"Maybe he knew there were quarters in the crocheted flowers she gave us."

"What, and Dan needed change for a parking meter?" Dinah said laughing.

"Good point. It's a lot of trouble to go to for some change." Just then I noticed that Dinah had a funny expression on her face. She seemed to be trying to tell me something, but what? I realized her eyes kept darting behind me. I turned and Barry was standing inches from me, holding a large sack of food.

"Is this your new hangout?" he said, eyeing the pile of greasy french fries. "And to think you have been giving me the evil eye about all the stuff I've been bringing home for dinner." He leaned in real close. "You might want to check, but I think there's a french fry in your hair."

Then he straightened and bid us "happy eating" and headed toward the door.

"That's it. I can't take it anymore. He keeps giving me dirty looks in *my* kitchen, in *my* house." I told Dinah about his comments when I'd been out all night.

Dinah laughed. "No matter what that man says, it isn't over between you two or why would he even care?"

"Well, it's over as far as I'm concerned and the sooner he moves on, the better. Mason has been very understanding, though he has a lot on his mind, at the moment anyway. Dealing with his ex-wife and the wedding disaster and the idea that in the not too distant future he could end up a grandpop."

"What's Barry excuse for not leaving? He's back at work, he doesn't limp unless he thinks someone is watching."

I reminded Dinah about the work he was having done to his place. "I sure hope they finish soon. I can't take all those disapproving shakes of his head."

We finished our fries and drinks and both left feeling full and swearing we never wanted to eat again. "That's what Barry doesn't get. It's only once in a while for us. He and Jeffrey are eating this stuff every day." Dinah looked at me and shook her head.

"If you're so anxious to get rid of him, why do you care what they eat?"

"I care about Jeffrey. He's a growing kid. He needs salad."

"Are you sure it's just Jeffrey's nutritional needs you're so concerned about?" Dinah said.

"He told me Barry thinks catsup is a vegetable." I might have sounded a little too emotional about that fact.

"Say what you will, but you haven't completely let go," Dinah said. I started to argue, but she gave me a knowing nod. Sometimes best friends know you too well.

CHAPTER 30

I DROPPED THE SHOPPING BAG OF SUPPLIES FROM Commander Blaine at CeeCee's house on my way to work the next day. She was just on her way out to a meeting with a director. She had transformed from the CeeCee we had at the crochet table to CeeCee the star. I figured she might have some insight into North Adams and took advantage of the moment.

"Dear, I have to fly," she said, giving a last-minute check to her hair. "I don't know North. I know who he is and he knows who I am, but that's it. People always think everybody in show business knows each other." She started to walk out and I followed her. "It is just a guess on my part, but I would imagine he lied about knowing Kelly because either he was just trying to stay out of the investigation. Or he's the one who shot her."

"What? You think he really might have killed her?" I said following CeeCee to her car.

"I've heard the man has some secrets. Suppose things started up between them again and oh, let's say he wanted to break things off and she threatened to make his secrets public." She gave me a knowing look. "The man knows how to handle a gun. And as for an alibi— I heard he claimed to have been in his trailer alone. No way to prove it or disprove it."

At that, she got in the car and pushed a button to open the iron gate across her driveway.

The fact that North was a legitimate suspect was swirling in my brain as I drove to the bookstore. But what could I do about it?

"Mrs. Shedd waved as I came through the bookstore. Mr. Royal was showing someone the gondola of hobby kits they'd just added to the store. Pretty soon we were going to have to change the name from Shedd & Royal Books and More to Shedd & Royal General Store. I automatically straightened the display. Someone had mixed up the boxes and I moved the origami sets off the stacks of the stamp and the coin collecting sets. Personally I was curious about the kit that promised you could make prints with sunlight.

I spent the morning working on our fall schedule of bookstore events while manning the information booth. When it was time for my lunch break, I headed back to the worktable in the yarn department, choosing crochet over food.

Adele was sitting at the table alone. She had a stack of cowls in front of her and was just finishing another to add to it. She had reluctantly switched to CeeCee's faster pattern. Even if they didn't sell, they would certainly make a pretty display at the Jungle Days Fair.

I sat down and pulled out the cowl I was making. Adele nodded with approval. "Are you still poking around in Kelly's murder?" Adele said. I was debating what to say and Adele saw right through my silence. "I thought if I said I was giving up, you would, too. Eric is right. Us amateurs should really leave it to the professionals." She stopped for a breath. "We were sort of partners on it. And if one partner quits, the other one should, too."

"I don't know where you heard that, but it doesn't work that way, and we weren't partners exactly. More like you were working on your own." I let out a sigh and put down my work. "But you know, I think I've gone as far as I can go with this case. I kind of hit a wall." Better to say that, than tell her what happened with the storage unit.

"Good move, Pink."

Adele was being entirely too supportive. It didn't take a building to fall on me to figure out why.

Call me contrary, but Adele's attitude suddenly made me want to do something. "You know, I think I'll give it another try. I'm going to talk to Dan again." I got up from my chair and Adele glanced at me with panic in her eyes as I mentioned going to the dollar store. Before I'd gotten two steps away, I heard the scrape of her chair and she came rushing after me.

"I'm coming, too," she said grabbing my arm. "I have some shopping to do."

All the way there, she went on about Eric. First, she was saying he didn't need to know where she'd gone. It morphed into she could just be shopping, and finally, she got down to the truth. She didn't want anyone, including a boyfriend, telling her what she could and couldn't do. Even though it was probably going to cause me problems, I told her I was glad she was standing up for herself.

More Bang for Your Buck was busy when we walked in.

Adele was trying to tell me we should do good cop, bad cop, but she couldn't decide which one she wanted to be. I just threaded my way through the shopping carts and found the office and Dan. I had learned from Barry that cops didn't necessarily tell suspects the truth. Maybe it would work for me, too. I thought if I caught him off guard, he might crumple and confess.

"You know there are video cameras at the bookstore," I jumped in, watching Dan as I spoke. "And we have you on tape taking those crochet pieces from the cabinet from the bookstore. My bosses are convinced you're the ringleader of those shoplifting kids." I let it sink in a little. "They are ready to press charges, but I think if you come clean me and tell me why you took those pieces, I might be able to get them to let the whole thing go. Were there more quarters in them?"

Adele stepped in and continued. "Yeah, I guess you weren't ready for your close-up, huh."

Dan's eyes darted back and forth and then he stepped away. "I don't know what you are talking about. I'd like to see that tape," he said with a little nod. "Now, if you'll excuse me we're about to have our dollar-of-the-hour special." He escorted us out of his office.

"That went well, Pink," Adele said as he walked away from us. An announcement of the impending special played over the loudspeaker and I saw people beginning to push their carts into position. I grabbed Adele's arm and pulled her toward the exit.

"You don't want to be here for that special."

Adele had insisted on driving, since my car was an antique in her mind, and hers was state-of-the-art. "Okay, what was that mumbo jumbo you said to him, Pink? Do we really have video cameras at the bookstore?" She started to throw a hissy fit, thinking Mr. Royal had installed them and not told her.

"No, there aren't any cameras at Shedd and Royal," I said trying to smooth things out. When it was so obvious it didn't work, I didn't want to answer her other question, but Adele was unrelenting.

Finally I told her about finding the crochet pieces and that I thought there might have been something in them, and when I mentioned the quarters in the little bags, she nodded. "Of course, it makes sense. They felt like they were weighted." She asked me some more questions about the quarters and I finally showed her the photo on my Black-Berry. "Pink, sometimes you just miss the boat. You're calling them quarters, when they're collectible coins. Didn't you look at the coin collecting set we're selling now?"

"I wish we looked inside the crocheted pins when we had them," I said, realizing Adele might be right.

"Well, thanks to Adele Holmes maybe you can," she said practically twirling on her toes. "I wasn't going to say anything about it because I thought you would get all weird about me taking any of Kelly's pieces out of the bookstore. But now it looks like I might have saved the day." Adele stopped to build up tension. I tried to act as if I didn't care, but it didn't work and I gave in.

"Just tell me what you did," I said, impatiently.

Adele leaned close and her eyes grew animated. "There was a smaller box in the bin. It had some of the bullion stitch flowers and a toy decorated with more of those stitches. I needed some samples to look at, so I took the whole box home with me." Adele had a self-satisfied smile. "I do detective work, even when I don't know what I'm doing."

"Could I see them?" I asked, beginning to want to grit my teeth. Adele wasn't going to make this easy. "Like, maybe now?"

"Well, they're at my house," she said. Her eyes moved back and forth as she thought about it before finally saying okay, and then we left. I'd never been to Adele's place. I didn't even know exactly where she lived and was surprised when she pulled into a parking structure below the building next to Barry's complex.

Adele had a one bedroom with a view of the driveway. I was shocked when I saw the inside. For all the colors that she wore, her place was all done in black and white. "It makes a better backdrop for me," she said. She got the box right away and brought it into her small living room. "These were the nicest pieces Kelly made," Adele said showing me the contents.

Adele picked up one of the flower pins. The two pieces of felt that made up the backing had been glued shut. Adele took a big needle and started to work the pieces apart.

"This is cute," I said noticing a small Amigurumi owl amidst the pins. It had a few bullion stitches as decoration on its chest. When I picked it up, I was struck by how heavy it was.

"She must have put rocks in there," Adele said.

"Or something else," I said. I hated to destroy it, but there was no choice. I cut into the side. Little plastic pellets fell out and then I poked inside and felt something metallic. When I pulled it out, I saw it was a man's gold watch. As I examined it, I noticed there was an engraving inside. It said "Love You Squiggie."

Adele got the pieces of felt open and a small gold coin fell out. When she checked the others, they also had gold coins in them.

"So, Detective Pink, what does all this mean?" I asked her to give me a minute to think it through. The first thing that struck me as obvious was Kelly didn't really give us the bin of things for the Jungle Days Fair booth. I thought back to the visit and how she'd gone to the door to answer the bell. When she'd come back in the room, she'd seemed agitated, upset. "She gave them to us because she didn't want the person at the door to find them," I muttered.

"Huh," Adele said peering at me. I hadn't meant to say that out loud, so I covered by looking at my watch, and appearing dismayed at how late it was.

"Our lunch break is over. We better get back."

Adele jumped right in and said we'd better hurry. "Unlike you, Pink, I adhere to the work schedule."

Adele put everything back in the box and I wanted to take it with, but she wouldn't budge. "The pieces are still here because of me and I'm keeping them in my protective custody." So instead I took pictures of everything with my BlackBerry before she shut the lid.

As I got ready to go, I glanced out the window toward Barry's complex. "Could you give me a minute?" I said. "I just want to check something." I explained about the proximity of Barry's place.

Adele rolled her eyes a few times, but agreed. I reached around in the carryall for my key ring. When Barry and I were together, he'd given me a key to his place. He'd never asked for it back and I had just left it on my key ring and forgotten about it—until now. I left my bag and rushed next door.

What harm could there be checking up on the work being done to his place? At least I'd have a real idea when he'd be moving out.

The key let me into the lobby and I walked through to a courtyard and went up the concrete stairs to the second floor. It was an older building, which here meant it was built in the seventies and there was no elevator. I stood outside the door a moment and then stuck the key in. The door opened easily and I stepped inside. It smelled like fresh paint and new carpet. I walked into the living room and looked around expecting to see Barry's rather sparse furniture pushed into a corner and maybe covered with a drop cloth. Instead, a wine-colored sofa sat next to a dark wood coffee table. Only the big screen TV looked vaguely familiar, but then all TVs looked the same to me. The dining room was complete with a long wood table and a sideboard with some silver accessories. There were no workmen or signs that they'd been working recently. Everything seemed very finished. I walked further into the place feeling uneasy. Had Barry decided to get all new furniture? I was certainly surprised by his taste. I'd never picked him for a wine-colored sofa type.

The bedrooms were up a short flight of stairs. I checked Jeffrey's room expecting to see his twin bed, wood desk and the poster of Al Pacino in *Scarface* gracing the wall. "What?" I said out loud as I stepped into the doorway. There was a twin bed all right, but it had a pink Hello Kitty spread. The desk was white and had a lamp with an embossed shade.

I rushed to Barry's bedroom. When I saw the elaborate bedroom set and his-and-hers dressers, I was stunned. I started opening drawers looking for something familiar. I picked up a handful of gold jewelry. I thought I heard some kind of noise, but chalked it up to something coming from the street. I looked through the gold chains, stunned. There was definitely something weird going on and I was going to ask Barry about it as soon as I could.

Suddenly the door slammed shut behind me and I jumped. I tried to tell myself that the breeze had blown it closed, but even so, I wanted to get out of there now. I pulled on the handle and nothing happened.

CHAPTER 31

THE COP PUSHED MY HEAD DOWN AS HE USHERED me into the back of the cruiser. I just wanted to say yuck at the hard plastic slightly stinky backseat. My hands were behind my back in handcuffs. It had been an awful walk of shame as they led me out of the apartment. It seemed like all the tenants had come out to watch.

I still had no idea what was going on. When Barry's bedroom door had finally opened there was a pair of cops on the other side. I tried to explain I was a friend of the owner of the condo and asked them to call. I showed them the key. But who were those people in the living room, glaring at me, saying I'd broken into their home and was stealing their jewelry?

At the police station, they handcuffed me to a bench and the two cops went off to do some kind of paperwork.

"You again?" a uniform said from behind the desk. Let's just say this wasn't the first or even second time I ended up there, though I'd never actually ended up in a cell. I pleaded with him to call Barry.

It seemed like I sat there forever, but it was more like an hour. One of the cops came and undid my handcuffs and I stood up just as Barry came in. His usual blank face was twisted in upset.

As soon as I was released, he put his arm around my back and ushered me out the door.

I didn't say a word until we were in his Tahoe. Then I turned to him. "Do you want to explain?"

He sighed deeply. "I could ask you what you were doing there," he said.

"Don't even try." I wasn't about to be put on the defensive.

"You remember the condo I showed you in Simi Valley?" he began. I certainly did. Barry had shown it to me trying to convince me it was the perfect spot for us to make a fresh start—if we got married. It was far from my job and friends and I had nixed it.

"I was so sure you'd like it and the real estate agent said someone else was going to make an offer on it."

"You didn't. You bought it?" I said, incredulous.

"Not quite. I put down a deposit on it and put my place on the market." He paused. "I never guessed my place would sell so fast. When we broke up, I tried to undo everything. I pulled my offer on the condo in Simi and got part of my deposit back, but the people buying my place wouldn't let me back out of the deal. I was still trying to work it out when I ended up in the hospital. The sale went through and escrow closed while I was staying at your place. Some of my buddies cleared it out for me. Those people are the new owners." He blew out his breath. "I haven't told Jeffrey yet."

Now I understood the argument I'd overheard. No wonder Barry had forbid his son to go to their place. "I can sort of understand, you not telling me, but how could you have not told Jeffrey?"

Barry looked at the ground. "I'm a lousy dad."

He'd never seemed so open and vulnerable. I thought back to how he'd flinched when I was struggling with the juvenile shoplifters and for the first time I really understood how much the incident had shaken his confidence.

"I have taken advantage of your kindness long enough. I'll tell Jeffrey the whole story and we'll move to that extended stay place until I can work things out."

I started to say something, but he put his hand up to stop me. "It's done." He started the motor and pulled out of the parking structure. He stared straight ahead and said nothing. I couldn't stand the silence so I began to babble about Adele and Eric and the coins and the watch with the weird inscription. He drove me back to the bookstore without saying a word.

I was shocked to realize it was late afternoon when I walked in. I found Mrs. Shedd and apologized for disappearing. I told her the whole story and she responded with a shrug and shake of her head. She'd gotten used to my crazy stories by now. She might have been upset, but all the business the film crew was bringing in kept her in a permanent state of bliss.

My next stop was the kids' department, hoping I'd find Adele. She was busy arranging some new books about school and fall that had come in. She looked up as I crossed onto the carpet with the cows jumping over the moon.

"What happened to you?" she said. "I waited for a while, but some of us worry about being at work when we're supposed to be. I had to leave." I gave her a brief explanation and asked if she'd brought my bag with. She went back to the cabinet at the back of her department and retrieved it.

"Pink, you got arrested again," she said, shaking her head. "If you had the open and honest relationship Eric and I have you wouldn't have to go sneaking around." I bit my tongue to keep from mentioning that just that afternoon she'd done something she didn't want Eric to know about. What would be the point?

After what I'd just gone through, I needed something normal and was relieved to work on the September calendar of events, though I was counting the minutes until I could leave. I wanted a shower as soon as possible to wash away all the ick I'd picked up in the backseat of the cruiser and on the bench in the cop shop. When I finally left, I didn't even want to wait until I got home and went straight to Dinah's instead. Maybe I wanted some sympathetic company, too. I looked down the sidewalk as I went up to her house. The production crew was still busy at work.

I was glad she was home. She took one look at me and said, "Okay, what happened?"

"Is it that obvious?" I said as I followed her inside.

"Probably not to the average person, but to me," she said with a knowing look. I realized I'd been holding my shoulders in a stiff position and finally let them relax. I could see she was getting ready to go somewhere. I pointed toward the glitter vest she'd put on, not her usual attire.

"You have something up with Commander, don't you?"

Dinah laughed. "I can't believe the costumes that man has gotten me to wear." She held out the glimmering green vest and said they were hosting disco night at the senior center. "They love it when we dress up." She took another

look at me and forgot about the vest and her upcoming evening and ordered me to spill.

"I need a shower first," I said. My friend didn't ask any
questions, just handed me a fresh towel and pointed me
toward the bathroom. Even though I had to put on the same
clothes that had been through the ordeal, I felt better after
washing my hair and showering. Dinah was eagerly await-
ing my story when I came back with a towel wrapped around
my wet hair. I thought her eyes were going to pop out of her
head when I told her about the condo and the strange people who were living there now, my almost arrest and Barry's
admission.

"What is wrong with that guy?" she said. I brought up
the shooting incident and how I thought it had affected him.

"But still," she said not letting him off the hook.

I went back to how my detour to his place had all come
about. As soon as Dinah heard I'd been to Adele's she wanted
to know what it looked like. She shook her head with amaze-
ment when I told her about the black-and-white decor. I
moved right on to the important part about the coins and
the watch and showed them to her on my BlackBerry screen.

We both figured the Rolex was worth a lot, but neither
of us knew anything about coins. We went to Dinah's computer and she did a search.

"Wow," Dinah said looking at the screen. I looked over
her shoulder and echoed her sentiment. Coins looking re-
markably like the ones I'd seen were worth fifty thousand dollars each. When we'd recovered from the shock, I
scrolled back through the pictures until I got to the quarters we'd seen in the package at Commander Blaine's.

"Maybe we should see what we can find out about these."

"It's amazing what you can find on the Internet," Dinah

said doing another search. It took a bit of checking, but she finally pointed to a screen at an auction site. "There's a coin like them." I bent down to get a better view. It was nothing compared to the value of the two gold coins, but each of the quarters we'd seen was worth fifty dollars.

"I think it's safe to assume that the whole box of flower pins had coins in them. No wonder somebody took them from the bookstore," I said. "And that's why when I found them in the storage locker, they were cut open." I thought back to all the discs with flowers on them. "The bullion stitch was her way of marking the pieces that had gold or silver in them. Even the owl had a few bullion stitches on the front and an expensive watch inside. Which is why I'm sure she never meant for us to sell those pieces at the fair. She shoved the bin on us because she was trying to hide them from the person who came to the door, and sent us out the back way so the person wouldn't see us."

"Of course, you're right. She had hidden the coins and watch in the crochet pieces, but she must have been afraid the person would find them anyway." There was a moment of silence as Dinah and I looked at each other.

"You're thinking what I'm thinking, aren't you? The reason someone shot Kelly was because of the coins and the watch," I said and Dinah nodded in agreement.

"We keep saying person, but don't we mean Dan?" Dinah said.

"I'm still going back and forth about whether it's him. Whoever it was, Kelly mustn't have realized how desperate they were. Anyone could have overheard Adele in her drama about the stitch and figured out where the pieces with the coins were in the bookstore and used the bookstore event as a distraction to take them." "I wonder where Kelly got the coins and watch?" Dinah said.

I thought back to her father and his design studio. There had been such an eclectic mix of stuff. I remembered the mounted stamp collection and the collage made out of old jewelry pieces and coins. I suggested they might have come from him. "But what's the difference anyway," I said. "None of this information about the coins is the smoking gun evidence Detective Heather needs."

"I hate to rush you," Dinah said. "But I have to go."

I wished Dinah a fun night with Commander as I left. She laughed about the night part. "To the seniors, night is six o'clock."

As I pulled into my driveway, the first thing I noticed was that Barry's Tahoe wasn't there. Nor was there a bike in the backyard as I walked toward the kitchen door. I could see Cosmo inside the glass back door waiting for me. The two cats circled behind him. And Blondie was no doubt sacked out in her chair.

When I opened the locked door, Cosmo greeted me before rushing outside. The cats made a beeline for their bowls, which were empty. The house seemed quiet, too quiet. I heard a key in the front door and a few moments later, Samuel walked in carrying some groceries. "Where are Barry and Jeffrey?" I asked.

"Gone," he said setting down the bag and beginning to unload it. I walked down the hall toward the room where Barry had been staying. The bed had been stripped. The top of the dresser was empty. Not even a sock on the floor. I went on to the room Jeffrey had used. It wasn't stripped quite as bare. The bed looked hastily made. The computer was gone from the desk and the closet was empty except for a dress shirt that had fallen off the hanger.

I went back into the kitchen. Samuel was putting some peaches in a bowl. "Were you here when they left?" I asked.

Samuel nodded. "It was all very tense. Jeffrey looked like he was going to cry and Barry seemed upset and in a hurry."

"Was anybody helping them?" I asked, thinking of Detective Heather.

"Some guy," Samuel said. "I think he might have been Barry's partner."

"Oh," I said, feeling guilty at my happiness that it wasn't the attractive blond detective.

"I guess that's that, then."

"What happened? Why did they leave so suddenly?" Samuel looked up at me with reproach in his eyes. "That poor kid. I felt sorry for him."

"I thought you were so upset I'd let them stay here."

Samuel went back to emptying the grocery bag. "They kind of grew on me." He took out a jar of almond butter mixed with honey. "I got this for Jeffrey. He really liked it." Samuel's brow furrowed as he looked at me. "Did you do something?"

I recounted the whole story and waited to see my son's reaction.

"So, the guy made a mistake," Samuel said.

"Now you like Barry?" I said, incredulous. My younger son had always seemed to be upset about him when Barry and I were a couple. Now he was defending him and I was the bad guy.

"I don't hate him," Samuel said. "And Jeffrey is an okay kid." Samuel finished putting away what he'd bought, then announced he was going out to hang with some friends. As soon as he left, the house seemed too quiet.

I showered again, still feeling some ick from my cop encounter, changed into fresh clothes and called Mason. I caught him in his car. "I have to get out of here."

"Ah, the detective driving you crazy?" he said with a chuckle.

"Nope," I said. "They're gone. Moved out, kaput. And the quiet is making me nervous. I had quite a day."

Mason said he'd picked me up in a few minutes.

I grabbed my carryall and went out the front door to wait. When I saw Mason's black Mercedes pull up to the curb, I went down the walkway and pulled open the passenger door. I jumped back when I saw the seat wasn't empty. Jaimee glared up at me as Mason leaned across the seat. "I hope you don't mind we have company," he said in a forced bright voice.

I got into the backseat. "We finally worked out a location for the wedding," Mason said looking over his shoulder. "We just have to pick out their wedding gift." He leaned his head toward me. "It won't take long. Then we can get dinner or something." I heard Jaimee snort in the front seat.

"Tell me about your day," Mason said.

"Later," I said. I was hardly going to talk about my ride in the police cruiser in front of Jaimee. Nor did I want to discuss the coins and watch. I almost got out of the car. It was a toss-up, which made me feel more uneasy at the moment. Being a third wheel with Mason and Jaimee or feeling jumpy in my too quiet house. It's good I didn't want to talk because I wouldn't have had a chance, anyway. As we drove across the Valley, Jaimee kept fussing about the arrangements for Thursday's honeymoon, which apparently was another gift from them.

I looked out the window as we cruised along the freeway and she went on and on. Personally I thought the annoying tone of her voice was grounds for divorce all on its own.

"If we do it your way," she said. "They'll have to stop in Honolulu."

"It isn't as if they have to change planes. They don't even have to get off if they don't want to. It just makes a stop to pick up passengers," Mason said in a tired voice. "I'm just happier with that airline," he said. Mason got off the freeway in North Hollywood and went to a warehouse district. Finally he parked and we got out. "Jaimee wanted to go here," he said gesturing toward a low building. It looked plain on the outside, but when I followed them in, I was amazed. It reminded me a little of Kelly's father's place, only much bigger. There was stuff everywhere. Odd pieces like old dress forms, and tables made out of unusual doors. Jaimee rushed off, but Mason hung behind.

"I'm sorry to have put you in the middle of this." He took my hand and squeezed it. "But you're probably keeping me from killing her, again." Jaimee had gone into a room with large carved horses and life-size bronze statues of cavorting nymphs. "I can think of a lot of other ways to celebrate the detective moving home," Mason said with a devilish wink.

"It's hard to feel exactly happy about it," I said before giving him the details of how it came about. Mason was dumbfounded when I told him about going to see how the work was coming in Barry's condo and my subsequent arrest.

"You should have used your phone call to call me," he said.

"It never got to that. Barry showed up and straightened it out."

"However it happened. It's good that he's gone and you can get on with your life." He turned to look at me and his expression grew warm. "And we can start acting like a couple." The words were barely out of his mouth, when Jaimee yelled for him to come look at what she was sure was the perfect gift for Thursday.

"Maybe Barry's living at my house isn't the only obstacle." I said. "Maybe after the wedding." I let it hang, but I was pretty sure Mason got my meaning. I wasn't going to be a girlfriend in the shadows. I didn't want any strings, but I wanted an all-access pass to his life. Being invited to the wedding would demonstrate that.

"Meeting Jaimee wasn't enough," he said with a laugh. I shook my head and followed along through the warren of rooms. Just as we caught up with Jaimee, I noticed a leaded glass lamp and detoured to look at it. Mason stopped with me and it took Jaimee about two seconds to get impatient with the delay.

"C'mon," she said in an annoyed voice. She seemed even more upset when the salesman came toward me. "Did I mention that I will probably be one of the housewives on *The Housewives of Mulholland Drive*?" she said trying to monopolize the salesperson's attention.

"It reminds me of the lamp I saw in Kelly's workroom and later was in the storage locker," I said as way of explanation to Mason. I turned to the store clerk. "What's the value of something like this?"

"This particular one is a Tiffany-style lamp. If you're talking about a real one. . . ." He whistled to indicate the price was way up there. Jaimee was doing eye rolls in the background. He asked me what the one I'd seen looked like.

"I don't remember exactly. It was blue and green and there might have been some flowers."

"It's probably a copy." He mentioned the real ones had a signature on the bottom. "An original similar to what you're describing was connected with a murder a while back. The police contacted us to ask if we'd seen it." He gestured toward the array of unusual items. "We get our pieces all over."

"I actually want to buy something," Jaimee said, pointing toward some fountains in a courtyard up ahead.

"You were asking about the lamp we saw?" Mason said. I had to break the news to him about my fiasco with Detective Heather. He didn't know about the coins I'd found or the watch. He seemed disappointed he was out of the loop. "You should have called me," he said. "Maybe I could have helped." Our moment was interrupted by Jaimee calling from the courtyard, commanding his presence.

I was amazed at Mason's self-control. No matter how much he wanted to kill her, he never let it show. I didn't do as well.

CHAPTER 32

WITH A WEDDING GIFT FINALLY CHOSEN, WE WALKED out onto the street. Actually, they'd chosen two. The fountain was going to be delivered and installed. The metal cherubs with the banner reading "Love Forever," Mason loaded into the trunk. Jaimee rushed and opened the passenger door as she prepared to get in.

Mason shut the trunk and said, "We'll drop Jaimee and the gift off at her house. Then we can—"

"That won't work," Jaimee said interrupting. "I want to take the cherubs to Thursday now." She trained her gaze on Mason. "You should come with." She swiveled her head in my direction. "And you shouldn't. Mason has always kept his women away from anything with our girls."

Mason stepped close to me and put his arm around my shoulder. "I'll make it up to you," he whispered in my ear. Jaimee was still half in and half out of the front seat and saw what Mason did. She groaned and rolled her eyes. "Oh my God, Mason, you're acting like some lovesick puppy."

I had to give Mason credit. He didn't react at all to what she'd said. Thankfully the ride back to my house was quick and I jumped out as soon as the car came to a stop at the curb. Mason cut the motor and rushed out of the other side before catching up with me.

"I'm sorry." He shook his head. "I'm so tired of saying that. I promise you when the wedding is over, Jaimee will be out of the picture. He hugged me and went to kiss me, but I backed away."

"Don't worry about it," I said. "You have your family thing to take care of." Yes, there was an edge to my voice. I didn't like the reference to "Mason's women" that Jaimee had made. It made me feel like I was just another female in the shadows. Right then I made the decision that it was best to continue to view Mason as just a friend, rather than let him move up into the spot of boyfriend.

Back at home I had the quiet house I'd been wishing for. What's that thing about being careful what you wish for . . . ? I checked the freezer and saw there was an unopened pint of Bordeaux strawberry ice cream. It had been a killer day. I was going to have to do something to make my life less dense.

What had started out like any other day had turned into a day where I got arrested for being in what I thought was Barry's place, followed by him coming clean about the situation and exiting my house and life. I'd found out that Kelly had been keeping valuable coins hidden in her crochet pieces and it probably had to do with why she'd gotten killed. To cap off the day, I'd had the encounter with Jaimee and Mason. I didn't even care about the leaded glass lamp information I'd gotten. Besides, now that it was gone there was no way to check if Kelly's lamp was an authentic Tiffany.

Well, I'd done it. I'd gone from too many men in my life, to none. And thanks to the whole episode with North Adams's gun and then the disappearing stuff in the storage locker, I'd lost any credibility with solving Kelly's murder.

After my ice cream dinner, I walked into what had been Barry's room. The sooner I got it back to my crochet room, the better. I needed to get my life back on track. I grabbed the keys to my storage locker and headed out to bring home my supplies.

It was the end of twilight when I pulled into the storage place. I knew I wouldn't be able to get everything in the greenmobile, but if I got all my yarn back, I'd feel better.

I parked the greenmobile as close to the rows of little garages as possible, sorry now that I hadn't chosen the deluxe ones that allowed you to pull your car right in front of them. I had dressed for moving stuff and left the tote bag I was using as a carryall at home. I had essentials in a tiny pouch I'd worn across my chest. Instead of making things easier, it felt odd, like something was missing and I kept thinking I'd left my purse somewhere. I was glad I'd brought a flashlight as the daylight was almost completely gone.

I thought I had memorized exactly where my locker was, but quickly realized I was in the wrong row. I had gone into the row where Kelly's locker had been. I recognized the spot of spilled white paint on the asphalt I'd noticed in front of her locker when I'd been there before.

I trained my flashlight on the blue pull-up door and saw there was no lock on it. I pulled it open just for the heck of it. Inside it was dark and empty. What was I expecting?

I continued down the row illuminating my way with the

flashlight. The beam of light hit the blue doors along either side of the walkway. The line of repetitive doors was making me a little dizzy until something made me stop.

Something on one of the locks glowed when the beam of light passed over it. When I got closer, I recognized there was a strip of reflective tape on the lock—just as I'd seen on Kelly's lock. Was it really her lock and had someone just moved everything to a new unit?

If it was the same lock, the key I had should still open it. I felt for my carryall and remembered I just had the pouch— so the key was back home. Maybe it was just as well. What could I do about it anyway?

Besides, it was completely dark now and definitely spooky. I wanted to get my stuff and get out of there. I found my own locker and loaded up what I could in the greenmobile and drove home.

By now the events of the day had caught up with me. I carried in the bags and bins of yarn and odds and ends of stuff and deposited them in the crochet room. I'd put everything away later. Now all I wanted was sleep.

The next morning I felt much better, but as I walked through the house followed by a parade of animals, I half expected to see Barry sitting at the kitchen table. I fed everybody and let them all out for some time in the yard before getting ready for work.

I skipped coffee at home and went right to the bookstore. On the way in I stopped in the café. Bob saw me and started making my red eye. I recognized several crew members from the production, carrying trays of drinks as they headed toward the door.

Mrs. Shedd smiled at me when I came in holding my red eye. I was on time and there for the duration of my shift. Not only would I be working the information desk, but I'd finish going through the file of events we were planning for the fall.

"Excuse me, but I need some help," a male voice said as I read over a sheet for a Girl Scouts' reading badge event.

"Mason," I said in surprise. He was dressed for work in a wheat-colored suit and a creamy off-white cotton shirt that probably had a thread count of a thousand. "I was worried. I tried to call you, but there was just voice mail everywhere."

I avoided his eye. The truth was I had deliberately not answered any of my phones. What was there to say?

"I finally called the bookstore this morning. Your boss said you should be here, but these days she wasn't sure anymore." He touched my arm fondly. "I thought we could at least get a cup of coffee."

I held up my red eye. Undaunted, he continued. "I am so sorry about everything. I wanted to call you last night, but it just went on and on," he said.

"I get it. Family comes first. You'll always do what's best for them. And even though you're divorced, Jaimee is still part of your family. I just can't handle being on the outside." Mason said he was going to get a coffee and would be back momentarily. I should have known he wouldn't just give up. He was a criminal lawyer and losing wasn't an option for him.

Mrs. Shedd walked up to the information desk holding a stack of books. I recognized the cover as being the one featuring Stone. She set them down on the counter in front of me. "Mr. Royal asked Stone if he'd sign these before he goes. He said he's stop by this morning."

"He's leaving?" I said. Mrs. Shedd shrugged in answer and said that was what Mr. Royal said.

"I'll send him over here when he comes in," my boss said.

Mason and Stone arrived at the information desk to-

gether. What a weird pair they made. Mason in a suit and
Stone in the khaki shorts, loose Hawaiian shirt and smelling
of suntan lotion. I was relieved that Mason understood dealing with Stone was part of my job and he hung to the side
while I took out a felt-tipped pen and opened the books to
Stone's picture.

"So, you're leaving," I said.

"In a couple of days. I want to go home, but first I have
to go back to Denver and finish what I came for," he said. "I
was in the middle of finalizing the partnership for the energy drink when I got the call about Kelly."

"I'm sorry I couldn't do anything to help the cops close
in on Dan," I said. He began to scribble his name along the
bottom of the photo of one of the books.

"I appreciate that you tried," he said. Mr. Royal joined
the little group and shook hands with Stone. He had the
same awed look he'd had when Stone did the event and
started talking about waves, riding tubes and how dangerous the pipeline was. I wondered if I should bring up the
storage locker. Since I'd already ended up looking foolish
once, and since I wasn't completely sure about the contents
being moved to a new locker, I kept quiet. I could see Mason
was getting impatient and was edging closer.

Mr. Royal had taken over Stone, so I turned my full attention to Mason. It didn't seem like the right time to discuss anything about us, so we made small talk until Mr.
Royal shook Stone's hand again and picked up the signed
books before they parted company. Mason watched it all
with a smile. "It's funny how people worship athletes. Even
one's who have given up being professional." Then he turned
the conversation back to us.

"Sunshine, if all this is about last night, you have to give
me another chance. I tried to get away, but Jaimee wouldn't

give up about the honeymoon trip. She kept working on Thursday, trying to get her on her side. Finally, I just said whatever. What was the difference?" I must have looked confused because he explained there had been a disagreement about the flight they should book for Thursday's honeymoon. "I can't believe you missed it. Jaimee was arguing with me about it nearly the whole time at that showroom."

"Why mess up a good thing? Let's keep it as just friends," I said. "I understand that you want to keep your family separate. It's just uncomfortable for me."

Mason's cell phone rang and he excused himself while he answered it. When he'd finished the call, he came back. "Sunshine, I have to go. I'm already late for an appointment. But this isn't over." He hugged me and then headed for the door.

"You're still here?" Adele said when she came out of the kids' department. "It must be a dull day for you. You haven't gotten arrested or led the cops on a wild-goose chase."

I rolled my eyes at her.

"Look who's here," she said, nodding toward the door. Dan had just come into the store. He had the usual energetic walk and cheerful expression.

He came up to us. "My kids are coming back tomorrow," he said. "It's been a bad time for all of us. I wanted to get them something. Maybe there are some books you could recommend." His glance went between us.

"Pink can help you. I'm meeting my boyfriend." Adele pointed toward the café and Eric waved from a table. Adele was wearing rosy pink overalls over a pink and white striped shirt. She had her hair pulled into a tiny ponytail. I wasn't sure if the outfit had something to do with story time or she'd chosen it for no reason.

Dan turned to me. "My kids are eight-year-old twins."

I began pulling out books. I noticed I was getting angrier and angrier as I did. Kelly was dead. Her future was gone. Her kids had no mother now. And Dan was just picking out books for his kids as if nothing had happened.

The time had come to confront Dan. After all, what did I have to lose?

"It's obvious you're going to get away with killing Kelly, but don't you feel any remorse?"

Dan stopped and looked at me. "You think I killed her, too?" He looked down and shook his head. "Why would I kill Kelly? I loved her. We had our differences, partly because we had both been married before. She had a hard time trusting and needed to have her own life, her own business. I admit I had trouble with that, but kill her?" His expression sank to the floor.

"I know all about the storage locker. How you moved it. I've already contacted the cops about it." I left it hanging.

"That detective asked me about a storage locker, too. She didn't seem that surprised when I didn't know anything about it. I didn't understand what she meant, but she said something about she should have known it was a wild-goose chase." Dan was beginning to get annoyed. I should have figured he wasn't going to confess. "I can't take the suspicion anymore. And you aren't the only one. I'm glad my brother-in-law is leaving. From the moment he called, no matter what I told him, I could tell he thought I'd done it." The cheerful look was gone. "Are you going to help me find some books, or just keep grilling me?"

CHAPTER 33

I FINISHED MY DAY AT THE BOOKSTORE WITH NO interruptions. For once, none of the Hookers came in and I didn't hear from Dinah all day. I really wanted someone to talk to about finding what I thought was the new location of Kelly's storage unit and whether there was any point to checking it out.

I went home to a quiet house and hungry animals. There was a message from Mason. He really wanted to see me and discuss our relationship some more, but now that they'd locked in a location for the wedding, he was tied up with making arrangements. There were a lot of "I'm sorry"s about the previous night and promises to make it up to me. Perhaps a trip to Carmel after the wedding. Had he even heard what I said about keeping our relationship as is?

I was glad when Samuel came home, but he'd only come home to change his clothes. And I tried calling Dinah, but she was tied up with Commander Blaine. They were chaperoning a dinner cruise excursion.

I made myself a cup of tea and took it out into the yard. The sky was dark and velvety. Cosmo and Blondie came out and sat with me, but it wasn't the same as a person. I hated to admit it, but I missed Barry's company. All that peace was like a vacuum longing to be filled and my mind went into overdrive.

I didn't like leaving everything hanging with Kelly's murder. Was there anything I could do about the storage locker? If I checked it out and the things had just been moved to the new unit, what could I do? I couldn't gather them up and bring them to Detective Heather. It would corrupt evidence. And there was no way I would get her to come to the locker. I had lost any credibility I'd had with her after the wild-goose chase.

Then I had a dark thought. When Detective Heather couldn't get any direct evidence, and Dan didn't confess, all the files and evidence would be filed in a box somewhere and it would become a cold case just like the ones Barry was working on. Frustrated, I decided to call it a night.

I AWOKE IN THE MIDDLE OF THE NIGHT TWISTED up in the sheet. I'd been having a bad dream and tried to recall the mishmash of images. I was standing in front of the Donohues' looking at the cars parked on the street. Dan was holding a phone and looking at a pile of rocks, while Mason and Jaimee were arguing about pineapples. They were sitting on the beach with giant waves and a plane landed on the beach in front of them. A yellow invoice floated through the air and Detective Heather was standing with her hand on her hip, shaking her head saying "You blew it." I was trying to tell myself something, but what?

In the morning, as I sat in the kitchen drinking my coffee, the images of the dream floated through my mind again. My thoughts were interrupted with a call from Mason.

"Have you thought about going to Carmel?" he said. I sighed and said he ought to just focus on his daughter's wedding and not worry about our relationship. I didn't even bring up being invited this time. But no one could accuse Mason of giving up easy.

"Sunshine, you're breaking my heart. When the wedding is over everything will be different. We got her gift, we settled the honeymoon flight. So, the flight will take a little longer with the stop. It's almost all done. How about I make those reservations for Carmel and you can think about it?"

"You can make the reservations if you want, but I'm still not sure about going." It was the best I could do, but it was enough to make Mason happy. He said he'd call his travel agent right away.

I got dressed and went to work driving the back way so that I went past Kelly's house. The street was lined with vehicles connected to the production and I glanced at them as I passed. Something about it was bothering me, but I couldn't put my finger on it.

"Good, you're here, Molly," Mrs. Shedd said when I walked into the bookstore. "Please don't tell me you're running off somewhere." She gestured around the store, which was quite busy.

When I got to the information desk to relieve Mr. Royal, he was looking through some books on a cart. He showed me a stack of biographies of North Adams and asked if I could use my influence with him to get them signed. More of the surfing books had come in, too, and he said Stone was going to stop in to sign the new batch before he left. I'd barely had time to settle in when a woman came up with a stack of travel books, wanting to know which one I thought was best. As she prattled on about her upcoming trip, something connected in my mind. Something that could turn the whole investigation of Kelly's murder upside down. As soon as the customer was gone, I called Mason.

He was more than happy to help, but was on his way to court. He said he'd have his assistant call me and get me any information I needed. Within an hour I'd gotten it all, but I still needed the evidence—the evidence I'd seen in the storage unit.

I really didn't want to go alone. I tried calling Dinah, but got her voice mail and remembered she'd said there was an all day, into the evening faculty retreat at Beasley to prepare for the start of the fall semester. Then I caught sight of Adele, who was just taking a break and was back at the worktable in the yarn department.

She was more dressed up than usual. She had on a tunic made of all black granny squares over a longer hot pink dress. Rows of ruffles peeked out from below the black. Her hair was held back from her ears with large pink crocheted flowers she'd attached to barrettes. She was humming to herself as she worked on a dark purple cowl.

I couldn't believe I was going to do what I was about to do, but I was out of options.

I slid into the seat next to her. "You know how you're always saying you like to be part of the action, that we're like the three, well, in this case two musketeers?" I said. Adele looked up and listened as I told her there was a storage locker I wanted to check for evidence. "If I'm right, I'm just going to take pictures of everything and then show them to

Detective Heather. Then she can get a search warrant and get the evidence she needs to solve Kelly's murder. I'd like to have a witness."

Adele swallowed hard. "Pink, I can't. I know I said I wouldn't let anyone tell me what to do, but I have definitely given up my detective work." She hung her head. "Eric said it was a deal breaker if I did any investigating. You've got to understand. Cutchykins gets who I am. I think he's the one, my soul mate, the yin to my yang—"

She was going to go on, but I cut her off. "I can't believe you are going to let someone tell you what you can and can't do," I said.

"Pink, I'm not letting him tell me what to do, it was my decision. All my decision. Besides, you're not even sure about the storage locker."

"Could you at least ask Eric a question for me?" The words were barely out of my mouth when Adele shook her head in a definitive no. "Don't you even want to know what I figured out?" I said. She started to weaken and then seemed to pull herself together and shook her head decisively.

It looked like I was on my own.

CHAPTER 34

AFTER ALL THE TIME I'D MISSED AT THE BOOK-
store lately, I didn't dare ask for some time off. There was no
choice, but to wait until the end of my shift. I was antsy to
see if I was right about the stuff just being switched to another unit. If I was wrong, well, the information Mason had
gotten me wouldn't mean much.

It was getting toward evening when I left the bookstore.
I had brought a lantern with me and my tote bag purse. I
wasn't going to be caught short this time. I parked as close
as possible to the unit in question and grabbed the lantern
and my bag. My heart was thumping as I rushed down the
aisle, using my light to find the reflective tape on the lock.

My breath was a little choppy with anticipation as I
pulled out the plastic bag with the key. I tried putting the
key in the lock and it didn't go. I sighed, thinking this might
be the end. Not wanting to admit defeat, I retried the key
and still it wouldn't go. Maybe the other way? I turned it so

the teeth went up and pushed it in the lock. It slid in and I turned until the lock fell open.

I pulled open the door and stepped inside. Everything had been rearranged in the move, but I recognized the markings on one of the boxes. It was the same stuff. The first thing I did was to take a picture of the outside with the unit number showing. Then I moved inside, hoping between the lantern and the flash on the phone, I'd get good images. I used a pen to poke through the boxes. I was curious about the leaded glass lamp, but my first priority was finding the gun. I moved further into the unit.

Suddenly I felt the hairs on my neck go up and I sensed I wasn't alone. I turned my head slowly and my fear was confirmed.

"What are you doing here?" I said with a squeak in my voice.

"Your friend at the bookstore said I might find you here. The one with the colorful clothes. I think you have something of mine," Stone said reaching toward my tote bag. "She was telling her boyfriend something about stepping down from investigating my sister's case and that she'd put the crochet things connected to it in your bag."

He fumbled with the pocket on the front of my tote bag and I saw a tissue-wrapped packet. He ripped open the top and I saw the owl and one of the bullion stitch flowers.

"Adele really told you that?" I said, getting agitated.

"Told might be the wrong word. It was more like I overheard them in the bookstore café. It doesn't really matter. I wanted to get these things before I left."

"You were the one who came to Kelly's door. You were the one who shot her," I said. The words tumbled out before I could stop them. Stone stood up and stared at me. He was wearing his usual khaki shorts, Hawaiian shirt and sandals, but his manner was different. The laid back surfer dude had been replaced by somebody with a cold stare.

He responded with a dismissive laugh. "Don't be silly. I was in Denver trying to close the deal for the energy drink. I showed the cops my boarding pass. It said departing Kahului arriving Denver."

"But with all the time changes, the detective didn't notice that the flight took longer than it should have." I had his rapt attention now. "Because the plane made a stop in Burbank before continuing on to Denver," I said. There was no plane change and therefore no need for more than one boarding pass. Since it was more than a two hour stop, they gave you the option of getting off the plane, didn't they?" I didn't mention that the information had come courtesy of Mason's travel agent.

I had his rapt attention now. "I know about the cab," I said. "You took it to your sister's and then back to the airport and got back on your plane."

Adele hadn't been willing to ask Eric my question, so I'd talked to him during my break. Between being a motor cop and working the production, he was very aware of what vehicles for the production were parked on Kelly's street. When I'd mentioned remembering seeing a cab, he'd been certain it had nothing to do with the filming.

Stone listened with a stoic expression as I continued with my final piece of evidence. "I knew that somebody else had a key to the lock and that person must have contacted the storage company about moving to the new unit. Not only did I find out it was you, but that Kelly's locker was originally rented to you. You left a credit card to be charged each month, but it expired. They tried to contact you and the phone number you'd left was Kelly's. According to their records, she took over paying for it and put it in her name.

I'm guessing you must have left the second key with her." I knew all of that thanks to Mason's contacts.

"WELL, AREN'T YOU THE AMATEUR SLEUTH," STONE said. He went to take the packet from my tote bag and I made a rush toward the door. All those years of surfing had given him lightning reflexes, and he got there first and pulled down the unit's door. Almost simultaneously he grabbed my arms, pulling them into a vicelike grip behind me. All the surfing had left him with muscles like steel and when I tried to move my arms, the pain was excruciating.

"I didn't plan to go to my sister's house," Stone began. "But I didn't want to end up with just a royalty for the coconut water energy drink. I wanted to be a partner, and that meant I had to invest in the company. I was just going to go to the storage unit, get some collectible coins I'd left there and get back on the plane. I thought I'd sell them when I got to Denver and use the money to buy into the business."

He seemed quite comfortable holding onto my arms. I was not. "Imagine my shock when the coins and other things were gone. I had kept one key and left the other in a box of things I left at my sister's when I moved to Hawaii. I knew that she must have taken the coins. I went to her house to ask for them. She said that she didn't have them anymore, that she had sold them all. I didn't believe her." His lips were in a straight line as he relived the moment.

He stopped and I thought he might have been finished, but his hold grew even tighter on my arms. "The way she kept looking around that room of hers, I was sure she'd hidden them somewhere. She argued that when my credit card expired and she'd taken over the payments for the locker, the contents really became hers. We argued some more and then she pulled out her trump card." He gestured toward the leaded glass lamp sticking out of a box. "She'd taken it home with her, too, with the idea of selling it. When she was trying to gauge the value, she found out some information about the lamp that could have caused me a lot of problems. She wanted to make a deal. I stop hassling her about the coins and she'd put the lamp back in the locker and never say a word about it. But that would leave me vulnerable. Any time she wanted to she could blackmail me again." There was a moment of silence as Stone collected himself.

"I'd brought along a gun from the storage locker as a last resort. I thought it might encourage her to give up the coins if she balked." He didn't finish, but the obvious finale was that he'd shot his sister because she knew too much. He said he grabbed the lamp and left.

Did he think I was going to be sympathetic when he complained that the cab hadn't waited like it was supposed to and he'd had to walk to Ventura and find one parked in front of Le Grande Fromage? He grumbled that he'd searched the house over and over for the coins and not found them. Then he heard people in the bookstore talking about having a box of his sister's crochet pieces. Stealing them was easy. Everyone was finding a seat waiting for him to speak. He just shoved everything in his backpack. The shoplifter kids had been a convenient distraction, including the mess they'd made in the yarn area.

He let out an annoyed snort. "What a wasted effort. I don't even know why my sister bothered hiding the coins behind those flowers. I got barely one thousand dollars for selling all of them. What had happened to the really valuable ones? I went through that house again. I looked on her computer and could tell she had never sold them or a Rolex watch I knew was missing from the storage locker. I'd almost given up, when I heard your friend talking."

We'd come full circle and it was making me uneasy. I had a whole list of questions like where the coins had come from and why keep them in a storage locker? What about the Rolex? Questions would stall him and give me time to think of an escape, but before I could ask the first question I heard a ripping sound as he tore a piece of duct tape off one of the boxes and slapped it across my mouth.

He loosened the hold on my arms for an instant, but then I felt him wrapping some kind of rope around them all the way up to my elbows.

This wasn't good. Not good at all.

My feet were still free and I made a move toward the door. He'd only pulled it down partway. Could I push it up with my foot and escape?

"I wouldn't do that," he said. I saw the lantern light reflect off of something metal in his hand. "I was afraid you might not want to part with that packet of stuff, so I borrowed my brother-in-law's gun. This could work out quite well. Dan's fingerprints are all over his gun." I could see that Stone had gloves on now. "So when I shoot you, that detective will finally have some hard evidence against Dan. And I can get on with my life."

Stone must have seen me glancing toward the boxes of stuff and figured what I was thinking. "The gun I shot my sister with is long gone. Once I realized someone had been in the locker, I knew it wasn't safe to leave it there, so I gave it a watery send-off from my surfboard."

He looked around at the interior. "I think I've taken care of everything. Let's see, where shall we do this?"

I was frantically looking for some way to escape when I heard the door rumble up.

"Molly, are you in there?" a voice called. In the split second it took me to turn, Stone was next to me and had the gun against my temple. As the door lifted all the way, Barry started to walk into the unit. "I saw your car," he began, and then his eyes got accustomed to low light and he saw the situation. His hand made a slight move.

"Don't even think about going for your gun or she gets it," Stone said. He was standing so close to me now, the sweet smell of his coconut sun lotion was making me sick to my stomach.

The color had drained from Barry's face and he seemed frozen just the way he'd been when I had been struggling with the shoplifter kids. Stone pushed me in front of him and we took a step toward the open door. I could feel the metal of the gun touching my skin. It was a terrible feeling.

I was afraid to breathe for fear it would make Stone pull the trigger, but I kept looking around, hoping to see something, anything that could help me out of this situation. Stone said something about us getting out of there. A bad sign. Once we got out of there, it seemed unlikely he was going to keep me as a travel companion.

That was when I noticed them. At first they didn't show up in the dim light, but the lantern reflected off one of their shiny black bodies. The big bugs I'd seen a few days before were moving around the floor. I tracked their movement and saw that they were headed toward Stone. It must have been the cloying coconut fragrance that was attracting them. Stone was too busy staring at Barry to notice.

"We're getting out of here," Stone said, giving me a push.

"Wait," Barry commanded. "Don't rush into anything. Let's think this out." Barry had made eye contact with me and I tried to direct my gaze to show him the parade of bugs headed toward Stone's exposed feet and legs, hoping he'd realize that once the insect army walked onto Stone's skin, he'd be distracted. But Barry's face was impassive and I couldn't tell if he'd gotten it. And even if Barry had understood my signal, when the moment for action came, would he freeze? Any hesitation on his part and the tiny window of opportunity would be lost.

Barry tried to calm Stone and asked him what it was that he really wanted. Meanwhile I watched the bugs get to the base of Stone's sandal and begin to walk up the strap. They were big and ungainly as they moved across the thin strip of leather that ran across his toes. One bug fell off and landed on his foot, then another. At the same time another contingent of insects had started walking up his bare legs. Even with all the adrenaline flowing, Stone felt something and looked down. He might have been a champion surfer with nerves of steel when it came to waves, but not bugs. He started kicking his feet out, trying to shake the insects off. The gun was wavering, and I felt it move away from my temple.

It had to be now. I threw Barry my most imploring look, but he seemed frozen. At any second, Stone would push the gun against my temple again. Just when I thought all was lost, Barry's expression sharpened as if something had kicked in. With precise timing, he rushed Stone and knocked the gun out of his hand before the surfer had a chance to react. At the same moment I elbowed Stone in his six-pack abs.

Our joint actions knocked Stone off his feet and Barry made him lie down spread eagle on the pavement, while he took out his handcuffs. Stone took an eye-level look at the congregation of shiny bugs and protested, but Barry ordered him to stay on the ground.

As he clipped the handcuffs on, Barry read Stone his rights, then checked him for more weapons and called it in.

When I looked over at Barry, he had turned away and

was pumping his fist in a victory move. His mojo was back. I would have said something like congratulations, but I didn't think he wanted anyone to know that he'd ever lost it. A moment later, he hugged me.

"That was close. Thank God, you're all right."

"Thanks to you and your fast reflexes," I said. "How did you happen by?"

He gestured toward Stone. "I was following him, hoping he'd throw something away with his DNA on it, but I lost him when he came to this place. Then I saw your car." I was confused and asked why he'd been following Stone.

"I don't know if you were paying any attention when I told you about the two cold cases I was working on." I guiltily admitted that all I remembered was the murder book, but as he described the wealthy Northridge man they thought had been killed by his maid, who'd been stealing from him but who had never been charged due to lack of evidence, it started to come back to me. The second case involved the death of a liquor store employee in what they thought was a robbery gone bad. There was no suspect in the second case. "In the beginning I was just hoping to find some new evidence on the maid, but then I noticed a lamp had been taken in both cases. The first case had come with an insurance company description of it. It was an original Tiffany lamp and worth big bucks. In the second case the girlfriend knew a lamp with a leaded glass shade was gone, but didn't know much about it. Could it have been the same lamp? A bunch of collectibles had been taken from the first case, including a valuable coin collection. As far as they could tell neither the most valuable coins in the collection nor the lamp had ever surfaced." At first when I heard you talking about lamps and coins, I thought it was just coincidence, but then I began to wonder. I knew the wealthy guy liked to hang out with athletes. On a hunch, I took a photo of Stone with my phone and showed it to the maid. The maid recognized him as being one of the regulars at the wealthy guy's endless parties. It turned out the victim of the other crime had a connection to the wealthy guy. The maid recognized his photo and said he'd delivered food and liquor for the parties. She was pretty sure the delivery guy sometimes ended up staying and joining the party.

"When I heard what was inscribed on the watch you found in the crochet stuff—the rich guy's nickname was Squiggie—I started keeping an eye on Stone."

Stone shook his legs and arms, trying to knock off the partying big black bugs.

"How about we make a deal," Barry said. "I let you get up and you make it easy on all of us and tell me what happened."

Stone said nothing. "He told me everything," I said.

Barry let out a sigh. "I'm afraid it's not the same." He tried to make me feel better by putting his arm around me in a supportive gesture. I told him that the Rolex and coins were in my tote bag and he said he'd make sure they got it as evidence.

It didn't take long for a bunch of cruisers to arrive, along with Detective Heather in her black Crown Vic. I'm not sure what was more upsetting for her—seeing Barry with his arm around me or having to admit I was right about the storage locker. I told her about the flaw in Stone's alibi. She was not happy realizing she'd missed it. Then I was old news as she and Barry went off to the side and began to talk. Barry looked animated and she kept fiddling with her hair, fluttering her eyelashes and touching Barry's arm in a possessive manner.

Oh, ick. Wasn't there some rule about cops flirting with each other while on duty?

Detective Heather finally took my statement before waving me on my way. She and Barry were deep in conversation when I finally headed to the greenmobile.

THEY BOOKED STONE ON A WHOLE LOT OF CHARGES. For attempted murder of me, for the murder of his sister and for the murder of Barry's two cold case victims. But there were all kinds of problems with the case. They knew by the casings that the same gun had been used in one of Barry's cold cases and Kelly's murder, but they didn't have the gun. I told them what Stone had said about throwing it in the ocean, but it had no effect.

Barry was able to identify the leaded glass lamp they found in the storage locker as the authentic Tiffany that had been taken in cold case number one, but there was no way to prove that Stone had taken it. It was the same with the Rolex. They couldn't even verify that the lamp, watch or the coins had been in the storage locker when it had been in Stone's name.

Barry and Heather knew that Stone was involved in all three murders, but they didn't have the evidence to prove it.

Even the charge that Stone had tried to kill me was in question. He claimed he was only trying to protect his family's property from being stolen by me.

Barry and Heather both tried to get him to confess, but Stone asked for an attorney before saying a word. And the attorney pointed out that although the plane had stopped in Burbank for two hours, there was nothing to say that Stone had left the airport. No cab company had any record of the trip. There was nothing to say that he was at his sister's when she was shot. If anything, the attorney tried to point the finger at Kelly for having the stolen coins, lamp and watch.

Detective Heather was still trying to come up with more evidence before the district attorney reviewed the case and decided if there was enough for a trial. In the meantime, Stone was let out on bail. He couldn't leave town and was staying with one of his surfer buddies until the situation was resolved.

Now I understood the frustration the cops felt when they knew someone was guilty, but there was nothing they could do about it.

DAN WAS RELIEVED TO BE OFF THE HOOK AND I profusely apologized to him. North and the prop guys never realized they'd been on the hook, though they were all glad it was settled. Still, they were sorry to hear it was Stone. Some of them were his fans.

I felt bad for Stone's father. There was no way he wasn't going to blame himself. Even if Stone never went to trial, everybody was always going to believe that he'd killed his sister.

CHAPTER 35

"OKAY, EVERYBODY," CEECEE COLLINS SAID AS THE Jungle Days Fair got ready to open. "Let's sell, sell, sell. Remember it will help all the dogs and cats." The proceeds of our booth were going to help her favorite charity, Hearts and Barks, and Meows, Too.

To say it was hot was an understatement. Yes, it was dry heat, but with the temperature close to one hundred, the lack of humidity didn't make a difference. It was like being in an oven.

The cowls were spread across the table like a rainbow along with Dinah's washclothes wrapped around bars of soap and Eduardo's bracelets and some other items we'd made. The whole bottom row featured Adele's version of Kelly's flower pins. The bullion stitch petals perfectly done.

"Those are lovely," CeeCee said. "Maybe you can show me how you made them. I've never mastered that stitch."

Adele's mouth fell open in shock. All her worry had been

for nothing. She picked up one of the pins and showed it off to the rest of us. "Maybe I should do a crochet clinic and teach all of you. There's a little secret that changes everything."

I noticed that Adele didn't say it was her secret, she just implied it. Actually it was Kelly's secret. When I'd really studied the yellow sheets I'd been carrying around, I'd found it. I wondered if Adele would remember that I was the one who had shown her how to overcome her Achilles' heel of stitches. Probably not. It had been hard enough to get her to admit that she'd put the coins and watch in my bag. But when she understood that Stone had almost killed me because of overhearing her conversation with Eric, she had thrown her arms around me and begged for my forgiveness.

Despite the heat, there was a crowd of people and they all stopped at our booth. The cowls got a lot of oohs and aahs at their colors, but when Adele demonstrated how to wear them, people seemed to start fanning themselves and dropped them back on the table. They were a lot more interested in buying the bottles of Crystal Gazer water Rhoda had brought in from Dan's store.

"Oh, dear," CeeCee said as midday approached and we hadn't sold one cowl. "I knew these were going to be a dud." Out of the corner of my eye, I saw Adele hanging her head.

"You people give up too easily," Rhoda Klein said. "No one wants something hot around their neck in this weather. But they would like something cool." Rhoda picked up a sunshine yellow cowl and poured some water on it. She squeezed out the excess and slipped it over her head. "Ah, my own personal air-conditioning," she said loudly. "This cool cowl is really great."

A few people turned at her voice, which wasn't a surprise because the nasally New York accent tended to carry. A woman brought a little girl over who was flushed with the heat. CeeCee picked up on Rhoda's cue and dowsed a bubblegum pink cowl with the rest of the water and asked the little girl if she'd like to try it.

"It feels nice," she said and her mother gladly bought it. Rhoda called out to them that they could recharge the cowl's cooling powers by dipping it in water.

Adele recovered and started swishing the cowls in the melted ice in the cooler to make colder cowls.

"I'll take one of those." When I looked up, Mason was grinning at me. He turned to the young woman next to him. "Which one do you want?" She pointed toward a cream-colored one. As I handed it to her, he said, "I'd like you to meet my daughter Thursday." He gave me a knowing nod. "Thursday, this is Molly, my special friend. She crocheted that beautiful hankie for you."

I was surprised when she leaned over the table and thanked me with a hug.

"This is great," she said putting on the drenched neck piece. She showed it off to Mason and then reminded him that they had to get to a dress fitting. "The wedding is in a week," she said.

"And Molly is going to be there," he said.

"See you then," she said with a smile. She moved on to another booth, but Mason hung back.

"Let's see, I invited you to the wedding, and introduced you to my daughter as my special friend. I think that counts as including you in my family. That's everything you wanted, right?" His eyes grew warm. "So, is the trip to Carmel on?" The best I could do was tell him the truth. I was still digesting what had just happened and I needed to think about it.

Detective Heather stopped at our booth. She was wearing a white sundress and it was the first time I remembered seeing her out of work clothes. She looked much less intimidating, almost girlish. She noticed me looking around and figured out I was looking for Barry. She pointed toward a bean bag game. Jeffrey and Barry were both trying their luck.

"I don't know if you've heard, but it looks like Stone is going to walk. Unless I can come up with something pronto, the DA is going to drop all the charges except threatening you. But Thomasville's attorney will probably twist things around, and the worst he'll get is probation." She looked at me intently. "I never thought I would say this, but I sure wish you could come up with something."

She bought a shell pink cowl and I chilled it for her. As I handed to her, I told her I wished I could, too.

As the day went on, the cowls kept selling. But so far Elise had kept the vampire ones she'd made out of the water. Finally somebody picked up one and asked for it wet. "I'm not sure it's the right thing to do for that one," she said trying to take it back.

"Anthony wouldn't mind," Eduardo said with a reassuring nod and Elise let it get the cold treatment.

Dinah had a marker in her bag and flipped the sign and wrote in "Chill with a Cool Cowl."

Needless to say, we sold out.

WITH EVERYTHING THAT HAD GONE ON, I HADN'T gotten a chance to get the rest of my stuff from the storage locker. It felt eerie to be back there, but I made sure I went in the middle of the day and I was relieved to see some other cars there. Regretting again that I hadn't sprung for a locker that you could park in front of, I was making trips back and forth to the car when I heard someone call my name. I turned and was surprised to see Barry. He was in jeans and a tee shirt and had the sweaty look of someone who had been moving things.

"What are you doing here?" I said.

He pointed toward a large locker. "You aren't the only one who had to store stuff. I had to empty the condo when it sold. Well, some of my friends did it for me."

I glanced down the driveway and saw a rental truck was parked in front of an open locker.

Barry wiped his forehead with his shirtsleeve and I saw that he had a bottle of soda in his hand.

He held out the bottle. "Want some?"

We really hadn't seen each other since the last time at the storage place. I accepted his offer and took a big sip of the icy drink. When I handed the bottle back, he put it to his lips and drank some. I don't know why, but it seemed very personal.

"Then you got a place?" I said. "Where?"

Barry's mouth curved into a friendly grin. "In Tarzana, over by Lindley. I took Jeffrey with me and we found a place that works for both of us."

"Good," I said. We stood there for a moment not saying anything. "Well, take care," I said picking up a box and starting to walk toward the greenmobile.

"Let me get that for you," he said taking it out of my arms. "I'm one hundred percent okay." To demonstrate he picked his leg up and jiggled it around. "I'm still getting physical therapy, but I don't really need it. Even without the resolution I wanted, the two cold cases I was working on are settled. At least the maid isn't under suspicion anymore." He let out a satisfied sigh. "And I'm back at my regular job. Thank heavens I'm done with that nine to five stuff. It is definitely not me." He sounded happy but there was this feeling that he wanted to say more.

He set the box in the trunk of my car and insisted on walking back to my locker and helping me with the rest. At first we walked in silence. Then he stopped, which made me stop, too.

"I want to tell you that I was wrong. I don't know what I was thinking. It was ridiculous trying to push you into getting married. And the whole thing with the condo in Simi—putting down a deposit and putting my place up for sale without telling you or Jeffrey." He took a few breaths and then looked me in the eye. "It was great staying at your house. Not the broken foot and leg part," he said with a chuckle. "But you were wonderful to Jeffrey and me. We'd broken up and you let us stay with you anyway. We both felt welcome, too." He halted again. "And I've missed you since we left."

We walked the rest of the way to my locker and he grabbed a box. I took some shopping bags. As we started back toward my car, he spoke again. "Remember how you asked if we couldn't just leave things the way they were when I gave you the ultimatum?"

I remembered it well. I couldn't understand why we had to get married or be broken up—why we couldn't find a common ground. I nodded.

"Is that offer still on the table?"

The truth was I missed him, too. The time we'd spent together while he was recuperating was different. Maybe because there weren't the pressures of being a couple. I had gotten to know him better. I had seen him when he felt vulnerable and then when he got his confidence back.

"Yes, the offer is still on the table—to be friends," I said finally.

He looked a little disappointed at the last part, but recovered. "I can deal with that." The words were barely out of his mouth when his cell phone rang. I heard him answer and by his voice I knew it was work. A body somewhere, a suspect to question or maybe a lead to follow. It was back to business as usual.

I DROVE HOME AND UNLOADED THE BOXES BEFORE going to meet Dinah. I told her about Barry as we headed down the street and she smiled knowingly. "I never believed you two were done. Do you think he'll really stop pushing you to get married?"

"Wouldn't he be surprised if someday I went and said yes." Then I laughed. "I just agreed to be friends, anyway."

We walked down the block and turned on Kelly's street—and did a double take when we saw what was going on. Though it was dark out, the street was bright as day thanks to the light atop a crane. The pavement was in the process of being wet down by several production assistants. Even without Adele's commentary, I knew that was to give it more contrast. Eric was in his uniform and stationed at the curb, prepared to stop any traffic that might want to go down the street. A group of neighbors were gathered near the Donahue house and their front yard was filled with equipment and more lights that were focused on their driveway. When I got closer, I saw that the whole backyard was illuminated as well.

Nanci Silvers stood on the edge of her front lawn, watching. Autumn was in the front yard, too. I did a double take when I saw who Autumn was talking to. The gangly kid in the baggy pants with a baseball cap at a stupid angle was none other than one of the juvenile shoplifters.

We stopped next to Nanci and I was going to say something about her daughter's choice of boyfriends, but Nanci spoke first. "I hope you ladies aren't here to complain. I've rethought the whole situation and I see that the production is great for our local businesses." She paused as though considering what she was going to say next. "I was afraid people might get the wrong idea, so I was keeping it a secret, but I'm Dan's partner. I want to do more with my life than be the PTA president. The dollar-of-the-hour special is all me." she said. "I have connections through my husband's business to get fabulous deals on merchandise. At first I didn't even tell my husband that I'd bought a share of the business with my nest egg."

"Sounds good to me," I said, looking at Autumn and her new boyfriend. "But is that who you want your daughter to spend time with instead of Jeffrey?"

"Who's Jeffrey?" Nanci said and I pointed to the boy on the bike at the end of the block. I pulled Nanci aside and told her what I knew about her daughter's new friend. Nanci's expression made it clear she'd gotten the message.

Because of the investigation, the *L.A. 911* team had never filmed the scene using Kelly's yard and driveway— until now. I felt a twinge of sadness. Kelly should have been out here enjoying the moment with the rest of us.

Dan came out of his house and crossed the driveway. "Well, this is it," Dan said as he joined the group standing on Nanci's front lawn. We had a perfect view of the backyard and the driveway.

The tall jean-clad director walked out to the sidewalk and waved toward Jeffrey and the production assistant near him. Jeffrey had tried to sneak into the shot so many times, the director had finally given in and said Jeffrey could ride his bike through this, the last scene they were shooting.

There was some more preparation and then the director yelled for everyone to settle and that they were ready to shoot. After a moment, he called for action. An actor dressed in creepy looking clothes came over the fence into the Donahue yard. He paused for a beat and ran through the yard and up the driveway. A moment later North appeared over the top of the same portion of fence. Though after it was edited, it would appear that he vaulted over the fence and landed on his feet, in reality, they put a ladder next to the fence and he climbed down. I think he was embarrassed at having us all watch the fakery, so to jazz it up a little, he jumped off the ladder before he reached the last rung. His move backfired and the tall ladder fell toward the house, hitting the row of poplar trees that had been brought into block the view. As it did something popped out of one of the trees and hit the ground.

"Cut," the director yelled, walking through the yard. We all inched closer to see what had fallen.

"Can't you people use the trash cans," he yelled.

Curious what was causing his irritation, I crept all the way into the yard. When I saw what they were looking at I yelled, "Step back. Don't touch that, it's evidence."

CHAPTER 36

Detective Heather walked across the back-yard while the film crew and actors watched. "I don't under-stand," the director said. "It's a piece of garbage. A broken plastic bottle."

"Do you want to explain or should I?" I said to Detective Heather.

"I'll handle this," she said stepping in front of me. "This piece of garbage proves that Stone Thomasville shot his sister. She pointed out the label, which though damaged still clearly showed that it was the coconut water energy drink, Stone was touting. "It wasn't available for sale anywhere, so the only way the bottle could have gotten there was if he'd brought it." She pointed to the missing bottom and explained he'd used the juice bottle to make a homemade silencer, which was why nobody heard the shot. It must have flown off the gun and gone out through the open sliding glass door and lodged in the row of poplar trees.

"If I hadn't seen a photo from a murder book," I said, "I wouldn't have known what it was."

Detective Heather stepped in again. "Since he probably was drinking from it, we'll be able to get DNA evidence to back it up. Through ballistic fingerprinting we were able to ascertain that the gun used to kill Kelly Donahue was also used to kill the liquor store employee. If we can tie Stone Thomasville to Kelly's murder, we can tie him to the other as well." Then Heather did something that completely surprised me. She gave me a high five. "With this piece of evidence, I am sure the charges will stick."

"Is this scene ever going to get finished?" Nanci said. Detective Heather bagged the evidence and stepped out of the way. The whole process of settling the crowd started again and the director yelled for action. This time it went through without a hitch. At the end of the scene, Jeffrey rode his bike across the driveway as North took off down the street.

"That's a wrap," the director called with relief in his voice.

Mrs. Shedd was so excited about all the business the production had brought to the bookstore, she was more than happy to have them throw the wrap party there. It was late, well after our regular closing time. Bob had made treats and they even brought in my son Samuel to work as a second barista.

When the party began to break up, my cell phone went off in my pocket and for once I heard it. It was my son Peter. "You have to take North home with you," he ordered.

I went over into a corner. "I'm not doing it unless you tell me what's going on."

Peter groaned and then finally spilled the story. It seemed North had a bunch of phobias connected with cars. He didn't drive and he only could ride on certain streets. Anything with too much traffic sent him into a panic. Good luck on that one in L.A., even in the Valley. He was always driven to and from the set in a limo, but he would only ride with a certain driver who knew his problems. Every now and then, there was a screwup and that driver didn't show up.

"Then he calls me," Peter said. "So, now you know. Please take him home with you and I'll pick him up."

The drive home with North gave me a chance to ask him why he had lied about knowing Kelly. His answer floored me. He hadn't lied. It was almost worse. He had no memory of their relationship. All he said was something to the effect that there were so many women, it was hard to keep track.

CHAPTER 37

SINCE I'D BEEN THE ONE TO FIND THE PIECE OF EV-
idence that positively tied Stone to his sister's death and the
liquor delivery guy's, Detective Heather let me watch when
they confronted Stone with the news. He didn't even ask for
his lawyer, but had begun to talk and talk. It seemed like
he thought if he explained what happened, the cops would
understand and make some kind of deal.

As if that was going to happen.

I was in an outer office viewing it all on a screen. "You
don't know what it's like," he complained. "One minute
you're a professional athlete with sponsors dumping money
in your lap, winning tournaments that dump more money in
your lap and then you get a little older and it all disappears.
You end up signing surfboards, being the surfer pro at some
beachfront hotel and struggling to keep afloat.

"But then you discover there are people who like to hang
out with movie people and athletes, like the guy in North-

ridge. He thought it made him look like a big shot. He had so much stuff and so much money. The whole place was done in expensive antiques. He had tons of jewelry, a huge coin collection, and all kinds of expensive doodads. He never paid much attention to any of it as far as I could tell. I was sure he wouldn't miss a piece of jewelry here and there and some coins from his collection so I began supplementing my income by taking something now and then. Eventually he did notice some things were missing, but he blamed it on the maid and fired her. I was just going to make one last score and figured if he noticed the ring missing, he'd think the maid took it before he fired her. It was before the guests were to arrive on party night and the guy from the liquor store had made a delivery and was looking for our host. Instead he caught me going through a drawer."

Stone took a deep breath before continuing because this was the big moment that changed everything. The delivery guy realized what Stone was doing and decided to help himself to a piece of jewelry, too. The problem was their host walked in on them. In a moment of panic, Stone had picked up the huge geode and knocked the host on the head. As he fell, he'd hit his head again on the corner of a table. When they checked, he had no pulse.

To make it look like a robbery gone bad, Stone and the liquor store delivery guy had taken a bunch of stuff. They'd taken the whole coin collection, the Tiffany lamp, a bunch of other collectibles and the watch off the guy's arm. The plan was to stash all of it in a storage unit and leave it there. Stone rented it, but the guy insisted on having one of the keys. Stone had felt safe when the cops seemed sure the maid had killed her boss as revenge for firing her. There was nothing to tie him to the murder.

"Just before I moved to Hawaii, I went to check on the

locker and saw that some stuff was missing. That jerk had the authentic Tiffany lamp on a card table. He was wearing the Rolex. When I objected and said we had to keep the stuff hidden he started threatening me, saying I was the one who had killed the wealthy guy. He could go to the cops and turn me in and look like a hero." Stone stopped talking at that point. Detective Heather had to fill in for him.

"You knew he had a gun, didn't you?" she said. "You took the bottle of orange juice the guy was drinking and used it as a silencer. Pretty clever of you to know how to improvise like that." When Stone didn't say anything, she prodded him. "Isn't that what happened?"

Stone was looking down and finally mumbled a yes and said that the guy's gun was sitting in plain sight on a table. "He worked in a liquor store," Stone said by way of explanation to why the guy had a gun. "And the silencer was nothing. I worked as a production assistant in props. You'd be amazed at the things we had to find or make." Stone's voice had grown very soft. "He went to the bathroom and when he came back I had the juice bottle taped on the gun. I shot him before he realized what was happening. I roughed up the apartment and took the Rolex and the lamp, along with some of his stuff, so it would appear he'd been a victim of a home invasion robbery. I dropped the stuff in the storage unit. Then I moved to Hawaii and put it all behind me."

There were no dimples or smiles as he talked. The expression on his face was hard and I couldn't believe he had ever seemed adorable. "I was never going to touch any of it, but then the opportunity for this energy drink came up. I didn't want to be just the face on the bottle. I wanted to be a partner. But that meant investing in the business. Time had passed and I didn't think any of the coins were traceable."

When he got to the part about what had happened at

Kelly's it was the same story I'd heard before. He'd killed her because once she knew the leaded glass lamp connected him with a murder, it left him too vulnerable.

By now it seemed as if Stone was in a trance, letting the story fall from his lips. "I used the energy drink bottle as a silencer. It flew off somewhere. I couldn't find it and figured nobody else would, either. I grabbed the lamp and rushed back to the storage place and put it and the gun in the locker. I got back to the plane just as they were going to shut the door."

Even though I'd heard some of it before, I was dumbfounded by his confession. How could it be that the self-deprecating surfer was really a serial killer? Everything was resolved, but I couldn't say it made me happy. A few minutes later, Detective Heather came over to where I was sitting. I thought she was going to thank me, but she was back to her usual self.

"Don't get any ideas, Nancy Drew. It worked this time, but if I find you mucking around in my business, I'll nab you for interfering with a police investigation." She jangled her handcuffs to emphasize her point.

A FEW DAYS LATER, I WAS RUSHING TO GET DRESSED. My suitcase was packed and ready to go. I looked at the big thick envelope with my name, hand done in calligraphy. There was no address on it. In addition to the verbal invitation, Mason had hand delivered a printed one and gotten me to confirm the trip to Carmel.

I'd gotten a new dress. It was peach-colored and ruffly and not at all the kind of thing I usually wore. I'd even gotten some matching heels. It had been down to the wire, but Mason had invited me to his daughter's wedding. He'd finally opened all the doors to his life. It was what I said I wanted, wasn't it? I checked myself in the mirror and then grabbed the suitcase before heading to the greenmobile.

The plan was that as soon as the wedding was over, we were leaving to drive up north.

The location Mason and Jaimee finally agreed upon had been staring them in the face all along. Mason's backyard. Though as I drove up in front, I could see it had been transformed. The whole backyard was tented. I knew they'd put a floor down over the lawn and pool. And that the tent was air cooled and done up as elegantly as any ballroom in the finest hotel.

A valet opened my door when I stopped the car. I got out and for a moment took in the scene. One valet slid in the driver's seat and another glanced toward the suitcase in the backseat. "Shall I put that in Mr. Fields' car?" The question hung in the air. What was it that made me turn and look to the other side of the street? I swallowed hard when I saw Barry leaning against his SUV. He was dressed in jeans and a dark green pocket tee shirt.

"Could I talk to you for a moment before you go in?" he said.

I finally knew what I wanted to do, and waved the valet on. He drove past us with the suitcase still in the car. Before Barry could say anything, I spoke. "Mason and I are just going to stay friends—like you and me."

A look of relief flooded Barry's face, but it was short-lived as we heard what sounded like a bloodcurdling scream coming from the wedding tent.

The Bullion Stitch

BY ADELE ABRAMS

Don't let anyone tell you the bullion stitch is easy. If I, Adele Abrams, Crocheter Extraordinaire, had trouble, anyone would. Molly Pink convinced me to share the secrets that turned the corner on the stitch for me.

The most important secret is to lay a large tapestry needle on your hook and wrap the yarn around both the hook and the needle. After you do your yarn over and are about to pull your hook through all those wraps, push the needle up so it covers the bent part of the hook.

Secret number two is to keep the wraps even and loose.

Secret number three is use yarn that doesn't split.

Secret number four is to be patient because it takes a certain amount of coordination to hold the tapestry needle in place while you do the wraps.

Kelly's Killer Flower Pins

Materials: K-10½ (6.5mm) hook
1 skein of Vanna's Choice yarn, worsted weight, 100% acrylic (about 170 yards or 156 meters, enough to make lots of flowers)
Tapestry needle
2 round pieces of felt approx 2¼ inches in diameter
Embroidery thread and needle
Pin back
Button for center of the flower
Glue

Stitches: Chain, bullion stitch, slip stitch

Finished size: Approximately 2 inches in diameter

Chain 6 and join with a slip stitch to form a ring.

Chain 5,** lay tapestry needle on the hook, including through the loop on the hook. Wrap yarn around hook 10 times. Put the hook through the ring and yarn over. Pull the hook out of the ring and push the tapestry needle over the bent part of the hook. Slowly pull the hook back through all of the wraps, leaving the yarn loose, chain one to lock the stitch.** One bullion made!

Repeat from ** to ** 9 times to fill the ring and attach to the first bullion with a slip stitch. Fasten off and weave in ends.

Use embroidery thread and needle to sew the flower onto one of the discs of felt. Sew the button in the middle. Either glue the two discs together or attach using a blanket stitch. Glue or sew on the pin back.

Adele's Cowl

Materials:	K-10½ (6.5mm) hook or hook needed for gauge
	1 skein Lion Brand Cotton, 100% cotton, worsted weight (about 189 yards or 172 meters)
	Tapestry needle
Stitches:	Chain stitch, single crochet, double crochet, slip stitch
Finished size:	Approximately 25 inches around and 7 inches tall
Gauge:	10 stitches and 7 rows = 4 inches

Chain 63 and, being careful not to twist, join to make a ring with a slip stitch.

Round 1: Chain 1 and work a single crochet in each chain around. Join last single crochet to first single crochet in the round with a slip stitch.

Round 2: Chain 3 (counts as first double crochet), work a

double crochet in each stitch around. Join last stitch to the first stitch of the round with a slip stitch.

Repeat Round 2, 9 times.

Last round: Chain 1, single crochet in each stitch around. Join last single crochet to first single crochet in the round with a slip stitch. Fasten off and weave in ends.

CeeCee's Cowl

Materials:	J-10 (6.0mm) hook or hook needed for gauge
	1 skein Lily Sugar 'n Cream, worsted weight, 4-ply 100% cotton yarn (about 95 yards or 86 meters)
	Tapestry needle
Stitches:	Chain stitch, single crochet, double crochet, slip stitch
Finished size:	Approx. 22 inches around and 6¼ inches tall
Gauge:	Approximately 13 (7 double crochets, 6 chain ones) stitches and 7 rows = 4 inches

Chain 84 and, being careful not to twist, join to make a ring with a slip stitch.

Round 1: Chain 1 and work a single crochet in each chain around. Join last stitch to first stitch in the round with a slip stitch.

Round 2: Chain 1, turn, and work a single crochet in

each stitch around. Join last stitch to first stitch in round with a slip stitch.

Round 3: Chain 4 (counts as double crochet and chain 1), turn, skip stitch, *double crochet in the next stitch, chain 1, skip the next stitch.* Repeat from * to * for the rest of the round. Join the last Chain 1 to the first double crochet in the round with a slip stitch.

Repeat round 3, 8 times.

Round 12: Chain 1, turn, and single crochet in each stitch around. Join last single crochet to first single crochet in the round with a slip stitch.

Round 13: Chain 1, turn, and single crochet in each stitch around. Join last single crochet to first single crochet in round with a slip stitch. Fasten off and weave in ends.

HOW TO MAKE YOUR COWL COOL
Dip finished cowl in cool water. Squeeze out excess water and put around neck.

Note: Colors may run, so check first.

Molly's Mac, Cheese and More

6 cups cooked elbow macaroni
1 10-ounce package of cut spinach prepared according to package
¼ cup cut-up sun-dried tomatoes
½ cup butter cut into cubes
3 tablespoons all-purpose flour
1 teaspoon garlic powder
1 teaspoon seasoned salt
1 teaspoon seasoned pepper
2½ cups of milk
2½ cups of shredded sharp cheddar cheese, divided
1 cup seasoned bread crumbs
3 tablespoons melted butter

In a 9 x 13 pan mix cooked macaroni, prepared spinach and sun-dried tomatoes.

In a saucepan, melt the cubed butter. Stir in the flour, garlic powder, seasoned salt and seasoned pepper until smooth. Gradually stir in the milk. Bring to a boil; cook and stir for 2 minutes or until thickened. Remove from heat. Stir in 1½ cups of the shredded cheese.

Pour sauce over the macaroni mixture and stir to mix it through.

Sprinkle 1 cup of cheese over the top of the macaroni mixture. Combine bread crumbs and melted butter, sprinkle over the top. Bake uncovered in oven preheated to 350 degrees for 20–25 minutes or until bubbly.

Molly's Hurry Up Chocolate Chip Cookie Bars

1 cup butter, softened and cut into slices
¾ cup white sugar
¾ cup brown sugar, packed
2 teaspoons vanilla extract
2 eggs
1 cup old-fashioned oats
1¼ cups all-purpose flour
1 teaspoon baking soda
1 teaspoon salt
12 ounces of semisweet chocolate chips
1 cup chopped walnuts

Cream butter, brown sugar, white sugar and vanilla together until creamy. Add eggs one at a time, beating after each addition. Pour the oats into a food processor or blender and blend until the oats look like sand. Mix processed oats, flour, baking soda and salt together. Beat into butter mixture. Stir in chocolate chips and chopped nuts.

Grease a 10 x 15 jelly roll pan and spread batter in it. Preheat oven to 375 degrees. Bake for 20–25 minutes or until golden brown. Cool on a wire rack. Cut into bars.

CHAPTER 1

YOU KNOW HOW THEY SAY WEDDINGS ALWAYS HAVE drama? Well, this one had an overdose. My name is Molly Pink, and the wedding in question was Thursday's, the daughter of my friend Mason Field. Yes, that's really her name. I wasn't invited to the actual ceremony, which was for immediate family only, but I, along with 200 or so others, had been invited to the reception that was being held in Mason's tented backyard. When I say *tent*, I'm not talking about some little open-on-the-sides thing. We're talking about a structure that took up the whole backyard. And it only looked like a tent from the outside—the interior was done up like an elegant ballroom. But I'm getting ahead of myself.

I would have already been inside the tent, but just before I was to go in, my friend Barry Greenberg, who is an LAPD homicide detective, happened to come by and stopped to chat. The title of *friend* was a step down from his previous

title as *boyfriend*. Don't get me started on that. *Boyfriend* for
a man in his fifties? C'mon. And I don't think his arrival was
an accident. It was a last-ditch effort to talk me out of doing
something. The friendship between me and Mason was supposed to move up a notch after the wedding. He and I were
to go up north for a get-to-really-know-each-other few days,
if you know what I mean. Barry didn't know that before he
had even arrived, I had already changed my mind and had
decided to keep my relationship with Mason at the friends-
with-no-benefits level.

Barry had looked relieved, almost happy, until we both
heard screams coming from the tent. Then we double-timed
it inside. It was easier for Barry since he was dressed in comfortable jeans, a T-shirt and sneakers. But then he wasn't an
invited guest and I was. The narrow bottom on my apricot
ruffly dress didn't allow for a wide gait, and the heels—well,
walking in them was a challenge, but running? Forget it.

When I got inside, it was as if the moment had frozen in
time. Nobody seemed to be moving or talking. The only
sound was the background music the DJ had put on.

I COULDN'T FIGURE OUT WHAT WAS WRONG, BUT
then I looked across the wooden dance floor that had been
laid over the grass and saw a long table at the back of the
tent. I didn't mean to gasp, but it was an automatic response
when I saw Jaimee Fields, the mother of the bride, sprawled
on the wedding cake, holding a bloody knife.

Barry had gotten up close to the table, and now he
flashed his badge and told her to drop the knife. It hit the
floor with a loud thud. You didn't have to be a detective to
know that a bloody knife meant somebody had been
stabbed. I was right behind Barry when he went around to

the other side of the table. I almost didn't see the tuxedo-clad man sprawled on the floor. My eye went right to the white dress splattered with red as Thursday Fields tried to help her new husband up. Thursday Fields, or should I say, Thursday Fields Kingsley.

The DJ finally cut the music, and I heard a gasp go through the crowd. I turned, and I saw that Mason Fields had just come in from the house. He had a happy smile and was carrying a wedding gift, oblivious to what he was walking into. When he caught a glimpse of the crowd, he seemed surprised. "What's going on?" His question was met with the sound of two hundred-plus people sucking in their breath, and he seemed perplexed by the reaction. "I go into the house for a few minutes and the party dies?" Then he looked across the tent.

Mason was an attorney, and he mostly dealt with naughty celebrities who got themselves into sticky situations. But I doubt anything he'd ever seen equaled finding his ex-wife sitting in his daughter's wedding cake. And that was before he knew about the bloody knife.

Barry ordered everyone to stay put and leaned down to check the groom. Mason and a dark-haired man in a matching tuxedo ignored the command and came behind the cake table.

The dark-haired man pushed me out of the way and fell to his knees when he saw the figure on the ground. While Barry searched for a pulse, the man—who I now realized was Jackson Kingsley, father of the groom—cried out in grief and disbelief. Then his eyes fell on Jaimee, who was somehow still stuck in the cake.

"You stabbed my son," he bellowed in a deep voice.

Barry had already called in the incident, and it took only a few minutes before the place was swarming with blue uniforms and paramedics. The paramedics checked Jonah Kingsley, but I saw them shaking their heads; clearly, it was too late. They still got some business, though. A number of women grew faint as they were hustled to the tables that had been set up for dinner. As soon as the area was cleared, two cops stretched yellow tape across the whole end of the tent, and the area around the cake and Jonah Kingsley's body was being curtained off with tarps. Somebody had finally helped Jaimee out of the cake, and she was surrounded by uniforms. Jackson Kingsley was standing nearby on the dance floor with a much younger woman, who, judging by the ring on her finger, seemed to be his wife.

"What are you waiting for?" Kingsley said to the uniforms. "How much more proof do you need? Arrest her." He pointed accusingly at Jaimee Fields. I got the feeling Jackson Kingsley was used to being in charge and didn't like it when he wasn't listened to. And he had that kind of deep, melodious voice that got your attention.

Thursday was with another cadre of uniforms, and Mason was rushing back and forth between the two groups.

All I could think was that poor Thursday had been married for only a few hours, and she was already a widow.

I stiffened when I saw Detective Heather walking toward me. Her real name was Heather Gilmore, but with her Barbie Doll looks, I'd taken to calling her Detective Heather, of course, not to her face. There was a certain amount of animosity between us. Even though I'd helped her with cases a few times, she didn't like my sleuthing.

She had her pad out and was ready to question me, when Barry interceded. "There's no reason to talk to Molly. She came in after the fact."

Detective Heather seemed disappointed, then almost annoyed when Barry explained that he and I had come in together. Apparently Heather still resented my relationship with Barry, even if he and I were just friends.

The whole tent had become a swirl of activity. Uniforms had spread out among the guests and help. The white-suited criminal-scene investigators had come in and were collecting fingerprints and DNA samples from the crowd. They had so much to deal with, it was mind-boggling.

After Detective Heather backed off, I watched the action, and for the first time, noted something odd. All the help had been gathered together, and they all looked the same. I mean, really the same. They all were wearing white shirts, black pants and white gloves, but it was more than that. For example, they all had their hair smoothed back, and if it was long, it was pulled into a small bun at the nape of the neck. And no one wore any makeup or jewelry. The androgynous, uniform look made it almost impossible to tell the men from the women or one person from another.

"Molly, it's okay, you can go on and leave," Barry said, coming up to me. As the police finished questioning the guests, each one was released and escorted out through the front entrance. Every time the door to the tent opened, I caught a glimpse of the newspeople already stationed out front. I dreaded going through the gauntlet of reporters.

Mason came by just as Barry was speaking. If it was possible, he got even more upset at Barry's comment.

"Oh," Mason said. I could hear the disappointment in his voice. "I was hoping you would stay, Molly. With your experience. . . ." his voice trailed off, but I knew what he meant.

I was the event coordinator for Shedd & Royal Books and More. Let's just say many of my events had a dusting of disaster about them. I'd had authors who got carried away with cooking demos and set off the smoke alarm, bringing the fire department. There had also been a Mr. Fixit, who broke the plumbing and started a flood. The thing was that, even with the touch of disaster, the events were always a success, and one way or another, we always sold a lot of books. But did Mason really think I could save this reception?

His head shot toward the knot of uniforms around his ex-wife. "They wouldn't listen," he said in an annoyed tone. "They're taking Jaimee in."

Jaimee appeared shocked and frantic. Her hands weren't cuffed, but there was an officer on either side of her, holding her arms. Her cappuccino-colored dress still had hunks of cake stuck to it, punctuated with an occasional petal from the fresh flowers that had decorated the cake. I could hear her arguing with the officers as they started to move en masse toward the door.

"My ex is guilty of a lot of things, but not killing the groom," Mason said. He turned toward the cops surrounding his daughter, who seemed to be in a holding pattern as she stared dazedly at her beautiful white wedding.

Mason turned to Barry. "You're a father. You know how you want to protect your kids. If you need to question my daughter later, no problem. Just please don't detain her now." He and Mason weren't exactly friends, and asking him a favor wasn't easy. Jaimee and her cop escorts were going out the door. "I have to go," Mason said, quickly. "Jaimee's likely to say something stupid and get herself in more trouble." He looked back at his daughter in her elegant dress spattered with blood. He let out a heavy sigh and asked Barry again not to detain her.

"Okay," Barry relented. "Your daughter can go. We've already got a statement from her, along with her fingerprints and a DNA sample."

Mason gestured to me. "Can you look after Thursday?

Her sister isn't much help." He pointed to a similar-looking young woman in a champagne-colored maid of honor dress. She was leaning against a young man in a dark suit as a female officer stood over them writing something down. "Nobody here is much help for her. Everybody is too upset themselves." Mason walked backward toward the door. "I don't know when I will get back here," he said. "This is a hard thing to ask, but would you take Thursday home with you, Molly?"

Then Mason turned to Barry. "And could you help Molly get her out of here so she doesn't have to go through that?" he said, pointing to the tent opening where the frenzy of reporters waited with their cameras and blinding lights.

Barry made a sort of grumbling sound, but agreed. Mason took off and Barry went over and talked to the uniforms surrounding Mason's daughter. A moment later, Thursday was standing next to me holding onto my arm for support. She seemed to pay no notice to the blood spattered on her arms and dress. Barry glanced around the tent. "There must be another way out of here," he said.

Thursday finally spoke and said the best way was to go through the house. Barry escorted us as far as a tent entrance that connected to French doors leading into the house, and told the uniforms guarding it that it was okay for us to leave. Then he went back to help his associates.

It seemed strange to go from the tent directly into the den. I was used to the room having a view of the pool and the backyard, not the white sides of a tent. I heard Spike barking from somewhere. Mason's toy fox terrier sounded unhappy about being locked up. I followed Thursday out of the den and down the hall to the master bedroom. She suddenly noticed the blood on her arms and seemed horrified. She didn't resist when I pulled her into the bathroom and wiped off her arms and hands. There was nothing I could do about the dress.

I'd never seen Mason's bedroom. It was done all in earth tones and, as expected, was large and luxurious. But I only got a quick glance as Thursday led us through the room to another set of French doors. They opened out to a small private courtyard with a fountain and beautiful landscaping, surrounded by a stone wall. There was no time to spend admiring the secret garden, because Thursday took me out through a gate in the wall, and I saw we were once again in the backyard

I was disoriented, but Thursday pointed out a walkway that ran behind the tent. "This leads along the back of the yard, past the garage to the driveway," she said, lifting her skirt as we went down the stone path in the darkness. She stopped as we passed an open flap in the tent. "I guess we could have gone out that way." I looked in and saw that it was a service area, now deserted.

A dry wind was beginning to kick up and pushed against the sides of the tent. Somewhere in the darkness, I heard palm fronds rubbing together in an eerie cry. The warm wind was blowing in from the desert, and the air felt warm and unsettled. As we reached the garage, the stone path turned to sidewalk bordered by neatly trimmed bushes backed by the fence. Suddenly, one of my feet began to hurt big-time. It was no surprise since heels and my feet weren't friends. I slipped off both shoes, and my bare feet practically sighed with relief. When I bent down to pick them up, I realized I was standing beside something white and crumpled.

Instinctively, I reached for it and picked it up. It was wet and slippery. When I held it up, there was enough light reflecting from the streetlight to see it was a shirt, and it was splattered with something dark. I couldn't see colors in the darkness, but something told me the splatters were red.

CHAPTER 2

SOME PEOPLE THINK SOUTHERN CALIFORNIA HAS no seasons. We do, they're just different from the ones most of the country is used to. September brings hot, dry weather and the beginning of the Santa Ana winds, or as some people call them, the devil winds. They stir up the wrong kind of ions and would have made Thursday and me feel edgy even if we hadn't just slipped away from her wedding disaster. Still getting out into the dark street was a relief. All the newspeople and exiting guests were around the corner in front of her father's house.

We stopped along the row of deserted catering trucks parked on the side street, and I said something about wondering how I was going to get my car because I'd left it with a valet. A moment later, we were bathed in the headlights of the greenmobile, as I called my old teal green Mercedes. It had come around the corner and pulled up next to us, and Barry got out, leaving the motor running.

"Thank you," I said with grateful relief. I reached out as if to hug him and leaned in close. "There's a white shirt in the yard. I think it has blood on it." I kept my voice to a whisper while Thursday went around to the passenger side.

He seemed a little disappointed when I didn't follow through with the hug. "I'll check it out," Barry said, going back to his detective persona. "I'm going to be lead detective on this case," he added, making a triumphant gesture.

"Oh," I said, suddenly understanding his manner. In the past, Barry had had to step down from a number of homicides because of a personal relationship with someone involved in the case, usually me. But that was when we were a couple. Maybe now that we were just friends, it didn't matter that I was a guest at the wedding.

"If it's okay, I'll call you later. I'm sure you'll want to know what happens," he said. I was stunned. In all the time Barry and I had been a couple, he'd never asked for permission to call me or come by my house. He'd always just shown up whenever and left the same way. I told him it was fine. Barry looked down at my bare feet and insisted I wear shoes to drive. I dropped the heels in the backseat and retrieved a pair of sneakers I had left on the floor.

"Nice outfit, huh?" I joked, doing a twirl in my ruffly dress and sport shoes.

He cracked a smile. "I'm sure it will be fine for the ride home." He started to leave it at that, but took a step closer. "I meant to mention before that you look really nice, even with the sneakers." He held the door until I got in and had my seat belt on, then he shut it, not stepping away until he'd made sure I'd locked it.

Thursday had crushed herself into the passenger seat and somehow managed to get her seat belt over the elaborate wedding dress. With its full skirt and train, it definitely wasn't meant for riding around in a car. As she adjusted herself in the seat, I heard the sound of fabric ripping and buttons popping off. Not that she seemed to care.

I put the car in gear and continued down the dark side street. For a moment I wondered what I'd gotten myself into. What if Thursday was like Mason's ex? Weren't daughters usually like their mothers? The thought of dealing with a junior Jaimee filled me with dread. Let's just say I could understand why Mason divorced her.

But Thursday didn't look like her mother. Even with her extravagant dress, professional makeup and flower petals twisted into her short hair, she was cute rather than pretty. I wasn't sure if it was the events of the evening or just the way she always sounded, but there was a little rasp to her voice that pulled at my heartstrings as she thanked me for helping her escape.

As I finally turned onto Ventura Boulevard and headed west for the short drive from Encino to Tarzana, I wondered how to make conversation. First I considered what I knew about her, which wasn't that much. All that Mason had told me was that she taught second grade at Wilbur Elementary, which was a few blocks from the bookstore where I worked. Mason had said little about the groom, other than he wondered if anyone would seem good enough for her. It seemed like a pretty common sentiment among parents, so I didn't take it to mean much.

I really wanted to ask Thursday about Jonah. If the cops hadn't asked her yet who might have wanted to kill him, they would soon, and probably again and again. Even though I wondered what kind of person her late groom was, I didn't have the heart to ask her while everything was so raw and fresh. And I certainly didn't want to let on that she would probably be viewed as a suspect or a *person of interest*, the toned-down term common nowadays that really meant the same thing as *suspect*. Instead I asked her about her job.

"Jonah wanted me to quit," she said, sounding amazingly calm. "I'm glad I didn't. I just took off the time for our honeymoon." Her voice didn't falter, and for a moment I wondered if she understood what had happened or was simply in some la-la land of shock. There was nothing to do but let her talk and be ready to catch her when she finally fell. She turned to me. "My dad was very vague about your relationship."

When I hesitated, she kept talking and seemed relieved to be talking about something other than the wedding. "I know he tried to keep his social life separate from us. But who did he think he was kidding? Both my sister and I knew he was seeing somebody. And then when he kept talking about you . . ."

"What did he say?" I asked, curious.

"He said you worked at a bookstore and were in some kind of handicraft group, and that you were some kind of amateur investigator, and that he helped you out sometimes. It sounded like he had a lot of fun."

"And you don't mind if your father sees someone?" I said, still surprised by the line of conversation.

She chuckled just like her father, then caught herself. "I hope you don't think it's odd that I'm talking about my father's social life." She looked down at her dress. "I'm still processing everything."

I let out a breath of relief before she continued. At least it showed she had some recognition about what had happened and might be letting the pressure out a little at a time, like when you dropped a bottle of soda on the floor and all the fizz built up inside. If you opened the top quickly, it erupted like a volcano, but if you loosened the top slowly and let the pressure out in little bits, there's no Vesuvius of drink. I told her whatever she did was fine with me.

"Okay then, no, I don't mind if my father sees someone. In fact I want him to. I wish he'd get married again. Anything so he'd be happy." She looked at me. "So?"

What could I say to her? Should I tell her that her father and I were just friends, that he wanted it to be more than that, but I was trying to keep my life from being so complicated for a while? I had been married for just about all of my adult life when my husband, Charlie, died. I'd been a wife and a mother and never just me. Now this was my chance to try my wings and fly solo.

The truth was that Mason claimed to want just a casual relationship, but for now, I was glad to keep both Barry and Mason at arm's length. I really cared about both of them. Maybe even the *L* word, but I wanted some space. But that was too much to lay on her at the moment. Besides, I viewed our whole conversation as just nervous chatter, avoiding the pink elephant in the car with us.

Thursday had grown quiet as I pulled into my driveway, and I wondered if this was going to be the moment her emotions erupted. Instead she just got out and walked across my backyard, waiting while I unlocked the kitchen door.

"I hope you don't mind cats and dogs," I said, seeing that my two dogs and two cats were waiting by the door. As soon as I opened it a crack, Cosmo, the small black mutt of indeterminate breed, ran outside. He screeched to a stop at Thursday's billowing white dress and began to sniff. Blondie was a terrier mix in name only and made a more hesitant move outside. She was one of a kind, a terrier with the aloof personality usually attributed to cats. She didn't even bark much.

I stopped the two cats before they walked outside. They'd

come with my son Samuel when he moved back home. We only let Cat Woman and Holstein outside with supervision, and never at night.

Thursday seemed taken aback by the menagerie. She looked down at the black dog making his way around the base of her dress. "Can I pet him?" she asked.

I was surprised by her manner until she explained. "I've never had a dog," she said, still seeming hesitant about how to proceed.

"What about Spike?" I said, referring to her father's toy fox terrier, who was all terrier in the personality department.

"The first thing my father did after my parents separated was get Spike. My mother doesn't like dogs, or cats, or birds, or fish," she said with a shrug. She finally crouched down and offered her hand for Cosmo to sniff, and then he moved in and offered his head to pet.

I suggested we go inside, looking at her dress. "I'm sure you'd like to change." I said it half as a question, and she nodded.

I took her across the house, and I offered her a pair of cargo capris and a T-shirt, which was my summer uniform when I wasn't at work. Our builds were a little different, and the outfit hung on her like she was a hanger. But just getting out of the dress seemed to take a load off her mind. I changed into cargo capris and a T-shirt, too. They were a lot snugger on me, but definitely went with the sneakers better than the fluffy dress. Still, she hadn't said anything about what had happened.

"I know I haven't eaten, and I imagine you probably haven't either." She followed me back into the kitchen.

Thursday started to shake her head and then looked down toward her stomach as it let out a rumble of protest. "Can I really be hungry after everything?" she said. I waited to see if she was going to say anything more about "everything," but she let it drop and said some food would be welcome.

I started to take out some cold cuts from the refrigerator until I noticed she looked uncomfortable. "Is there something wrong?"

"Do you have peanut butter?" she asked. When I nodded, she said she could make herself a sandwich.

"That's not much of a meal." I went to get the peanut butter for her, but something didn't feel right, and then I had a thought. "Are you a vegetarian?" I asked. She nodded, seeming relieved.

"I don't like to mention it. It's easier just to eat around stuff than answer people's questions or listen to their lectures about why they don't think it's healthy."

"How about eggs?" I asked, putting the peanut butter back in the refrigerator. When she nodded, I decided to make us both omelets with some salad on the side, along with toasted bagels. She wanted to help, but I urged her to sit at the built-in kitchen table. Exhaustion was beginning to show in her face.

I was back to having trouble starting a conversation again. Everything I thought of saying sounded wrong. But silence made me feel tense, so I chatted about the animals and how they'd come to live with me. I whipped up the food and set it in front of her. She ate everything on her plate, and I could tell she was still hungry, though too polite to say anything. "How about some ice cream?" She agreed without even asking what kind.

I took out my stash of McConnell's Bordeaux strawberry. It was my personal favorite, and I'd been known to make a dinner of it. She scraped the bottom of the bowl, but when I offered seconds, she said she was full.

"Thank you," she said softly. "For everything." I heard the front door open and close. My son Samuel came into the kitchen a moment later.

"Do you know what happened?" he said before he was fully in the room. When he saw Thursday, he almost swallowed his tongue. My sandy-haired younger son was a barista by day and a musician by night. In all the excitement, I'd forgotten that he and his group were supposed to have been the after-dinner band at the wedding.

"Do you know Thursday?" I said, faltering when I got to her last name. I supposed it was Kingsley, even if Jonah was dead and she'd only been married for an hour or so. Obviously Samuel had recognized her, and before he could say the wrong thing, I got up and escorted him into the hall. He was already asking what she was doing there. "Mason asked me to get her out of there," I said.

Samuel said when they arrived at the reception, the cops had stopped them from bringing in their instruments and told them everything was canceled. He took a deep breath. "Is it true that her mother stabbed the groom?"